Shortlisted for two Dead Good l...
Reichs Award for Fearless Female Character and The Cat
Amongst the Pigeons Award for Most Exceptional Debut

'Lori Anderson is back with a bang in *Deep Blue Trouble* – a sharply written, fast-paced thriller with bucket loads of heart. With a heroine who jumps off the page and a fantastic supporting cast, this series is a sure-fire winner for anyone with a pulse' Susi Holliday

'Another adrenaline-fuelled, brilliant thriller from Steph Broadribb. Trouble has never been so attractive' A. K. Benedict

'Second in the Lori Anderson series and another electric humdinger of a read. Bounty hunter Lori is thrown in the deep end when she agrees to hunt down a murderer in order to strike a deal with the FBI. The clipped, almost unsentimental tone allows the fast-paced story to explode from the get-go. *Deep Blue Trouble* has an intense energy, it cements Lori Anderson as a fabulous main lead ... long may this series continue' Liz Robinson, LoveReading

'One of the freshest series around. The second outing is just as exhilarating as the first, but Steph ramps up the tension and then some' The Book Trail

'Yes, kick-ass Florida bounty hunter Lori Anderson is back in *Deep Blue Trouble*, which is even better than the first book in the series. It's fresh, fun and a roller-coaster read. I read it in just a few hours' Off-the-Shelf Books

'In Lori Anderson, Steph Broadribb has created a genuinely authentic, kick-ass, realistically flawed heroine who I will now follow anywhere – a breath of fresh air on a hot summer's day blowing right through the thriller genre and turning it on its head' Liz Loves Books

'The plot twists and turns like a waltzer car at the fairground and Broadribb kept me on the edge of my seat, on my toes, and my fingernails are now bitten down to the quick ... *Deep Blue Trouble* is a great book. If you're looking for fast-paced, by-the-seat-of-your-pants action this is the series to read' Bloomin' Brilliant Books

'This is romping entertainment that moves faster than a bullet' Jake Kerridge, *Sunday Express*

'Reads like an action-packed Hollywood movie' The Book Review Cafe

'An absolutely great read' TripFiction

'Superb ... right from the start' Have Books Will Read

'Full of excitement, tension, energy and romance' Emma the Little Bookworm

'At times it had us gasping, others excitedly punching the air ... this book is riveting' Ronnie Turner

'Loved, loved, LOVED IT, from start to finish' My Chestnut Reading Tree

'This debut author has the chops to stand alongside the giants of the crime thriller genre' Reader Dad

'If you like your action to race away at full tilt, then this whirlwind of a thriller is a must' Deirdre O'Brien, *Sunday People*

'With convincing, gritty local detail, unflinching violence, and a subplot of red-hot romance, all narrated by a likeable, fast-talking heroine, this punchy and powerful adventure will leave you wanting more' *The Mirror*

'Stripper-turned-bounty hunter Lori, with her sickly young daughter in tow, gets into high-octane escapes when she sets out to bring her former lover and mentor to justice. Lively' *The Sunday Times* Crime Club

'The non-stop twists and turns draw in readers like a magnet and keep them hooked to the action right up to the emotional conclusion' Pam Norfolk, *Burnley Gazette*

'Sultry and suspenseful, it marks a welcome first for an exceptional new voice' *Good Reading Magazine*

'Gripping, entertaining and utterly addictive, this is a cracking start to an enthralling new crime series' *Lancashire Evening Post*

'Fast, confident and suspenseful' Lee Child

'Like *Midnight Run*, but much darker ... really, really good' Ian Rankin

'A real cracker ... Steph Broadribb kicks ass, as does her ace protagonist' Mark Billingham

'Pacey, emotive and captivating, this is kick-ass thriller writing of the highest order' Rod Reynolds

'Crazy good ... full-tilt action and a brilliant cast of characters' Yrsa Sigurðardóttir

'Broadribb's writing is fresh and vivid, crackling with life ... *Deep Down Dead* is an impressive thriller, the kind of book that comfortably sits alongside seasoned pros' Craig Sisterson

'Fast-paced, zipping around the South Eastern US with chases, fights, ambushes and desperate escapes ... there's a sensitivity in the telling of Lori's struggle to save her daughter that gives *Deep Down Dead* a bit more depth than other action thrillers' Crime Fiction Lover

'Steph Broadribb deals with the topical issues of child exploitation and sexual abuse with an intensity and maturity that leaves you gasping and with your heart in your mouth' *Shots* Mag

'Once I began reading *Deep Down Dead* I knew I was reading something special ... might just be my favourite debut novel ever' Book Addict Shaun

'An action thriller with heart and compassion, combining the darkness of film noir with a family story and the ruggedness of a Western' Finding Time to Write

'Perfectly paced. Edgy. Tense and with a lead character you will want to root for. *Deep Down Dead* ... will grip you as it has that elusive "one more chapter" magic' Grab this Book

'With constant twists and turns ... a wealth of characters, explosive action and a heroine who is absolutely perfect ... *Deep Down Dead* is a cracker' Random Things through My Letter Box

'A very engaging and exhilarating read ... If you're a fan of high-octane thrillers you won't want to miss this electrifying debut' Novel Gossip

'*Deep Down Dead* is pure entertainment. It has action, suspense, a touch of romance ... and a cliffhanger ending that left me desperate for more ... completely immersive and addictive' Crime by the Book

'A steadfast page-turner of a first novel and if she can keep this up for the next couple of books she'll set herself up as a force to be reckoned with' The Library Door

'Steph Broadribb has really blown my mind ... the reader's imagination is instantly grabbed hold of and dragged ... onto a Hollywood set' Swirl & Thread

'Broadribb writes like she has been doing this for years. She has that special *something* that some authors may spend a lifetime trying to find' P Turners Book Blog

'I just loved it. Broadribb excels at creating atmosphere. She gives Lori a distinctive voice and makes you want to listen to her' Blue Book Balloon

'This is the book that every other book has to beat this year to become my favourite read of 2017 ... Superb' Damp Pebbles

'It's hard to believe that *Deep Down Dead* is Steph Broadribb's debut ... a slick, fast-moving race against time with a whip-smart sassy female bounty hunter' The Nut Press

'*Deep Down Dead* takes the reader on a tumultuous, frenetic ride, one where the pace never lets up' From First Page to Last

'This is a fast-moving, adrenaline rush of a story with a relatable protagonist who it is hard not to cheer along ... As you turn those pages, remember to breathe' Never Imitate

'There're some great debuts out there, but *Deep Down Dead* ... is superb. Hard to believe it's her first' Neil White

'*Deep Down Dead* is an ass-kicking thriller of the highest order. I can't recommend it highly enough!' Bibliophile Book Club

'A fast-paced, nail-biting, hard-hitting novel that not only takes you on an all-guns-blazing action adventure but will also take you through the emotional ringer' Chillers, Killers and Thrillers

'This is abso-fluffing-lutely blinkin' brilliant. Fast-paced, high-octane action and with great characters' Jen Med's Book Reviews

'Steph has delivered a *great* thriller, steeped in Americana with settings and characters that feel completely authentic and with a plot that insists you don't put it down' Espresso Coco

'Once you start reading this book, you won't be able to stop' Mrs Bloggs Books

Steph Broadribb was born in Birmingham and grew up in Buckinghamshire. Most of her working life has been spent between the UK and USA. As her alter ego – Crime Thriller Girl – she indulges her love of all things crime fiction by blogging at www.crimethrillergirl. com, where she interviews authors and reviews the latest releases. Steph is an alumni of the MA in Creative Writing (Crime Fiction) at City University London, and she trained as a bounty hunter in California. She lives in Buckinghamshire surrounded by horses, cows and chickens. Her debut thriller, *Deep Down Dead*, was shortlisted for the Dead Good Reader Awards in two categories, and hit number one on the UK and AU kindle charts.

My Little Eye, her first novel under her pseudonym Stephanie Marland will be published by Trapeze Books in April 2018.

Follow Steph on Twitter @CrimeThrillGirl, and on Facebook at *Facebook.com/CrimeThrillerGirl/*, or visit her website: *crimethrillergirl. com.*

Deep Blue Trouble

Steph Broadribb

**ORENDA
BOOKS**

Orenda Books
16 Carson Road
West Dulwich
London SE21 8HU
www.orendabooks.co.uk

First published in the UK in 2018 by Orenda Books
Copyright © Steph Broadribb 2017

A catalogue record for this book is available from the British Library.

ISBN 978-1-910633-93-9
eISBN 978-1-910633-94-6

Typeset in Garamond by MacGuru Ltd
Printed and bound by CPI Group (UK) Ltd, Croydon CR0 4YY

SALES & DISTRIBUTION

In the UK and elsewhere in Europe:
Turnaround Publisher Services
Unit 3, Olympia Trading Estate
Coburg Road,
Wood Green
London
N22 6TZ
www.turnaround-uk.com

In the USA and Canada:
Trafalgar Square Publishing
Independent Publishers Group
814 North Franklin Street
Chicago, IL 60610
USA
www.ipgbook.com

In Australia and New Zealand:
Affirm Press
28 Thistlethwaite Street
South Melbourne VIC 3205
Australia
www.affirmpress.com.au

For details of other territories, please contact *info@orendabooks.co.uk*

Deep Blue Trouble

To Karen, for everything.
Kick-ass female. Publishing marvel. Amazing friend.

Prologue

They met just before dawn in the unremarkable parking lot of an out-of-town motel. Dodge arrived in his sedan dead on five forty-five; the man in the convertible showed a few minutes later. They parked hood to trunk, driver's-side windows level. Neither wanted to get out.

The man in the convertible rested his elbow on the top of the door and leaned towards the sedan. His body language made it clear that he believed he was in charge. He had a sporty ride, better-cut suit and designer shades. He spoke with the authority of a man used to getting what he wanted. 'Have you decided?'

Dodge chewed his gum real slow. Nodded. He spoke no more than was necessary – he was too smart and too cautious for chit-chat. He'd taken the job because it paid four times more than his usual commission, but that didn't mean he trusted the man in the shades, not even a little.

'Good.' The showy guy took an envelope from the inside pocket of his jacket and held it out the window. 'Half up front, as we agreed.'

Dodge took the envelope and slipped it inside his jacket. He was old school, didn't like bank transfers and online whatnots. Cash was better. Less chance of being traced, getting identified. His business thrived on anonymity and he guarded his own fiercely.

'Not going to count it?'

Dodge kept chewing the gum, a slow rhythmic grind. Shook his head. There was no need. The showy guy had been less careful about his anonymity. He'd sent emails to one of the many intermediary addresses. Lots of emails, with specific details. They knew everything about this man. They could get to him fast and easy, and if the money wasn't right, retribution would be swift.

'You don't say much, do you?'

'No,' replied Dodge.

'Don't let them get too close,' said the showy guy. He shifted in his seat and lowered his elbow from the convertible's door; subtle signs he was getting spooked.

It didn't surprise Dodge none, people usually got twitchy after handing over the money. It tended to be the moment reality hit them; when the guilt of what they'd put in motion kicked in. Not this guy though. He doubted this guy felt anything. It was something about the look in the man's eyes, barely visible behind the tint of the shades, but still somehow empty and hollow.

Killing could do that to a man. Dodge recalled the pictures he'd been shown of the yacht's interior: fresh blood splatter across a page of *Vogue* magazine; bloody fingermarks smudged on a half-completed Sudoku puzzle; two bodies – one male, one female – punctured with bullet holes; a child's ragdoll saturated with blood.

'Timeframe?' asked the man in the convertible.

Dodge hated that question. It was impossible to be specific when so many variables were in play. 'It takes as long as it takes.' He glanced at the sky. The sun had started to rise. It was time to leave. He looked back at the man. 'There's a woman in the mix now – a hired professional. She could be a problem.'

The man grimaced. His voice was hard and cold as granite when he spoke. 'Watch her. If she gets too close, end her.'

Dodge kept his expression solemn. Chewed the gum in the same steady rhythm. Nodded again. 'Whatever it takes.'

1

'If he's so innocent, tell me why he confessed to multiple homicide?'

Special Agent Alex Monroe kept asking me the question. He looked real pissed, like I'd messed with him bad, yet he knew what'd happened on my last job right from the get-go. We were supposed to be confirming the details of a new, off-the-books job I'd agreed to do for him; instead, he seemed fixated on the recent past.

'I told you already.'

Monroe ran a hand over his unruly brown hair. 'You told me a version of what happened, but from the way Tate tells it, things went down a whole lot different.'

'He's lying.'

'One of you is for sure.' Monroe looked at me over the top of his shades. Frowned. 'You want the deal we made to hold? Then convince me I'm not exchanging one killer on the loose for another.'

I looked away, across the coffee house to where my nine-year-old daughter, Dakota, was sitting cross-legged on a beanbag chair, reading a book about horses as she sucked her strawberry milkshake through a straw. The bruising across her left cheekbone had faded from blue-black to yellow-tinged purple. I knew it'd take a damn sight longer for the horrors of the previous week to pale, but she was alive; we all were. If James Robert Tate – JT – hadn't been with us, none of us might have survived to tell any kind of version of the truth.

'It's not right for JT to take the fall,' I said. 'He didn't kill those people.'

'Convince me.'

I sighed. 'When I took the job to fetch him back from West Virginia I hadn't seen Tate in ten years. It was supposed to be easy money – just a collect and deliver.'

Monroe nodded. 'I've seen the job details. Tell me, the two of you were real cosy back in the day. What happened?'

I held Monroe's gaze. Knew he was trying to figure out the nature of our relationship. I could tell him in two words – damn complicated. Ten years ago JT had trained me to be a bounty hunter and we'd become lovers. Then it all went to shit.

Monroe cleared his throat. Sounded impatient. 'Did you fall out?'

I looked down into my mug, swirled the dregs of my Americano around the bottom. Old Man Bonchese, the head of the Miami Mob, believed JT was responsible for the disappearance of Thomas 'Tommy' Ford – my husband, the Old Man's enforcer, a man he thought of like a son. But the Old Man didn't know the half of it. JT wasn't the cause of Tommy's disappearance; I was. Tommy murdered my best friend and, when I'd tried to take him in for it, he'd taunted me, threatened me, and I'd shot him dead at point-blank range. JT helped me hide his body, and we'd split soon after. Until the previous week I hadn't known he'd taken the blame and lived with a price on his head, exiled from Florida by the Old Man, for ten years. I hadn't spoken to JT in all that time, not even to tell him we had a daughter.

I looked back at Monroe. 'We had a professional disagreement.'

'But you're backing him now. Why?'

I said nothing. I was fed up with going over it. What I needed right then was for JT to be free and out of danger. With him locked up in the Three Lakes Detention Facility the Miami Mob could reach him, kill him and get their revenge real easy.

Monroe looked irritated. 'You came to me, don't forget that.'

It was true. What should have been an easy job had turned out to be anything but, due to JT having been framed by a man named Randall Emerson – an amusement-park owner who made kiddie porn to order. When Emerson's henchmen kidnapped Dakota we were forced to take the law into our own hands to get her safe, and the damage and body count kept on rising. That the Miami Mob had been gunning hard for JT as well had added a further complication. 'We did what had to be done.'

Monroe raised an eyebrow. 'We?'

I knew what he was implying. JT hadn't been my prisoner the whole time, even though it'd started out that way. We'd gotten close again – emotionally and physically. I'd trusted him. We got Dakota back, brought Emerson to a rough kind of justice – one that meant he'd never harm another child – and then I'd had to take JT to jail in order to get the bond percentage that would help me pay some of the sky-high medical bills Dakota's leukaemia had racked up. That's when JT'd been charged with multiple homicide.

Monroe had offered me a way to clear JT's name, and what with the DA saying they'd go hard for the death penalty, I'd been all kinds of desperate to get JT free. Without Monroe's help, our only chance would be for the state trooper shot by Emerson's man to wake from his coma and say JT was innocent. That didn't seem likely real soon. I held Monroe's gaze. Shrugged. 'It's just a turn of phrase.'

Monroe shook his head. 'He's confessed, and he looks guilty as hell.'

'But he isn't.' I balled my hands into a fist. JT wasn't supposed to take the fall. He was meant to stay silent. But if he'd confessed to things he'd never done I could guess why: he wanted to stop any blame falling on me, to make sure his daughter stayed with her momma. By confessing to stuff he hadn't done, he thought he was keeping us safe.

He was wrong.

Ever since we'd split I'd been so determined to be independent, to prove I didn't need a man to take care of me, be responsible for me, that I'd not told him about Dakota's illness. Even when she was sick I kept putting off contacting him, telling myself I'd do it just as soon as she needed a donor – if she needed a donor. So I'd never told him about the cancer or that, if it returned, she'd need a bone-marrow transplant. Or that, as I'd already been tested and failed to be a compatible match, he, as Dakota's father, would be her best chance of life. I realised now how selfish I'd been, but the mashed-up emotions of love and fear oftentimes threatened to overwhelm me. They made me vulnerable and I hated that. But still I regretted not telling him about Dakota's condition. She needed him alive. I needed him alive. I couldn't let him be sent to the electric chair.

So there was no way out. I'd studied it every which way and come up with a big fat zero. We might have been sitting there all civilised in that brightly lit coffee place, but metaphorically Monroe had backed me against the fence of the corral, ready to sack me out and get me broke. There was no play to be had. I was all out of options. I needed the deal.

'Look, enough with the navel gazing,' I said. 'Let's do this. You going to get me to sign something?'

Monroe pushed his shades up onto the top of his head. 'Nope. You get our guy, your service gets recognised, and I'll get Tate free. Screw up, and you're on your own.'

Get *their* guy, not mine – Gibson 'the Fish' Fletcher. He'd been serving triple life in supermax until the previous week. After an emergency transfer to hospital for a bust appendix, he'd gotten free – killed three guards and disappeared. Monroe thought, because I'd caught Fletcher before, one time when he'd skipped bail, I could catch him again. I guessed it was probably true. Thing was, back when I'd caught him the worst I thought he'd done was some high-value thieving. The double homicide he'd been charged with – and found guilty of later – wasn't a part of that bond ticket.

'It's high risk.'

Monroe shrugged. 'It is what it is.'

I studied Monroe for a long moment. His words were don't-give-a-damn tough, but there was a nervousness in his expression, different to his usual Kentucky cool. Seemed he needed me on the job, so perhaps there was a play to be had here after all.

I narrowed my gaze. 'Before I do this, I want to see him.'

Monroe didn't answer. He took a mouthful of coffee and swallowed it slowly. We both knew it was a stalling tactic. 'Not going to happen.'

'You've made me a deal that isn't even written on a piece of paper. A deal I'm going to risk my life for.' I glanced over at Dakota. She was still reading the horse book, her milkshake almost finished. 'That deal means I've got to leave my daughter right after all the shit that just happened. The least you can do is give me and JT a little bit of time.'

Monroe's jaw tightened. 'It's been three days already. Meantime Fletcher is still in the wind. I need you on him as of now.'

'Tomorrow. I'll start then, just so long as you get me a visit.'

'Goddammit, Lori.'

I held his gaze. Didn't look away. Didn't blink.

Monroe exhaled hard. Flipped his shades back down over his eyes and stood up to go. 'Fine. No promises, but I'll see what I can do.'

'There's something else you should know.'

Monroe turned back to face me.

'I think I'm being followed.'

2

I checked the rear-view mirror. The black SUV was still there. I inhaled slow, trying to keep my heart rate steady. Looked across at Dakota sitting in the passenger seat and forced a smile; didn't want her to see I was worried.

But I was worried, real worried. The SUV had been tailing us for seven miles. I'd seen it idling at the side of the street as we turned out of the parking garage of our Clearwater Village apartment. They'd pulled out when we were five cars clear, and stayed at that distance ever since. No faster, no slower, no jostling for position like the other vehicles on the freeway. And they'd made no obvious moves; that's why they stood out as suspicious.

Monroe hadn't put any store in my concerns, but that didn't mean I was wrong. That black SUV was following us, I just didn't know why. My chest tightened as fear gripped me. After all that had gone down in the past week, I could not allow my daughter to get caught up in another dangerous situation.

Pulling across the freeway, I accelerated. Knew I needed to get rid of the tail before we got closer to our destination – Camp Gilyhinde. I'd figured the kid's summer camp would be the perfect place for Dakota to stay while I was hunting down Gibson Fletcher; somewhere she'd be kept safe from danger. But that safety would be shot to shit if I couldn't lose the tail.

Five cars behind us, the SUV pulled into our lane and matched our pace. My stomach lurched. I was going to have to take more evasive action.

I looked at the navigator on the dash, assessing my options. Glancing at Dakota, I tried to keep my tone light as I said, 'I think I've found us a cut-through, might save some time.'

She said nothing. Stayed slumped in the passenger seat with her arms folded across her stomach, her eyes staring straight ahead, very pointedly ignoring me. The thing of it was, she didn't want to go to camp.

'Look honey, it'll only be a few weeks. Three at the most,' I said. In truth I'd no clue how long it'd take to hunt down Fletcher. It'd been hard enough getting Dakota a late entry to camp. Harder still to have them believe me when I warned them about her bruises and how she'd gotten them. In the end, I'd enlisted Monroe's help, pacified them with his FBI credentials. 'You'll have fun, and I'll be back before you know it.'

Dakota leaned forwards and turned up the volume on the radio.

I clenched my jaw. Looked in the rear-view mirror again. The SUV remained five cars behind.

Gripping the wheel tighter, I pressed the gas and set us head-to-head with a huge eighteen-wheeler. I assessed the distance to the next exit ramp and planned my next move. I'd have one shot at it. I had to get it right; it was all in the timing.

I turned down the radio, looked at Dakota, my concern making my tone sound harsher than I'd intended when I said, 'Sit up straight.'

Dakota glared at me, rolling her eyes. 'Why are you leaving JT in jail? He's not a bad man.'

We were three hundred yards from the exit ramp. I glanced at Dakota again. 'Because I have a job.'

'That sucks.'

She was right. It did. So I didn't pick her up on the cuss, not this time. 'I wouldn't be going if it wasn't super important.'

'I don't get why you're going. It's like you don't even care.'

'I care.' We were two hundred yards from the ramp. The SUV was five lengths behind us. We were neck and neck with the eighteen-wheeler. I needed to focus.

Dakota turned to me, pouting. 'Then *why* are you leaving?'

I didn't answer. We were a hundred yards from the ramp and closing. I accelerated harder and nosed ahead of the eighteen-wheeler. Concentrated on the speed, holding hard for the perfect angle. Kept my breathing regular.

'Momma?'

'Hold on,' I said, flooring the gas. We shot a length ahead of the truck and I yanked the wheel hard, turning across its path, my focus on the exit ramp. The tyres squealed on the blacktop. Dakota shrieked. The truck driver blared his horn as we cut across him. No warning, no blinker, and barely an inch to spare.

I checked the mirror. The black SUV was blocked by the eighteen-wheeler and a pick-up truck; it couldn't switch lanes in time. It didn't make the ramp.

We were free and clear.

I exhaled hard.

'Momma ... what ... why did you...?'

'Sorry, I nearly missed our exit.'

Dakota narrowed her eyes. She didn't believe me. Sounded sad as she said, 'Won't you tell me why you're really going?'

There's nothing harder than saying goodbye to your child, especially when you've just gotten her back. The last thing I wanted to do was leave her. I wanted to bind her to me and never let her out of my sight, but I couldn't. What with tracking the fugitive – Gibson 'the Fish' Fletcher – for Monroe, and the mystery tail I seemed to have picked up, I figured she'd be a hell of a lot safer at camp than she would be with me.

I was too choked with emotion to answer her. Checked the mirror – no black SUV.

She put her hand on my arm. Squeezed it a little. 'Please?'

I looked over at her. Nodded. Back when she was little I promised I'd always be straight with her. I, more than anyone, knew the hurt that could come from secrets; the damage and the danger they caused. 'The truth of it is, JT's in big trouble. The cops have him charged with murder and the only way for me to help him is to do this job as a favour to an important lawman who can help JT.'

Dakota's eyes widened. Her lower lip trembled. 'Murder? That means he could get—'

'I can't let that happen.' I cut her off. Couldn't hear her say the words *death penalty*. 'That's why I have to go.'

3

It wasn't the most romantic of settings, but then I've never been a candles and roses kind of a girl. Armed guards, metal doors and security cameras do create a certain type of ambience, but it was nothing that I hadn't handled before in my line of work. As a bail runner, you get familiar with the county's law enforcement facilities. Still, going to that place to visit with JT made it feel real different. Personal. That time, I felt afraid.

Monroe had pulled strings and gotten me a visit at the Three Lakes Detention Facility faster than the usual seven-day wait. He made sure we were given a private visiting room, and for that I was grateful. Me and JT, we had a whole bunch of things to talk about, and I knew some of that conversation wouldn't come easy.

'Take good care of our daughter, you hear.' They'd been the last words JT had spoken to me before the cops took him into custody. Eight words that told me he'd guessed the truth about Dakota, said in a moment that gave me no chance to explain. That'd been four days ago – a long time to think on the things I should have said.

But even now I still hadn't managed to wrestle the words I'd rehearsed so they fitted together right. Yes, he had a daughter. *We* had a nine-year-old daughter; and I hadn't told him. I'd decided before she was born that I'd *never* tell him. And, if it hadn't been for my last job bringing us back into contact after ten years apart, he still wouldn't know.

The sound of the door unlocking behind me jolted me from my thoughts. I turned and saw the guard – a younger guy, as tall as JT but maybe twenty pounds heavier – step into the room. He nodded towards the table and two chairs bolted to the floor in the centre of the space. 'Take a seat, ma'am.'

I did as he asked. The guard pushed the door open wider and nodded. JT limped into the room.

He wore a grey sweater and training pants. Fresh bruises, in dark, eggplant shades of purple, were layered over the yellowing ones he'd got as we fought off Emerson and his men, determined to get Dakota safe whatever the cost. 'What happened to your—'

'It's nothing,' he said, sitting down.

I reached out to touch JT's face. 'Looks like a damn hard dose of nothing.'

The guard cleared his throat. 'No contact, ma'am.'

I put my hand back on the table.

As JT eased himself back in the chair his gaze didn't quite meet mine. Trouble had found him again for sure. The price on his head set by Old Man Bonchese – head of the Miami Mob – was still in force, so even if JT wasn't speaking about it, as long as he was in jail, he would be in danger. There'd be plenty of people inside loyal to the Old Man.

'Why'd you come here, Lori?' he said. His tone sounded defeated rather than angry. I hadn't expected that.

'I needed to see you.'

'I'm fine.'

'Yeah,' I said, gesturing to his face, and the arm he was holding all protective across his ribs. 'Sure looks that way.'

He stared at me. Stayed silent. I couldn't read his expression, but truth was he didn't seem pleased to see me. I felt tension tightening at the base of my throat. Thought we'd gotten close again on those three days chasing Dakota's abductors across the South. We'd gotten physical, and at the time it'd felt like it meant something to the both of us. I wondered if I'd made a mistake.

'I've made a deal.'

He frowned. 'Tell me.'

So, I told him what Monroe wanted me to do – about catching Gibson Fletcher – and why I'd agreed to do it, for the most part anyways. All the while JT stared at me, his expression unreadable.

'So that's the deal. I find Fletcher. Monroe gets you free.'

JT raked his hands through his dirty-blond hair, pushing it back from his face before letting it fall shaggy across his forehead again. He shook his head. 'Walk away from this, Lori.'

'I'm not going anywhere.'

'You've got Dakota. You can't take the risk, not now. Not for me.'

'I can, and I will.'

'I don't want you to.'

'It's not up to—'

'You only just got her safe.' His tone was no-nonsense tough. 'She had a hell of a shake-up – getting snatched by Emerson's men, being held prisoner and watching a man die, almost drowning as Emerson's boat sank into that swamp.' He held my gaze. 'Meeting me.'

I looked down at the table. Traced the cracks in the plastic laminate with my gaze. 'The DA's talking about going for the death penalty, making you his career case. I can't let that happen. I had to get Monroe to—'

'I didn't ask for you to do that.'

'You didn't need to.'

He sighed.

'I don't get why you're taking the fall. We had a plan, so why confess to a bunch of things that weren't your fault? Why are you lying?'

JT flicked his gaze towards the guard and gave a tiny shake of his head.

Never trust no one. That was JT's first rule. Either he didn't want to speak on it, or the men inside loyal to Old Man Bonchese included some of the guards. From the way JT was acting, I figured what we had going on was most likely a half of both.

Frustration and the fear of what would happen next fireworked in my stomach. I slammed my hands down on the table. Watched the plastic top vibrate from the blow. Wanted more than a one-liner-style conversation, and needed JT to answer me straight. The stakes were top-dollar high; there wasn't room for ambiguity. 'Enough of the silent act already.'

He slid his hands across the table towards mine, stopping them so our fingertips were a couple inches apart. 'How's Dakota?' he asked, his tone softer.

I exhaled hard. 'Honestly? Not so great. She won't talk about what happened.'

'I get that. Those three days, they were a whole lot for anyone to deal with, and she's just a kid.' He looked real thoughtful. 'But she's strong, like her momma. You give her time. She'll talk when she's ready.'

I nodded. I knew he was right, I'd been telling myself the same thing, but it didn't make it any easier.

I looked into his eyes. 'What you said before, about Dakota being your—'

'Don't, Lori. Okay? Not here, not now.'

I stared at him. Thought about telling him why I'd never told him about his daughter; that it was easier to rely on myself because, in my experience, men always let you down; better to never depend on them in the first place. I knew I should tell him about her illness; about how, although she was in remission, there was the ever-present threat that the cancer could return, about how, if she needed a bone-marrow donor, he would be her best shot at a match because I wasn't a viable candidate. But I didn't want that conversation to be this way: him with his barriers up, me all angry and confused. So I said nothing.

He exhaled hard. 'You should go.'

'I only just got—'

'You coming here, it ain't right.' He sounded real determined. 'Go, Lori. Please.'

His rejection stung like a bitch, but I gritted my teeth, refusing to show the hurt. 'I'm doing this to get you out faster. To stop them—'

He shook his head. 'I don't want you to take the deal.'

'Yeah, I hear that.' I felt the anger building inside me. Pushed my hands against the table and stood up real fast. 'But it doesn't mean I'm going to listen none.'

I strode away from JT. Left him sitting in that dreary box of a room with the table and chairs bolted to the floor. As I passed the guard he nodded. I tried real hard to ignore the pity in his eyes.

I went back through the security checks and the airlock doors in a daze. I was taking the deal, whatever JT said. It was the right thing to do, the *necessary* action to take. And sure, I knew I should have told him about Dakota's illness, but he frustrated the hell out of me. I didn't have time for his strong-and-silent bullshit; I needed him alive, for our daughter's sake, and I was going to make damn sure that happened. Everything else, I would just have to leave to fate.

The final set of doors clanked shut behind me and I emerged blinking into the sunlight. I inhaled the fresh, hot air – it sure tasted a whole lot sweeter than the stale environment of the detention-centre compound. The image of JT, battered and bruised in his prison-issue sweats, floated into my mind. I pushed it away, fought the urge to feel sorry for him, knowing I had to stay strong. I'd got work to do.

I was so lost in my thoughts that I was almost at my truck when I noticed. My breath caught in the back of my throat. I halted. Looked around.

The driver's door was open.

I drew my Taser from its holster and stepped towards the truck. Scanned the area for signs of life.

Saw nothing.

What the hell was going on?

4

The mutterings had started the second day JT was there. Nothing concrete, just rumours relayed to him during exercise, always by the more squirrelly, nervous types, looking to get in with the hard men for protection.

'There's a price on your head.'

For sure, tell me something I don't know.

'Price just got doubled.'

Just means the more stupid of you will try your luck.

'They're saying you didn't kill Thomas Ford. They're saying a woman did it.'

He'd said nothing. Walked away. Clenched his jaw so tight his teeth started aching. Pretty soon the fidgety, anxious types left him alone. Realised he wasn't going to give them protection. That he didn't pick favourites. That he kept himself to himself.

He didn't go looking for trouble. Made a habit of that, just like when he was on the outside. But if someone else chose to start something, he sure as hell would be the one finishing it. He'd said that to the few who'd gotten all up in his face. Seemed that they hadn't believed him.

He looked at his knuckles, purple and black against the grey marl of his sweatpants. Remembered the look on Lori's face when he'd batted away her questions about the bruises – hurt and confusion, mixed with irritation. He knew that if he'd answered she'd have fired more questions at him. Questions whose answers he wouldn't have wanted to say in that room; answers for no one else to hear but her. Given the situation, it had been better to say nothing.

He flexed his fingers. Winced. Knew it'd be a couple of days before the swelling went down.

Trouble had found him a couple of hours before Lori's visit. The cells had unlocked for morning exercise and his cellmate, who snored like a hurricane but was bearable enough, scooted out fast. Moments later two guys – one tall and stringy, one heavy-set and bulky, both shaven-headed – entered his space. They looked wired, ready for action.

'What?' JT had said. He'd stayed sitting on his bunk. Acted casual.

The stringy one spoke first, his voice nasal with a whiny twang. 'Word is you been killing our brothers. Started with Thomas Ford.'

JT didn't respond. Kept his expression neutral, showing no reaction to the name of Lori's former husband, the man she'd killed. A murder JT had covered up ten years before.

The stringy guy continued, 'Gunner Zamb. Richie Royston. Johnny Matthews.'

JT recognised the names – soldiers from the Miami Mob. They'd held him captive in West Virginia the previous week, waiting for Ugi Nolfi, one of Old Man Bonchese's top enforcers, to come collect him. Lori had bust him out before Ugi arrived. They'd left the three men tied up and alive.

'They were still breathing when I left the ranch.'

Stringy glanced at the heavy-set guy then back to JT. 'What about Ugo Nolfi? Heard you left him shot up in an amusement park. That's kind of sick.'

JT clenched his jaw. Ugo Nolfi had been a good guy. They'd talked and struck a deal, but Ugo had been shot by Emerson's henchmen before he could tell the Old Man. 'Not me.'

The heavy-set one cocked his head to the side. 'Not you, huh? So tell us about the bitch.'

JT clenched his fists. He wouldn't tell them shit about Lori. 'Don't start something you can't finish.'

They didn't take the warning. The skinny one grinned. Cracked his knuckles. After that JT knew it could only end one way. He was going to have to fight.

Two guys were easy. Like a walk in the park on a Sunday, even with him still bashed up after the business that went down with Emerson.

Even though the bullet wound in his thigh wasn't fully healed. Hadn't mattered. Two men, one of him – a quick one-two to the heavy-set one to get him dazed; an uppercut and roundhouse to the stringy one, and he went down. The first came back for a little more, and a triple right hook finished him off.

JT doubted either got more than a single punch in but he didn't feel bad. After all, it wasn't like he hadn't warned them. He lived by the motto: *You throw the first punch, it'll be me that throws the last.*

He could take care of himself, always had and always would. But Old Man Bonchese's men were asking about Lori. They'd linked her and the killings, and that made him real twitchy. Because, problem was, now they'd connected her name to the Mob men who'd died, JT knew it wouldn't end there. And from the inside of a jail cell there was nothing he could do to keep her safe.

5

'Did they take much?' Monroe slid onto the bench beside me and held out an iced tea. It felt like a peace offering of sorts, showing he was taking my concerns about being followed more seriously, now that it was too damn late.

I took the go cup, shook my head. 'They'd tossed my stuff, but nothing was missing.'

'We swept it for bugs. Found this.' He passed me a black box, a couple of inches long by a half-inch wide. 'They'd stuck it way back under the dash.'

'A GPS tracker?' I guessed that explained why I'd seen no sign of a tail when I'd left my apartment that morning. They could track me on-screen, no need for a visual. 'Why'd they break in? Why not just use a magnetic one under the wheel arch?'

He shrugged. 'Could be they thought you'd be less likely to find it inside. Guess you coming out of your visit early surprised them and they had to abandon the vehicle before they'd finished.'

'You heard about that?'

'My contact told me you stayed less than a half-hour...'

'Yep.'

'You get what you needed?'

I took a sip of the iced tea. Had I got what I needed from my meet with JT? No, not even close, but that shouldn't have been a surprise. No good ever came from dreaming on a man, I knew that, but the thing was, I'd let myself get caught up in the moment, thinking on the possibility of some kind of happy ever after. I knew it was fantasy – some bullshit peddled by hopeless romantics and greeting-card sellers. The best I could hope for was guaranteeing a straight plain *after* for JT, and so safeguarding one for Dakota.

I met Monroe's gaze. 'I told him about our deal.'

Monroe nodded. 'So you're ready?'

I studied him a moment. He was wearing his trademark shades, which made his expression hard to judge. His suit looked a little more crumpled than usual. I wondered why he'd chosen this spot on the edge of Palatlakaha River National Park to meet. Me, I preferred to sweat in the heat than kowtow to formality and air-conditioning, but I had a feeling he'd rather have been sitting inside. 'Why aren't we meeting at your field office?'

'Because this isn't an official operation – you're an asset, not an operative.'

Yeah, that was for sure. I was expendable, a means to an end, he'd already made that clear. And I kind of appreciated his frankness – meant I knew where I stood. 'So tell me, what's the deal on Gibson Fletcher?'

'You know from when you chased him before that his rep is as a largely opportunist jewellery thief, taking from boat owners and tourists along the Florida coast. That changed when he tried to rob a Chicago businessman, name of Patrick Walker, who was vacationing with his wife, Ailsa, and their eight-year-old twin girls, Hayley and Ana, on the Keys. Fletcher misjudged the timing of his break-in, got spooked when he was interrupted by the family coming on board the yacht. He killed Mr and Mrs Walker. Left the kids covered in blood and catatonic.' Monroe took a gulp of iced tea. 'The inside of that boat looked like a goddamn abattoir.'

I bowed my head, thinking of those two girls witnessing the brutal murder of their parents. They'd been just a year younger than Dakota was now. No wonder they'd been catatonic.

'What happened to the kids?'

Monroe gave a wave of his hand, like it didn't matter. 'They went to live with Mrs Walker's parents. Had a tough time adjusting I heard, they hadn't had much contact with their grandparents until then.'

Parcelling those girls off to virtual strangers straight after such a tragedy seemed cruel, although at least, as twins, they'd got each other. My stomach flipped as I realised that was exactly what I'd done to Dakota in sending her off to camp. Except she didn't have a sister; she was alone in a strange place with strangers.

I swallowed down the guilt. Told myself it wouldn't be for long. That, after what had happened on the last job, I would never take my daughter with me on any kind of job, easy or not. Still, it had been crazy tough to leave her. When we said our goodbyes, her lower lip had trembled as she said, 'Keep safe, Momma.' It'd felt like my heart was being squeezed to busting.

I took a breath and pushed the memory from my mind. Needed to focus on the job – have it done fast and get back to Dakota.

I looked at Monroe. 'So what made him freak? He didn't have a history of violence; I checked that out when I took the skip trace on him before.'

'We don't know. He said nothing in his defence at the trial, and nothing since. But there's more to Fletcher than small-time thieving. Stuff that isn't on his official file.'

'Oh, yeah?'

Monroe waited for a group of hikers to stride past, arguing over the best trail to take, and then said, 'He had another line of business that was more niche, kept off-the-record: specialising in antiquities – finding and liberating unique items to order.'

It was news to me. 'Like what?'

'It's a long list, but the thing that got him on our radar was the theft of a set of chess pieces that were used in a special game in Vegas between two legends back in the eighties; showcasing the old guard and the newest talent. It was the fall of '89: Christophe Lenon vs Bradley Eston. It was the victory match that made Eston the household name he is now. Back then the match was the most glitzy, expensive one in history. The set itself was a work of art.'

I nodded. Had a vague recollection of it. 'The Billionaire Face-Off match?'

Monroe nodded. 'Yep.'

'So what happened to the chess set?'

'It was bought at auction by a private collector, and that was it, until it disappeared from the owner's collection ten days before Fletcher was arrested for minor thefts from tourist cabins on the commercial vacationers' yacht, *Sunsearcher*. It hasn't been seen since.'

'I'm guessing the set was worth a lot. How come its theft got the attention of the Bureau, though?'

'Sorry. That's need-to-know.'

He did look kind of sorry, but I wasn't tolerating any bureau bullshit. 'And I don't?'

'It's not relevant to the job you're doing.'

'Is that right? Because it sounds real relevant.' Irritated, I tried a different angle. 'So if you knew he was lifting this high-end stuff, why didn't you arrest him?'

Monroe exhaled. Pushed his shades a little further up the bridge of his nose. 'We've got no evidence. Nothing that ties Fletcher beyond reasonable doubt to the antiquity thefts.'

I took another draw on my iced tea. Frowned. 'You were working the case before he got busted though, am I right?'

Monroe shifted awkwardly on the bench beside me. Didn't answer.

'Yep, guess I am right.'

He gulped down the rest of his drink. Tipped the ice out onto the grass and scrunched the plastic cup into a ball in his fist. 'Look, whatever I was or wasn't doing at that time, I can tell you the trail went cold as soon as Fletcher got arrested.'

I looked at him sideways. 'So me finding Fletcher, it's not just about taking a dangerous man back to jail is it?'

Monroe stayed silent a long moment, then shook his head. 'I need some time with him – off-the-record kind of time – before he goes back to supermax.'

There was something about his tone, and the way his voice broke slightly as he said the word 'time', that made me think this wasn't just about work. It was personal too. 'Why?'

Monroe stared at me, silent, his expression impassive aside from the frown lines between his brows. The dark lenses of his shades masked the look in his eyes.

'Yeah, yeah, don't tell me. Need-to-know, right?'

He nodded. His expression stayed unreadable.

I figured I needed to play the long game to find out what was going on behind those shades of his. From what I'd learned about Monroe in that last week, he was as smart as he was guarded, and that's a hard combination to crack. So, much as I wanted to push him harder, I didn't force it, not just then, even though a personal element between fugitive and lawman introduced an extra layer of complication that had me feeling real uneasy.

I switched topics. 'So you told me Fletcher got loose after an operation?'

'Yep. After a kerfuffle in the yard he was diagnosed with a bust appendix. The medical on site couldn't deal with the complications, so he was transferred to the hospital for urgent treatment. The op was successful. But a few hours later Fletcher killed three guards and shook off the marshals.'

'How'd he kill them?'

'Faked collapse. Took the first's weapon when he came over to check his breathing and shot him point blank. Uncuffed himself then took out the other two when they stormed the room. Emptied the gun at them. Messy, not economical.'

'Same as on the Walkers' yacht?'

'Close enough.'

'That's pretty special for someone who'd just had major surgery. You sure he didn't have help?'

Monroe shook his head. 'Cops found no trace of it. They never got him in their sights.'

I narrowed my gaze. 'The cops didn't. What about you?'

'We got in on it late. Almost twenty-four hours after the fact. The usual jurisdiction bullshit, local PD didn't want to give up the case.'

'And now?'

'We have confirmation Fletcher crossed the state line. It's a federal case, no question.'

I nodded. 'So when he hightailed out of state, do you know which way he was heading?'

Monroe gave a half smile. 'I can do better than that. I've got a confirmed destination.'

'So why'd you need me? You could go fetch him yourself.'

The smile on his lips died real fast. 'It's not that simple.'

It never is, but the more complicated a situation, the more chance there is of things turning out bad. I felt a twist of tension in my stomach, and fixed Monroe with a hard stare. 'Yeah, yeah, I know, you need a time delay. If you catch him, you'll have to bring him straight back; no detour, no off-the-record chat. You use me, and the timeline can be a little more flexible. And "use" is the key word here, am I right?'

'Lori, it's more—'

'It's damn messed up, is what it is. You're using me – exploiting JT's situation as leverage, so you can appear to keep your hands clean.' I clenched my fingers tighter around the iced tea. Heard the plastic start to creak. 'I don't like it, and I do not like being a part of it. Whatever's gotten a burr in your saddle about Fletcher, I need your assurance that once I have him you're not gonna go all vigilante. I will not have another person's blood on my hands, you understand?'

'It's not like—'

'I asked you a question. You give me your word, or I walk now.'

Monroe stared at me, most likely trying to figure out if I was bluffing. He ran his hand over his wayward hair – a nervous tic of his – and exhaled hard. 'Alright, agreed. You have my word. Fletcher will be returned to jail in one piece and with a fully functioning pulse. I just want to talk to him.'

I held his gaze a couple more beats, then nodded. 'Okay then.'

The bluff had paid off, so long as Monroe's word held good. It was the only guarantee I had that JT would be exonerated and that whatever grudge match Monroe and Fletcher had going on wasn't going to turn deadly. I was pinning a whole lot more than was wise on a promise, but still I had to take the risk. The only other living witness who could confirm JT hadn't shot the state trooper was the man himself, but he was in a coma and the doctors said things didn't look good. Unless he came right, and could remember what had happened to him out on the shoulder of the highway in Florida, the deal with Monroe was the only way I could get JT free.

'So where is Fletcher?' I asked.

'As of this moment, I don't know. We tracked him to a small airfield outside San Diego two days ago. Trail ended there.'

I figured Fletcher was most likely heading for the border. Wondered what business had caused him to stop in California. 'Tell me about your eyes in San Diego.'

Monroe stayed silent.

'What, that's need-to-know, too? Enough with the bullshit, give me something to work with here!'

Monroe looked thoughtful. Nodded. 'A local informant. Young guy who works cargo at a storage place near the airfield. He took a photo on his phone.'

'Message it to me. The guy's name, too.'

Monroe looked uncomfortable. Sweat beading on his forehead. After a long pause he said, 'Okay.'

'No sightings in that area for two days?'

Monroe shook his head. 'Nope. That's all she wrote.'

'And you need for me to write the next line.'

'Something like that, you ready to do this?'

I'd got Dakota safely to camp and I'd told JT about the deal. My go bag was packed and checked, my Taser and cuffs were ready. I felt the pre-job nerves fizz in my stomach. Knew this was what had to get done. I couldn't tell Monroe to go to hell and walk away; I had to do this for JT and for my daughter.

'Yep. I'm good.'

He nodded. Handed me a ticket. 'You fly out of Tampa. Wheels up at 17:15. Don't be late. We've booked you into this place.' He passed me a print-out for a booking at the Carlsbad North Inn. 'It's close by the airport. Nice, and clean, but not high profile. Should be a good base.'

'Thanks.'

He took a burner cell phone – a pay-as-you-go, unregistered, old-school, non-smart variety – from the inside pocket of his suit and gave it to me. 'Use this to stay in contact. Update me twice a day – at 08:00 and 20:00. My number's stored in the contacts; it's the only one.'

'What about a number for your San Diego contact?'

Monroe looked irritated. 'I'll message you his details.'

I nodded.

'If you don't check in, I'll assume you're in trouble.'

'And if I'm in trouble, I'm on my own?'

'Get Fletcher for me, Lori. Fast as.'

I pocketed the paperwork and the phone. 'I'll report in when I've arrived.'

Monroe nodded then stared out across the grassland towards the lake. I took that as the cue our meet was over. Getting up, I strode back along the trail to the parking lot, thinking on my next move.

There was someone tailing me and I didn't know why or what their end game was. I had a fugitive in the wind; a start location, but no leads. I wanted to know why Fletcher had gone to San Diego, why he'd risked travelling out of state, and why, as he'd left Florida and seemed to be heading to Mexico, he hadn't gone straight there? It didn't stack up right. Not yet. But if I could find what motivated him to stop in California, I'd have a damn sight better chance of finding him once I got out there.

Back when I'd caught Fletcher the first time, I'd had a little help from a retired investigator of sorts. If anyone could help me figure out what Fletcher had waiting for him in California, I reckoned it would be him.

I had six hours before I had to be on the plane. If fate had any sense of justice, she'd let me find the old investigator right where I'd found him before, at the Deep Blue Marina, Tampa.

6

There's something real peaceful about the marina.

The drive had been easy enough, straight down the I-4, through Polk City and into Tampa the back way through Brandon. No sign of the black SUV. I got into town near on midday, and the sun was beating hard.

Up ahead I saw the sign for the Deep Blue Marina – orange script across bright-blue, the smiling fish pointing towards the words. Turning across the traffic, I drove through the open gate and took an immediate left into the parking lot.

As I turned off the engine, I looked out past the lines of boats bobbing in their moorings towards the ocean. The place looked just as I remembered it. It was neat and clean, but wasn't as fancy as some – more for houseboat dwellers and Florida residents with smaller yachts than for the big vacation boats and millionaire cruisers you saw further into vacationer central. I liked that. Made it feel more homely.

Jumping out of the truck, I made my way to the white security hut. It looked empty at first glance. It was only the loud snore that made me look twice. Reclined back on his chair, chin resting on his chest, was a young guy in board shorts and a white polo shirt with 'Deep Blue Marina Security' on the pocket. He was unshaven, wore shades and, from the alcohol fumes coming off him, must have come straight to work from a party.

I was about to say something when I heard tyres on the gravel behind me. Turning I spotted a silver sedan stop on the edge of the parking lot closest to the security hut. It was twenty yards away – close enough for me to see that the driver was staring right at me. Watching.

My breath caught in my throat as I recognised him – black hair, mirrored shades – the same guy who'd been driving the black SUV. The tail was back.

I'd had enough already. I needed me some answers. Dropping my purse, I sprinted towards the vehicle. Covered the ground fast – taking long strides, arms pumping, exhaling hard through my mouth. Kept my eyes focused on the driver.

Surprise flashed across his face. He scrabbled for the ignition.

I reached the sedan. Bashed my fists on the door. Tried to yank it open but it was locked. I kept thumping – on the door, the roof. Yelled, 'Who the hell are you? Who do you work for?'

The man's face was flushed. He didn't look at me. Put the gear into drive. The engine caught.

'Why are you following me?' I pounded my fists against the window. 'Tell me what the hell you want!'

The sedan accelerated out of the lot, tyres squealing, back end fishtailing, gravel spitting in its wake. Left me cussing and none the wiser. Bastard.

'Hey, you okay, ma'am?'

I turned. Saw the young security guy hurrying towards me with my purse.

He handed it to me and gestured at the exit. 'You had some kind of trouble?'

I forced a smile. Knew I needed to find out who was tailing me, but didn't want the authorities involved, not yet anyways. 'Nothing I can't handle.'

He rubbed his bloodshot eyes. Seemed relieved I wasn't going to ask him to file a report. 'You visiting with someone?'

'I'm here to see Red.'

The altercation with the driver of the silver sedan had me worried and pissed in equal measure. Were they connected somehow to what had happened at the amusement parks or was their interest in me due to my job for the FBI?

As I headed out along the wooden walkway between the boats I tried to put the questions flying around my mind to one side and focus on the job for Monroe. I only had a few hours before my flight to get what I needed. Glancing around, I hoped I could remember how to find Red's boat. It'd been two years since I'd last visited, and the boat-lined, well-trodden walkways all looked real similar.

I remembered he'd been moored at the end of one of the jetties, that he liked it that way on account of him not getting any passing foot traffic. I paused at a point where four walkways intersected. Instinct told me I needed to go along the jetty to the left. When I did, I recognised the boat, and the man, straight off.

The houseboat had the same immaculate green and gold livery, and Red was upfront, cleaning the exterior, just like he had been the first time I visited with him. The memory of how he'd inducted me into the ways of the boat community and helped me figure out Gibson 'the Fish' Fletcher's way of getting into yachts – by approaching them from the water rather than land – made me smile. It also made me wonder if all he did these days was work on that boat. Maybe that was how he spent his retirement. Except a man like that, I doubted he'd ever truly retire.

As I got closer, he looked round, squinting towards me. Grinned. 'Miss Lori? Well, hell, aren't you a fine sight.'

He wasn't bad himself. Barefoot, wearing sun-faded jeans and a grey tee, his deep tan made his silver-streaked hair all the more striking. He must have been in his mid-sixties but was still a disarmingly attractive man – fit and rugged, with a boyish smile that age couldn't dim. Made me wonder a moment if that was how JT would look when he got older; if the state allowed him to get older.

'Hey, Red. How's it going?'

He scooted around to the side of the boat. Held out a hand to help me aboard. 'You know what they say. You do stuff, then you die.' He looked down, brushed a dried flake of gold paint off his jeans. 'I'm still here, so I must be doing something.'

I took his hand and stepped onto the boat. 'Guess so.'

'People like us, they don't like to be bored.' He winked. 'Lack of adventure, that's what kills you in the end.'

'Live hard, die young?'

'Something like that.' He narrowed his gaze. 'Fun as it is to shoot the breeze with you, Miss Lori, I'm thinking you didn't journey out here just for the conversation. What's the job, and what help are you after?'

I held up my hands. 'You got me. I need to find Gibson Fletcher again.'

'Uh-huh. They got you back on that one?'

'Yeah, he escaped.'

'Saw that. I watch the news. Not sure I believed it mind. Seemed a mighty effort for a man just out of surgery.'

'I thought so, too, but the cops and the FBI are saying it's true.'

'And you trust them?'

Oftentimes trusting people, especially those that want something from you, is a foolishness, and I do not like to be taken for a fool. 'Let's say I'm humouring them.'

Red nodded, then rubbed his chin, thinking. The frown lines between his eyes deepened. 'Why'd they want you on this? No disrespect, you're damn good at what you do, but the man's a fugitive from the law, a cop killer not a bail skipper.'

'It's a little complicated.'

'Always is.' Red gestured for me to sit. He opened the cooler beside one of the deck seats and handed me a soda. As he opened his, he said, 'Why don't you enlighten me?'

So I told him the bones of the thing – that things went bad on my last job and some folks ended up dead. That JT was taking the rap for it, but it wasn't his mess, so I'd taken a deal with the FBI to bring Gibson Fletcher back on the promise they'd make sure JT never got put on death row. I didn't mention JT was Dakota's father. Red was a smart guy, I knew he'd figure out what the spaces between my words meant.

He looked real thoughtful. Drained the last of his soda before speaking. 'I get your motivation, but I'm still wondering on theirs. Why bring you into it? Why not fetch him themselves?'

'There's the rub. The agent in charge, he's got something else going on with Fletcher. Need-to-know, he says. Means he wants a gap between Fletcher getting caught and arriving back at supermax.'

'You don't want to be involved in some dick-waving federal bullshit, Miss Lori. No good can come of that.'

'Yep, for sure, but if I don't, I'm leaving JT to rot … or worse.'

'You say JT told you not to take the deal.' Red held my gaze. 'You ever think it was good advice?'

I looked away.

'It's not what you wanted to hear, I get that, but it seems the man was trying to look out for you is all.'

I didn't want to talk about JT. I stared out across the water, to the far horizon, where the ocean met the sky. I tried to keep my tone even as I said, 'I came to ask you about Fletcher. We going to talk about him, or should I be leaving?'

Red let out a long whistle. 'Well, damn, if you aren't still quite the firecracker.'

I raised an eyebrow. 'Is that a yes?'

He laughed. 'Sure, why not, but when this whole FBI thing comes back and bites you on your ass, don't say I didn't warn you.'

'Duly noted.' I smiled. 'So, what I need to figure out is, what's in San Diego that made Fletcher go there rather than straight to Mexico?'

'Good question.' Red thought for a moment. Took a fresh soda from the cooler and took a swig. 'As far as I remember, his folks are from around here, his brother, too. No cause to trek out to California for them.'

I remembered Fletcher's parents from when I was hunting him before. They were cold people – hard faces, unkind eyes; and not just towards me because I was looking for their son. Their dog, some kind of terrier, had cowered every time Fletcher senior had moved his right hand.

'His brother Donald's close by, isn't he?' I said.

'Yup. He's still in that place just out of town.'

The brother had been more helpful. Not friendly as such, but less openly hostile. 'I'll pay him a visit on my way out to the airport.'

'Good thinking.'

'Fletcher has a wife, doesn't he? Where's she at these days?'

Red shook his head. 'Don't know, although from the way that marriage was heading I'd put money on her filing for divorce as soon as he was put away. It's an angle needs looking at for sure. You want me to help on that?'

'Can you?'

'Wouldn't offer if I couldn't.'

'Then yes, look into the wife, and also any link you can find to San Diego, I appreciate it.' I glanced at the other boats moored up along the jetty. 'Do you know if Fletcher still owns that boat?'

'I saw it listed for sale after he was convicted. Sold pretty damn fast. It was a nice little vessel too.'

I nodded. 'Look, if you're going to help me on this you should know I'm being followed. Don't know by who.'

'Given what you've told me about what's been going on, I'd say you've pissed off a fair few people recently. You got a dash cam?'

'No.'

'I reckon you should. Stick one on the dash, and another out the rear window. Record what they're up to. Might help you work out who they are.'

'Good thinking.' I scribbled my cell number – my personal one not the burner from Monroe – onto a scrap of paper and handed it to Red. 'Look, I'm heading out to California in a couple of hours. Call me if you find anything?'

He took the paper and tucked it into his shirt pocket. 'I'll call you anyways.'

I smiled. Shook my head. He always was the charmer.

7

The mosquitos were out in force. The minute I stepped out of the car I could feel them getting to work on me. Still I dawdled. Even in the blistering heat and bright sunlight there was something about Fletcher's brother's house that gave me the chills.

I glanced around. The neighbourhood seemed quiet. Little traffic noise, the afternoon siesta time punctuated only by a lone dog barking somewhere in the distance. No sign of the black SUV or the silver sedan.

The houses were older here, their structures less uniform than the new builds springing up in the neighbourhood around them. Two-storeys stood shoulder to shoulder with one-storeys, stucco beside wood, modern beside traditional. The nature of the place seemed more organic, more natural – unfenced yards, a feeling of community. Welcoming. Not Fletcher's brother's property, though. That was altogether different.

It was a square two-storey, stucco finish, painted mid-brown with high, narrow windows and a second-level sundeck. On paper that would sound just fine, but in reality it seemed too tall for the plot it occupied. The shadow it created blocked out the sunlight to the neighbour on its right, and a six-foot-high wire-mesh fence blocked people from entering. As I walked to the front gate I spotted it was secured with an automated lock and monitored via a video intercom. I wondered why Donald Fletcher needed such a high level of security.

As I pressed the intercom button, I spotted a red light appear underneath the camera; I was being recorded. I stared into the lens and waited for someone to answer. It didn't take long.

'What do you want?' The voice was male, hostile.

'Donald Fletcher? I'm Lori Anderson. I'm looking for your brother, Gibson. Can we talk?'

'You got the wrong place. There's no Gibson here.'

In my business folks tell you you've gotten it wrong eight out of ten times, but that isn't often the truth. 'Sure, but you know him. And you know me. Check your camera feed – we met before, remember? When your brother skipped bail? I was the person who picked him up.' I smiled into the camera, gave a little wave. 'I won't take much of your time.'

I waited a long moment, then I heard a clunk as the automatic bolt on the gate unlocked, and the man said, 'You've got five minutes, that's all. Make sure you close the gate behind you.'

I did as he asked and walked up the white concrete path to the front door. It was only as I got closer that I realised the door was made of metal. I wondered again what made Gibson's brother so security conscious. He lived in a good enough neighbourhood; I doubted the crime rate warranted all this.

As I stepped up onto the stoop I heard a vehicle out front. I turned and saw the back end of a silver sedan disappear around the corner and out of sight. My heart rate spiked. Were they watching me or had it just been a random drive-by? I clenched my fists. If they'd been tailing me they'd been smarter than before; I'd been careful on my drive over, checked the mirror regularly, looking for a shadow. It worried me I might have missed them this time.

The scrape of bolts being pulled back pulled my attention back to the reason I was here. The door inched open. A man stood in the doorway. I recognised him, but only just. He was about five feet ten, which I'd expected, but he'd lost a lot of weight since the last time we'd met. I remembered Donald Fletcher as a larger guy, not especially fat, just untoned – unlike his brother, who carried his extra weight in muscle. The man in front of me now was slim verging on gaunt. His clothes hung off him, emphasising the fact. His cheeks were hollow, his skin pale and waxy. I noticed far more greys in his black hair, and reckoned his hairline had receded at least a couple of inches. It seemed odd; he couldn't have been more than forty-five years old. I wondered what had aged him so fast. Had he gotten sick?

He didn't speak, just opened the door wider and stepped aside so I could enter, his eyes focused behind me, darting back and forth along the street the whole time.

Inside the house it was cool, the air-conditioning unit cranked up high to combat the afternoon heat. As I followed him through to the living space I was surprised at how stylish the place was: wooden floors, bright couches, large modern-art paintings with splodges and dashes hanging on the white-painted walls.

He gestured for me to sit. 'I'm not offering you a drink. You're not staying long.'

I figured my five minutes had already started so I got straight to business. 'Gibson killed three guards and escaped from hospital a few days ago. Have you seen him?'

'Why should I have?'

'Why shouldn't you?'

Donald sighed. 'Look, I get that you're just doing your job, but I don't talk about Gibson these days. None of us do.' He grimaced. 'All he's brought is shame and embarrassment. I live my life, I pay my bills, and I try not to remember I have a brother.'

The discomfort on Donald's face looked genuine. Got me to wondering if all the security was to keep Gibson out.

'Then I'm guessing you want him found quickly, too?' I said.

'Yeah. Before he does another stupid thing.'

Stupid seemed an odd way to describe multiple homicide. 'More stupid than murdering two citizens and three prison guards?'

Donald exhaled hard. 'Much more stupid than that.'

Something was going on here. I needed to know more. 'Like what?'

Donald looked away, shaking his head. 'You know my folks were destroyed over this? Friends they've had thirty years won't look them in the eye these days. They got cast out of their community. It's not right. What did they ever do?'

I remembered how Fletcher Senior's terrier had flinched every time he moved his hand, and figured Gibson and Donald's parents weren't so innocent. But I needed to get Donald on my side, so I tried real hard to look sympathetic. 'That's a tough deal. I get that it's difficult to talk about him, but to help me find him and get him back to jail, I need to know if you've seen him.'

Donald gave a bitter laugh. 'I'd be the last person he'd come to.'

'Why?'

'Because I'd rest easy even if he was on fire in front of me and I was using the flames to toast marshmallows.'

'Why?'

Donald frowned. 'Long story.'

I checked my watch – quarter after two. I had another half-hour before I'd need to leave for the airport. 'I've got time.'

Donald looked like he was weighing things up, although what things I didn't rightly know. Nodded. 'Alright. The problem with Gibson is he's impulsive. He does things without thinking of the consequences. And he's never been good with money. However much he gets, it's never enough.'

'Same for most folks,' I said. Sure as hell felt that way to me.

'Yeah, I guess. But he's more extreme.'

'Does he have a gambling problem?' I was no stranger to that particular addiction. My husband had been a compulsive gambler, I knew the fallout from a losing streak could be dramatic; I'd experienced the bruises first hand.

Donald shook his head. 'Not gambling, no.'

'Women?'

Donald sighed. 'Yes. But not in the way you're thinking.'

I glanced at my watch. I needed Donald to get to the point. 'Tell me then.'

He rubbed his forehead, as if just thinking about it made his brain ache. 'So you know Gibson was married, right, with a couple of kids, in their teens now?'

I nodded.

'Well, there's another woman. A woman with a husband and a son.'

'A long-term thing?'

'Kind of, but it was complicated.'

I leaned forward. 'Go on.'

'The other woman is married to an influential guy. An important guy in a tough world. Not the sort of man you want pissed at you, you know?'

'Can you give me a name?'

Donald looked away. Scratched at a spot on his forearm over a faded tattoo of a red heart. The name 'Jamie' was tattooed beneath it. 'You don't want to go poking around this; it'll only lead to trouble.'

No doubt. But it was a new angle to the situation with Gibson Fletcher. I couldn't let it drop. 'Perhaps, but I need a name anyways.'

'Marco Searle.'

'And Searle's wife and Gibson were seeing each other right up to Gibson going to jail?'

'Yep, as far as I know. It's been going on a long time. The Searles must have been married near on fifteen years. Their boy's eleven now, but Gibson and Searle's wife started way before that, when we were in our twenties. Gibson and me were boxers of note back then, locally famous, you know what I mean? Searle, he was our manager. That was when it all started. Searle found out and some shit went down. Searle thought it had ended, but they never stopped, they just got better at hiding.'

'And the woman's name?'

'Mia.' He spat out her name like it was poison.

I went with a hunch. 'And you fell out with your brother over her?'

He raised his eyebrows. 'Damn, you ask a lot of questions.'

I didn't reply. Waited for him to answer.

'Yeah, I guess. In a roundabout way.'

'Why?'

He exhaled hard. 'Back then, when Searle found out what they were up to, he went after Gibson one night after a match. Gibson, he was pumped back then, lethal, could have taken out Searle with one punch, but when Searle went at him he just stood there and let the guy pummel him. He didn't even try to block the blows.' Donald exhaled hard. 'So, like a damn fool, I stepped in to defend him. I hadn't been fighting that night, but I had been drinking. Landed a punch wrong. Fractured my hand and screwed my boxing career. I never fought again.'

'And you blame Gibson?'

He frowned. 'It fucked my career. I had to start over. I'd been aiming for the big fights. Vegas. Championship stuff. In one punch, my future was gone. So, yeah, I blamed him alright. Wouldn't you?'

'And Searle never knew Mia and Gibson carried on seeing each other?'

Donald shrugged. 'He must have had an idea, but I'd say he definitely found out about them before Gibson got put inside. There was some kind of bust-up. Searle moved Mia and the boy out of state real fast.'

'Can't have been pretty when the guy found out Gibson and his wife had been seeing each other all those years.'

Donald looked away, started rearranging the magazines on the glass coffee table. 'There were a lot of accusations and threats made, but nothing came of it.'

A man like that sounded the sort to make good on a threat for sure. That he hadn't didn't ring true for me. 'How so?'

'Gibson was caught thieving that same week. Got bailed. You know the rest.' Donald shook his head. 'I guess once he'd been banged up for life Searle decided there wasn't any point pursuing it. Gibson was out of the picture.'

I wondered if that was true. A proud-sounding man like Searle – a guy willing to punch out his own cash-cow boxing star over a woman – didn't sound like the sort of man to let a thing like that go. A man like him, who knows what he'd do to get even? In my experience, anger and pride were never a peaceful pairing.

'Where did Searle move to?'

'Chicago initially. Then he moved again pretty quickly. Mia went with him. I think the boy's in a boarding school somewhere upstate.'

'Where'd they end up?'

Donald glanced at his watch and I guessed my five minutes were done. Standing up, he took a step towards the door. 'As far as I know, some place out in California. San Diego.'

I'd figured as much.

Good job I was heading there next.

8

People do stupid things for love. If Gibson Fletcher's trip to California was down to issues of the heart, he was doing a very stupid thing, taking a massive risk. The safer option would have been for him to go direct to Mexico. Still, that he'd gone to San Diego gave me an advantage. I just hoped he'd stay there a little while, saying his goodbyes and whatnot. It'd be a damn sight easier catching him stateside, that was for sure.

Before I boarded the plane I messaged Red. Filled him in on what Donald Fletcher had told me about his brother and about the other woman, Mia, and her husband and son. Asked him to look into it, try and find me some background details on her and this Searle character, and to search me out an address.

Red hadn't gotten back to me. Didn't surprise me though. He didn't do internet messaging – WhatsApp or whatever. The fact that he even used SMS's was new. So even though the plane's wi-fi was pretty good, I still felt cut off from the search. To stop myself constantly checking, I switched off my cell phone. Figured I'd conserve its energy and my own. I had a feeling things were going to get real hectic once I got onto the tarmac.

Cramped up in my seat, wedged between a large guy in a suit and the window, my legs felt jittery and restless. I needed to move, take action. Instead I ate a cream-cheese bagel and a pack of mint Oreos, and tried not to think on why JT had pushed me away again. Instead the question of who'd been tailing me bounced around my mind. The six hours and fifteen minutes from Tampa to San Diego felt like a lifetime. By the time the doors were being reset to manual I was clawing to get gone.

I cleared the airport terminal in just shy of two hours. It took a whole lot longer than I'd expected due to a delay in the checked bags being hauled to the carousel. That's the downside of checking a bag rather than only having carry-on, but there wasn't much to be done about it. It was a necessity: the only way I could fly with my Taser.

At the Avis counter I handed them the prepaid voucher Monroe had given me, took the keys they offered and signed for receipt of the vehicle. The cars were housed in the lower level of the parking garage. I took the elevator down.

The garage was huge, but with its low ceiling and spaced-out strip lighting it felt gloomy and claustrophobic. I stepped out of the elevator and, as it rose back up, I headed towards the rows of vehicles in their numbered bays, searching for 384.

I'd reached bay 229 when I heard the elevator descend again and the doors open. I kept walking, still looking for my bay. Then I heard footsteps.

I turned. The footsteps stopped. No one was there, or no one I could see anyways. Was I being shadowed? Had the man tailing me in Florida followed me to San Diego?

I hurried along the row, crossed to the next one, and then the next. I'd reached bay 304 before I heard the footsteps again. It sounded as if they were a little ways behind me, to my right.

Halting, I spun round. Heard a scuffle, like a shoe skidding to a stop on the concrete. Then silence. The garage looked deserted, but I wasn't convinced.

Putting a growl in my tone I said, 'Show yourself.'

My words echoed in the gloomy space. There was no reply. No sign of movement. Whoever was there didn't want to be seen. To me that meant things would go one of two ways; either they'd follow me from a distance, or they'd make a move as I got to my vehicle, and most likely try to snatch me. I couldn't let that happen.

Crouching down behind a dark-blue Merc, I unzipped my carry-all and felt inside for my Taser. But I couldn't feel it. The footsteps started up again, getting closer. I had to move. By my calculation, bay

384 would be two rows over and across to my left. I flung the strap of my carryall over my shoulder, and readied the rental vehicle keys. I'd need to do this fast.

Keeping low, I ran along the line, then swerved left, cutting through to the next row. The footsteps started again. Further away now, but still closing. I kept focused on bay 384, pumped my arms, sprinting hard, gulping in the warm, gasoline-scented air.

In bay 384 was a red Jeep Wrangler Sport. I accelerated towards it, pressing the key fob. The lights flashed as it unlocked. Behind me, the footsteps quickened. I wanted to look behind, but that would slow me down. I leaped for the driver's door.

It was stuck. Wouldn't open.

I pressed the key fob again. The lights flashed and I heard the door unlock. Then, *clunk*, it immediately relocked.

Shit.

The footsteps were closing fast.

My mouth was dry. I had to get out of there. I tried again. Stabbing my finger against the key fob and, as the doors unlocked, yanking the door handle. This time it worked. I threw open the door. Jumped inside. Chucking my carryall onto the passenger seat, I fired up the engine. Heard the clunk as the doors locked again. *Safe.*

I jumped at a banging on the driver's-side window, loud and angry. A man's voice shouted, 'Get the fuck out.'

I shoved the gear into drive. Turned. The man – medium build, around six foot, blond hair – yelled again at me to stop. He pulled a Glock from beneath his jacket.

Flooring the gas, I gunned the Jeep out of the bay. In the rear-view mirror I saw the guy raise his gun. I accelerated harder, scooching down in the seat to make myself a harder target. Kept looking for the exit.

He opened fire.

The first shot hit a Corvette to the right of me. The second hit a pillar on my left.

I pushed the Jeep faster, fishtailing it around the end of the row. Exhaled in relief as I spotted the exit. And hightailed it out of there.

That had been too close for comfort.

The man tailing me in Florida had dark hair, not blond. Who the hell was *this* guy?

Carlsbad North Inn was an easy ride along Palomar Airport Road. As I drove I kept checking my mirror, looking for a tail, but there were no vehicles behind me. At first I felt relief, but it came with a chaser of suspicion. I'd expected the guy from the parking garage to pursue me. That he hadn't seemed wrong. I inhaled sharply as a thought hit me – maybe he'd got a tracker on the Jeep.

Pulling over, I opened the glove compartment. I took out the paperwork and ran my hand around the nooks and crannies, did the same around the dash and underneath, checking all the places a GPS tracker could be hidden. Found nothing.

I checked my rear-view again, got out of the Jeep and checked each wheel arch, then used the torchlight app on my cell to search around the lower trim of the fairings. Still nothing. As far as I could tell, the Jeep was clean.

Still feeling uneasy, I climbed back inside and continued to the inn.

It looked welcoming enough – a boxy new build, its yellow-stucco façade illuminated by ground-level spotlights, and the Stars & Stripes flying from the flagpole beside the lobby. I parked around back and headed inside.

It was a fancier kind of place than the motels I usually stayed in, for sure. Pale-coloured walls with black-and-white framed prints, cream stone floor tiles, and a wood-panelled check-in counter. The lobby was quiet, the couches and easy chairs empty, which was standard for this time of night I guessed.

The glossy-haired woman behind the counter looked up as I approached, a well-practised smile on her face. 'Good evening, ma'am, and welcome to the Carlsbad North Inn.'

I forced a smile and handed her my ID. 'You have a reservation in the name of Anderson for me?'

She took my driver's licence and tapped my details into her computer. Looked up at me. 'You're all set. Your room is seventy-four. Take the elevator to the second floor, then you're all the way along the hall to the left. Breakfast is served between six and ten. Enjoy your stay.'

Taking the keycard she was holding out, I thanked her. As I headed to the elevator, I tried to push the tiredness away and figure out what the hell was going on.

Inside room seventy-four I threw my carryall onto the bed closest to the door and took a look around. Everything seemed just fine. The room was clean and adequate, the colour scheme all inoffensive beiges. Could have been orange and silver for all I cared. Form and function was what mattered. The room had a bed and a lock – right then, everything else was incidental.

As always, I planned to sleep in the bed furthest from the door – more chance to react to an intruder that way – and to fix the sturdy-looking desk chair up against the door handle when I turned in. It wouldn't stop someone real determined from forcing their way into the room, but it was a more effective warning than relying on the weak-assed security chain. Given what had happened in the parking garage I figured I needed all the security precautions I could get.

Fatigue had started to dog me, the adrenaline of earlier turning into a heavy ache in my legs. Still, I paced the layout of the room, memorising the number of steps from the bed to the door, from the bathroom to the desk, making a blueprint in my mind, just as JT had taught me way back when I was a rookie and he was my mentor. I waited a minute, then walked the room again, eyes closed this time, just to be sure.

Old habits die hard.

I glanced at my watch. It was well past one in the morning. That meant it'd be gone four am in Florida, what with them being three hours ahead. My check-in with Monroe was at eight am, so whether I went by my time or his, it was too early for that. It was too early for calling Dakota, too, yet the urge to speak to her was as strong as hell. Either I'd been followed from Florida to San Diego or someone other than Monroe and Red knew I was heading here on that specific flight. Neither option was a comfortable thought. It made me wonder what else these people knew about me and my life, and whether Dakota really would be safe at camp.

I switched my personal cell phone back on, dialled the camp number. As I'd suspected I would, I got the office answer service. I left a message: 'Hi, this is Lori Anderson, Dakota's mom. I'm calling to check that Dakota is doing okay? You're aware of the, erm ... situation that happened the week before Dakota joined you. Please call me if you have any concerns, or see anything out of the ordinary, no matter how small. Thank you.'

I wanted them to know they could call me, anytime. I needed to know Dakota was safe. The fact that I'd taken her to camp – away from our home and the normal routine that anyone watching us would have observed – made me feel a little less twitchy about leaving her. But still I hated being apart from her. I needed to get this job done fast and then hurry home. Every minute away from her felt like an age.

With nothing else to be done right then, I wedged the desk chair beneath the door handle, stripped off and stepped into the shower. Let the water cascade over me, washing away the grime of my travels.

As I shut the water off, I heard a beep from my cell. Wrapping a towel around me, I padded back into the room and checked the screen. The voicemail had sent a notification. But the time on it showed it was delayed by a few hours ... while I'd been travelling I'd had a voicemail from a withheld number.

My heart pounded against my ribs. Was Dakota okay? Had something happened at the camp?

With trembling hands, I dialled the answer service.

I breathed out hard, smiling in relief as I heard the deep voice of the man who'd left the message and imagined him sitting out on the deck of his boat in the dusk as he called me. Red said he'd found something of interest about Fletcher. He said he hoped my flight had been good, and asked me to get in touch when I could. He left his cell number.

It was two o'clock my time. Five am in Florida; too early to call Red back, given he'd not said that it was urgent. So I saved his number into my contacts, took my Taser from my carryall, put it on the nightstand, and got into bed.

The mattress was comfortable, but my ribs were still bruised from where the butt of a gun had been jabbed between them during the fight to get Dakota safe. The pain was a constant reminder of how lucky I'd been to get her back in one piece. It made getting settled real awkward and sleep ever more elusive.

Turning off the lamp, I lay on my side, a pillow cushioning my ribs. I closed my eyes, and hoped that sleep would claim me. But the events of the day swirled in my mind – Monroe, Red, Donald Fletcher; being followed in Florida; the man who'd chased me in the airport parking garage. I needed to think through the facts, figure out my next move, but first I needed sleep.

But as I tried to clear my mind, a person I had no control over appeared in my head and straight up refused to fade away again.

JT.

No matter how I tried to ignore them, all those feelings I'd got so good at keeping buried were back, jabbing at my heart. The physical damage inflicted over those three days on the road from West Virginia to Florida was already starting to heal. But it seemed the hurt of letting JT back into my life again, and of maybe losing him a second time, had opened a wound that would take a whole lot longer to fix.

9

It was there when JT returned to his cell after exercise.

Whoever did the drop had been real bold – propped the photograph against his pillow, tucking the bottom edge into the fold of his blanket. Taken time. Wanted to make an impression, get his attention.

They succeeded.

He snatched up the photo and stared at the image. Lori was outside, leaving an apartment – hers he assumed – with Dakota walking alongside her. He traced the outline of his daughter's face with his finger. The bruises that had been deep purple and black when he'd last seen her had faded to green and yellow. She was wearing a Taylor Swift T-shirt. He wondered if Swift was her favourite singer. Hated he'd missed so much of her life, her growing up. Wished he'd got to know her better. Wanted to keep her safe.

He clenched his jaw. This photo wasn't left for him as a keepsake of his daughter. It was a message.

Lori's face was angled towards the camera. She had her go bag with her, and he guessed the photo had been taken before she came to see him, sometime in the last day or so, before she headed out on the job to find Gibson 'the Fish' Fletcher. Whoever had taken the picture must have been waiting for her outside her apartment. JT wondered if she knew she was being watched. Thought most likely she did. He'd been impressed with her skills, and her tenacity, as they'd tracked Emerson – getting back Dakota and putting a stop to Emerson's sick sideline. Lori had always been smart, but in the years they'd been apart she'd developed a resilience and strength that put her up there, at the top of her game. He hoped it was enough.

The two goons, String and Bulky, had asked about her. They'd said the Old Man suspected she was involved in the Miami Mob deaths, but what did they really know for sure?

JT tightened his grip on the picture. The paper buckled beneath his fingers.

He needed them to focus on him. Blame him. That was the way to keep Lori and Dakota safe. If he failed, the gamble he'd taken would be shot to shit; he'd have made himself a fish-in-a-barrel target in the detention facility and left them exposed on the outside. He hadn't warned Lori about the threat. He hadn't told her of the mutterings, of his suspicions. Instead he'd let her walk away. Again.

JT shook his head. Cursed himself for not saying more.

The photo was more than a message. It was a threat, no doubt.

Across the top of the picture they'd written one word: '*REVENGE*.'

Lori's eyes had been scratched out.

10

I woke suddenly. Heart banging. Disorientated by the unfamiliar surroundings. My hand reaching instinctively for my Taser.

Then the noise came again. Three raps on the door.

A woman's voice: 'Housekeeping.'

Taser in hand, I slid out of bed and padded silently to the door. Checked through the spyhole. Through the slightly distorted lens I spotted the woman. She *looked* like housekeeping, with her navy tunic dress and pissed expression. The cart stacked with supplies for the room seemed authentic. Still, I left the door closed, and said, 'No thanks.'

Through the spyhole I saw her smile. Glad to skip a room, no doubt.

'No problem,' she said. 'Have a good day.'

I waited by the door until she moved along down the hall, just to be sure. Heard her knock on the next door, wait, then use a keycard to open the room and go inside. A few moments later I heard the vacuum start. It seemed she was genuine, so I was thankful she'd knocked on my door rather than just letting herself in. If I had woken to find a stranger in my room I would have acted on impulse. It would not have been cool to Taser the maid.

I checked the time: a quarter after ten. It seemed the blackout blinds had stopped me from waking with the dawn. Whether I worked on my time or Monroe's, I had missed my first check-in. Damn. I hurried to my purse, grabbed the burner and switched it on.

Missed Call (11)

Double damn.

I dialled the only number programmed into the contacts list and waited.

'You're late,' Monroe said, irritation mingled in with his usual Kentucky drawl.

I figured I should probably apologise. 'Sorry about that. Late night, you know.'

'Where are you at with Fletcher?'

'Nowhere as yet.'

'What's your next move?'

'I'm going to head back to the airport – visit the storage depot he was spotted at, and see if I can get a fix on where he headed from there. Do you have the details of the flight he arrived on?'

'No. All I have is the eyes on sighting.'

Seemed strange to me that Monroe hadn't checked the flights. 'Can you get me the passenger manifests for the flights that came in that day? If I know how he got here, it could help me figure out where he headed.'

'I'll try.'

'Good. In the meantime, I need you to message me the details of your contact. I need to speak with them, find out exactly what they saw.'

There was a short pause, then Monroe said, 'Yeah, okay, I'll do it now. Keep me posted on your progress.'

'Sure. Will do,' I said, ready to hang up.

'How's the hotel? You like it okay?'

The questions surprised me. For Monroe I was a means to an end; I couldn't imagine my comfort was real high on his priority list. 'It's fine.'

'Good. Okay, check in later. Don't forget.'

'Yep.' I ended the call, swapped the burner for my own smartphone and dialled the number for Dakota's summer camp. Needed to hear my baby's voice. Check she was okay. Feel less guilty.

The call connected but no one answered. I stayed on the line, waiting. Eleven rings, twelve, thirteen. Finally a girl picked up: 'Camp Gilyhinde. This is Sasha. How can I help you today?'

'This is Dakota Anderson's mom—'

'We got your message, thank you. Camp Director said to let you know we'll be vigilant, and there's no need to worry, we have the best security.'

'Okay. Thanks. Can I speak to Dakota please?'

Pause. Then Sasha's sing-song voice said, 'I'm sorry, Ms Anderson, but she's out day-trekking. She'll be back just before sundown.'

I felt a pang of sadness deep in my chest. It was more than twenty-four hours since I'd last heard my baby's voice. I hated that. I cleared my throat, tried to make my tone normal. 'Could you tell her I called, and that I love her, and that I'll call her later?'

'No problem, ma'am.'

The line went dead. I stood holding my cell, staring at the screen as it faded to black. It felt like my connection to Dakota was fading too. I swallowed hard. Bit my lip to stop it quivering. Told myself to get on with the job.

On the bed, the burner phone beeped. I glanced at the screen and read the message from Monroe:

Clint Norsen. Twenties. Dark hair. Warehousing Team B. Southside Storage. Be gentle, this is his first gig.

Forty-five minutes later I was sitting in my Jeep out front of a grey building – all metal struts and concrete blockwork – with 'Southside Storage: Warehouse B' on the sign above the entrance. It'd been easy enough to get to, not being airside, just a case of finding it among the rabbit warren of warehouses that populated the space south of the air-field. I'd doubled back on myself a good few times, made sure I wasn't being tailed. Seemed I'd managed to shake off the blond-haired guy from the previous night, but it didn't stop me wondering who he was and what the hell he wanted. Still, for now I needed to remain focused on the job.

Monroe had told me his contact worked cargo. That seemed to be exaggerating the situation a little. I'd watched the place twenty minutes and seen several transits and the occasional truck drive up to the floor-to-ceiling doors and get unloaded or loaded. This was a storage depot of sorts; a place for items in transit to be deposited and collected. I wondered how the guy had managed to spot Gibson Fletcher; if Gibson had flown in he'd have been on a passenger plane, not cargo. I also wondered if the ID was genuine, or whether Monroe's contact was a little too eager to help. Hoped to hell I hadn't been sent out to San Diego on hearsay rather than fact.

Thinking back to the last conversation I'd had with Monroe I recalled him saying his guy had taken a photograph of Gibson. I'd asked him to send it to me, but he never had. Was that tardiness on his part, a deliberate evasion, or something else? Figuring there was only one way to find out what his contact knew for sure, I climbed out of the Jeep and strode across the blacktop to the warehouse.

I bypassed the reception. They'd stall me, no doubt – I didn't have a legitimate reason for being there, no licence as a bounty hunter in California, and I could hardly use the FBI name to gain access. So I undid an extra button on my shirt, put a little extra wiggle in my walk, and headed for the open loading-bay doors around the side – the place I'd seen the transits back up into.

Inside was a huge, cavernous space – as tall as a three-storey house and then some. With no windows it was strangely gloomy, even in the midday Californian sunshine. A group of guys in blue coveralls were unloading boxes from the back of a white flatbed truck. The nearest one, wearing a dusty-blue ball cap pulled low over his eyes, nodded at me. 'You looking for someone?'

'Clint Norsen. He about?'

'Who wants to know?'

The guy's tone wasn't hostile, but not exactly friendly either. I decided to play the stereotypical dumb-blonde card, and use the irritating way some folks judge us women to my advantage. I tilted my head to one side, curled a lock of my hair around my finger and looked at him all seductive. 'I'm Lori. I'm a … *friend* of his.' I lingered over the word 'friend', figured the guy would get my meaning. 'Just wondered if Clint might fancy a bit of … *lunch*.'

From the ball-cap guy's leer I reckoned he'd caught my meaning clear enough. 'Lucky Clint,' he said, nodding towards the rear of the warehouse. 'He's down in row Q44. Doing inventory.' He gave me a wink. 'You go on back and have some "lunch". I won't tell.'

I thanked him, and hurried across the loading bay and into the main body of the warehouse, the heels of my pink-suede cowboy boots clonking loudly on the concrete floor as I made my way between the metal racks holding boxes of who-knows-what towards Q44.

Monroe's contact was halfway along the row, standing on a ladder, checking things off on a clipboard. He wore the same blue coveralls as the team who'd been unloading the truck, and a blue ball cap turned backwards. A tuft of dark-brown hair poked through the gap between the strap and the main body of the cap. It made him look kind of comical.

I hid my amusement. Kept my tone friendly but businesslike. 'Clint Norsen?'

He flinched. Looked down at me. 'Erm, yeah, who wants to know?'

'I need to speak with you.'

He frowned. 'What about? Who are you?'

'It's official business. Urgent business.' I glanced around – for show; I'd already checked we couldn't be overheard – and kept my voice low. 'I work with Special Agent Monroe.'

I'd never seen someone shift so fast down a ladder. He pulled off his cap as he reached the bottom, face flushed, eyes searching mine. He was nervous, for sure. 'Is this about—'

Out of the corner of my eye I saw the lead guy from the unloading team peering around the far end of the stack; checking up on us. I met Clint's gaze and gave a quick glance towards the guy, then I put my hands against Clint's chest and pushed him against the racks. Rubbed myself up against him and whispered in his ear, 'Your co-workers are watching. They think I'm here for some lunchtime fun. Make it look real.'

He kissed me harder than I'd expected. Slid his hands around my ass and grabbed a feel. I tried not to recoil. Had to make it look convincing so his buddies didn't suspect.

I let it continue twenty seconds, twenty-five tops. When I glanced towards the end of the stack the team leader was gone. I pulled away from Clint. 'Okay, now we need to talk.'

He nodded. His face was more flushed now. 'Yes ma'am.'

Courteous; I liked that. 'I'm here to find Gibson Fletcher. Monroe says you IDed him three days ago, getting off an airplane. I need for you to tell me the details.'

'It was late, after ten o'clock at night; three days ago, like you said, but I didn't see him getting off a plane.'

'What did you see?'

'I was on retrieval duty that night, and a request came in for an item in our vault.' He lowered his voice. 'We don't hold so many things in there. Mostly folks store bulky items with us. It gets ticketed and stowed here on the racks. This was different, stood out from the norm. The guy did, too.'

'How so?'

'Kind of twitchy looking. Not just in a rush. Most people are rushing when they come here – on their way for a flight, or on their way home from one. This guy looked worried. He kept looking around like he thought someone was following him or something. When Chad came into the office and let the door slam, the guy almost leaped clean out of his skin. Seemed strange, especially given he looked like a man who could handle himself, if you get my meaning.'

I nodded. 'Monroe said you took a photo?'

'Sure.' Clint pulled a cell phone from the pocket of his coveralls. Swiped through some pictures before holding the cell out to me. 'This guy, yeah?'

The picture quality was a little grainy, but it was Gibson Fletcher for sure. I looked back at Clint. 'What was the item he collected?'

Clint shook his head. 'Don't know. It was packed in a cardboard box. About the size of a shoebox I guess. He signed for it and left.'

I remembered what Monroe had said about Gibson's little sideline – stealing high-value items to order. Could be the missing chess pieces had been in that box. 'Do you know how long it'd been in your vault?'

'No ma'am.'

'Do you know who checked it in?'

Clint shrugged. 'I don't.'

I took a scrap of paper from my purse and jotted my cell number on it. 'I'm going to need to know, okay?'

He nodded.

I handed him my number. 'You've done great so far, Monroe will be pleased. Find out the details, then call me. Message me that photo of Fletcher, too.'

Using my fingers, I messed up my hair, pulled my shirt a little to the side and wiped off what was left of my lipstick. I smiled at Clint, gestured back towards the loading bay. 'Remember to tell the guys you had a nice *lunch*.'

His cheeks flushed red as I turned and walked away.

11

Lunch was coffee and grilled cheese, eaten alone in a diner by the airport. The air-conditioning was up high, making goosebumps rise on my arms. But what made me so jittery was not that, it was the frustrations of the job, the start-stop nature of the thing.

I checked my watch: almost two-thirty. Dakota would be back from her hike now surely? I pulled out my cell and dialled Camp Gilyhinde. Sasha and her sing-song voice answered on the third ring.

'Hey, Sasha. This is Dakota Anderson's mom again. Is she back from her hike?'

'Mrs Anderson, hello. Yes she is, and she's waiting right here in the office for your call. Let me put her on for you.'

The joy I felt that my baby was there stopped me picking Sasha up on adding 'Mrs' to my name. I wasn't anyone's missus, and I never would be. I'd learned that lesson the hard way, punch by punch. I'd never again let myself get tied to a man.

'Momma?'

Tears filled my eyes. I wiped them away, determined to keep the smile in my voice. 'How are you? How's camp?'

'I love it! It's so fun, Momma.'

'And you're sure you're okay?'

Dakota laughed. It sounded genuine. 'I'm good. I was nervous at first, but everyone is nice. I'm in cabin six and I've got a top bunk. Jenna is on the bottom. She's my best friend now.'

She sounded excited. I was relieved – happy that she was happy. But it didn't make being apart any easier. 'How was your hike?'

'Totally amazing. Counsellor Megan was our guide. We sang songs as we hiked, and I saw a turkey buzzard and its babies real close, and there was this...'

As she was talking, I heard a double buzz from my purse – a message alert on the burner from Monroe. I ignored it. Focused on my baby.

'...and tonight they're showing us how to make a camp fire and light it by rubbing two sticks together, just like JT does, and we're going to cook marshmallows and make s'mores.'

I remembered JT showing her how to make a fire when we were stuck outside overnight in the mountains after crashing the truck in West Virginia. 'That sounds a lot of fun.'

'And tomorrow I've got my first horseback riding lesson.'

She'd always wanted to go riding, but what with her illness and my money problems it hadn't been possible until now. Now I'd got the money to pay for it, I couldn't be there with her. I felt a pang of disappointment. I was missing so much. Tried not to let it show in my voice. 'I'm so glad you're having such a great time.'

'Are you okay, Momma?' She sounded worried, and I hoped she hadn't picked up on my sadness.

'I'm doing just fine. The job is going well. I just miss you is all.'

'I miss you, too.'

I heard the tremble in her voice. Hoped that her enthusiasm for camp life was true and not put on for my benefit. Knew I had to stay upbeat, for her sake. 'I'm so glad you're enjoying camp. I'm very proud of you. Have all the fun.'

'I will, Momma. I love you.'

'I love you too, baby. So very much.'

I heard a voice in the background calling her name.

'I've got to go now. Jenna's waiting. We need to go to the fire circle.'

'Of course. You have fun y'hear. Love you.'

'Bye Momma.'

The call ended. It had been good to speak with Dakota, but my cheeks ached from the effort of forcing a smile and faking happiness. I put the phone back in my pocket and drained the last of my coffee.

The faster I got this job finished, the faster I could be back in Florida with her.

The waitress came over. Nodded at my empty cup. 'You want a refill?'

I shook my head. 'Just the check please.'

As I watched her walk over to the register, I remembered the buzz from the burner phone. I pulled it from my purse.

New Message (1).

It was from Monroe. Short and specific, the words knocked the breath from me like a sucker punch to the chest.

JT stabbed. Call immediately.

12

A shank. A makeshift weapon, fashioned from an old toothbrush sharpened to a point at one end. Eighteen stab wounds. Some shallow, some deep. According to the prison, no one saw anything – not the inmates, not the guards, not even the CCTV.

He almost bled out, right there on the bathroom floor.

'And now?' My voice sounded tight, half strangled. I felt as if I could hardly breathe. 'How is he?'

'He's in the detention facility's infirmary. Biggest worry is the punctured lung, but they're saying he's stable.' Monroe was matter-of-fact. His Kentucky drawl made him sound unconcerned that JT had almost died.

'Is he safe?'

'As safe as anywhere.'

'So not safe.' I clenched my fingers tighter around the burner. 'He's unconscious, lying in an infirmary bed, and he's not safe? That's no way near good enough. I'm out here in San Diego because of you. You want me to keep working, I need to know he's going to survive long enough for you to be able to uphold your end of the deal.'

'Steady. Look, I—'

'Don't you go telling me to be goddamn steady!' I hissed. 'He nearly died, and you don't seem to think it matters a damn. Well it matters to me and I need for you to ensure his safety.'

Monroe sighed. 'It's a prison, these things happen.'

'Not to JT they don't. For them to stab him eighteen times there would have had to be a bunch of them – a big bunch of them. It was a planned attack. They meant to kill him.' I remembered the price on his head put there by Old Man Bonchese. It'd become active as soon as he'd crossed the state line onto the Miami Mob's Florida turf. I reckoned someone had tried to collect on it. 'They'll try again. I need you to make sure they don't succeed.'

Monroe was silent. I waited, heart banging, mouth dry, my whole body feeling like it was on fire. If JT died, so did Dakota's best chance of a bone-marrow donor. If she got sick again her chances wouldn't be good. 'You need to—'

Monroe exhaled hard. 'I'll do what I can.'

'Get him into a private room in the infirmary. Have one of your guys stand guard.'

'Lori, it's a prison. I can't put an FBI—'

'Do it, or I'm walking away.'

'Fuck, Lori. I—'

'Do it. Or, believe me, I'm done. Only reason I'm on this job is to get JT safe. You can't keep him safe, we have no deal.'

Silence.

'Guess you don't need me to do your dirty work for you after all.'

Still nothing.

'Okay, I'm hanging up and I'm heading straight to the airport.'

'Lori, wait. Look, I'll talk to the prison. Try and get a protection detail on JT. But, Jesus, you need to deliver Fletcher for me fast.'

'I've got a couple of leads. I'm doing all I can.'

'Good. I need—'

'Message me when the protection is in place,' I said, and ended the call. I couldn't stop the fear flooding through me from distorting my voice any longer. *Never show weakness*, JT had always told me, *not unless it's a part of your play*. Well, what I was feeling wasn't a play; it was full-throttle real.

JT had been stabbed.

He almost died.

I felt sick, light-headed. As I put the burner down beside my coffee cup, its image blurred as tears distorted my vision. Fighting back nausea, I gripped the edge of the table and tried to stop my hands from shaking.

It didn't work.

There were nearly six thousand miles between JT and me, and I hated it. Hated being apart from him. Hated the feeling of helplessness; that we were divided by circumstance and there was nothing I could do. Hated that I wanted to drop the case and go sit by his side in the infirmary. I felt afraid of what that meant, of what I had allowed myself to feel for him ... again. Knew for sure that me loving him was the biggest damn fool move of my life.

13

Coffee can be a cure for many things, but it couldn't change the distance between me, JT and Dakota. When you're that many states apart, moping and wishing on things being different are pretty much a waste of time, and I didn't have the time to go wasting. The only thing that could get me back to Florida and JT out of danger was my finding Gibson 'the Fish' Fletcher. So that was what I turned my attention to.

But on that front my options were still limited. Clint Norsen – Monroe's contact at Southside Storage – had been eager to help but, until he got back to me with the details of the package Fletcher picked up, I couldn't move that particular line of enquiry forward.

I needed another lead. By my reckoning, one of the reasons Fletcher had been drawn to San Diego had to be the woman he'd been secretly seeing: Mia Searle. As far as I knew their relationship was still on, so I figured if he'd come into town he'd have made contact with her. I needed to speak with her fast. Maybe Red had gotten her address by now.

I checked the time. Just gone three-thirty in California – meant it was a little after six-thirty in Florida: a reasonable time to call. Taking my cell from my pocket, I dialled Red's number. It rang nine times before he picked up. When he did, he sounded a little breathless.

I noted a slight wheeze in his voice as he said, 'Miss Lori? Y'all doing okay?'

'JT got attacked.'

'I'm sorry to hear that. Nothing serious I hope?'

'Serious enough, but stable.'

'Well, that's a blessing.' He sounded genuinely concerned.

I appreciated that, especially after Monroe's indifference. But I

DEEP BLUE TROUBLE **63**

didn't want to dwell on JT's situation. Couldn't trust myself to stay strong if I did. 'Red, I'm keen to get moving out here. I wondered if you'd had any luck getting that address for Mia Searle?'

He chuckled. 'As it happens I have.' He paused a moment and I thought I heard a woman's voice speaking in hushed tones in the background. It didn't surprise me none. A man like Red, he liked his own space for sure, but he didn't strike me as the kind who often slept alone. There was a rustle that sounded like paper, then he spoke again. 'You got yourself a pen?'

I pulled a notebook and pencil from my purse. 'I do.'

'Okay, so Marco and Mia Searle live at 1147 Ocean View Boulevard. It's a fancy piece of real estate from what I've heard – impressive house, big yard, with its own jetty out onto the water. Mr Searle moors a yacht there.'

Interesting – another person with a yacht. 'I'll pay them a visit.'

'Be cautious with this one, Miss Lori.' Red's tone was serious. 'There's a bunch of myth and rumour surrounding this guy Searle. Bad stuff, told in whispers.'

'Like what?'

'Match-fixing, doping and potentially some things a whole lot more sinister.' He cleared his throat and I got the impression he didn't want to go into more detail in front of whatever company he was entertaining for the evening. 'Could be something, or nothing. I'll dig deeper and let you know.'

'I appreciate it, really.'

I could hear the smile in his voice as he said, 'It's a pleasure, Miss Lori. I'll be in touch.'

Forty minutes later I was sitting across the street from 1147 Ocean View Boulevard. I'd been parked up ten minutes, watching. I couldn't tell if the Searles were home. There were no vehicles parked in the street aside from mine, and there were no cars in the Searles' driveway.

There was a fifty-fifty chance they were parked in the garage, but there were no lights or movement inside the house either.

I glanced along the street. Red had been right, it was a fancy neighbourhood for sure. High-value detached properties with plenty of space around them. Perfect lawns and manicured flowerbeds. Long yards leading back to the ocean, space for yachts or jet skis. Like a picture postcard of the Californian dream – in this place extravagant facades and big money were king.

Here, people parked up on the street stood out as strangers. I knew there would be eyes on me. In my red Jeep I was bold and obvious, disturbing the equilibrium of the place. I figured I couldn't stay sitting there much longer without someone coming over to check on my business.

I took the cardboard box that had contained the rental sat nav from beneath the seat of the Jeep and put it under my arm to give the impression I was delivering something. Then, climbing out of the Jeep, I crossed the street and made my way up the block-stone driveway to the Searles' house. Aside from the breeze coming off the ocean and the sound of sprinkler systems working overtime on neighbouring lawns, the place was quiet, almost eerie. I felt self-conscious. I didn't belong here; it was too neat, too ordered, and way too silent. In my experience, tidy and smart are a way of hiding the mess behind closed doors. From what I knew of the Searles' situation, that was surely true. I'd need to play this real careful.

I pressed the buzzer. Waited a couple of paces back from the door. Respectful.

No one came. No movement behind the frosted glass panel in the door.

I rang the buzzer a second time.

Nothing.

I checked my watch: almost five o'clock. Could be they were out at work, although from what I'd heard it didn't sound like Marco Searle was a conventional businessman, and Red had made no mention of Mia having any form of employment. I stepped off the porch, glancing towards the back yard.

That's when I saw it. The gate to the yard was ajar. Just by an inch or two. Stepping towards it, I pushed the gate wider and poked my head around.

There was a woman in the garden, on her knees beside a flowerbed about ten yards away. Her long green skirt was bunched up around her thighs, her bare feet tucked underneath her. She was digging the soil with sharp, angry-looking thrusts of her trowel. Beside her was a basket of bare-rooted seedlings, ready to plant.

I watched her a moment then called out, 'Mrs Searle?'

She flinched. Turned. The look on her face was fear. Flight or fight – that was the decision in her mind.

When she saw me her expression changed. She was still tense, possibly angry, but the fear had gone. She stood up. She was taller than me by at least a couple of inches, slimmer, too. Her long black hair was twisted up onto her head in a messy knot. She wore no make-up, and she didn't need to; her dark eyelashes and brows defined her features naturally. Her movement was elegant, with the grace and strength of someone who works out; yoga, no doubt. She looked at the parcel under my arm.

'Can I help you?'

'Are you Mia Searle?'

She frowned. Eyed me warily. 'I am.'

I let her come to me. Sensed that approaching first might spook her. As she stepped closer I held out my hand. 'I'm Lori. I'm looking for a friend of yours – Gibson Fletcher.'

She glanced towards the house. Ignored my hand, folding her arms across her body instead. 'You should leave.'

I followed her gaze towards the house. 'Is your husband home?'

'What's that got to do with anything?' she snapped.

I looked back at her. Held her gaze. 'Everything I would imagine.'

Her shoulders dropped. 'What do you want?'

'I'm working with the FBI. I need to find Gibson. Trust me, he'd be a lot better off giving himself up to me than trying to make it to Mexico. I know the two of you have history.'

Mia shook her head. She looked tired. 'He hasn't been in touch.'

Something about the way she said it – the air of hope in her voice, how she glanced away from me as she spoke – told me she was lying. 'You sure about that?'

She looked back at me. Held my gaze firm. 'Completely.'

I nodded. Went as if to turn away, then turned back and said, 'Only, when folks are in a jam, they usually turn to the ones they love.'

Mia's cheeks coloured.

'He's turned to you, hasn't he?'

She bit her lip.

'It must be hard, I'm sure. You've got your husband to think about ... and your son.'

'What could you possibly know about anything?' Mia snapped.

'I have a daughter, she's nine, so I know, as a mom, you do all you can to protect your child. And it seems to me you wouldn't want to be involved in a situation that could end up in a man gunned down by a hail of police bullets. Because that's the difference between me finding Gibson and the cops getting him first. Trust me, you'd be doing right by everyone if you tell me what you know.'

She held my gaze for four long beats. It was a stand-off of sorts – both of us waiting for the other to yield.

Mia exhaled. 'When you're young you think being an adult will be so simple, that you'll have things sorted and life will be good.' She shook her head. 'Things have never been—'

The sound of tyres on the driveway out front stopped her speaking. The engine cut off, then a car door slammed shut.

She looked at me, panic on her face. 'You need to leave.'

I glanced towards the front of the house. 'Is that your husband?'

She nodded. 'Go, please.'

'Tell me about Gibson first.'

'I really can't. There's nothing to say. You must leave. Please.'

I needed her to tell me more. Knew I had to ask her more questions, find the truth. But the way she looked at me – a panicked combination of terror and pleading – made me stop. I knew what it was like to fear the one who was meant to love you. I'd lived with my husband Tommy's temper and fists for many years before I'd got free. The look in Mia Searle's eyes told me she was still held in that place. A captive.

'Okay, I understand,' I said. I took my card from my purse and held it out to her. 'If you remember anything about Gibson you think could help me – help all of us – then call.'

She stared at the card then back to me. Shook her head. 'I can't.'

Oftentimes I'd have left the card there, tucked it into her shirt pocket, or put it somewhere for her to pick up later if she reconsidered, but if Mia feared her husband I couldn't do that. Couldn't take the risk that Marco Searle would find it and punish her. So I nodded and put the card back into my purse. 'I'm staying at the Carlsbad North Inn over by the airport. If you think of anything, you can get hold of me there.'

14

The next day I woke early.

Although I'd had seven hours I didn't feel rested. My sleep had been patchy, with dreams of JT slumped in a prison bathroom, bleeding onto the grimy tiled floor, haunting me every time I closed my eyes and mixing with fleeting images of shadowy figures following me. No matter how hard I tried, I could never get a clear look at their faces. In both dreams I felt powerless, angry. I woke with a strong urge for action.

Checking in with Monroe came first. I'd missed my evening check-in the previous night – on purpose rather than by accident. Figured we'd spoken a few hours previously, and after his casual attitude to JT's injuries I was in no mood to speak with him again so soon. But much as I hated it, I needed to give him an update and keep him onside; for now he was a necessary evil.

Grabbing the burner from my nightstand I typed a quick message: *Have poss lead on Fletcher. Following up today. JT news?*

Switching cells, I checked my smartphone. No messages, no calls. Florida was three hours ahead – it was nearer lunchtime than breakfast for them. I figured Dakota would be out horseback riding already. Red was most likely looking into the rumours around Searle he'd mentioned, or could be still curled up with his previous night's company. Either way I had nothing more to work with.

It was obvious to me that Mia knew more than she'd let on. The more I replayed our conversation in my mind, the more I was convinced I felt that she knew where Gibson Fletcher was, and that gave me a problem. I'd gotten the strong impression she wasn't going to give the information up easy, which left me with one other viable way to find it out. I was going to need to tail her.

Stakeouts aren't how they look in the movies. Oftentimes they're dull and it's trickier when you're alone. The bathroom breaks are troublesome, and you have to work hard at not being noticed. A woman sitting in a vehicle for hours on a street with little traffic stands out, which is no damn good because stakeouts are all about blending in.

So I parked further along the street this time. Way back, so that the Searles' house was barely visible, and I wasn't immediately obvious to them. You see, most folks when they enter and exit their homes only give their surroundings a cursory glance. We're too used to being comfortable, feeling safe, in the places we know. We think that familiarity brings protection, when in fact it's most often our weakest spot – we're less vigilant, an easier target. So I figured Mia wouldn't notice me, whereas I had her driveway in my sights, ready to make a move just as soon as she left the property.

I'd been waiting a little more than two hours before anything happened. Two hot, sticky hours with the Californian sun beating ever stronger down onto the blacktop, making the air seem to warp and haze as I watched the Searles' property through my windshield. Waiting. I'd put my hazard triangle out at the side of the Jeep, to fool anyone wondering why I was parked up so long into thinking I'd broken down and was waiting on the tow truck. The downside was that, without the engine, and therefore the air-conditioning, running, the inside of the vehicle was like a regular sweatbox.

Finally there was action. The garage door opened and Mia reversed her silver Ford SUV out of the driveway. Starting the Jeep's engine, I kept it idling until she'd pulled off, turning away from me. I waited until she was almost out of sight before grabbing my warning triangle and following her. Ocean Drive Boulevard was a long, straight road with few side turns. I knew I'd be good for a half-mile before she'd have the option to turn off, so I kept my distance.

As it was, she followed Ocean Drive Boulevard along the waterfront until the signs for a bunch of stores had her take a left. I hung back, let a couple of other drivers slot between us, before I took the same left turn into the parking lot of a BJ's store.

I parked a few rows behind her and waited as she hurried across the lot to the store entrance before I got out of the Jeep. To look a little different from the previous day I pulled my red-and-blue plaid shirt on over my black T-shirt, tucked my hair up under my Red Sox ball cap and slipped on my aviators. Wearing shades inside wasn't something I'd usually do – more often than not, it drew more attention than it deflected – but this was California, folks wore shades as standard. I figured it'd make me blend in more.

A half-hour later and the only thing I'd learned about Mia Searle was her strict diet; unsweetened, organic wholefoods were the only things that she put in her basket. I grabbed a carton of juice, a box of mint Oreos, and a pre-packed chicken salad. Paid at the cashier four stations along from where Mia bought her goods and left the store ahead of her this time. I waited in the Jeep while she loaded her bags into the SUV, and watched her ride out of the lot.

She didn't go straight onto the highway. Instead she took a right and looped back around the retail stores to the drive-thru of First American Bank. I stayed sitting in the parking lot, watching. Used the zoom lens on my smartphone to see what she was doing. Her transaction was fast; a simple cash withdrawal. I couldn't tell precisely how much – more than one note, less than twenty. Could have been housekeeping money or something else. I wondered if it was something else – for a friend; Gibson, perhaps. As she pulled away from the bank I put the Jeep into drive and followed.

At first I thought Mia was returning home, but we didn't turn off onto Ocean Drive Boulevard; instead, we carried on heading along the coastline towards the beach. I kept four cars between us, maintaining a steady speed. Did nothing to attract attention. The freeway was three lanes wide and free flowing. The Jeep was a regular vehicle. It seemed Mia still hadn't noticed she had a tail.

Four miles later she turned off the main freeway and took a road signposted for the beach. I followed, three cars behind. When she parked up on the street I drove on past. Kept going a while before pulling a U-turn and heading back towards her. I parked a couple of hundred yards away on the opposite side of the street and waited to see what she did.

She got out of the car. I noticed then that she'd made an effort to alter her appearance, too – her long black hair was hidden beneath a headscarf tied fifties-movie-star style, and big, oval shades covered her eyes. As she set off along the sidewalk I jumped out of the Jeep and followed.

It was real crowded. Rollerbladers mixed with dog-walkers and joggers. Tourists stood out here, their untanned faces in stark contrast to the locals' beachy looks. I fitted in, my Florida tan a match for the California look, or close enough anyways. The breeze coming off the ocean was cool against my skin, a welcome respite from the heat of the midday sun. Out on the waves I saw the ripped torsos of surfers catching the waves. Thought it looked a fun way to spend a day.

But I didn't have time for fun. With every step I felt the ticking of the clock, the stopwatch counting how long it was taking me to catch Fletcher, how many minutes I'd been separated from my baby girl, and how long JT had been lying vulnerable in the prison infirmary bed.

We walked a good twenty minutes, and I got to wondering if that was all Mia was doing – walking. Maybe this was her regular routine, a place she came to stretch her legs. I started to doubt my tailing her would lead to anything useful.

Then I saw her glance behind. Not a long look, as you might do if you'd spotted someone familiar pass by, but a quick, half-turn of the head; the kind folks going somewhere they shouldn't use. Maybe I was right after all. I kept back, part-hidden behind a muscular guy walking three tiny terriers and a long-haired greyhound, and watched.

Mia slowed her pace and glanced round again. Another few steps and she turned off the sidewalk onto a wooden pier. I lengthened my stride, ducked around the dog-walker, and along to the place Mia had turned off.

I read the sign. 'Pier 61: Coastal Surf Cottages'.

The whitewashed pier had been divided into lots. Each housed a single-storey, weather-boarded cabin with a white-railed fence around it. I counted twenty of them. Pretty, with a perfect view of both the beach and the ocean, I figured they must be summer homes or vacation rentals.

Mia was heading along the walkway between the cabins. Her stride was purposeful, determined. Like she knew where she was going and wanted to get there fast. I needed to follow her, but it was tricky. The walkway was the only route down the pier, but as the only purpose of it was to access the cabins there wasn't much foot traffic. Aside from Mia there was a small boy practising riding his bike, and his mom. If I followed Mia I would be out in the open without cover. Not good. So I hung back. Watched from a little way along the main pier. I leaned over the railings towards the ocean as if I was studying the surfers, but behind the shield of my shades my gaze was trained on Mia Searle.

I watched her open the gate in the white picket fence surrounding the furthest cabin on the left of the pier. Stepping through, she went to the door and knocked twice. She looked nervous, her posture rigid and her hands clasped tightly in front of her. No one answered the door.

She stepped closer and cupped her hands against the glass, trying to peer inside. I figured she didn't see what she was hoping to, as she soon moved away from the door. She stood for a moment, her shoulders hunched, head down – the rigidity gone. Then she rummaged in her purse and took out a piece of paper and a pen. I watched her scrawl something onto the paper and then fold it neatly in half. She moved back to the door. There was a white mailbox to the right of it – smaller and squarer than the usual residential boxes, and decorated with painted pink roses. Leaning down, she opened the box, put the note inside and closed it again.

Turning away from the cabin, she moved back to the walkway and hurried back along the pier. I shuffled a little further along the fence. Made a show of waving towards the surfers, as if I knew them, giving them the thumbs-up. But all the time kept my peripheral vision focused on Mia.

Reaching the end of the pier, she stepped out onto the sidewalk and carried on past me, head down, hands in her pockets, seemingly oblivious to anything around her.

It looked like she was crying.

15

Oftentimes folks don't understand it's the little things that give them up. I'd been telling the truth when I told Mia that people on the run often turn to those they love. What I'd not said was that it's often those loved ones that lead to the person getting caught – and not necessarily because they've co-operated.

It was obvious Mia had been expecting to meet someone at the cabin on Pier 61, and it was no big leap that got me to thinking that person was Gibson Fletcher. I figured if I could find out what Mia had written on that note I might be able to prove my theory. So I waited until she'd got back into her SUV and driven off, then made my way along Pier 61 to the furthest cabin.

The little boy and his momma were still on the walkway, the child wobbling on the bike, his training wheels stopping him from falling. I smiled to his mom as we passed. Acted like I was meant to be on the pier, like I was staying or visiting with a friend. Kept my stride real easy and relaxed.

I let myself in through the whitewashed gate and stepped up to the cabin. The door was half wood, half glass – giving a clear view of the room. It looked as clean and pretty inside as it did on the outside – the same whitewashed weatherboards with pale-blue shutters at the windows, rattan furniture with blue cushions and a blue rag rug laid over the varnished floorboards. I saw no one inside, but there were signs that someone had been there recently – a plate by the sink, a half-drunk bottle of red wine sitting on the counter. I wondered if that person was Gibson Fletcher.

To my right was the mailbox. Kneeling down, I glanced around quickly to check I wasn't being watched, then opened the box. Inside it was empty aside from the folded note I'd watched Mia put there. I took it out, unfolded it and read the three words: *'Where are you? Xox'*

Could be for Fletcher, could have been for someone else. For all I knew, Mia had another lover that she was due to meet with, or a girlfriend of hers was vacationing in the cabin. But my gut told me my original assumption was correct – her upset at not finding the person home seemed too raw for him or her to be a regular friend. If Fletcher was staying in the cabin I was getting closer to catching him. It meant Mia was a valuable asset in the hunt; but, as he'd not been there to meet her, it also meant something could have gone wrong. I needed to find out what.

As I walked back along the pier I spotted a sign for the office and headed towards it. Inside the room was a desk, various filing cabinets and a small bookcase filled with books about San Diego, all colour co-ordinated in white and blue, just like the furniture in the cabin. The woman sitting at the desk smiled as I entered. She wore a yellow sundress that showed off her tan and had flawlessly applied make-up.

'How can I help you today?' she asked.

'I wanted to ask about cabin twenty,' I said, the lie coming easy. 'My family's coming out for the summer. Do you have any availability in the next week or so?'

She tapped a few keys on her keyboard and peered at one of the two computer screens in front of her. Shook her head. 'I'm sorry, ma'am, that cabin's booked up as a permanent let. All the cabins are rentals, but occupied at the moment. Some of the vacation lets end second week of September. I have a few short breaks coming in right after that, but could give you a week at the end of that month. How would that be?'

I moved closer. Stepped a little more to the right so I could get a clearer view of the screens. 'Darn. That'll be too late. It's such a beautiful place you have here.'

The woman gestured to a poster on the wall showing a row of wooden cabins above the dunes. 'They're a little further out of town, but you could try one of our beach properties perhaps? Everything's all booked for the next two weeks, but number sixteen is free after that.'

I kept my face towards her, but behind the cover of my shades I was reading the computer screen. 'I kind of had my heart set on the pier.'

'I'm sorry I can't help. Maybe another time?'

I nodded. 'Yes, maybe.'

I wanted to find out who'd taken a permanent rental on cabin twenty, but the cool efficiency of the woman made me think she'd not disclose such details. In my experience it's only those who don't care about their position, and take no pride in their work, who'll compromise confidentiality in that way. Sure, if I could have mentioned the FBI's name it would have been a whole lot easier, but as Monroe had made clear, I was operating off the books on this job, so I had no formal credentials to persuade the woman I was for real. Without them, I figured I'd not get far.

It was easier to keep her talking while I looked at the double-screen display. On the right-hand screen the booking system still showed the record for number twenty. The cabin had been let out for the past two years just as the woman had told me. It also showed the name of the person it was booked out to: Mrs M. Searle. Whoever Mia had left the note for was staying in the cabin as her guest.

Lunch was a take-out burger and coffee in a go cup eaten back in my hotel room. A functional meal, basic fuel was all. As soon as I was done eating, I picked up my cell and called Camp Gilyhinde. Sasha answered the phone and told me Dakota had gone swimming in the creek, but she'd left a message to tell me she'd had a fun time horseback riding. Usually no cell phones were allowed at camp, but in view of what had happened to Dakota in the previous couple of weeks, I'd been allowed to leave one for her to use in their office, so long as she did it under supervision. Sasha told me she'd have Dakota call me at five-thirty. I said that I'd be waiting.

I was starting to think on my next move with Mia, when the burner started ringing. Monroe was calling early, hours before check-in. I snatched up the handset and answered the call.

'Lori, we need to talk.' His tone was real serious.

My heart started racing. 'Is it JT? Is he okay?'

'His medical condition is the same – stable – if that's what you mean. But I've got a problem.'

Relief gave way to wariness. I felt the hairs on the back of my arms stand on end. 'What kind of a problem?'

'Firstly, a protection detail for JT in prison – that's not going to happen.'

I felt sick. Swallowed down the nausea. Without protection, JT was an easy target for anyone with an eye on collecting the price the Miami Mob had put on his head. 'You promised me you'd arrange it.'

'I said I'd do what I could. And believe me, Lori, I've done everything I can, but my hands are tied here. My boss has vetoed it, therefore it's a no.'

I clenched my fists. 'And what am I supposed to do with that?'

'You're supposed to get on with the job you've got.'

'Why would I when JT is at risk? The reason I'm out here is to get him safe. You've just taken that reason away.'

Monroe sighed. 'No, Lori, I haven't. He might be in the infirmary, but he's still breathing. I've impressed upon the prison authorities the importance of him staying that way. I'm confident they'll make sure he—'

'Why? Because they've done such a great job so far?' I felt heat flush across my skin as the emotions jolted through me: anger, frustration, fear.

'Sarcasm. Nice. I've done what I can. You still have a job to do.'

'That's not the way I'm seeing it.'

'Well you should be, because, assuming he survives just fine, if you don't finish your job for me, the thing that'll be waiting for him once he's all patched up is a one-way trip to old sparky.'

'Bastard,' I hissed.

Monroe didn't miss a beat. 'I've been called worse, but for now you have to work with me.'

I hated feeling as if I had no choice. Putting my faith in Monroe had been hard enough before, but now, without him or his boss willing to get additional protection, I knew the next attempt on JT's life could come at any time. I also hated that Monroe was right: without his help, JT was more than certainly looking at death row and a visit to the electric chair. Monroe knew that, too, and would play on it to keep me right where I was. Didn't mean I had to be civil though. 'You said "firstly"; what else is going on?'

Monroe sighed. 'My boss isn't happy with our progress – there's a lot of public outrage that Fletcher is still on the loose – badmouthing of the department on social media, questioning our competence and the rest. It's the usual, really, but my boss is getting restless, wants it done.'

'Meaning what?'

'He's drafting in more manpower, increasing the size of my official team, so he can convince the media we're doing all we can. It's not my choice, but I can't turn down the resource, it'd look bad.' His voice became more strained. 'You have to find Gibson Fletcher before the official team, Lori. They can't get to him first.'

'Why?'

'Don't ask me that again. All you need to know is that if the team find Fletcher first, our deal's off and your friend JT goes to death row.'

I clenched my fists. 'Does your boss know what you're up to?'

Monroe stayed silent a moment. Exhaled hard. 'Everyone answers to someone.'

Yeah, and right then he had me over a barrel. Shaking my head, I hung up without responding. The clock on the job had just started ticking faster. I had to find a way to accelerate my progress.

I dialled Red's number from my own cell. I needed to hear a friendly voice – it felt like I was fighting for the survival of my family, and in that moment I wanted to feel like I wasn't doing it alone.

There was no answer. The call disconnected and left me staring at a blank screen.

When the landline rang I almost jumped clean out of my skin. I snatched it up, expecting it to be Monroe, pissed at me having put the phone down on him.

I could not have been more wrong.

16

Mia calling me at the hotel must have taken a whole lot of courage. That she wanted to meet, to talk, clearly took a whole lot more, especially given how nervous she'd been the previous day. I wondered if her aborted rendezvous at Pier 61 had something to do with it, and what she thought she was gaining from speaking with me.

But I didn't ask her any of those questions when we met thirty minutes later at Hayley's Diner – a brightly lit, fifties retro place close to the beach and buzzing with lunch trade. I joined her in a booth in the far corner of the room, slid onto the red bench opposite her, and waited for her to tell me why she'd called.

'The iced tea is for you,' she said, nodding towards the glass on my side of the white tabletop.

'Thanks.'

She was wearing the big shades again, so although she was looking right at me I couldn't really read her expression when she said, 'I wasn't always unfaithful, you know.'

I hadn't figured I'd be taking her confession, so her statement took me by surprise. I tried real hard not to show it. 'Doesn't matter to me either way, I'm not here to judge.'

'But you will anyway. Everybody does.'

I fought the urge to ask her straight up about Gibson. I sensed she needed careful handling and that coming to the point her own way was key to her trusting me. So I tried not to think on the ticking clock and the need to find Gibson before the FBI team, and said, 'I'm more interested in why you've changed your mind about talking to me.'

She stared at me a moment, then lifted the oval shades from her eyes, pushing them up onto her head. Fresh bruising shaded the area around her right eye. She held my gaze. 'My husband didn't enjoy his meal last night.'

I nodded, waiting for her to tell me more. She put her shades back in place and took a sip of her iced tea. Didn't seem in any hurry to talk. I glanced away, looked at the four teens in cut-off jeans and strappy tops sipping milkshakes at the round table in the middle of the room, then the pair of young moms having club sandwiches while their babies snoozed in their prams. Tried to hide my frustration.

It must have been near on a minute before Mia started to talk. Her voice was quiet and hesitant at first. Then the bitterness crept in as she continued. 'The first time he hit me I was in shock. He said it would never happen again. He was this big shot, an important man, and he liked to have money. The business was having a few problems; he said he lost his temper because of the stress. Young fool that I was, I believed him.'

I looked at Mia. I knew how that kind of scene played out. I'd been there. Heard all the 'I'm so sorry's. Believed all the empty promises.

'But he did do it again...' I said.

'Yes. But by then I was his wife.'

'So you stayed.'

She pursed her lips. 'I did.'

'And he carried on hitting you?'

'You must think I'm so weak. Of course you do; *I* think I'm weak.' She clasped her hands together. 'You know, I wasn't always so pathetic. When I was pregnant I actually bought a gun. Imagine how ridiculous I must have looked walking into a gun store, the bump of my second trimester clearly showing.' She sighed. 'But I couldn't risk him hurting my baby...'

I stared at her. Till that moment I'd made the assumption Mia Searle was a mother in name only, that she was a woman who preferred others to raise her kid in boarding school miles away from her. I realised now that I'd been wrong, and I felt bad for the disservice. She was a mother protecting her child, even if the best way she could do that was for them to be split apart.

'And did he?' I asked.

She shook her head. 'No, at least not physically. But he can be so cruel.' She stared into the distance a moment, lost in a memory, then looked back at me. 'You know, I learned how to shoot my gun. The instructor at the range said I had a real eye. Sometimes I wish I'd had the gumption to use it...'

I remembered how my best friend Sal had died: shot dead at point-blank range in my kitchen by my husband, Thomas Ford. Killed because she stood up for me when he'd gotten violent. I leaned forwards, put my hand on Mia's arm. 'Trust me, taking the law into your own hands doesn't end well. Call the police and let them handle it, that's my advice.'

She shook her head. 'It's too late. This is my life now.'

'And Gibson?'

A smile briefly flicked up the corner of her lips, then died just as fast. 'He was just this sweet guy.'

The sweet-guy description didn't fit right with the images I'd seen of the inside of Patrick Walker's blood-splattered yacht, or with the pictures of the three guards shot dead in the hospital when Gibson Fletcher escaped. Still, I didn't say anything. Wanted to see where this was going.

'He was kind and funny and I needed some of that.' She looked at me all intense, like she needed me to understand. 'With Marco I felt like I was being ... caged.'

My husband Tommy had had a real bad temper. I shuddered at the memory. I knew all about how claustrophobic a marriage could be, and how those first few slaps could escalate – moving all the way along the line and ending in murder.

'And Gibson made you feel free?' I asked.

'In the snatched moments we had together, yes.'

'So why'd you stay with Marco? Neither of you had kids back then. You could have left – had more than a few snatched moments. What held you back?'

She looked down at the iced tea. 'Marco would never have let me leave.'

'Did you try?'

Mia shook her head. 'I was too weak. At first I didn't have the money to support myself. I threw myself into my work – my art: making life-size sculptures in wire of animals and birds. But nothing ever came of it. Marco didn't want me to pursue art as a career, he preferred for me not to work…'

'And you did as he said?'

'Yes.'

'What about when you knew you were pregnant? You said you were worried he'd hurt the baby – why didn't you leave then?'

'Gibson begged me to.'

'So why didn't you?'

'I ask myself that every day.'

'Get any answers?'

She dropped her gaze. 'Yes.'

I waited.

'If I'd have left, Marco would have killed Gibson. Probably me and the baby, too.'

I thought of the dead bodies Fletcher was responsible for. 'It seems Gibson can handle himself.'

'You're wrong.' She shook her head. 'He didn't kill those people. The guy I know … he's just not like that.'

I narrowed my eyes. Didn't doubt Mia believed what she said, but that didn't make it true. Love puts blinkers on you. It stops you seeing the things you won't like about a man. It makes fools of us all that way. 'How can you be sure?'

She looked down. Snatched up the paper napkin and started fretting the edge of it. 'This is all my fault.'

I felt my cell buzzing in my pocket. Glancing at the clock on the wall I realised it was two-thirty. Damn. I knew the call would be from Dakota, ringing me from her cell phone in the camp office at five-thirty Florida time. I wanted to answer real bad but had to keep questioning Mia. She was the best lead I had on Gibson, so I couldn't let this go, not now the clock was counting down in double time.

'How so?' I said.

Mia didn't answer. She clutched her iced tea and took a sip. As she set it down on the table I saw that her hands were shaking.

'Where do you think Gibson is now, Mia?'

She met my gaze. Didn't blink. Didn't hesitate as she said, 'Mexico.'

My cell stopped buzzing. I tried not to think of Dakota sitting in the camp office, wondering why I didn't pick up. I pushed away the thought, the guilt. Had to keep my mind on the job.

'How do you know?'

Her lower lip trembled. 'Because he told me that's where he was heading – he pleaded with me to go with him.'

'And you refused?'

She nodded. 'How could I leave my son?'

'You could have taken him with you.'

Mia sighed. Didn't speak.

My cell buzzed twice in my pocket. A voicemail. I fought the urge to listen to it right away. Instead I asked, 'You're sure he's not hiding out some place around San Diego?'

'He was, but he's gone now.' Her voice broke as she said the word 'gone'.

'Where in Mexico is he headed?'

'He didn't tell me.'

She sounded truthful, but she'd not been straight with me before, so I asked, 'So when I asked you yesterday if you'd seen him and you told me no, that was a lie?'

She held my gaze. 'I didn't know if I could trust you.'

'What's changed?'

'He's gone.'

'So you've said. Did you expect him to wait for you?'

'I always thought that he would. If he loved me...'

I didn't tell her that I thought it strange he'd made the detour to come see her before heading to Mexico in the first place. 'When did you last see him?'

'Yesterday morning. There's a vacation rental I have a retainer on. It's a bolt hole, somewhere to retreat when life with Marco gets too much, a kind of home-from-home. Gibson found me there.'

'Where is it?'

'Near here.'

That she didn't want me to know the exact location of the Pier 61 cabin was real interesting. It told me she didn't really trust me, and also that she hadn't completely given up hope of Gibson coming back for her.

'And you're sure he's heading for Mexico?'

Mia nodded.

'So why tell me now?'

'Because I'm afraid what will happen there.' She took another napkin from the dispenser and started shredding it. 'Marco has friends in Mexico. Not good people...'

I nodded. I could imagine what Marco's friends would do if they got their hands on Gibson. Understood then that she was talking to me as a measure of last resort.

'You think prison is better than death?'

She gave a bitter laugh. 'Don't you?'

I thought about JT lying weak and unprotected on an infirmary bed. 'For some men.'

'He's a good person. He's not a killer.' She reached across the counter, took my hands in hers and pressed a slip of paper into my palm. On it was her name and a cell-phone number. 'I need you to tell the people you work for, the FBI, that he's not a killer.'

From the hope-filled expression on her face I could tell she believed it. Still, a person's belief can be a real long way from the facts. Gently, I removed my hands from her grip. 'I'm sorry, I can't do that.'

Her expression hardened. 'Why not?'

I looked her straight in the eye. 'All of us have the potential to kill. We just don't know if we'll do it until we find ourselves in that situation.'

She frowned. 'Even you?'

Sliding out from the bench seat, I threw a five-dollar bill onto the table for my iced tea and said, 'Thank you for telling me about Mexico. I can't vouch for Gibson because as far as I know he's guilty. But if you have evidence proving he didn't murder Patrick Walker and his wife, I can pass the information to the FBI and help you clear his name. That's the best I can offer.'

She was still staring at me when I turned and walked away.

17

Dakota had left the office to get dinner when I called back at two fifty-five, just before six o'clock her time; she'd not been allowed to wait any longer. Even Sasha's sing-song voice seemed to have a hard edge of disapproval when she spoke to me. I knew I'd let my baby down. It made me hate the miles between us even more, and doubled my determination to get Gibson Fletcher found fast.

Back at my hotel, I got busy. Monroe had emailed me the passenger manifests from the days between Gibson Fletcher's escape and him being spotted in San Diego – hundreds of lists, thousands of names. I propped my smartphone up on the in-room entertainment guide and ate Chinese food from a carton as I scrolled through the documents, looking for Gibson's name.

It took a while. And I found nothing.

I cussed under my breath. Rubbed my eyes. They felt dry, sore from staring at my cell's screen for hours. Glancing up, I saw Gibson Fletcher's face on the TV. The news banner beneath his picture read, 'FBI Manhunt Continues'. I unmuted the audio. Listened to snippets of the commentary as images of Gibson's initial arrest, the Walkers' yacht and the hospital he escaped from appeared on-screen.

'...Gibson "the Fish" Fletcher remains at large ... FBI directing extra resources to the search ... top priority ... do not approach ... armed and extremely dangerous ... call this toll-free number...'

Damn. The FBI team had numbers on their side – their own and the public. All I had was me, with a helping hand from Red and whatever snippets Monroe threw my way. The odds were against me getting Gibson first, but I had to give it my all. I wasn't going to let myself get beat.

That meant I had to be fast and smart. Faster than I'd been so far, and think smarter than the FBI team. The passenger manifests had been a long shot. That Gibson would've have used a commercial airline was a gamble, and that he'd have used his own name was a down-to-my-last-dollar bet. Twenty percent chance at most, but I'd had to check. Needed to check. *Be thorough and be curious,* JT had always told me. *Notice everything.*

If I knew how Gibson had got from Florida to here, the way he'd travelled and the level of care – high or low – that he'd taken to disguise his identity, it could help me track him now. How his travel had been booked could also tell me if he'd had help, and who from. And if he'd gone to Mexico I'd need the details to follow his trail.

Mind you, Gibson may not have flown into San Diego at all. Sure, Clint at Southside Storage had spotted him two days after he'd escaped, but being near the airport didn't automatically mean he'd just got off a flight. If he'd been strong enough to fight three guards, he could've driven to California. It would have made it a whole lot easier to avoid detection: no ID checks, no hidden cameras, a greatly reduced risk of being spotted. I didn't know how quickly his name had been put on the no-fly list, but it must have been fast. Even if he'd flown under another name, his face would have triggered an alert as he passed through security. Taking a flight just didn't stack up.

I also figured that, for either option to work, he would have needed some help. This'd been a nagging doubt in my mind since Monroe had first told me that Gibson had fought his way out of hospital just hours after surgery. Question was, who helped him? Was it Mia? Or was it something to do with the valuable chess pieces Monroe had talked about? And where in Mexico was he heading?

I needed to look into all the angles. I also knew I should call Monroe and update him. But I just didn't have the stomach for it – I was still pissed at him for not fighting harder for a protection detail to guard JT – so I sent him a message:

Update: Gibson not on commercial manifests. Send private plane/ other traffic landing lists? Source says Gibson gone to Mexico – uncon- firmed at this stage. Awaiting more details. LA.

Through the thin walls I heard people moving along the corridor, heading out for the night. The man in the room next to me had been watching some kind of action film with the sound turned up high; the gunshots and explosions were as loud in my room as in his. I was glad when the soundtrack stopped and a few minutes later his door slammed shut. I prefer silence in unfamiliar surroundings. It's easier to hear danger approaching that way.

I rubbed my eyes again and thought about what Mia had told me, and what Monroe had shared with me about Gibson's escape. There had to be something I wasn't seeing.

Focus on the facts – JT had drilled that into me all those years ago when I'd been starting out. What was it that I knew to be true about Gibson Fletcher? Kicking off my boots, I lay back on the bed as the reported facts and hearsay about Gibson jumbled in my mind. *Look at the timeline,* JT would have said. *Sort the facts from the assumptions. Look for a pattern in the target's actions.*

I curled onto my side. Pulled a pillow close to me and felt my eyes closing. As sleep claimed me one question echoed around in my mind over and over: *What's my next move?*

JT always planned four steps ahead – oftentimes more. But four moves, that was his minimum. He didn't like surprises. Wanted every base covered, every possible option assessed and countered. Always worked real strategic, like a game of chess, he said; each move played out one-on-one until the capture of the fugitive was inevitable. And that was how he'd trained me.

I got the theory, but I'd not always found the practice easy. So ten years back, when I had been learning about the business, JT coached me on it regular, using each job we got as a chance for me to hone my skills. I remembered sitting out on the porch of his cabin, nestled deep in the forest in Georgia, watching the chipmunks scamper in the yard as we worked through the options, checking every which way that a fugitive might run.

My natural inclination was to focus on the where. It'd been that way with the case of the nineteen-year-old pizza delivery girl and wannabe blues singer – Katy Vance – who'd stolen nine hundred dollars from her last drop of the day, robbing a family of vacationers from England at gunpoint. The judge had set bail high, and the indication from her legal counsel was that she'd be serving jail time once they found her guilty at the hearing. When she didn't show for court, we were given the job of finding her. I was a real tadpole rookie back then, maybe five weeks in the job. I was out on the porch the evening we'd been given the job, and handing JT my notebook; written on it was a list of places I figured she might have run.

JT smiled as he reminded me I was skipping a move. 'It's not about where, kiddo, not straight off, otherwise all you're doing is guesswork. Being professional, that's about the why and the how. When you know a person's motivations and the help they've got, knowing where to find them comes easy.'

Easy? I'd thought. How could it be easy? There were so many places, so much distance a person could cover. I stared off the porch at the tall trees surrounding the cabin. They grew close together like soldiers in formation, the dense canopy shutting out the sunlight as effectively as any blackout blind. I shook my head. Finding a person wasn't easy; it was like looking for a bobby pin in the forest. I told him as much.

JT disagreed. 'Work out their anchors, Lori. What is it that keeps them here? Who's important to them?'

'I don't—'

He shook his head. 'Family, friends, freedom – that's the order a fugitive thinks on things when they're on the run. I've done thousands of jobs. It's the same every time. Everyone thinks they're unique, but they're not. The pattern is the same.'

I nodded.

'Anticipate their next move, Lori; where will they go first?'

I thought a moment. 'The vacationers said she seemed desperate, that she was near on pleading with them to give her more dollars, even though she'd already got nine hundred. My guess is she needs more cash. She'll get that first.'

He nodded. 'How?'

'Can't use her cards, because we'll trace them and she's smart enough to know it. So she'll have to steal or borrow.' I thought a moment. 'We know she's not on speaking terms with her family, so she'll go to a friend.'

'Who?'

I picked the file off the porch floor and flicked through it. Alongside the mugshot was a picture of Katy Vance in happier times, her arms around a twenty-something guy with long black hair and an eyebrow piercing. 'Could be she goes to her boyfriend first.'

'But?'

'It depends on why she ran.'

'Exactly.' JT gestured to the file. 'Tell me more about the boyfriend.'

'They live together, been seeing each other over two years. In a band together. No obvious signs they're not happy.'

'He put up her bail?'

I checked the docket. Nodded. 'Yeah.'

'So he's pissed that she skipped out?'

'Real pissed.' I thought back. I'd spoken to the boyfriend after his girl hadn't showed in court. He *was* pissed, but also worried. 'He said she'd been feeling sick recently – stomach cramps, sickness and getting more tired. He was worried she had something wrong that she'd not told him about. Kept pressing on her to see a doctor.'

JT raised an eyebrow. 'Sick?'

Shit. The most likely reality of Katy Vance's situation hit me. 'She'll go to her best friend from the neighbourhood first, then her favourite female co-worker. Boyfriend only if the others can't help.'

'Why?'

'Because with sickness, stomach cramps and tiredness, I'm guessing she's pregnant, and as her boyfriend doesn't know I'm thinking she wants to keep it a secret.'

JT looked real thoughtful. 'Abortions aren't cheap.'

'So she stole the money as a last resort...' I shook my head. 'Damn.'

We'd found Katy Vance hiding out at an old school friend's condo later that evening; she was the only person Katy still had contact with from her early life. She hadn't wanted her boyfriend or any of her new friends to know she was pregnant; they all had dreams of their blues band making it big. She said she'd felt she had no choice but steal the money. Felt she didn't have time to be pregnant, couldn't care for a child, that she was only just done with being a child herself. But as we drove to the police precinct she told me she'd changed her mind; that she'd decided she was going to have the baby. That maybe her and her boyfriend were strong enough to make it work.

Without figuring out her motive for running, I'd never have worked out who she'd have gone to for help, and where to find her. JT was right. Just learning the search and tracking techniques wasn't enough. You had to study the person, understand them and their anchors, and then play your moves according to how they behave – that was how you found a fugitive.

Family. Friends. Freedom. They were the key.

Every time.

In the moments between sleeping and wakefulness I stretched out my arms and felt surprised JT wasn't there. I woke feeling his loss more acutely than I had in years. Forcing myself out of bed before I could dwell on it, I took a shower, using the powerful jets of water to try and clear my head, washing the memories of JT away: how it felt to be with him, to have his hands on my skin, to feel him inside me. Reminded myself that there's no sense pining over a man. I was my own woman, and I had a job to do. I sure as hell was going to get it done.

If Gibson Fletcher had gone to Mexico how would I find him?

If Gibson had gone to Mexico.

Mia had left a note saying, *'Where are you?'* in the post box at the cabin on Pier 61. So she hadn't known where Gibson was. The more I thought on it, the more I suspected her saying he'd headed for Mexico was a guess, an assumption. She knew his end goal was all, and as he'd gone AWOL she had assumed he'd left already. Me, I had my doubts. Family. Friends. Freedom. So far Mia seemed to be Gibson's strongest anchor, and she was right there in San Diego.

But I needed to work both sides of the thing, to cover all the options; to think four moves ahead. So far, the main factors in play were these: Mia – Gibson had been drawn back to her, and I doubted he'd run without her; the package from Southside Supplies – whatever had been inside was important to him, and I needed to know what it was; and Mexico – for Mia to assume he was heading that way most likely meant seeking sanctuary there was their end game.

Three factors influencing Gibson's behaviour based on two of the factors JT said fugitives thought about when they ran. Mia was kind of family, the package and Mexico were about freedom. I wondered if there was something else, something to do with his friends – something I'd not uncovered yet. Either way, I had three factors and three moves; I needed to figure out a plan to mitigate them.

I'd never been to Mexico. It wasn't a place that looked kindly on folks in my line of work, so crossing the border raised the stakes on this job in a big way. I had no contacts there. I didn't speak the language. And I had no clue as to where Gibson would hole up. It was a vast country so Gibson could disappear forever once he'd crossed the border. One thing was real clear; if I couldn't get a better sense of why Gibson had run and who he was getting help from, this job was dead in the water.

18

Turned out Monroe had a plan for how I'd track Gibson. He called me at morning check-in and got straight down to business. 'Lori, you need to get Fletcher out of Mexico.'

'I figured that for myself,' I said, irritated at his tone.

'You worked out how yet?'

'No.'

'So you need a plan?'

For a moment Monroe reminded me of JT – *always have a plan*, he'd said. Thing was, this situation wasn't as straightforward as Monroe was thinking.

'I'm not real convinced Fletcher is in Mexico,' I said. 'My source hasn't been honest before. It could be a bluff.'

'Yeah, it could, but it needs investigating, and we don't have time to wait around. The expanded team is in place – you need to get to Fletcher first.' The casual edge to Monroe's Kentucky drawl had slipped.

'So you've said, and I'm working on it. I'm just not sure we should focus all my efforts on Mexico.'

'Noted. But my decision stands.'

'I thought you brought me in on this because you believed I could find Fletcher. If that's so, seems strange you're not listening to my view.'

Monroe didn't speak. I heard passing traffic at his end. It seemed he was outside and on the move – hiding his association with me by calling me away from his desk. Again I wondered what it was that had made Monroe want to use me for this job. Maybe it was happenstance that JT's arrest fitted real neat with the job Monroe needed doing. Maybe he needed a patsy. Like a bobcat sizing up a fresh deer carcass in a place outside their territory, I needed to say alert, cautious. Monroe was not my friend. I needed to remember that.

'Fine,' I said at last. I kept my tone all business.

'I have a guy – Dez McGregor. He's a local bounty hunter, specialises in extractions from Mexico. It's a high-risk operation, but I'm sure you know that. He's the best there is.'

'So you're handing him the job to find Fletcher?' My heart rate quickened. If Monroe was giving the job to someone else then our deal was off. Where did that leave JT?

Monroe laughed. It sounded stilted, false. 'No, I'm pairing the two of you up. You know Fletcher. McGregor knows Mexico. Working together will expedite the process of finding him.'

I didn't let my relief show in my voice. Stayed cool and professional. 'And assuming we get him, then what?'

'*When* you get him. Our deal stands: you tell me, and I'll give you a location to rendezvous. You, me and Fletcher spend some time talking. Then he goes back to jail.'

'Okay.'

'All that's different is you'll be part of a team now. Dez has a lot of people in his employ. More eyes and ears should speed the process along.'

Not always true. The more people you work with, the more potential there is for things to get screwed up. It was one of the reasons JT worked alone. I'd learned everything from him; used his methods and preferred not to have to rely on others.

'I'm not sure that's going to work for me,' I said.

'Well, you're going to have to make it. McGregor is expecting you first thing this morning. I'll message you his details.'

'So I have no say?'

'Consider it a management order.' Monroe's tone was firm.

'Fine. But don't think you ordering me about is going to make this job work out any better.'

'Let's agree to disagree on that.'

'For sure,' I said, and ended the call.

I flung the handset down onto the bed. Pulled on my jeans and a black T-shirt, all the while seething with frustration. Anger. I knew the way Monroe had handled the situation with JT getting stabbed was still influencing my view of him, and it hadn't made the conversation between us flow any easier.

The burner beeped – a new message from Monroe with the address of McGregor's office. As I was reading it a second message appeared from Monroe: *Hurry, hurry. Clock's ticking.*

Cussing, I chucked the burner and my own smartphone into my purse, slid my feet into my cowboy boots and headed out into the corridor. I was hungry. Dez McGregor could damn well wait.

The smell of eggs and baked goods wafted its way from the breakfast room, making my stomach growl as I drew closer. Inside only a few tables were occupied; a family of four was talking loudly about their plans for the day at their spot over near the window, and a solo woman was eating cereal while reading a mystery novel at a table in the middle. None of them looked up as I entered.

Breakfast was a self-serve buffet with filter coffee warming on a hot plate at one end of the line. I poured myself a mug of coffee, heaped my plate with eggs over-easy, pancakes, bacon and maple syrup, and headed to the table in the back corner – the one with a clear view of the whole room.

There wasn't much going on. I glanced at the television on the wall showing CNN news. The sound was muted, but the subtitles were switched on. As I ate, I read about the latest politician in the middle of a sex-scandal shitstorm. I'd had four mouthfuls before my smartphone buzzed.

I pulled it from my purse. Checked the caller ID, then answered. 'Red, hey.'

'Saw I had a missed call from you, Miss Lori. You doing okay?'

I nodded, even though I knew Red couldn't see me. Forced a smile too. 'Sure, I'm good. Just run into a snag is all.'

'What kind of snag we talking?'

I glanced at the woman at the middle table; she seemed lost in her book. The family on the far side of the room was still talking real loud. Even so, I lowered my voice when I said, 'Could be a Mexico-type snag.'

Red let out a long whistle. 'Yup. That's a problem for sure. You got a plan?'

'I'm working on it. Monroe's wanting me to work with a local guy here – specialist in extraction.'

'Not a bad idea.'

'He works teams.'

For a moment Red stayed quiet. Then he said, 'Ah, one of them.'

I nodded again, knowing precisely what he meant. If you ran teams of bounty hunters you didn't operate like us; you weren't traditional, old school, like the way JT had trained me, and the way Red worked. 'Yeah.'

'Still, if you're going into Mexico, could be best to have someone with you who knows the place.'

That Red thought it could be a wise move made me feel a little more positive. I hated the way Monroe had ordered me about and teamed me up with a local bounty hunter that I had no knowledge of and no trust in; but it was true that his experience of extraction across the border *could* be helpful. Perhaps I needed to give this a chance.

'I guess,' I said. 'Anyways, cheer me up, what have you got for me?'

Red laughed. 'I've found some more about our friend Marco Searle that puts an interesting twist on things.'

'How so?'

'Those rumours of violence? Well, they're more than just rumours. He's been taken into custody more times than I can list, but no charges have ever stuck.'

I thought of Mia's black eye. 'Against his wife?'

'Some of them, yes, but not exclusively. There's a whole bunch of folks, and a big range of injuries – broken arm, broken jaw, broken ribs. But every case ends the same: charges are never brought.'

'You find out why?'

'With his wife they're always dropped. She refuses to give evidence and the cases crumble. The others are more complicated. There's always a reason why he never gets charged – oftentimes lack of evidence – but according to my cop friend the paper trails are as holey as the slowest draw in a gunfight.'

I'd seen this a few times before. In my experience, if it happened more than once there was a simple explanation. 'So someone's protecting him.'

'Yeah. And I've done a bit of digging and found out who. Seems your boy Searle has connections with the Cabressa family in Chicago.'

'The Chicago Mob?'

'Yup. Goes back twenty years at least. And that's not all; he's also done business with the Miami Mob – with Lucano Bonchese to be specific – the Old Man's grandson. I'm told that they're friends of sorts.'

Damn. It seemed everything I came into contact with these days had a connection to the Miami Mob. 'So the Mob are fixing his problems, paying off cops and putting pressure on good folks to turn a blind eye?'

'I'd say so. You need to tread careful, Miss Lori. Searle isn't the forgiving kind.'

'At the moment his wife is my only source of information on Gibson.'

'Like I say, be careful. If Searle clocks you sniffing around he'll take evasive action. Don't matter what you're doing, if he thinks you're a threat he'll warn you off and it's not likely to be gentle.'

'Thanks for the heads-up.'

'You're welcome. Just make sure you watch your back.'

I nodded. I'd spent the last ten years watching my back, and Dakota's. Putting a roof over our heads, feeding us, keeping us safe. I wasn't about to stop now. 'I always do.'

'Good girl. You had any more problems with a tail?'

Somehow, from Red, being called a girl didn't seem patronising. 'No, nothing since the day I arrived. Guess I shook them.'

'Guess you did.' Red didn't sound real convinced.

I changed topic. 'You had any luck with Gibson's ex-wife?'

'Not much, but I'm on it.'

'Did you find her yet?'

'I've got an address, some place out in Lake County. She's remarried, changed her name and all. I've gone over to visit a couple of times, but there's never anyone home. I'm thinking they've gone out of town for a while.'

'You think it's connected to Gibson escaping?'

'Could be. I doubt they parted on good terms, seeing as he was jailed at the time of the divorce and she would only communicate with him through her legal representation. The ex-Mrs Fletcher and her new man most likely aren't wanting to risk it, given Fletcher's conviction for double homicide.'

A good point, I thought. 'Unless he already got to them.'

'True.' Red was quiet a moment, like he was thinking on the probability of Gibson murdering his ex. 'No doubt she'll turn up soon either way. When she does I'll let you know.'

'Thanks,' I said. Mia didn't think Gibson was the murdering kind, she trusted him. But if his ex-wife had done a runner it was possible she didn't think the same way. Interesting. Wife and mistress: two women who'd known Gibson most of his adult life – two different takes on the same man. One trusted him, one not so much. Sometimes trusting the wrong person could be the difference between staying alive and getting dead. I hoped to hell that the bad feeling I'd had about the safety of Gibson's ex-wife was wrong.

It made me consider my own actions, though, and the people I was trusting. I thought back to my training. *Never trust no one.* JT had always been real clear about that, and I'd stayed true to his rule on it for the past ten years.

But with this job I'd slipped. Sure, I'd pulled Red into my confidence to a point, but I was kind of comfortable with that; we'd worked together previously, and he'd proved he was as honourable as I could reasonably expect a man to be. Monroe was different. Our deal was built on necessity, on a final Hail Mary for JT. He was FBI, sure, but he had something else going on where Gibson Fletcher was concerned, that was real obvious. And that meant I couldn't trust him. Yet most of my facts had come from him. So now I was wondering whether I could believe the things he'd told me about Gibson. What was really true here?

I thought back to Mia. Even if Gibson's ex-wife hadn't trusted her husband, Mia had seemed sure Gibson wasn't capable of murder, and she'd known him a long time – longer than his wife. Maybe I should pay a bit more attention to her disbelief.

'Red, would you do me another favour?'

He chuckled. 'Sure thing, Miss Lori.'

'Find out all you can about Special Agent Alex Monroe.'

19

Dez McGregor rubbed my fur backwards from the get-go.

His base was a bail bond shop downtown next to a Subway sandwich place – a simple white storefront with a big sign above the door that said 'BONDS'. I parked the Jeep on the kerb outside and crossed the sidewalk. The door was propped open with a fire extinguisher. Good for getting the air circulating, sure, but useless as a first line of defence warning. It'd be real simple for someone to sneak into the shop unnoticed. Not good if they had mischief on their mind, and, in my experience, bail bonds-men and bounty hunters attracted plenty of trouble.

I stepped inside. First thing I saw was the mess. Paper, stacks of it, cluttering up most of the four workstations in the room. There was no reception desk, no waiting area. Only the workstation in the far corner was occupied – a muscular guy in a Miami Dolphins ball cap was tapping away at a computer. He didn't look round.

I cleared my throat. 'I'm looking for Dez McGregor.'

The guy in the ball cap looked over his shoulder. He seemed surprised to see me, like he'd not heard me come in. 'And you are?'

I stood up a little taller. 'Lori Anderson.'

The guy nodded. 'You come here from Florida?'

'Yeah.'

'Cool. Grab a seat.' He picked up a cell from the desk and tapped something into it. I heard a whoosh as the message was sent.

I raised an eyebrow. 'And?'

He looked back at me. 'And what?'

'Is Dez about?'

The guy grinned. He glanced up at the ceiling. 'Kinda. Give him five, yeah?'

As if on cue there was noise above us, creaking, like someone walking about on the floor above. 'His office is upstairs?'

The guy shook his head. 'He lives there. Just give him a few minutes to get his shit together and he'll be down.'

I checked the time. Almost ten. It seemed Dez McGregor was a late riser. Monroe had told me Dez was expecting me early – I'd figured I was already kind of late. Ten wasn't early. Hell, nine wasn't early. Him still being in his bed made me question just what kind of an operation McGregor ran here.

As if reading my mind, the guy in the Dolphins cap said, 'Late pick-up last night, you know how it goes.'

I nodded. 'Sure.'

'You want a coffee or something?'

'That'd be good, thanks. Black with nothing.'

The Dolphins guy smiled. 'Good job you like it black. We don't got any cream. None of us drinks it here.'

'How many of you are there?'

'Nine all told, though we don't work here every day.' He got up from his desk and walked through the archway at the end of the room. 'Dez has a bunch of other bond shops around the state. We swap in and out of jobs depending on the skills needed.'

I followed him through the archway and stopped. Rather than another room, the space beyond the arch was little more than a closet-sized alcove, just big enough for a sink, coffee-maker and an icebox. I reversed out and perched on the nearest desk, taking care not to disturb the papers heaped all over it. Watched the guy grab a chipped white mug from the drainer and fill it with coffee from a pot warming on a hotplate.

'You specialise?' I asked.

'Some of us, not me though; I do whatever comes in. Some guys focus on search, some on retrieval. Jorge and Monty only do over-the-border stuff.'

He walked across to me and handed over the mug of coffee. As I took it the door at the back of the office opened and a man in cargo pants and a black T-shirt came in. He was in his fifties and obviously in good shape – lean and muscular; not an ounce of extra weight on him. His grey hair was cropped short and his beard tightly clipped.

His dark eyes were staring right at me. 'I see you've met Four-Fingers here,' he said.

'*Bobby* Four-Fingers,' the guy in the Dolphins cap added, giving me a wink. 'I got a real name, too.'

It was then I noticed the thumb of his left hand was missing.

Bobby caught me looking. He laughed. 'Pretty aren't I? Ex-polis. Got injured in the line of duty. The guys reckoned Bobby Four-Fingers was a sweeter name than Bobby No-Thumb.'

I smiled. 'It's pretty sweet.'

'That's enough of the love-in,' the older guy said. 'This is a place of work, and we've got jobs on the clock.'

I looked back at him. 'And you are?'

'Dez McGregor, and you're Lori, yes?'

There was something in his tone that irritated the hell out of me – patronising, with a hard edge of know-it-all. A bad combination. 'Lori *Anderson*,' I said.

He nodded. 'Got it. You're Alex's associate. Here to give us a hand finding the escaped con.'

That he called Monroe by his first name gave an indication of their relationship. That he viewed me as an extra pair of hands to help him rather than the other way around told me more about McGregor. 'I think you've got that backwards. Monroe told me he was bringing you in to help *me*.'

McGregor stared at me a long moment. I tightened my grip around the mug and stared right back. Had to stand my ground. This was my case, McGregor needed to understand who was the lead.

Bobby Four-Fingers shifted his weight from one leg to the other. Cleared his throat. Looked real uncomfortable.

Then McGregor laughed – a single 'ha'. He pointed at me and said, 'Okay then, Lori Anderson, what do you know about Gibson Fletcher?'

I told him the bones of what I knew about Fletcher – his criminal history, and the time I'd tracked him before. I missed out about the lack of love between him and his folks, and what Monroe had told me about the chess pieces. Then I started telling him how I'd come to San Diego on Fletcher's tail, and what I'd been looking into.

McGregor held out his hand to stop me. 'You went alone to question the mistress?' It was impossible to miss the surprise in his voice.

'Yeah.'

Dez frowned. His expression implied criticism of my decision. Personally, I'd rather folks just said what they felt.

'You got a problem with that?' I said.

'Going in alone was a risk. You didn't know if she'd be hostile; you could've got jumped or trapped.'

'I'm a big girl and I've been doing this a while. I know how to assess the risks of a situation. It was—'

'We don't fly solo here. This is a team. To be effective every link in our chain needs to be strong, united. If you're working with us you need to be on board with that.'

I stared at him. He sounded more like some corporate bullshitter than a bounty hunter. And he was wrong: Mia Searle wouldn't have opened up to a 'team'. If he only ever hunted in a pack then using his method I'd never have gotten anything from her. I shook my head. 'I usually work alone.'

'Not here you don't. Not on my watch.' He nodded towards the open door. 'If that's your attitude, best you leave now.'

Seemed we had ourselves a stand-off. Bobby Four-Fingers didn't speak, but his sharp intake of breath told me he felt it, too.

I shrugged. 'Monroe says he wants us working together.'

'He does. And on my pitch you play by my rules, or you don't play at all.'

I gritted my teeth. Monroe had been real clear on us needing McGregor's expertise to extract Fletcher from Mexico. That meant I had to work with McGregor for JT's sake, and for Dakota's future. The way McGregor talked grated on me real bad, but I forced a nod – wasn't much else I could do. For the time being anyways.

'Guess I'll have to accept that,' I said.

McGregor narrowed his eyes. Watched me a moment. Bobby Four-Fingers looked nervous. He glanced from McGregor to me and back to McGregor. The bond shop might be messy as hell, but from the way Bobby watched his boss it seemed McGregor was more ordered in how the chain of command worked.

In my head it was real clear though. I might have to play by his rules on his pitch, but I was still the captain of my own team, even if it was a team of one.

I broke the silence. 'So are we good?'

McGregor cracked a smile. 'Alex is a friend. You respect the way we work here, things will be just fine.'

I nodded. Played nice to broker a truce. 'Then let's get this done.'

'Our target's in Mexico, yes? So that's our focus.'

'As I said, I've talked to Mia Searle, and she's—'

McGregor cut me off. 'She tell you exactly where he's at?'

I put my mug down, the coffee untouched. 'No.'

'Then that's what you're bringing to the party,' McGregor said, his tone dismissive. He turned to Bobby Four-Fingers. 'Call in Jorge. Tell him to get here by two.'

McGregor looked back at me. 'We'll work this as a team – me, Four-Fingers, Jorge and you. We start prepping this afternoon.'

I didn't need to ask who the team leader was; McGregor's authoritative tone made that real clear. But this was my job, and I'd do whatever it took to get it done, and the hell to whatever rules McGregor thought we should all play by.

I wondered how long our truce could possibly last, because the bad feeling in my gut told me things sure weren't going to be easy.

20

The beeping woke him. Incessant. Rhythmic. It took him a while to figure out what it meant.

JT opened his eyes to confirm his suspicions. Saw the cannula first, taped to his hand, the line of the drip snaking over the side of the bed to an automatic pump. Sometimes he hated being right.

He took a moment to get his bearings. The starched white sheet and beeping machine, the drip and all the other medical paraphernalia meant hospital, but the metal bars across the window and the uniformed guard a few feet away told him something quite different. He remembered then where he was. Jail. In the holding section of the detention facility, for prisoners not yet convicted. Grey jumpsuits. Slip-on shoes. Awaiting trial.

Yup. He remembered it all now. He was in jail, and things hadn't been going so well. The bastards had got to him in the shower. He wondered how much damage they'd caused. He took hold of the bed sheet with his free hand, and lifted it. Padded dressings were taped to his chest, across his abdomen and beyond – their whiteness bright against the tan of his skin.

Damn. Not part of the plan. They'd gotten bolder much faster than he'd anticipated.

He tried to sit up. Gritted his teeth as a sharp pain stabbed into his side, making him breathless. They'd caught him between the ribs. Bust a couple of them, damaged his lungs, too. Bastards. They'd learned from the first attempt. The second time they came for him they'd brought reinforcements.

JT closed his eyes. Nausea was making the room spin. He tried to distract himself, thought back and remembered how it'd started. He'd been in the shower. It'd been a busy time. Other guys were waiting in line; the stalls were all occupied. Some theatrical-type along the line was singing in the shower about rainbows or some such nonsense. There'd been heckling from those waiting. JT tuned out their noise, ignoring them all. He'd been rinsing shampoo from his hair when he realised the singing had stopped real abrupt. It'd sounded odd, involuntary, like a hand had been slipped over the guy's mouth to silence him.

JT had shut off the faucet. Listened. Heard no other showers running, and knew something wasn't right. Pulling the towel from the hook, he wrapped it around his waist and stepped out of the cubicle. Looked around. The line was gone; all the cubicles empty. In front of him, waiting, were two guys – lean, wiry types with bad facial hair. They were looking right at him. No question about why. Then six more stepped into the shower room.

So, eight this time.

One of him.

Tougher, but possible.

The first two went down easy; a couple of uppercuts, a hook and an elbow to the nose; job done. But this wasn't a backroom bar fight, or random chancers that fancied their luck – these guys were co-ordinated, they knew their moves. He realised too late that they had themselves a game plan and were executing it in full.

The first two guys had been cannon fodder, there for sparring, for sport, to bait and test him a little while the rest got their game faces on. Once those two guys went down, the shanks came out. Six guys, six shanks – not easy. Add water, tile and soap to the situation and the odds shifted even more dramatically.

JT scanned the room, looking for an out, but all the exits had sentries; prisoners on look-out. No sign of the guards. Shaving foam had been sprayed over the CCTV cameras. Bad news. No record, no exit.

He looked at the biggest guy – a man with a shaved head, crooked nose and full-sleeve tattoos; he was the one that the rest got their lead from.

JT shrugged. 'We could always talk about it.'

The shaved-headed guy raised an eyebrow. 'Who killed Thomas Ford?'

'You're looking at him.'

'Not according to the Old Man.'

'Really? News to me. Last I knew he was baying for my blood over it.'

'Word is, you took the fall for a woman.'

'Not my usual style.'

'Word is she's got a kid.'

JT didn't speak. Didn't like where the conversation was going. They had connected Lori and Dakota to him. They'd connected Lori to Thomas Ford's murder. That put her in danger; Dakota, too. He couldn't allow that, needed time to think on the best play to be had.

The shaved head guy laughed. 'Not so chatty now? What's that about?'

The guys stepped in closer, started circling. Time just ran out. JT knew what was coming. Knew nothing he said would change what they planned. The only way was to fight.

'Didn't you hear me, boy? We heard you're protecting a woman.' The shaved-headed guy stepped closer, got up in JT's face. Shouted louder. 'The Old Man wants confirmation of her name.'

JT stared into the man's bloodshot eyes. Never going to happen. He'd always protect her. JT saw Lori's face in his mind. He needed the Old Man's anger – the kill contract – on him not her; only on him. He glared at the shaved-head guy and shook his head. Still he said nothing.

They set on him as a pack. No order, no etiquette. Jabbing with their pig-sticks, punching with their fists. JT fought back. He took several down, two maybe three, but slipped after deflecting, and dropped to his knee. The bullet wound still healing in his thigh made him slower than usual. He wasn't quick enough to get up.

The pack engulfed him.

He had still been thinking about Lori as the first blade went in.

21

By four, the cracks in my truce with McGregor were starting to show. He'd taken me, Bobby Four-Fingers and Jorge upstairs to what he called his 'command centre'. We'd spent a couple of hours going through Gibson Fletcher's history – rap sheet, family, associates, prison time and the way his escape went down. McGregor used the back wall to create a search board – he pinned Fletcher's mugshot at the top then added photos of known associates, maps of locations he'd been spotted, pictures and media clippings about his crimes and convictions.

'So, this is our guy.' McGregor tapped the picture of Fletcher that was pinned to the wall. 'That's the background check done: ex-wife in Florida, mistress in San Diego, five dead at his hand in total. We're looking forwards from now on in.'

Jorge cleared his throat. He'd been the quietest of us so far. Athletic and toned, he wore cargo pants and a tee the same as McGregor, but his frameless oval glasses gave him a preppy look. 'This is an FBI favour, am I right? Did they give a prediction about the target's movements?'

'So far as we know, our target hasn't been to Mexico before. He'll be a new guy in town, so he'll stand out.'

Jorge nodded. He started tapping on his smartphone. Getting his people into action, I guessed. It seemed he was a man of few words.

'A fish out of water,' Bobby Four-Fingers chuckled. He winked at me. 'See what I did there?'

I smiled. 'Gibson "the Fish" Fletcher out of water – nice word play. Smart.'

'Minds on the job, people,' McGregor said. 'Time is money.'

I leaned closer to Bobby. 'Is he always like this with the bullshit?'

Bobby glanced at McGregor to see if he was watching – he wasn't – then nodded. 'Yup.'

McGregor turned back to us. 'As I was saying, the focus is finding the target in Mexico. Jorge, get your spotters in-country on the lookout. Four-Fingers, you're tracking the tech – cell, cash withdrawals, card use, all the usual – and speak to your police department friends, see if they've got anything we can use.'

I caught McGregor's eye. 'And me?'

He frowned. 'What would you usually do?'

'Work the contacts I've made. I don't think Mia's told me all she knows, and I'm waiting on more from the eyewitness who placed Fletcher here in San Diego a few days back.'

'Okay, you do that,' McGregor said, his tone implying he didn't give a damn what I did. 'I prefer hard data rather than hearsay, but follow your process if you want. It can't hurt.'

I exhaled hard. The man sure knew how to get my hackles rising. 'Don't expect to get much from the tech. When Fletcher skipped bail before he left his cell behind and never touched his cards.'

'Phishing,' Bobby Four-Fingers said, chuckling again.

McGregor and I both glared at him.

Bobby shook his head. 'Jeez, you two need to lighten up.'

McGregor ignored him. 'The difference is, the last time Fletcher had planned on running. This time it's opportunistic. He'll have been improvising from the start. We can use that to our advantage.'

'What if it *had* been planned?' I said.

'You can't fake a burst appendix,' McGregor said, his tone dismissive. 'The man had surgery.'

I stood my ground. 'Yeah, he did. But maybe it wasn't a surprise. Maybe he did something to cause it.'

Bobby Four-Fingers frowned. 'Took a beating on purpose?'

'That's what I'm thinking.'

McGregor rubbed his chin. 'A couple of hard punches? I guess it's possible. But they'd have had to be very precise to make his appendix rupture.'

'Painful as hell, too,' Bobby Four-Fingers said, holding his side as if he'd taken a beating himself. 'And dangerous. If he'd not got medical help in time...'

'For sure,' I said, 'but maybe he thought it was worth it to get clear of the prison compound. Freedom can be one hell of an incentive.'

'Your point being?' McGregor asked.

'You said we're only looking forwards from now on, but I'm thinking we can learn a lot that'll help us predict his future movements if we dig deeper into how the escape went down.'

'What do you propose then?'

'Relationships are how these things get set up, and it's not always the most obvious ones, either. The tech can't tell you who Fletcher was working with.'

McGregor held my gaze. 'If they talked on their cells it can.'

I clenched my fists. Tried to keep my tone even, non-emotional, as I said, 'So you're saying I should butt out and let you find Fletcher your way?'

Bobby looked from me to McGregor. McGregor didn't speak.

I shook my head. 'So that's a yeah?'

McGregor sighed. 'Look, we're not relying on the tech alone. Jorge is running his spotters. They're the best in the business. If Fletcher's run over the border they'll find him. And when they do, we'll go fetch him back. So trust me, the people stuff is covered.'

I frowned. Felt real pissed at him talking to me like I was some hick-ville rookie on their first hunt. 'Trust you?' I shook my head. 'Hell, I don't even like you.'

'Your choice,' McGregor said. He turned away from me, back towards Jorge, who was still tapping on his iPad, and started giving him instructions in hushed tones I couldn't hear.

Bobby looked embarrassed. Getting up, he mumbled something about getting on with the job and went downstairs. McGregor continued to ignore me. Shaking my head I followed Bobby back to the main office.

McGregor was wrong, I felt sure of it. The key to finding Fletcher was discovering who helped him get out of prison and across the country without being spotted. His escape had gone too smoothly to be improvised. My money was on him having help, and the more I thought on it, the more I felt convinced that every bit of the escape – from the timing of the burst appendix, to the shooting of the guards and running from hospital, to turning up in San Diego – was carefully planned. Two questions hung in my mind, though: who helped him, and why?

If McGregor wasn't interested in these then that was just dandy. But I sure as hell was going to find out.

I called Monroe early, didn't wait till check-in. As soon as I'd got back to my hotel room I dialled him on the burner, my fist clenched tight around the handset, the frustration and anger at McGregor's casual dismissal of my methods still stoking the fire in my belly.

Monroe answered after five rings. 'Lori, what's up?'

'Your man McGregor is an ass. He's—'

'The best at across-the-border extraction. We need him in our corner.'

'You *think* you need him.'

'Don't be petulant. We both need Fletcher. So we both need McGregor's expertise.'

'Only if Fletcher *is* in Mexico.'

Monroe sighed. 'Let's not do this again. It's getting boring.'

I bit my lip. Seemed everyone was hell-bent on not listening to me. Good sense told me I was beat. There was no point banging on to Monroe when it was clear he wasn't interested. I'd check into things myself. I worked better alone anyways.

'Fine,' I said. 'Tell me, did you get the private plane information I asked for?'

'I'm working on it.'

'I need it soon as.' I walked across the room to the coffee-maker.

Added a coffee pod and switched it on. 'Also, I need you to get me copies of the prison visitor logs for Fletcher.'

'For what time period?'

'All the way back to the start of his sentence preferably, but at least the last six months.'

'I'll do what I can.'

The coffee-maker grumbled into action, the coffee filtering through into the cup below. I watched it impatiently. Needed a caffeine hit. 'Thanks, I appreciate it.'

'Noted.' There was a hint of a smile in Monroe's tone. 'You not focusing everything on Mexico, then?'

'McGregor is. I've got some other ideas I'm following up.'

'You're playing nice though?'

I took the coffee from the machine. Had a sip. Strong – just as I liked my coffee and my men. 'I'm trying.'

Monroe laughed. 'You sure?'

'Kind of.' And then thought, as much as I was willing to try and work with him.

Monroe's tone became serious again. 'We need him Lori. Getting people back from over the border is dangerous.'

'Yeah.' Not to mention illegal.

'He's the best.'

'So you said already.' I took another sip of coffee. 'Look, I'm not getting in his way. We just do things differently. It won't affect the job.'

'Good.'

'I'm following up a few things here, and I've got Red looking into Fletcher's arrest record and his family life back in Florida.'

Monroe took a sharp intake of breath. 'What has his arrest got to do with anything?'

'I don't know yet, but there's something not right about all this. I need to know what.'

'The deal is with you, Lori, not some retired PI. You've got Dez and his team now. Cut Red loose.'

I shook my head. Knew for damn sure that wasn't going to happen. 'I need a hand from someone I trust. He's my guy.'

Monroe cussed under his breath.

I ignored his swearing. 'So are we done?'

Monroe didn't reply, but it felt like he had something else to say.

'What?' I prompted.

He cleared his throat. 'I didn't know whether to tell you. Don't want to raise your hopes. But JT gained consciousness earlier today.'

I felt a jumble of emotions surge through me, all jostling for top spot: anger at Monroe for not calling me immediately; hope that JT was getting better; fear that he hadn't been in touch with me himself. Relief won.

'Can he speak?' I asked. 'Did he say who attacked him?'

'He's weak, but the doc says he should be able to talk.'

I frowned. Didn't like the sound of that. '"Able to"?'

'He's not said anything about anything yet.'

'Not even about who attacked him?'

'No, not that I know of.'

'Did they ask?'

'Lori, I don't know. I—'

'I need to talk to him.'

'I'm not sure he's—'

Monroe was still speaking as I ended the call. JT was awake. I needed him to tell me who attacked him. But, more than that, I just needed to hear his voice.

22

JT wouldn't speak to me. Wouldn't take my call.

The guard, or nurse, or whatever the man in the infirmary who answered the phone was, put me on hold. The carefree melody of a Taylor Swift song beat out of time with the way my heart was pounding crazy fast inside my chest as I waited. When the music stopped and the man came back on the line he told me in plain words that Tate wasn't up to talking. JT was too weak, he said. But I didn't believe it. If JT had talked to the guy on the end of the line, then he could have talked to me. If he'd wanted to speak with me he would have done, no matter how weakened he was.

That he hadn't hurt real bad.

Still, I didn't dwell on it. Knew nothing good could come from trying to analyse the whats and wherefores. I knew him as well as anyone, but in many ways JT was still an enigma. Maybe that was what made him both so intriguing and so frustrating.

Be tough, I told myself. *You've got this. You don't need him.*

The only person you can ever truly rely upon is yourself.

I'd not expected to hear from Clint Norsen anytime soon, figured I'd most likely be having to chase him on the task I'd asked him to do, so his message surprised me. He wanted to talk. Had more intel. In truth it was a welcome distraction.

So, less than an hour after my aborted call to Monroe and JT's refusal to speak with me, I was sitting in a whiskey bar just inside the good part of downtown, waiting for Clint Norsen to show. I thought it was a strange meeting place for him to pick – I reckoned he wasn't yet twenty-one, so getting served would be trouble. Still, that was his problem. I sipped my drink – an old fashioned made the proper way, with a slice of orange and a cherry – and surveyed the rest of the clientele.

My drink was a good match for the setting. This was a traditional bar – dark wood, polished counter, low lighting – not a brightly lit tourist place. The drinkers around me, most sitting alone as they nursed their drinks, were male and by my reckoning all on the wrong side of forty. The bartender, with his slicked-back hair and neat moustache, looked like he'd been first stationed there in the fifties. He wore a short white apron over his black pants and shirt, and had a white, slightly grubby dishtowel permanently draped over his right shoulder.

He noticed me watching him and flashed a smile. I nodded back, and took a sip of my drink. The glass was almost empty now. The events of the day had made me real thirsty.

I paid no mind that I was the only woman in the place and that several of the guys were looking over their glasses at me. I kind of liked the attention. After all, there's only so much rejection a woman can take before she starts feeling down on herself, and none of the guys looked the type to be giving a girl the wrong kind of trouble.

The jukebox in the corner was playing on free selection. It loaded a fresh CD and I recognised the opening bars of an old Billy Joel tune, the lyrics sounding like they'd been written about a bar just like the one I was in. Draining the last of my drink, I wondered how much longer it would be before Clint Norsen showed and whether I should get myself another.

As it was I didn't need to decide. The guy a couple of stools along the bar put a ten-dollar bill on the counter and slid it towards the bartender. 'Get the pretty lady another of whatever she's having.'

A slightly sexist comment possibly. A come-on for sure, but nothing I couldn't handle. And if he wanted to get me a drink, who was I to argue?

The bartender looked my way, waiting for my agreement. I nodded and turned to the chancer paying for my drink. 'Thanks.'

'You're welcome, ma'am,' he said, nodding towards my pink-suede cowboy boots. 'Great boots.' His accent sounded more Texan than Californian. The shiny buckle on his belt and the black cowboy boots he wore backed up that theory.

'Yours, too.'

He smiled. Leaned a little closer along the bar towards me. 'You from around here or passing through?'

'Passing through.'

He nodded and raised his glass to me. 'Here's to a good trip.'

I raised mine in return. 'And to you.'

The Texan slid down from his stool and for a second it looked like he was all set to come join me. That was the moment Clint Norsen made his entrance.

'Sorry to be tardy,' Clint said, climbing onto the vacant stool between me and the Texan, and signalling to the bartender for a beer. He looked different out of the Southside Storage coveralls; the jeans and short-sleeved shirt he was wearing made him look less gawky, more mature. I figured it was a good job, given our location.

'You invited me here,' I said. 'I didn't expect to be kept waiting.'

Clint didn't get asked for ID. He paid for his beer and took a swig. 'The baby took longer than usual to put down. Teething, I think. Lots of crying.'

I looked at him, surprised. 'Baby?'

'Joni Mae,' he said with a grin. 'I'm a single dad. Couldn't leave her with the sitter until she was settled.'

I smiled. Decided to cut him some slack. 'I understand that. I often-times had the same when my Dakota was little.'

He looked surprised. 'You got a kid?'

'Sure do, she's nine. Why, does that shock you?'

Clint blushed, and he looked more like the gawky kid from the warehouse. 'I didn't mean anything by it. It's just, with your line of work, I figured having a family would be tough.'

'Yeah, it is.'

'Worth it though, right?'

'Sure is. Every moment.' Right then I felt the one-two punch of both missing my daughter and feeling guilt at having left her. I looked away and took another sip of my drink. Be professional. Focus on the job, I told myself. Dakota was just fine. I looked back to Clint. 'But you didn't ask to meet just to discuss kids. What have you got for me?'

He glanced around the bar, then leaned closer, keeping his voice low. 'I found out those details you're after.'

I nodded. 'Go on.'

'The thing is, the package had been stored with us longer than any of the other items in our safe. It arrived before we went fully digital so I had to dig through the archives to find the sender's information.'

'How long ago was it sent?'

'Almost two and a half years ago – March 7th.'

Monroe had told me the chess pieces used in the Vegas game between the two legends disappeared ten days before Fletcher was arrested for the thefts from the *Sunsearcher*. That was the bond he'd skipped on – the one that had put me on his trail almost two and a half years before. The dates matched. The smart money said the chess pieces had been in the package held at Southside Suppliers all this time. Monroe would spit feathers when I told him.

'So how'd it get to Southside?'

'It was sent from Florida via courier. Not our usual service, but an independent company. I managed to get a copy of the documentation, though. Whoever checked the package in did a thorough job.'

'Did it give a description of the contents?'

Clint shook his head. 'Nothing specific; just said "board game".'

Specific enough. 'Who sent it?'

'Well, that's the thing. Most things seemed in order, but when I looked at the sender and collector details there was something that didn't add up.'

The bartender hovered close by, wanting us to order more drinks, no doubt. I shook my head. Waited until he'd moved away to the other end of the bar before asking, 'In what way?'

'Well, on the documentation it says that the guy who picked the package up and the sender were both called Fletcher.'

'I'm sensing a but?'

'See for yourself.' Clint pulled out his cell. Flicked through his photos and showed me two signatures.

'They don't match. No way near.'

He nodded. 'Exactly.'

Taking the cell from him I enlarged the picture. The most recent signature – given when the package was collected a little under a week before – clearly said Gibson Fletcher. I recognised the big, loopy flourishes of the G and the F from when I'd taken him in. Back then I'd thought it looked more like he was giving an autograph than getting signed into jail.

But the first signature – the one given to enter the package into storage – was totally different. Small letters, tight loops, barely legible. I enlarged it again. Peered closer. Inhaled sharply as I read the name. 'Well, shit. And he said they'd been estranged for years.'

'You know who it is?' Clint asked.

I nodded. Re-read the name, just to be sure.

Gibson Fletcher's brother – Donald.

23

Donald Fletcher was on my mind as I drove back to the hotel. It was real late, but I needed to find out what was going on between Gibson and his brother. Despite what Monroe had said, there was only one person I trusted enough to help me. I switched my cell to speaker and dialled Red's number. It rang three times before he picked up.

'You're working late today, Miss Lori.'

'Guess I am. Hope you weren't sleeping?'

'Dozing is all. I tend to sleep light. What's on your mind?'

'I met up with that local bounty hunter – Dez McGregor. He made it clear he was in charge and they didn't need me. So I've been following up some leads of my own. I met with the guy from Southside Storage and there's something odd in their records. Makes me think *Donald* Fletcher could be involved.'

'Interesting.'

'Yeah. Look, can you add another thing to that to-do list of yours?'

'You know I'm an old man, right?'

I laughed. 'You're not old.'

'It's nice that you think that.'

'Can you find out what contact Donald Fletcher had with his brother? He said they weren't on speaking terms, but now I'm thinking that's not true.'

'Sure, I'll get on that. I might have something else on Fletcher, too, but I need to do more checks before I'm certain.'

'Like?'

Red waited a beat before he spoke. 'It's to do with that initial arrest – the vacation thefts. I took a look at the file and—'

'How did you do that?'

He chuckled. 'A good investigator never reveals his secrets.'

'But?'

'Let's just say I still have friends who are polis. I'm meeting one tomorrow. I'm hoping she'll be able to fill in a few blanks.'

I wondered if this female cop was the woman I'd heard in the background when I'd spoken with Red a couple of nights previously. 'Okay. Keep me posted.'

'I'll update you in the morning. Goodnight, Miss Lori.'

I ended the call as I pulled into the hotel parking lot. It was fuller than I'd seen it before, lines of vehicles filling the slots. I drove between the rows. Eventually I found a slot; but had no choice but to park the Jeep in the far corner, further from the building than was my preference. It was late, and I figured there must be some kind of function being held for the place to be so busy. Locking up the Jeep, I set off across the lot to the hotel. The only sound aside from the noise of the nearby highway was my footsteps on the asphalt as I weaved through the lines of cars.

It was real dark. There was no lighting at this end of the lot and the moon was hidden behind cloud, but I knew my way well enough; the spots around the building guiding me to the hotel like a homing beacon. As I walked, I was thinking on Donald and Gibson. On why the package had been stored at Southside Storage for over two years, and on why Donald hadn't mentioned it to me when I'd questioned him about Gibson's motive for stopping in San Diego.

Maybe that's why I didn't see it coming.

I felt him first. Felt his hand around my mouth, another around my waist clamping my arms tight against my sides, yanking me backwards, unbalancing me. He smelled of chilli corn chips. His calloused fingers were rough across my cheek.

He outmatched me in both height and weight. The angle of his arms indicated he was at least a foot taller; the width of them showed he was a hell of a lot stronger. I had no weapon with me – my Taser was in my hotel room – so my only defence would be my fists. I fought the natural instinct to pull against him, knowing his size and momentum would give him the advantage. Instead I pushed back hard – the opposite of what he'd expect. Then, using this moment of surprise, pulled forward and twisted left – aiming to get free and to face him, see him.

He was far stronger than I'd anticipated though. Smart too. He didn't fall for my trick. Blocked me from turning. Didn't let go. Kept pulling me backwards, my heels dragging against the tarmac as I tried to root myself, thrashing beneath his hold. He weaved between the vehicles. There were three lines of cars between us and the hotel door. I could see the light behind the glass entrance door to the lobby; blurred shapes of people moving inside. I tried to yell, but his hand muffled the sound.

'Shush,' he hissed. There was alcohol on his breath. 'Don't go causing a fuss.'

I fought beneath his grasp, but with my arms pinned I had no leverage. So I went limp, then tried to jerk my right elbow into his ribs. He shifted left, blocked me, so the impact wasn't as great. Cursing, he slammed me against a black SUV, trapping me tight with his body weight.

I squealed. Bucked against him and kicked back hard. Felt my foot connect with his leg, and heard him wince. But it wasn't enough. I'd missed his knee. Caused pain but not enough damage.

'I said no fuss,' he growled, pressing himself harder against me. 'Hold still.'

Never. To hold still was to give in, admit defeat. I would not be taken down easy. I thought of my baby girl; of her sweet face, her big blue eyes looking up at me as I left her at camp, and of my promise I'd be back soon to collect her. Felt love and fear and the need to see her again ricochet through me. No fuss my ass! I'd be damned if I'd ever surrender.

I lurched to the left, faking another escape attempt. As my attacker moved with me, I raised my leg forward, pressing my knee against the side of the SUV and, using it as leverage, thrust myself backwards. I threw my head back and felt my skull connect hard against his chin. Heard him grunt. And, in his moment of recoil, I twisted hard to the right.

He didn't release me, but the sudden movement caused his hand around my mouth to slip. I bit down on his fingers, hard as I could. Tasted blood mixed with chilli corn chips. Felt the flesh tearing between my teeth.

He howled in pain. Flung me against the SUV. My head slammed into the window. Glass shattered. The vehicle's alarm started wailing. I hit the ground hard.

Vomit rose in my throat. My head throbbed. My vision went hazy.

Blinking, I tried to focus. Had to escape. Reached up for the door handle, tried to pull myself up but my legs were like Jello. I couldn't stand. My balance was shot. The car alarm pierced into my brain with every shriek. I swallowed hard, trying not to vomit. Through the haziness I saw the dark shape of the man towering over me. I tried again to scramble to my feet. Failed.

The car alarm stopped. In the silence I looked between the cars towards the entrance of the hotel, the light. No one was coming. No one would help.

He crouched beside me. I turned, trying to crawl free, but he grabbed my wrist with his good hand and wrenched me back towards him. Grabbed my arms and pinned them to my sides again. Put his leg across mine, stopping me from kicking.

I spat in his face. Still fighting.

He shook me hard. I felt a stabbing pain in my head. Tasted bile on my tongue. My vision was blurred, useless. My eyes tried to shut. I fought to keep them open, blinking, trying to focus on the man in front of me: dark hair, real muscular, tall.

He pressed his lips against my ear. His voice just audible as he said, 'Leave this alone, Lori. Go back to Florida. And tell Monroe to leave me be. He owes me that.'

Back in my room, I stood in the bathroom and stared into the mirror. My lips were stained with blood, my chin, too. My mascara had run, painting dark circles around my eyes. A bruise was blooming down one side of my face. I looked like a vampire who had lost a fight.

But I'd won, hadn't I?

In truth I wasn't sure. But I was alive, and my injuries were superficial, so that counted for something. Turning on the faucet, I wetted one of the white washcloths and scrubbed my face clean. As I rinsed it out, I watched as the water changed from clear to red to pink and back to clear – the evidence of the attack, washed down the drain. Didn't matter. It wasn't like I would be going to the cops, anyways.

A sharp stab at my temples made me gasp. It felt like someone was drilling into my brain. I grabbed the sides of the basin, gritting my teeth as the pain vibrated through me. As it began to reduce I glanced down and saw the toe of my left boot was scuffed, the pink suede torn into a jagged flap. The knees of my jeans were bloodied and ripped. There was a bloody smear across my left forearm – not my blood. I rubbed it with the washcloth. Winced from the pressure. When the blood was gone I saw dark bruises, hand-shaped, had formed beneath.

The drilling in my head started again and I thought I might vomit. Shutting off the faucet, I staggered back to the bed and slumped down onto it, waiting for the pain to stop. I knew this was the aftershock of reverse head-butting my attacker. It would pass in time, I was pretty certain of that, wouldn't be nothing permanent.

Leaning forward, I rested my head in my hands. I'd been tailed in Florida and followed in the garage at San Diego airport a few days before, but since then nothing. Tonight had been different. My attacker had me pinned; I was beat. He could have done whatever he'd wanted, and although I'd have fought, I'd have lost. But he hadn't taken advantage; instead he'd backed off. Why?

I'd been real groggy, but I'd heard his words clear enough. I replayed them in my mind: *Leave this alone, Lori. Go back to Florida. Tell Monroe to leave me be. He owes me that.*

My vision might have been too blurred to see his face, but I knew that voice. Recognised it from two and a half years previously: Gibson Fletcher.

He'd taken one hell of a risk, revealing himself to warn me off. But it hadn't just been about me. He'd been warning Monroe off, too.

I tried to think on what that meant. Tried to force my aching head to concentrate through the pain. This was important. Gibson had sought me out for a reason. He could have gone direct to Monroe. He could have just run.

Why hadn't he?

I'd told Mia Searle I was working for the FBI, sure, but I'd never mentioned Monroe to her. Fletcher must have worked out that Monroe was involved. And from the way he spoke it sounded like they knew each other. I didn't understand how, and I didn't understand why Fletcher thought Monroe owed him; but from the anger in his voice my guess was there was a whole load of history between them.

I massaged my temples. Surely it wasn't Gibson behind the men tailing me in Florida, though? I hadn't met Mia until I'd come to San Diego. For him to have been watching me in Florida he'd have to have learned about my deal with Monroe right from the get-go. But how? It didn't make any kind of sense. I kept massaging my temples. Tried to stay logical and focus on the facts I *did* know. Top of the list – Gibson wasn't in Mexico. Mia had been in recent contact with him. Gibson had connected me to Monroe.

Tell Monroe to leave me be. He owes me that.

I'd had my suspicions, but now I knew for sure. This wasn't a straight fugitive recovery; there was a whole other hidden agenda going on between Monroe and Gibson. Back when I'd taken the job, Red had warned me against federal bullshit. Now I feared that the bullshit surrounding this job wasn't federal, it was personal between Monroe and Gibson.

And I needed an answer.

24

Next morning, I called Monroe early, before I left for McGregor's office.

Unsurprisingly, he quickly got real evasive.

I held the line. 'I want to know what you're not telling me. Why does Gibson Fletcher think you owe him?'

Monroe sounded irritated. 'I said it's need-to-know, Lori.'

I kept my tone no-nonsense firm. Wished we could be having the conversation face-to-face rather than by phone. 'If I'm getting jumped in parking lots, I *do* need to know.'

'I'm sorry that happened, but you know the risks of the job.'

Son-of-a-bitch. 'But that's the thing. I don't know the risks, because you're not telling me.' I took a breath. Knew that getting Monroe all defensive wouldn't help none. 'I'm trying real hard to do a good job here, but with patchy data my chances are limited. The more you give me, the better the chance I've got.'

'It's a clearance thing.'

'Clearance, my ass.'

Monroe sighed. 'Just do your job, okay. Work with Dez and fetch back Fletcher.'

'I am. But Fletcher knows I'm onto him, and he knows you sent me.'

Monroe didn't seem at all surprised Fletcher had figured out I was working for him. 'We've got history is all,' he said. 'That's enough for you to know.'

'What kind of history?'

'It's not relevant to the job.'

'First, I didn't have clearance, now it's not relevant. Seems you're grasping for any kind of reason not to tell me, Monroe. That makes me uneasy. Tell me why you need the gap between Fletcher being taken into custody and him getting returned to gen pop.'

'I've told you, I need a conversation with him.'

'Why?'

Monroe was silent. I could just make out his breathing; it sounded shallow, rapid. He was nervous for sure.

I decided to push him a little harder. Kept my tone firm. 'I asked you a question.'

'This conversation is over, Lori. Unless you've got something new, just message me at check-in tonight.' The burner beeped as he ended the call.

Slinging it into my purse I thought on my next move. Monroe had been real evasive about his history with Fletcher. He'd given me no answers, and I was no further forwards. He said their past had no bearing on my job, but I couldn't believe that was true. Back when JT was my mentor he'd told me a person's past behaviour – the people they confided in, the actions they took – was key to predicting their behaviour and reactions in the present. *Don't make assumptions*, he'd said, but the more you knew about a person's relationships and everyday patterns, the more successful you'd be at working out where they'd be and what they'd do in any situation.

If Gibson thought Monroe owed him something then their history was a whole lot more than some brief contact. Something had happened between them and that something was a big hole in my understanding of my target. Their history had caused Gibson to jump me and use violence to warn me off – something I'd not predicted, because the details of his past with Monroe were unknown to me. That hole in my knowledge made me vulnerable. I hated that; it scared me. If he'd wanted to, Gibson Fletcher could have killed me last night.

He didn't, because he wanted me to deliver a message to Monroe – to get him to back off. But Monroe wasn't going to; he was upping the chase – raising the stakes by adding Dez McGregor and his team into the mix. That would make Fletcher pissed. Could be he'd come after me again, to finish what he started.

The risks of the job were just getting higher. I didn't know how far Fletcher would go to get me off his tail, but I couldn't rule out him attacking me again. I wondered if the risk was worth it. Glanced at my carryall by the foot of the bed. Five minutes and I could be packed and out of there. Go to the airport, and catch the next flight to Florida. It was real tempting.

Then I thought of JT all cut up in an infirmary bed in jail, and Dakota at camp – finally able to be a kid, enjoying hikes and horseback riding rather than being sick and enduring treatment after treatment. I sighed. If I wanted to get JT away from the Miami Mob, and Dakota's future safeguarded, I *had* to stay on this job. *Had* to catch Gibson Fletcher, and *had* to give Monroe his time with the fugitive before hauling him back to Florida.

One thing was for sure, though – if I was going to finish this job successfully, safely, I needed to fill in the Monroe-shaped gaps. I had to know what had gone down between him and Gibson. If Monroe wasn't going to tell me I'd just have to get the information another way.

Grabbing my cell, I tapped out a message to Red: *Let me know how it went this morning. Also I need intel on Monroe asap. Call me soonest. LA*

Then I grabbed my coat and headed for the door.

25

A team is a lonely place when you're the one that doesn't fit. Dez clocked the bruise down my face soon as I walked into the bond shop. He raised his eyebrow. 'Get into some rough stuff last night?'

Bobby Four-Fingers guffawed. 'Maybe that's how she likes it.'

I narrowed my eyes. Glared at Bobby. 'I pretty much like it any which way just so long as it ain't with you, sweetie.'

His cheeks flushed. 'I was only having some laughs.'

Shaking my head, I turned my attention to Dez. 'I got jumped in the parking lot of my hotel last night. It wasn't a random attack. The guy gave me a message for Monroe, telling him to back off. The guy was Gibson Fletcher.'

That wiped the grins off their faces. Dez glanced at Jorge, who was sitting quiet in the corner, hunched over the computer as usual, then back at me. 'You sure it was Fletcher?'

'One hundred percent. I recognised his voice.'

Dez frowned and gestured to my bruised cheekbone. 'You didn't get close enough to see his face?'

'I got plenty close enough, but he jumped me from behind and by the time I was face-to-face with him I'd had my head bounced off an SUV so my vision wasn't all that.'

Bobby Four-Fingers let out a long whistle. 'Shit, girl.'

Dez's frown deepened. He ran his hand across the stubble on his chin. Shook his head. 'So you can't be certain it was Fletcher?'

'I'm sure.' I stood my ground. 'Once I hear a voice, I remember.'

He glanced over at Jorge again. 'Only, the thing is, we got ourselves a confirmed sighting of our target last night. He lost the tail we had on him, but they said it was definitely Fletcher.'

'Where?'

'Rosarito, Mexico.'

My local geography knowledge wasn't so hot. 'How far from here?'

'An hour maybe.'

'So he could have moved from here to there last night.'

'He could.' Dez's tone made it sound as though he doubted that'd happened. 'Or one of us had a mis-sighting.' He stared at me real hard. It didn't take a genius to know he was thinking I was wrong.

'I know it was Gibson Fletcher who attacked me.' The way I saw it, an hour's drive was nothing. Sure, he'd have had to get across the border twice, but otherwise the journey was easy. 'What time was he spotted in Rosarito?'

Dez glanced over at Jorge.

'23:48,' Jorge said. He had a soft, melodic voice, his accent making even the time sound romantic.

Damn. 'I got back to my hotel around eleven-thirty.'

'Man couldn't be in two countries at one time,' Dez said, rubbing his forehead.

I nodded. 'Yup, I figured that.'

'So what's the next move, boss?' Bobby Four-Fingers asked.

'We wait for another spotter to confirm Fletcher's in Mexico.' Dez sounded tired, the rush of thinking he was close to his target gone. 'No sense in moving before we get that.'

'Why? If you really think he's there what's to stop us taking a look.' I gestured to Bobby Four-Fingers and Jorge. 'If we're there as a team there'd be a whole lot more chance of finding him – four more pairs of eyes to spot him.'

Dez shook his head. 'I told you before, it don't work that way.'

'I don't understand why it—'

'Because *I* say so.' Dez gestured to my face, scowling. 'And from where I'm standing you don't look nearly tough enough to be going over the border.'

I put my hands on my hips. 'I'm just as tough as—'

'Enough!' Dez thumped his fist down on the desk. A pen rolled across it, and fell onto the floor. A stack of files wobbled and cascaded down, covering the keyboard of the computer next to them. Cussing, Dez turned and stomped out of the office. Moments later I heard a door upstairs slam. Then silence.

'Prick,' I muttered. I looked at Bobby Four-Fingers and Jorge. 'What the hell was that about?'

Jorge said nothing. He looked real uncomfortable.

Bobby nodded towards the desk opposite the one Dez had been sitting on. It didn't have a computer on it, just a bunch of files stacked twenty high. 'That workstation wasn't always empty.' Something in Bobby's tone told me things hadn't gone well for the person who'd sat at that desk.

'What happened?' I asked.

Bobby didn't say anything. He glanced at Jorge.

Jorge met my gaze for the first time since I'd been at the bond shop. He shook his head. 'Mexico isn't so friendly to bounty hunters.'

'So I've heard, but it's not exactly a safe job, anyways. I don't get why we can't—'

Jorge shook his head. Looked sad. 'You talk a lot, but talking isn't always so smart. Over the border, talking is one of the things that'll get you killed.'

I frowned. It seemed odd to me. These guys were real worked up over Mexico, yet this was their line of work, their world. I gestured to the empty desk. 'Is that what happened to your friend?'

Bobby Four-Fingers adjusted his ball cap. Looked real uncomfortable. 'We don't talk about that.'

I raised my eyebrows. 'Well, you kind of brought it up.'

'Cartels don't like bounty hunters.' Jorge spoke slow and steady, kept his eyes on mine, not blinking. His tone was neutral, matter-of-fact, but the muscles in his neck were tight, his posture rigid with tension. 'Any bounty hunter who steps across the border has an automatic price on their head, doesn't matter who they're chasing or why. The cartels want the hunters to stay out, and killing is the best deterrent. That and making an example of them – murder with a flair for the dramatic.

Dragging them between vehicles till their bodies break; leaving them buried up to their necks in the desert; having them trussed up and used as target practice. Videos taken. Photos of...' Jorge's voice trailed off.

'I'm sorry about your friend,' I said. Couldn't think of anything more to say.

The memory of cradling my best friend Sal as she died in my arms from a gunshot wound ten years previously replayed in my mind. When you lose someone through violence, no words can make it okay. Nothing can bring them back. The pain stays raw. I knew that from experience.

Jorge nodded. He turned back to his computer and started tapping away at the keyboard again. I looked at Bobby Four-Fingers. His face had flushed, his eyes a little watery.

He gestured towards the other desk. 'If you need somewhere to work you can set up camp here. It's Dez's, but he doesn't use it. He has another upstairs. Prefers things that way since what happened.'

'Thanks,' I said. I knew not to push further for the specifics on what the cartels had done to their colleague. Could see the sharp knife of fate was still close and bloody. 'Can I use the computer? I need to access some documents on my email and it'd be a whole lot easier to read through them on a big screen.'

Bobby wiped his hand across his face. Nodded. 'Sure. The password's EASYRIDE.'

I switched the PC on and as I waited for it to whirl into action I checked my cell for messages. There was still nothing from Red, yet it'd be gone lunchtime in Florida. Opening the message I'd sent him earlier I saw its status said delivered. That meant he'd not read it, and Red always looked at his messages as they came in. That he'd not read it yet made me feel real uneasy.

Hours passed, but there were still no further sightings of Fletcher. I was starting to feel stir-crazy corralled in the bond shop with just the whirl of the ceiling fan and the constant, rhythmic sound of Bobby Four-Fingers chewing gum as a soundtrack.

I buried myself in the details. Monroe had sent through the prison logs and the manifests for all the other aircraft that had landed at the airport in the time window between Gibson Fletcher's escape and Clint Norsen's sighting of him. I went through the flight lists first; pages of names, none of them Gibson's. It was looking ever more likely that he hadn't flown.

At one pm I walked next door and bought a Subway sandwich – tuna melt on Italian – and an iced tea. I brought them back and had them at my desk. Jorge had gone out with Dez on a job, leaving me and Bobby Four-Fingers alone in the office. Bobby was filling out paperwork while listening to a ball game on the radio – the Yankees were playing a smaller team for charity. It made me think of JT. He loved the game. Loved the Yankees. It'd been a source of friendly friction between us when I was training with him – jibes about my team, the Red Sox, used to motivate me through the exhaustion. I smiled at the memory.

'Come on, Lori. You'd be too slow even for the Red Sox.'

I gritted my teeth. The hill was my nemesis. It had been ever since the start of my training, although back then I just had to hike up it. Six weeks later, JT expected me to run and filled my backpack with rocks to make it harder. Told me it was good for me; that I needed stamina and determination; that I had to be able to hit the wall and push through it. That afternoon he wanted me to shave thirty seconds off my previous time.

Eight miles. Near on vertical ascent. All during the hottest part of the day. I was glad that the forest offered some shade, making it maybe eighty-five degrees rather than ninety. Still, the zigzag pattern of the pathway, the humidity and the kamikaze desire of millions of bugs to fly straight into my mouth took their toll on me as we neared the last mile. I was on track, though. I was beating my previous best.

Then things went wrong. Reaching the final turn in the path I slipped as I tried to avoid a tree root sticking up across the narrow track. I felt a muscle twinge in my knee. Grimaced. Knew there were only another sixteen hundred yards to the top.

I limped a couple of strides.

'Don't slow.' JT instructed.

I pushed on through the pain. Shot a look at JT. He'd barely broken a sweat. Looked as if he'd been out on an afternoon stroll.

'Swing your arms harder,' he said. 'Strong legs.'

Damn. He made me want to kill him and kiss him all at the same time.

'Lean into the slope. Eyes on the top.' He surged ahead of me. 'Race.'

It was all I could do to stay upright and keep breathing. I cussed under my breath and he lengthened the distance between us.

JT looked back. Grinned. 'Don't you quit on me.'

'I'm not a quitter.'

He beckoned me on. 'Show me.'

I pumped my arms harder. Determined to beat my previous time. Determined to catch JT.

We sprinted up the path. JT in front, me behind. It was too narrow to run side-by-side here. I stayed on his heels. My breath was loud in my ears, my legs were screaming from the strain, the rocks in my backpack rhythmically banging against my spine.

At three hundred yards to the top JT pulled four paces ahead of me. I pushed myself harder. Fought to keep my breathing controlled and even. Focused on the summit.

'Keep it going,' JT shouted.

I said nothing. Shortened the gap to two paces between us. I remembered what he'd told me before about hill running – take shorter, quicker strides rather than longer ones to increase your speed. I accelerated.

The last twenty yards of the path broadened out again. I saw my chance. Swung left and sprinted around JT, my legs strong, my arms pumping, my focus on the finish, giving it one hundred percent.

I beat him. Turned, and as I did I stumbled. Fell. Hit the dirt with my shoulder and then my hip. Rolled onto my back, lay arms-out like a beached starfish, and laughed.

JT stood over me, checked his stopwatch. 'Nicely played. Thirty-six seconds faster, too.'

I raised my fingers to my forehead in salute. I was still breathing heavily, getting the air back into my lungs. 'I'm not a quitter.'

'Always knew that.'

I smiled. 'So what's my reward?'

'I'll think of something.'

He held out his hand to help me up. I took it, and made as if I was going to stand, then lay back and pulled him down to me.

He didn't put up any resistance. Grinned, and kissed me on the tip of my nose. For a man who said he preferred to be alone, he sure seemed to enjoy us being together. Not that he'd say as much, of course. Not that he'd talk about us, even on the odd occasion I grew bold enough to raise it.

I reached out to him. Stroked his face, my fingertips trailing across his stubble. 'You know, I think you like me being here, really.'

He didn't answer, not with words. Kissed me instead, long and slow, like we had all the time in the world.

Afterwards, as we lay on the forest floor, looking up at the birds singing above us in the tree canopy, I felt happy for the first time in a long while. Of course, I knew even then that it couldn't last.

JT often quoted some saying about men being islands as if it were written just for him. He worked alone. Lived alone. Made out that he wanted the uncomplicated life of no worries about anyone or anything. Wasn't true, though. Not when I looked back at how he'd been, how *we'd* been. The only trouble was that he'd never admitted to wanting me.

I stared at my screen and tried to focus on the scanned prison logs. But the memory of JT lingered. The uncertainty of what we had, if we had anything at all, made my stomach flip.

Why wouldn't he speak with me when I called?

Why wouldn't he talk about Dakota being his child?

Why did he push me away when I was trying to help him?

I shook my head. He was the most frustrating man I'd ever known, but he was also the most exciting. Thing was, he was wrong about the whole each of us being islands thing. Neither of us were islands. We were more like planets drawn together by each other's magnetic fields, messing with each other's atmospheres and trying our damnedest just to stay intact.

The current situation might just break both of us. I couldn't let that happen. I was far tougher than McGregor gave me credit for and I was going to prove to him that I was more than his equal. I pushed the thoughts of JT aside, and made a start on the prison visitor log.

26

Gibson Fletcher wasn't an island, at least not on the first Tuesday of every month. According to the prison visitor logs, for the past year Gibson had been receiving a regular visitor – his brother, Donald.

Every month Donald had visited for one hour, bang on – no more, no less. It was right there on the scanned copy of the visitor log open on my screen, signed and dated and witnessed. Grabbing my cell, I compared the photo of Donald's signature on the Southside Storage form that Clint Norsen had given me. It was a perfect match.

Busted.

No contact. That's what Donald had told me. He'd said he and Gibson had fallen out years before, that they didn't see each other and he had no desire to help his brother. He'd been bitter, made it sound genuine. But his own signature seemed to be telling me different; he'd sent the package and he'd visited Gibson every month in jail. I scrolled back through the pages of the log and checked them twice. Made sure there was no mistake.

There wasn't, but there was an anomaly; a change in the pattern the final time they'd seen each other. Donald had visited Gibson the day before his appendix had burst. Which hadn't been a Tuesday, and which wasn't at the start of the month. And that day he'd only stayed seventeen minutes.

Donald's story didn't stack up anymore. I'd caught him in a lie and that got me to thinking there was something underhand going on between the Fletcher brothers. Why else would Donald hide the fact they were on speaking terms. I wondered if he was embarrassed, and kept the contact between them secret due to his folks being so disapproving. Or maybe there was a more sinister reason, something more criminal, and the feud was a smokescreen to hide something else. I wanted to know what Donald was hiding and why he'd lied to me.

Reaching for my cell, I checked my messages. Still nothing from Red, and he hadn't looked at my earlier message either. I dialled his number. The call connected, ringing unanswered until it switched to voicemail. I tried again, same thing happened.

My stomach flipped. Something was wrong. It'd be late afternoon in Florida now. Red should've called me before lunch. I needed to know what was going on.

I glanced over at Bobby Four-Fingers. He was leaning back in his chair, eyes closed as he listened to the game. Dez and Jorge were still out and he was happily taking advantage. There'd still been no calls giving fresh sightings of Gibson in Mexico. Yet the clock was counting down and time was wasting.

'Bobby?' I said.

He opened one eye. Didn't look at all guilty he'd been caught slacking. 'Yup?'

'I need to follow a lead out of town, okay.' I scrawled my cell number onto a piece of scrap paper and tossed it across to him. 'Call me if there's news on Gibson.'

He took my number, propped it between his keyboard and computer screen, and closed his eyes again. 'You got it, momma.'

I grabbed my purse and headed out to the Jeep. Whatever was going on in Florida, and whatever secrets Donald was hiding, I sure as hell was going to find out.

27

It was late when I arrived back in Florida. The marina was in darkness. The only sounds at the far end of the jetty were the soft roll of the ocean and the distant hum of traffic from the highway. Inside Red's houseboat a single light burned in the main cabin. I felt myself relax. If Red was home, maybe he'd lost his cell and that's why he wasn't answering my calls. Maybe he was fine and the bad feeling I had in my belly was wrong.

As I reached for the handrail to haul myself on board I froze.

Blood – a crimson smear across the handrail, illuminated in the glow from the window.

Someone had left the boat with blood on their hands.

My heart rate accelerated. Drawing my Taser, I stepped up onto the deck and hurried, light-footed, to the cabin door. Paused outside, listening, but aside from the lapping of the water against the boat all was quiet. I eased the handle down and stepped inside.

The usually pristine cabin was in chaos. Drawers had been emptied out, crockery smashed, papers flung across the floor, dirt and blood trodden into the debris. What the hell had happened? Had Red been robbed? Where the hell was he?

I moved quickly, searching the boat. The office, the restroom – all ransacked, But no sign of Red. I opened the bedroom door. Gasped.

'Red ... no ... oh Jesus!'

His eyes were shut. He wasn't moving.

He lay on his side, still bound by duct tape to a chair. His face was a bloody pulp. Dark red streaked through the silver of his hair. Purple bruises swelled across his eyes, his cheeks, his jaw. Trails of blood had dried crusty brown over the silver tape blocking his mouth. His shirt had been ripped open. Black and blue bruising mottled over his chest and abs. A metal rod, maybe a couple of foot long, that he used to winch the sail, lay coated with blood on the floor.

I ran to him. Knelt beside him. 'Red? Red, can you hear me?'

Nothing.

Putting my fingers to his neck, I felt for a pulse. Prayed that he'd be okay. Swallowed down the fear and concentrated on what I was doing. His pulse was weak, but he was alive.

I exhaled hard. 'Red, can you hear me?'

Still nothing.

I kept talking to him as I cut the duct tape binding him to the chair and pulled the tape from his mouth.

His eyes flickered open. 'Miss Lori ... I...' He gasped in pain.

'It's okay, you're safe.' I helped him up. Watched him grimacing with pain from each movement. 'You need a doctor.'

He eased himself down onto the bed. His breath was laboured. 'No hospital ... Go into one of those places when you're my age, chances are you'll never come out.'

I didn't agree. I fetched him a glass of water and started bathing his wounds with antiseptic as he drank, and refilled the glass each time it was empty. God knew how long he'd been lying here, I figured he was dehydrated, and from the slight tremor in his hands most likely in shock, too. He should have been in the hospital, but he was stubborn as a mule and I knew it wasn't a fight I'd win even with him in such a weakened state.

'What happened?' I finally asked.

'They were here when I returned from the meet with my polis contact.' Red winced as I applied the antiseptic to the cut across his cheekbone. 'Place was a mess. Three young guys – all fancy clothes and smart backchat – were in here waiting. When they grabbed me I figured I was a goner for sure.'

I threw another bloodied cotton pad into the plastic bag I was using for trash and dipped a fresh one in the antiseptic. 'They beat you pretty bad.'

'That they did.'

I wiped the blood from his split lower lip. 'They tell you why?'

'The one with a hat – cocky little son-of-a-bitch – asked about you.'

I felt a cold chill down my spine. Shivered despite the heat of the night. 'And what did you say?'

Red grimaced. 'Told him to go fuck himself.'

Typical Red. I smiled despite the situation. 'Bet he loved that.'

'Sure did.' He glanced at the winching bar lying on the floor. 'That's when he started getting handy with the tools.'

I put my hands on his chest. Felt his ribs, checking for breaks. He gasped. Couldn't disguise the pain in his expression fast enough. 'You've got cracked ribs for sure,' I said. 'You need a doc.'

'Told you no, Miss Lori. Bit of rest and I'll be fine.'

I held his gaze. 'I don't think—'

'I'm dog-tired. If you fetch me a couple of painkillers from the cabinet and another glass of water, I'm going to swallow them down and have me some sleep.'

I did as he asked. Helped him into bed and pulled the blankets over him. 'We'll talk more in the morning. I need to find out who did this to you.'

He curled onto his side and closed his eyes, his voice already slurred and heavy as he said, 'Yes ma'am.'

I watched him until his breathing changed to the slow rhythm of sleep, then padded out of the bedroom and closed the door behind me.

As I straightened out the main cabin, sleep was the last thing on my mind. I felt wired – crazy-sick from guilt at having dragged Red into whatever trouble was following me; angry that these goons had beaten on him; fearful at what they might do next and to whom.

28

Next morning I rose early, just before dawn. My neck was cricked from lying on the narrow couch, my head fuzzy from a few hours of restless sleep, but that didn't dampen my determination to find out what Donald Fletcher was holding back, and who the hell had beaten Red half to death.

Red was still sleeping. I didn't want to wake him, so I left a note saying I was going to see Donald Fletcher and that I'd be back by lunchtime. I told him to rest up, no heroics.

As I hurried to my truck, I called McGregor's office. Put it on speaker as I drove. Bobby Four-Fingers answered.

'Any more joy with Fletcher?' I asked.

'Nah. Couple of unconfirmed sightings but by the time the spotters got there he'd long gone.'

'Same locations as before?'

'Different, and really spread out.' Bobby whistled between his teeth. 'Man can't be in all those places.'

'Let me know if you get anything concrete.'

'Will do. Where you at?'

'Following up a lead. I'll tell you more when I'm back later.'

'You coming in today?'

I thought of Red. Of the beating he'd taken. Knew I needed to do right by him before I flew back to San Diego. 'Maybe tonight. This errand might take a while.'

Bobby lowered his voice to a whisper. 'I'm covering for you with Monroe. Haven't told him you're out of town.'

'I appreciate that.'

'No worries, momma.'

Thankful for Bobby's help, I ended the call and stepped harder on the gas. It was time to find out why Donald Fletcher was lying.

To say that Donald wasn't pleased to see me would have been an understatement. He buzzed me into his wire-fenced compound without a word, but kept me waiting on the porch for near on five minutes. I was just starting to think he'd forgotten me when the door opened. He was unshaven and had the look of a man who'd just got out of his bed: hair all stuck up at odd angles, his feet bare below his track pants. He glared at me real hostile. 'It's early. What do you want?'

It was nine-thirty. Not so early in my world. 'I've got some more questions.'

He scowled. Leaned against the doorframe, keeping the metal front door half closed. He didn't invite me inside. 'I've nothing to say. I told you all I know about Gibson.'

I narrowed my eyes. 'Well, you see Donald, that's the problem I've got. I'm not sure that you did.'

He scratched at an insect bite on his arm. Didn't look overly concerned. 'What are you implying?'

'Let's go inside first.'

He glanced past me, checking the street. I turned, anxious to see if there was a sign of the man who'd tailed me before.

A cab passed along the road. Aside from that there was no traffic. The neighbourhood was quiet. Donald shook his head. 'No. You can say what you've gotta right here, and then you can go.'

Fine, if that's how he wanted to play it. I put my hands on my hips. Stood tall. Kept my tone businesslike. 'You lied to me, Donald. You said you hadn't seen Gibson in a long while, but I know that's not true. I've seen the visitors' logs from Gibson's time in jail. You visited once a month, every first Tuesday. So what I want to know is why'd you lie about it?'

Donald scowled. 'You're the one who's lying. I've never visited Gibson in that place.'

Denial. I guess I'd kind of expected that; but I hadn't expected the genuine look of confusion on Donald's face. Still, I kept my tone firm. Knew he was most likely trying to throw me off the scent of whatever scam the two of them had cooked up. 'Your signature's right there in the log. You visited your brother every month, without fail.'

Donald stepped back, and started closing the door. 'You're talking crazy, I don't know what game you're playing, but it won't work. I told you before, I've not seen him.'

I thrust my leg out, sticking my boot against the doorframe, blocking him from shutting the door. 'I need answers, and I'm not leaving until I've gotten them.'

He cursed. Glared at me. 'Get the hell off my porch.'

'Not until you tell me the truth.'

'Goddammit. I've not seen Gibson in years. I—'

'How many years?'

'What?'

'Answer the question. When exactly did you last see him?'

Donald shook his head. 'I don't remember, and I don't give a damn.'

'Was it two and a half years ago? More? Less?'

'Why does it matter?'

'Because I've got a shipping document that says you sent a package to San Diego for him on March 7th, two and a half years ago.'

'You're just making shit up. Why would I do that? What package?'

I held his gaze. Spoke slow and measured. 'You tell me.'

He exhaled hard and pulled back the door. I thought he was backing down, letting me inside. I was wrong. He lunged forward, grabbed my shoulders and shoved me hard.

I lost my balance. Stepped back. 'What the...'

Before I could recover, he had slammed the door shut. Shit. I pounded on the metal with my fists. 'Open the door, Donald.'

'Just leave,' he shouted from inside. 'I didn't send any parcel.'

'I know that you did.'

'Horseshit.'

'I've got proof.'

'Impossible.'

'I've got photos on my cell.'

A couple of seconds passed, then I heard the sound of a bolt unlocking. The door opened again. Donald stared back at me. His face was ghostly white. 'You can't have.'

Either he was genuine about not knowing, or he was one hell of a good liar. I couldn't be sure which. 'I've got a copy of the parcel despatch documentation, and copies of the prison visitor logs. It's your name. And the signatures match.'

The anger of earlier had left him. He looked deflated, beat. 'Show me.'

Taking my cell phone from my purse, I held it out to him and flicked through the pictures; first the photo of the signed parcel documentation, then the copies of the prison logs. 'It's all here in black and white.'

He stared at them for a long moment, then shook his head. Looked confused. 'That's not my signature.'

'What?'

He pulled his wallet from his pants pocket and flipped it open. Showed me his driver's licence. 'Look. This is how I sign my name. Always has been.'

I looked at the card. My stomach lurched. The signature on Donald Fletcher's driver's licence was tall and loopy, not squat and tight. The signatures didn't match.

Donald was telling the truth.

29

Who'd been impersonating Donald Fletcher? That was the question that occupied my thinking on the drive back to the Deep Blue Marina. It was someone who didn't want to be associated with Gibson, that was for sure – not on record anyway. But they'd have needed ID to prove they were who they said they were to get into the prison as a visitor, so they'd have had to have faked that, too. Not cheap, and not easy.

So they'd gone to a lot of trouble and risked the authorities spotting them in the lie. And they'd specifically wanted Donald's name in that prison log. Could be it was a part of the plan for Gibson's escape – they wanted his brother in the frame. Question was, why?

I remembered once again JT's strategy on tracking a fugitive – family, friends, freedom – use past behaviour to predict future actions. If it was a personal thing between Donald and the person who used his identity, the connection that sprung to my mind was Gibson and Donald's old boxing manager, Marco Searle. Searle had a relationship of sorts with both brothers and there was bad blood between them, with Gibson over Mia, and with Donald over the punch-up twenty-odd years ago. As motives went, I'd seen folks killed for less.

Keeping one hand on the wheel, I messaged Monroe. I kept it brief, didn't tell him about Red, or what I'd found out from Donald and my suspicions; instead, I said I needed the CCTV from the prison visits. I wanted to see the visuals from the times Donald Fletcher signed that visitors' log. I needed to be sure Donald wasn't trying to double bluff me and, if he wasn't, I needed to see the person using his identity.

I was so caught up in my thoughts I didn't spot the black SUV until I was three blocks from the marina. I didn't know how long it'd been following me, but as it mirrored each turn I took, I knew for sure it was on my tail.

I looped around the block, deciding my next move. When I slowed down, the SUV slowed, too. I sped up and they kept pace. I could see there was one person inside – a man – but he was too far behind for me to see him clearly.

I clenched the steering wheel tighter. I was sick of this. Needed to know why they were following me and what they wanted. Pulling my Taser from its holster, I kept it on my lap as I drove to the marina. Decided that when they followed me into the parking lot we were going to have a serious talk.

But they didn't turn onto the lot after me. Instead they carried on along the highway, not even glancing in my direction. I braked to a halt. Felt cheated. Angry. I *needed* to know what the hell these people wanted. *Had* to know. Especially now they'd targeted someone close to me. The gloves had come off, and I was not going to stand for it.

Red was up and had lunch waiting when I rolled in. We ate outside, balancing plates of shrimp gumbo on our knees, cold beers sitting by our feet on the scrubbed-clean deck. His face was swollen, bruised, and I could tell from the way he chewed his food that his jaw was real tender.

'Who got to you?' I asked at last.

Red shook his head. 'Can't say for sure. Young Mob guys, I'd reckon, but they didn't do any formal introductions. Didn't say what they wanted either, other than your whereabouts.'

'I had a guy following me again this morning. Sped off before I could challenge him.' I put my hand on Red's arm. 'I'm real sorry I got you involved.'

He shrugged. 'Don't be. This isn't the first beating I've taken.'

'It's the first you've taken because of me.'

'I'll live.'

'But the next time—'

'I'll be better prepared.' He pointed his fork at me. Looked real serious. 'Don't you go retiring me off just yet. You need a hand on this.'

I nodded. Could tell he wasn't going to budge any. 'I appreciate it.'

'I know that.' Red took a swig of his beer, then changed the subject. 'So what's the deal with the brother?'

I told him about the prison logs showing that Donald had visited Gibson every month on the same day for the same amount of time, and that the day before Gibson had been taken sick he'd visited him on a different day and stayed less time.

Red ran his hand over his grey stubble. Looked doubtful. 'And you're sure it was him?'

'I was. Visitors have to sign in and out. I compared the signatures on the logs with the signature on the package sent by Donald to Southside Storage and they matched. But when I talked to Donald this morning he showed me his driver's licence – his signature is totally different. Whoever signed the log and sent the package wasn't Donald, or if it was, he forged a different signature.' I shook my head. 'It makes no sense.'

Red leaned forwards. 'What's your feel on him? What does your gut tell you?'

I didn't know much about Donald Fletcher aside from him being Gibson's brother and that they boxed together in their twenties. He had a big fancy home, seemed to live alone, and was real paranoid about his security. 'It tells me something else is going on between the brothers and I need to know what that is.'

'I'll add Donald Fletcher to my list.'

'Thanks.' I took another mouthful of gumbo. Stared out across the ocean. 'The more I dig into his thing, the bigger the mess I'm trying to unravel.'

Red let out a long breath. 'True that. You want me to tell you about your friend Monroe?'

I nodded. 'What'd you find?'

'I'm still working on it, but I've got some background. He comes from Crestwood, Kentucky. It's a little town northeast of Louisville. Same as most places out there, but with kinda elevated status due to its good living standard and low crime rate.'

I'd never visited Kentucky, but I'd seen plenty of pictures. 'Horse country?'

'Yeah, real close to the home of the Derby and all, not that it seems Monroe's folks are racing people.'

'What kind of people are they?'

'The political kind. Monroe's mother – Elizabeth – her family are deep in the system, but through funding rather than acting. Her father is a Republican, just as his father was and his father before him. Their money is from business, but they've ploughed a hell of a lot into the political game.'

'And Monroe's father?'

'Alexander Monroe Senior was the longest-serving mayor of Crestwood. Well respected, from what I can gather, a real man of the people. He's retired now, but is still on the scene as an adviser to the new mayor.'

'I'm surprised Monroe went into law enforcement. Surely his folks would've been pushing him towards politics?'

Red nodded. 'I reckon they did, but it didn't take. He was a good student, graduated high school with top grades and went to Stanford to study political history. Seems the Bureau recruited him while he was there, as the moment he'd graduated he shipped out to Quantico for his twenty-week training. He's been with the FBI ever since.'

I frowned. My knowledge on the workings of the FBI was a little rusty, but that didn't sound quite right to me. 'I thought you had to have experience in the real world before the Bureau would take you?'

'I guess his daddy pulled a few strings.'

Made sense. It made sense of Monroe's manner, too – the self-entitlement and assumption that things would go just as he said; he wasn't a man used to being told no or having the rules that the rest of us lived by apply to him.

'You know anything about his time at the Bureau?'

Red shook his head. 'Not much. I'm still working on that.'

I put the last forkful of gumbo into my mouth. Chewed slow. From what Red had discovered so far, there was no obvious connection between Monroe and Gibson other than work, but I still felt uneasy about whatever was going on between them, and what Monroe's intentions might be towards Gibson when I found him.

'I did find some interesting anomalies on Gibson's arrest record,' Red said.

I put my plate down on the deck. 'Oh yeah?'

'Yeah. It's like a piece of Swiss. Real holey.'

I leaned forwards. 'How so?'

'His custody records don't make sense, and there are gaps in the evidence I could put my arm through.'

'Yet he was convicted.'

'You could probably explain some of the custody records on sloppy paperwork, but the gaps are what concern me. The biggest thing is that the initial eyewitness statements are missing.'

'From the two girls?'

'Yup.'

The noise of the water lapping against the sides of the boat seemed to grow louder. 'A filing error?'

Red frowned like he was musing on the question, then shook his head. 'There are second statements taken from each girl thirty-six hours later, and a whole bunch of other addendums, but the initial statements have gone. I checked the legal pack. They weren't submitted into evidence by either side.'

'How do you know they existed at all? Maybe they gave the girls time. They were so young, and they'd witnessed their parents being butchered—'

'I know because their statements are referenced in the handwritten notes of one of the cops working the case. He's retired now; that case was his last. I'm trying to speak to him to verify.'

I drained the last of my beer and put it down on the deck beside my empty plate. 'You figure it's deliberate?'

'Could be.'

'Damn.'

We sat in silence for a moment. Seemed there was nothing straight-forward about Gibson Fletcher. Everywhere we looked there were anomalies; no fully accurate picture of his past to help anticipate his future moves. JT's strategy of three rang in my head like an echo – family, friends, freedom: Donald and Mia; Monroe; Mexico. Each one of them had a stake in Gibson's past or his future. Each one added another layer of mystery. 'Any news on the ex-wife?'

'Not yet. I've been over to her place in Lake County, but wasn't any sign of her and her new husband. Place looked the same as the last time I checked. I'd say she's still out of town.'

That the ex-wife was still missing gave me a real uneasy feeling, and I wondered if foul play was involved, and whether it was connected to Gibson. I looked at Red. 'Will you stay on it?'

'Sure I will. Donald, Monroe, and Gibson's arrest record, too.' He smiled. 'You've given me a puzzle to be solved, Miss Lori, and I do enjoy that.'

I held his gaze. He was trying to hide it but he looked dog-tired – the drama of the last twenty-four hours, the swelling on his face and the cuts and bruises had aged him dramatically. He'd said he thought young Mob guys were behind his beating, but I remembered how Monroe had told me to stand Red down and how I'd refused.

I hoped to hell the puzzle and this job wouldn't be the death of both of us.

30

I stayed with Red as long as I could, but by six o'clock I knew I had to get gone. He knew it, too. Near on pushed me off the deck and onto the jetty, grumbling at me to stop fussing over him like he was a goddamn invalid. I was worried about him for sure, but I didn't argue. I had a job to do and needed it done.

As I hurried back to the parking lot I scanned the area, looking out for the black SUV and silver sedan. Saw nothing, until I reached my truck.

I was a couple of yards from it when I spotted the paper under my wiper blade – a single sheet, folded once. Halting, I looked around. My hand instinctively going to the Taser holstered beneath my jacket. But the lot seemed deserted.

With my heart punching at my ribs I stepped forward, yanked the paper free and read the handwritten note.

'FACE WHAT YOU DID OR YOU'RE NEXT BITCH.'

My mouth went dry. My stomach flipped. 'Face what I did' – what the hell did that mean? Was this about Gibson Fletcher, JT or Monroe? And why were they watching me and leaving threatening notes rather than beating on me the way they had with Red? It didn't make any kind of sense.

Shoving the note into my jacket pocket, I jumped into the truck and headed towards the airport. I kept vigilant, but saw no sign of a tail. Leaving the truck in the lot, I headed into the terminal building for my flight. It felt like I was running away.

Next morning, in San Diego, I tried to put the note out of my mind and concentrate on the job. The way I saw it, if the lines of enquiry me and Red were working had got some folks riled, that could only mean we were on the right track. So I swallowed down my fears and focused on my next move.

I'd called Bobby, but he said there'd still been no confirmed sighting of Gibson Fletcher in Mexico. McGregor and Jorge were out on another job and I saw no reason to wait around in the bond office – I'd got some leads of my own to follow.

Top of my list was Marco Searle. All the things Donald and Mia had said about him made it seem he and Gibson were enemies, but as everything about the job was out of whack and so many secrets were being kept, I didn't want to discount the notion that they were still in contact before checking it out. Given what Red had said about Searle's violent nature and Mob connections, I couldn't risk approaching him direct until I had hard evidence. But there was another route I could take to get the information I needed.

After I'd called her, I waited for Mia in a booth at the back of the fifties-style Hayley's Diner. It was early afternoon, and aside from a few surfing types, the place was empty, the waiting staff having a breather in the lull between the lunchtime rush and the evening crowd. I ordered a coffee for me and an iced tea for Mia, and sat listening to Elvis playing on the jukebox until she arrived – 'Hound Dog', 'Heartbreak Hotel', 'Jailhouse Blues' – songs about heartbreak and prison that sounded far too happy for their subject matter.

The bell over the door rang as Mia entered. She wore a simple shift dress with wedge sandals and had her long dark hair pinned up in a messy bun. As she hurried across the diner towards me, she pushed her shades up onto her head. There was no trace of the bruising around her right eye I'd seen a couple of days ago. I figured it'd faded enough for her to cover it with make-up.

She slid onto the bench opposite me. She looked worried. 'What's this about? Is Gibson okay?'

I remembered his hand around my mouth. The pain of impact as he flung me against the SUV, and the anger in his voice as he'd given me the warning to stay away from him, and for Monroe to leave him be. I thought of the note, telling me to face what I'd done – maybe from Gibson, maybe from someone else.

Still, I kept my expression neutral as I said, 'I'm sure he's just fine.'

'Did you find him?'

I shook my head. 'Not yet.'

She frowned. 'Then why did you ask me here? I don't have long, I'm supposed to be at beach yoga.'

'I need your help.' I pushed a piece of paper across the red vinyl, gingham-print tablecloth towards her. On it I'd written the days Donald Fletcher's signature had been faked on the prison visitor's log. 'Was Marco out of town on these dates?'

As Mia read the dates she bit her lip and an emotion passed across her face real quick – too fast for me to place it. She looked back at me. 'I don't know. Maybe. He's out of town a lot for business.'

'I need to be sure. Can you check?'

She glanced back at the list. Read it again. 'I'd have to go through his schedule. It's on his computer in the study, but he keeps that room locked. If he found out I'd—'

'I wouldn't ask if it wasn't important.'

She exhaled. 'Will it help get Gibson safe?'

'I don't know, but it will help me find out who helped him escape and why.'

'You think he's running from them?'

'Do you?'

She stayed silent. Took a sip of the iced tea, then another.

I bent forwards a little. 'Tell me what's going on here, Mia.'

She shook her head. 'I don't know. But I think Gibson's scared, and not just because of the cops and jail.'

'Why did he stage his escape now?'

Mia shifted uncomfortably in her seat. 'I don't know.'

'Who helped him?'

'I don't know; he never told me. I asked, but he wouldn't say.'

'And if you had to guess?'

She held my gaze. 'I really don't know. We never talked about business. When we got time together we just … It was our time, not for business or real life. Do you understand?'

'Sure.' And I did understand. I understood that if all you got with the person you loved was the occasional snatched moment, then talking business would be the last thing on your mind. I got that, but it didn't mean I believed she knew nothing about Gibson's business dealings. They'd been together a long time, over twenty years. I was pretty sure she was hiding something. I needed to find a way to get her to tell me the truth.

Monroe wasn't happy. As I walked along the beach, away from the diner, I had to hold the burner away from my ear because he was jawing on so loud. 'What the hell, Lori? You just left San Diego and flew back to Florida? You didn't think to run it pass me first?'

'I needed answers, and the only way I could get them was from Donald. I thought he'd lied to me. I needed to see his face when I called him on it.'

'You *thought* he'd lied?'

'Turns out the signatures in the prison visitors' log were faked. The sender's signature on the parcel documentation from Southside Storage, too.'

'Shit.'

'Yeah. That's why I need you to get me the CCTV from the prison. If we know who impersonated Donald Fletcher we should be able to connect them to the escape – maybe even the theft of the chess pieces and the murder on the yacht.'

'I'll do what I can.' He didn't sound happy. 'Might take a while.'

I decided not to tell Monroe what had happened to Red, knowing he'd use it as more ammunition for his argument against me working with him. I didn't tell him about the note either. 'I'll be waiting,' I said.

'And you're sure it wasn't Donald? He could have lied to you about it not being his signature.'

I stopped. The sand was hot beneath my feet; the heat burning the soles of my feet. 'Look, I'm not some rookie, tadpole bounty hunter. I checked Donald's driver's licence – the signature is totally different. Someone pretended to be him.'

'For two and a half years?'

'Pretty much.' I carried on walking.

Monroe was silent. I could hear his breathing; rapid, shallow. I guessed he'd not expected this. When he spoke his cadence was steadier, the volume of his voice more measured. 'They've been planning this from the beginning.'

I'd been thinking the same. 'It looks that way.'

'If that package at Southside Suppliers was the chess pieces, could be whoever they were stolen for is helping Gibson now.'

'Yep. So you going to tell me who that is?'

Monroe exhaled hard. 'I don't know for sure.'

'But you've got suspicions?'

'Yeah.'

'And?'

There was a pause before Monroe spoke. His voice had a defeated tone; like he was telling me more than he thought was wise. 'Patrick Walker was a Chicago businessman, an accountant. He had no arrest record, seemed perfectly legal on the face of things, but there had been rumours for a while. Nothing substantiated.'

'You suspect Gibson Fletcher killing him wasn't just because of a bungled theft.'

'Exactly. I think Walker was a middle man for the theft of the chess set.'

I remembered what Red told me about Marco Searle – that he had connections to the Chicago Mob. That made two people who Gibson had been in contact with who had links to Chicago and the seedy side of the city. I didn't believe in coincidence. 'I'll look into it.'

'On the quiet though, Lori.' Monroe's voice had an urgency to it that I didn't wholly understand. 'Don't tell Dez McGregor about this. He doesn't need to know.'

I shook my head. That was Monroe all over, always working on a need-to-know basis, never telling anyone the full truth. I guessed that was why I didn't tell him about Marco Searle and my suspicions.

Everyone needs to keep some secrets.

31

I didn't go back to Dez McGregor's bond shop that afternoon. I was tired from the travelling and the time difference, and figured Dez wouldn't miss me; hell he'd probably be glad of the time without me. So I headed back to my hotel with the idea of calling Dakota on my mind.

As it was, she beat me to it. Back in my room, I kicked off my boots and pulled my cell and the burner from my purse, and saw I'd just received a bunch of messages. I smiled when I opened them.

Mom hey. Cabin trip Mont. Town. Very fun. Swimming in river with horses 2mrw – Beauty my fav horse. Here's art I did. Counsellor Jen let me take pic. Says I could be art major! Love u. Miss u xox

I guessed she'd been allowed to use her cell to message me from the office, and I was real glad for the contact, but there was a deep ache in my chest. I missed my baby. Hated us being apart. But still, I felt proud at how she was coping.

I scrolled to the photo. Exhaled hard.

The picture was taken in daylight, Dakota was holding a painting towards the camera. She was grinning, but the picture in her hands was a jumble of angry, vivid colours. I tapped the screen, enlarging the image. It looked like oil paints layered onto canvas. There were dark shapes, the shadows of faceless people in the middle distance. A small figure, painted in yellow, was in the foreground. Thick crimson slashes criss-crossed the image. It was beautiful, and shocking. Mesmerising and violent. I'd never seen Dakota draw like that before.

I reduced the photo. Stared at my baby's face, smiling into the camera, and wondered how much darkness her smile was hiding. I knew that, after everything she'd experienced recently, it must be a lot. She'd seen things no nine-year-old should ever have to see and I couldn't undo that, no matter how much I wished I could.

So I didn't mention the darkness, the angry red slashes, in the pictures. Instead I messaged her back:

Wow. Sounds awesome. And your art is stunning. I'm so proud of you. Missing you too. All my love xxx

Her reply came a few seconds later so I reckoned she must still be in the camp office: *How's JT? I miss him*

I messaged back: *He's doing fine. He misses you too xxx*

The white lie came easy enough. I couldn't tell her the truth; didn't want to upset her by saying how worried I was; that he'd been attacked and I'd not heard anything other than that his condition was stable. That he wouldn't speak to me when I called. That he was in danger. Old Man Bonchese had people everywhere. I needed JT out of jail and cleared of the wrongdoing to which he'd falsely confessed. But most of all, I needed him to speak to me and, even if he didn't care about getting the death penalty for himself, I needed him to understand why it was so important he stayed alive.

He'd refused to talk the last time I called, but I wasn't going to accept that any longer. I've never been a quitter, and I damn well wasn't going to quit now.

I flicked through my recently dialled numbers and called the infirmary at the Three Lakes Detention Facility. When it connected I asked to speak with JT. Told them I had special permission, gave them Monroe's name. They didn't argue.

I waited.

Heart banging. Throat dry.

The line crackled. No one spoke.

'Hello?' I said.

No words. But I heard breathing. Someone was there.

'JT, is that you?'

'I asked you to leave things be.' His voice sounded weak. The gravelly tone was rasping, but I'd have known it anywhere.

'I can't.' I said. 'There's something you need to—'

'I wanted you safe. Dakota, too.' A sigh. Barely audible. '...They know, Lori. I've ... failed.'

I shook my head. Blinked back tears. Hated hearing him sound so weak. 'You didn't fail. We're fine. And you'll be fine, too. I'll get you free and—'

'They'll never let that happen. You can't be connected to me ... too dangerous...' His voice was getting fainter. 'They'll come for me again, I...'

There was a clatter at JT's end of the line, as if the phone had fallen to the floor, then a rapid beeping as an alarm began to sound.

Oh Jeez.

'JT? Can you hear me?'

No answer.

I heard voices, footsteps.

In the distance, a woman's voice. 'He's crashing.'

More footsteps, rushing. The beeping became a continuous sound. More voices. I couldn't make out their words.

'JT?' I screamed his name into the phone. 'JT, answer me, please!'

The call disconnected.

'Shit. Oh, Jesus.' With shaking hands I redialled the infirmary.

No answer.

Redialled.

It rang and rang.

Redialled again. A man answered. Not JT.

In a voice that sounded unlike my own I explained what happened. Asked to speak to JT. There was a pause, then the man told me James Tate had suffered a cardiac arrest. They were trying to stabilise him, but it was too early to tell the prognosis. Call back in a few hours, he said. They might know more then...

He left the rest of the sentence unspoken: ...if he's still alive.

Dropping my cell onto the bed, I pulled my knees up to my chest, and hugged my arms around them. I couldn't hold back the tears any longer. Felt the fear of losing JT in every sob, every heave. Cried until there were no more tears and I felt as dry and empty as a husk.

I stayed that way until I got the call.

Bobby Four-Fingers' voice sounded urgent, breathless. 'The spotters have a confirmed sighting. We've found Fletcher.'

32

We crossed the border into Mexico at sundown. McGregor and Jorge travelled in the lead truck; I rode shotgun with Bobby Four-Fingers in the second. We'd left our weapons at the bond shop – easier to cross the border that way. Jorge's spotters would sort us out their side of the border. It was part of the deal.

The mood was tense, the conversation minimal. Even Bobby turned serious as we approached the rendezvous point – a patch of land surrounded by dirt and scrub, about ten miles east of Palm Valley.

I checked my cell phone. It was almost three hours since I'd spoken to the prison infirmary. Call back in a few hours the man had said, and the fear had been eating away at me ever since. What if they couldn't keep JT stabilised? What if he died? I had to know he was okay. Couldn't wait any longer. I dialled the infirmary number once more.

Nothing. Then the call aborted.

I checked the screen: no bars – meaning no signal. I cussed. Felt fear tighten in my chest.

Bobby glanced at me. 'You doing alright, momma?'

'Yep.' I didn't tell him about JT; couldn't trust myself not to break down. 'Phone signal's out.'

'Always goes around here, that's why McGregor has us use the radios rather than cell phones for comms.' Bobby smiled. 'It's not just because he likes things old school.'

We travelled on in silence. A couple of miles later, in what seemed like the middle of nowhere, McGregor turned his truck off the highway and kept going across the baked wasteland, along a barely visible track. Bobby followed. I gripped the seat as we bounced over the rutted ground, dust flying out behind us. Wondered if this was their usual meeting place, or if McGregor was working off co-ordinates. Aside from a few scraggy trees and cacti there were no obvious landmarks.

The light had all but gone. The country around us was cloaked in darkness, leaving just the stars and our headlamps to keep us from blindness. I was in an unfamiliar country, with a team of guys I'd never worked with, hunting a fugitive with a history of extreme violence. The combination had me feeling real uneasy, but that wasn't what was making me sick to my stomach. The nausea was caused by the memory replaying in my mind, over and again: the frailness in JT's voice, the beeping of the machine going from intermittent to continuous, and the infirmary nurse telling me JT had suffered a cardiac arrest. I was in the toughest place in the world to be a bounty hunter and my head wasn't in the game.

McGregor's voice crackled over the comms channel; the tiny earbuds and mics we wore connected to a set radio frequency. 'ETA one minute. Be ready to meet our spotters. We'll do a quick briefing, then it's time.'

Bobby glanced at me and I nodded. I waited for the familiar energy buzz to kick in; for my mind to get clear and sharp, ready to act and react fast like I was taught, but it didn't happen. My head stayed full of JT, my emotions overriding my training, saturated with the fear that he wasn't going to make it. I checked my cell phone again; still no signal.

A few yards ahead, illuminated in our headlamps, was a white pick-up truck. McGregor's vehicle came to a halt in front of it, and Bobby swung us around to park alongside McGregor. A man and a woman climbed out of the pick-up. McGregor and Jorge joined them.

Bobby opened his door and gestured for me to get out. 'You ready?'

I nodded, even though it wasn't the truth.

Told myself to focus.

The man was Ortiz and the woman Rosas. Both had black hair and wore dark clothes, the bulge of their guns obvious beneath their jackets. Ortiz was as lanky as Rosas was petite. Introductions were kept minimal: no first names, no details, just family names and nods of hello – that was all we had time for. They'd been tailing Gibson Fletcher since he'd been spotted three hours earlier, and had tracked him to a small shack in the wasteland, surrounded by nothingness.

Turned out our meeting place was a mile from the shack, over a ridge that concealed our location. Time was short; every minute without line of sight on the shack was a minute Fletcher could get away unseen. Conversation centred on the best way to extract him.

Rosas led. She kept her voice low, as if she feared Fletcher could hear us, but there was no doubting the conviction of her words. 'It's a good location for him. Approaching unseen is impossible. There's only one way to do this – we go in fast and hard.'

Bobby Four-Fingers glanced at McGregor. 'That's risky.'

'It's high risk however we do it,' Rosas said, her tone firm, her expression serious. 'This way we don't give him too long to think about it.'

'But if it's open ground he'll see us coming as soon as we go over the ridge.' Bobby sounded worried. 'There'll be no element of surprise.'

Rosas frowned. 'We do what we can. Go in dark, no headlights. Take two vehicles. Minimise the chances he'll see us until we're close and it's too late for him to get away.'

Jorge looked at the three trucks we had surrounding us. 'Two vehicles?'

Ortiz nodded. 'Four people in the lead vehicle. Two in the secondary, approaching from the opposite side in case he gets spooked and runs.' He looked at McGregor. 'We brought guns for each of you, as instructed. Tasers, too.'

Rosas looked at McGregor. 'So are we agreed on the approach?'

McGregor nodded. 'Yep. Hard and fast. There's six of us and one of him. He's outnumbered and outgunned.'

Don't make assumptions, JT had always told me. I looked at McGregor. 'As far as we know.'

He glanced at me as if noticing I was there for the first time. 'What?'

'Ortiz and Rosas said they'd not seen anyone else enter or exit since they tailed Fletcher there. Doesn't stop someone from being inside before they arrived.'

Rosas nodded. 'She's right. We can't be sure he's alone. It's likely, but not certain.'

McGregor ignored me, kept eyes on Rosas. 'So what do you propose?'

'Two vehicles, three people in each. Equal teams to the front and rear. There are no side windows, only two exits. We sweep the building even once, we have him.' She looked at me. 'No assumptions. We make certain it's clear.'

'Sure,' I said, trying to keep the irritation from my voice. Even if McGregor paid no mind to my input, at least Rosas had listened. 'I'm comfortable with—'

'Agreed,' said McGregor, his gaze still on Rosas. 'I'll take the front. Jorge and Rosas, you're with me. Ortiz, you're with Four-Fingers and Anderson. Communicate using the comms channel. Hold the front and the back. Only merge once the fugitive has been contained.' His tone made it pretty clear I was not part of the A team.

As we hustled to Bobby's truck I told myself McGregor's disrespect didn't matter. I was only working with him because that's what Monroe wanted. He was a means to an end. I didn't need to like the guy. Once we had Fletcher I never needed to see McGregor again. For me, that time couldn't come soon enough.

At the truck Ortiz handed Bobby a Glock 18 and a semi-automatic X2 Defender Taser, then offered the same combination to me. I lifted my jacket and tightened the bottom tabs on my concealed body armour, then took the X2 and tucked it into the waistband of my jeans.

Ortiz looked me up and down, frowning. 'You brought a gun?'

'No.'

He raised his eyebrows. 'Then why aren't you taking this one? You crazy?'

I climbed into the passenger seat, turned to Ortiz as he settled in the back. 'I prefer the Taser.'

'I prefer both.'

'With my history, you'd change your mind.'

'Wouldn't get the chance,' Ortiz said. 'Without a gun, in my job, in this place, you'd already be dead.'

Bobby Four-Fingers exhaled hard and tapped his palms against the steering wheel. 'Come on – enough, yeah?' His voice sounded strained. He put the truck into drive. 'I'm trying to concentrate here.'

I met Ortiz's gaze. He nodded, and I turned back round. Bobby was looking real nervous. Not a good sign. I knew it, and I could see Ortiz did, too. Nerves made people unpredictable, more prone to overreaction. Nerves made everything more dangerous.

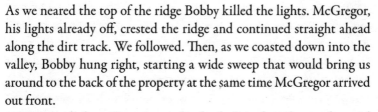

As we neared the top of the ridge Bobby killed the lights. McGregor, his lights already off, crested the ridge and continued straight ahead along the dirt track. We followed. Then, as we coasted down into the valley, Bobby hung right, starting a wide sweep that would bring us around to the back of the property at the same time McGregor arrived out front.

We stayed silent. Our eyes on the shack. Our thoughts on the need to move real fast as soon as our feet hit the ground.

Five hundred yards from the shack I glanced at Bobby. 'You okay?'

He nodded, but he didn't look okay. His jaw was clenched and he looked real tense.

I looked back at Ortiz. 'Ready?'

'Yep.' At least he looked it; one hand on the door release, the other braced against the seat, poised ready to leave the vehicle the moment we stopped.

Two hundred yards out, I noticed the nose of a vehicle parked on the far side of the shack, and saw a low light was glowing inside the building. The place looked tiny; one room, two at the most. There'd be nowhere much for Fletcher to hide.

On the other side of the shack, McGregor's truck accelerated fast towards the target. Bobby stepped on the gas.

One hundred yards and closing.

I heard Ortiz draw his weapon behind me.

At twenty yards, Bobby braked. McGregor did the same on the other side.

It was time.

'Go!' McGregor's instruction came through my earbud.

We jumped out of the truck, our boots stamping onto the dirt. No time for stealth. Crouching low, running, we spread out; me in the centre, Ortiz on my left flank, Bobby on my right. I couldn't see the others, but I knew they'd be doing the same, approaching the front as we went for the back.

There was no sign of movement from inside. No clue as to whether our fugitive had seen us. Either way, it didn't matter none. We had him trapped, and that could be good or bad – he might surrender, or he might try to fight his way out. Whatever happened, I needed him alive. Monroe had been real explicit on that.

Reaching the back door, I turned the handle and felt the catch release. I signalled to Bobby and Ortiz to follow me. We entered and found ourselves in a small utility room; crates of dusty supplies were stacked against the wall, in the corner was an ancient toilet and wash-basin. No sign of Fletcher. The air tasted stale. The smell of decay was strong and fuggy in the air. I fought the urge to gag. Stayed focused.

'Back room, clear,' I said, hoping the mic picked up my voice. 'Moving towards the front.'

'Confirmed,' Rosas said, her voice a whisper in my earbud.

I heard a crash from the front of the shack – McGregor kicking his way inside.

Rapid footsteps. Friendly or not, I didn't know.

'Situation?' I said.

No response on the comms. I hated not knowing what was going on. Working in a team this way felt alien to me.

I heard shouting in the next room, McGregor's voice: 'Gibson Fletcher, give it up. Hands in the air. Keep 'em high.'

There was a loud crash. More shouting.

McGregor's voice yelled, 'Put the weapon on the floor. Put the weapon on the floor.'

'You need help?' I said into the mic. Again, no response.

I hurried to the connecting door. Tried the handle – locked. We were supposed to be covering the back and we'd gotten it secure, but the action was going down in the front and we had no clue what was happening. It sounded as if Fletcher was armed. Did McGregor need our help?

I looked at Bobby. His expression was grim. Ortiz was behind me. I took a snap decision. Launched myself forward, shouldering the door. It broke on contact, splintering apart, and I burst into the room.

Halted.

McGregor, Rosas and Jorge had their weapons raised. On the far side of the room, in front of a battered couch with an upturned plate of beans and a spilt beer beside it, a man stood facing away from them. I couldn't see his face but he was Gibson Fletcher's height, muscular and dark-haired. He wore a plaid shirt, dirty jeans, and scuffed black sneakers. In his right hand was a gun.

'Put the weapon on the floor and turn around, Fletcher,' McGregor said.

The man didn't respond. Ortiz and Bobby raised their weapons.

McGregor kept his weapon high, his finger tight against the trigger. 'We've got five guns on you.'

Everyone was real tense. Fletcher didn't move. He still had his gun raised, and in not putting it down, seemed he was thinking on his next move. It was real hard to assess what would happen. He was outgunned for sure, but, like a cornered grizzly, he might decide his only choice was to attack. I had to avoid a firefight. I needed Fletcher unharmed.

I took a couple of steps into the room. 'Put the gun down, Fletcher. Don't do anything crazy. Think about Mia. This doesn't have to end badly.'

Two beats passed. No one moved. I held my breath. Felt my heart punching against my chest. What happened next was live or die; my deal with Monroe would succeed or fail.

Fletcher lowered the gun, and put it on the ground.

I exhaled. 'Kick it away.'

He did as I asked. It rattled across the floorboards and stopped when it hit the edge of the brick hearth.

McGregor glared at me. Then said to Fletcher, 'Hands high. Turn, slowly.'

He put his hands up. Turned to face us, his expression one of anger. 'I want you to get the hell off my property.'

I cussed. Shook my head, glanced at McGregor.

McGregor looked furious. 'Who the fuck are you?'

The guy scowled. 'I could ask you the same damn question. My name isn't Fletcher.'

He was right about that.

33

'What the fuck was that?'

McGregor was real pissed, and that made him meaner than usual. He'd had to pay off the guy in the shack: a few hundred bucks to fix the doors; a few more to keep him quiet. Dollars worth spending, given the situation, but we were still no closer to finding Fletcher. As we debriefed back at our original meeting location McGregor was getting more agitated with every minute.

'We acted in good faith.' Rosas sounded defensive. 'Ortiz sent a photo, you confirmed it was the fugitive.'

Jorge nodded. 'In the picture he looked like Fletcher.'

'But it wasn't, and now we've revealed our hand,' McGregor said. 'That makes everything harder and the risks higher from hereon in.'

'Yes,' Rosas said. 'But it was an honest mistake.'

McGregor glared at her. 'Honest or not, mistakes cost lives in our business. It's unacceptable.'

I didn't know what McGregor wanted from Rosas. Maybe he wanted her to feel bad, maybe he just needed an outlet for his anger. Whatever it was, I'd had enough of this aggressive navel gazing. It wasn't constructive, and it sure as shit wasn't helping us find Fletcher.

I cleared my throat. 'What's done is done. We need to work out our next—'

'We're done when I say we are.' McGregor turned on me, furious. 'And what the hell did you think you were doing? I told you to cover the exit, not barge your way through the building. You could have got us all killed.'

'We were blind. You weren't communicating. I had no idea if you needed help or had things under control.'

Ortiz took a step back. Bobby Four-Fingers kept his eyes on the ground, and shifted his weight from one foot to the other. It was clear neither of them wanted to be a part of this conversation.

'I'd have told you if I needed you.' His tone implied he'd never want my help.

'Yeah, I doubt that. You've either ignored me or put me down ever since Monroe sent me your way. What the hell is your problem?'

'I work in a team, and I work with professionals. I've asked around; I know who you are, who trained you.' He looked at me like I disgusted him. 'You're a loose cannon. You've no discipline. There's no place for insubordination on my team.'

'You never gave me a chance.'

'And yet you proved me right as soon as you could.' He gestured towards the shack. 'What the hell were you thinking in there, challenging me for leadership in the middle of a stand-off?'

'I was trying to prevent a firefight. You were just waving your dick around. If that'd continued it was real likely that guy would have tried to shoot it off.'

'It's my team. My decision.'

Blasting through the door had been risky for sure; I could have waited for McGregor's signal. But JT had trained me to use my initiative and I'd needed to be certain they had Fletcher. My fear for JT's safety had spurred me on. So I glared at McGregor. Refused to back down. 'You're not my boss.'

'Whatever. But on my team, you play by my rules.'

'You told me that already, and I said *you're* the one who's supposed to be helping *me*.'

McGregor shook his head. Grimaced. 'As a favour to Monroe, yes. And Lord knows I've tried, but you're making it damn near impossible.'

'I'm trying to get the job done.'

He stepped closer to me. 'No. You're letting your emotions rule you. Whatever deal you've brokered with Monroe, it involves that disgraced mentor of yours, doesn't it? And whatever's going on between the pair of you is messing with your judgement.'

I clenched my fists. Felt my nails digging into my palms. 'My judgement is just fine.'

'Blasting into a room where I've got a man who's pulled a gun cornered? Getting close to him without a weapon drawn? Not having yourself a gun? That's three counts of poor judgement in my book. You were reckless and that put the team at risk.'

I shook my head. 'I took the initiative. I have to find Fletcher.'

'The only thing you'll be finding if you keep going the way you're heading is an early grave.'

'I—'

'We need to move.' Jorge's voice sounded strained as he interrupted us. 'That guy could talk. If the message goes out bounty hunters are in town, we can't be here.'

McGregor exhaled hard. Nodded. 'Agreed.' He looked at Rosas and Ortiz. 'Keep searching. Be certain next time. I don't want another fuckup.' He turned back to me. 'This conversation isn't over.'

No, I thought, as I walked back to Bobby Four-Fingers' truck. It sure isn't.

34

It was gone midnight when I got back to the hotel – and was three hours later in Florida – but I called the jail infirmary anyways. I'd been trying the number every fifteen minutes since I'd had a signal on my cell. So far they hadn't picked up, but there was no way I could rest without knowing JT was alright. Please. *He had to live.*

This time they answered.

They couldn't tell me much, just that he was comfortable and had been sleeping. His condition seemed stable, but they weren't sure what had caused the cardiac arrest. I could hear it in the tone of the doctor's voice – the unspoken message that JT might not survive. I ended the call with shaking hands and sat on my bed as the shock of the situation ricocheted through me.

I thought of our last few conversations; of how pissed I'd been at him, and how stubborn he'd been; of how neither of us had been able to express our feelings properly. I longed for a do-over, to tell him that what really mattered to me was him and Dakota, for us to give being together as a family a chance, and for him to tell me the same.

Things had never been easy between us but, still, I couldn't lose him.

With some men you never know where it is you stand, and JT was one of those men. Even though I knew that, it ate me up that he never spoke about how he felt or what he wanted when it came to us being together. Ten years back, I'd tried to mirror his behaviour, tried to act like what we had was just casual for me too; that I didn't want more, that I expected to move on once my training was done. Oftentimes I managed to act that way. Oftentimes, but not always.

The morning I said it, I'd woken real early. The pale morning sunlight was filtering through the gaps around the shutters, and I could hear the birdsong waking up the forest outside, like nature's own alarm clock. It was early fall, but still warm enough to sleep with just a cotton sheet covering us. JT lay on his side, facing me, the cover pushed down to his hips, the deep tan of his skin dark against the white of the sheet.

I lay there a moment, watching him sleep. Noted how his dirty-blond hair had flopped across his forehead, and how his eyelashes fluttered as he inhaled. Watched the rise and fall of his torso. Noticed the grey hairs mingling amongst the blond ones across his chest; reached out and traced them with my fingertips.

He murmured something I couldn't make out and pulled me to him. His arms tight around me, his skin warm against mine. I relaxed into him. Felt safe, happy. I kissed his chest and slid my hand around him, caressing his back.

I felt him harden. Let him turn me onto my other side, and pressed myself back against him. Exhaled as he entered me. I moved with his rhythm, slow and sensual, savouring the moment, the feeling. Then getting faster, harder, more urgent. Needing him. Wanting him. Racing each other to the climax until we were both spent.

Afterwards, we lay on our backs, catching our breath. I reached out and touched his face, ran my fingers across his stubble. He smiled. Kissed my palm. Pulled me to him, and kissed me long and slow. Delicious.

I smiled. 'I love you.'

He didn't speak. A couple of seconds passed, then a few more. The silence seemed deafening. I didn't know what to do. Put my head on his chest, my face hidden from his as I blinked back the tears of hurt and humiliation.

I never should have told him that I loved him. It was the truth, but it was a fool move and I knew it. We were a temporary deal; he'd told me that from the very start, and I should have known better than to fall in love.

I glanced up at him. He looked at me all intense, his expression impossible to read. Still he said nothing. Instead he ran his hands up my arms and pulled me to him. Pressed his mouth against mine, and kissed me like his life depended on it. I kissed him back, but I felt real sick. I'd put my feelings out there, told him how I felt about him, and he couldn't even acknowledge what I'd said.

I knew right then how it would end: in pain, with him walking away, and me being alone again. I could see our path real clear, and yet I couldn't stop going along it. I didn't want to stop; even the fatal inevitability of the situation couldn't dim what we had right then.

A little while later, me killing my husband, Thomas Ford, did that; JT asked me to leave and I went. But I wasn't alone for long; nine months later Dakota was born. We had each other. I didn't need a man, JT, anyone. And it had been that way ever since. Except him coming back into my life near on ten years later had upset the balance, made the memories of what we'd had before resurface. Messed with my head.

On that event-filled drive from West Virginia to Florida we'd gotten close again. We'd both changed. I'd toughened up. He'd got less reclusive. It felt like we had another chance.

I wiped the tears from my cheeks. Told myself all this thinking on the future wasn't helping nothing. Maybe McGregor was right and I wasn't acting as neutrally as I usually would on a job. But I couldn't just switch off my emotions when JT's life was on the line. I needed to bring in Fletcher and get Monroe to pull strings to get JT out of jail. I needed him safe. And I needed to be back home with my child.

Sitting on the bed in my hotel room, sleep tried to claim me. I fought it, trying to figure out a plan, my next move; one of JT's rules was to *always have a plan*. But rather than a plan forming, what buzzed around in my mind were the questions still unanswered about this job: who had been impersonating Donald Fletcher? Why did Gibson want Monroe to leave him be? Why was there missing information in Gibson's police file? What else did Mia know? Why did Monroe need my help with catching Gibson when he had the resources of the FBI at his command? Who was after me in Florida and why had they beaten on Red, but only left me a note?

The more I investigated, the more questions this job raised. None of it made much sense, but it did give me a whole bunch of trails to chase down. If fate took my side – and Lord knows she kind of owed me – one of them had to lead to Gibson Fletcher.

35

Monroe's call woke me. I'd missed morning check-in again and he was real pissed.

'McGregor tells me you messed up last night.'

I rubbed the sleep from my eyes, propped myself up against the pillows. 'That's one version of events.'

'So what's yours?' Monroe's Kentucky drawl was clipped, his tone all business.

I got out of bed, switched on the coffee-maker and started to pull on my clothes. 'The spotters got the wrong guy.'

'That much I know. Tell me what happened in the cabin?'

So I told him how things had gone down. How McGregor had put me on the B team, and that once we were inside the shack we were blind to what was happening with the target. How there'd been shouting, confusion, and that McGregor hadn't answered on the comms channel, so I'd taken the door down to make sure they weren't in trouble and that they had Fletcher.

'That's not the way I heard it. McGregor said you tried to take over. That you put the team in danger and nearly got everyone shot.'

I cussed under my breath. 'The man had a gun and McGregor was acting all macho. I talked him down. If I hadn't, things would've been a whole lot worse.'

Monroe didn't speak for a moment, but I could hear him breathing. I wondered what he was waiting for, what he was thinking. I felt the tension tighten my chest. 'Monroe, you still there?'

'I'm here. Look, McGregor's view is you're a liability. He wants you off the team and off the job, says he'll find Gibson Fletcher without you.' Monroe sighed. 'Personally, I'm wondering if that might be the best way to go.'

Fear knotted tighter in my chest. I felt breathless. I needed to stay on the job for the deal to be in effect – for JT to get free. For Dakota.

'So you're taking McGregor's side over mine?' I said. 'That's real nice. I broke down that door because I was worried they were in trouble, to be certain we caught Gibson for you. I talked him down so the bullets didn't start flying and people – Gibson – didn't end up dead. And because of that you're threatening to fire me?'

'Lori, I—'

'McGregor had an issue with me from the minute I arrived. He doesn't like the way I'm trained, and he doesn't like who I trained with. I'm thinking he also doesn't like that I'm a woman; that he's got some kind of problem working with women. He was the same with the female spotter last night – laid all the blame about them getting the wrong guy on her, aimed nothing at her male partner.'

'He's a straight-up guy, I've never known him have a—'

'How many women has he recruited to his team?'

Monroe was silent a moment, then said, 'I can't remember any.'

'Yeah.' I grabbed the cup from the coffee-maker. Took a sip. 'That's what I thought.'

Monroe exhaled hard. 'Okay, look, stay on the job, on Fletcher, but don't keep rubbing McGregor up the wrong way. He's letting you work with him, but if there's any more shit I doubt he'll let that carry on. If that happens, you're off the job and our deal is off. I need McGregor's extraction team more than I need you right now.'

So whatever I said, as far as Monroe was concerned, the issue between McGregor and me was mine to fix. I shook my head. Swallowed down the anger. 'Got it.'

White-hot fury burned through my veins as I ended the call. Monroe was losing patience, and I didn't know how much longer I'd be able to stomach McGregor's patronising bullshit.

On the screen of my cell was a photo of Dakota at the fourth of July parade; her face was painted with the Stars & Stripes, ribbons in her braids, a funnel cake in her hand as she grinned a sugary smile at the camera. I stared at the picture. I'd taken it less than a month ago but it seemed like a lifetime. She looked so carefree – a world away from the sick little girl not expected to survive long enough to see her tenth birthday. But her birthday was just weeks away now, and the cancer was still in remission. I had to make sure it stayed that way. If it wasn't for her, and for JT, I'd have gone from this place and this job a long while ago.

And now McGregor had tattled on me to Monroe and tried to cause trouble. He was an escalating threat; he had sway with Monroe and it was real clear he wanted me gone. Bastard. I couldn't have him jeopardising the deal with Monroe. JT's life and therefore Dakota's future depended on it. He wanted me off the job, but there was no way I was going to give him that satisfaction. We needed to get past our dislike of each other and get on with finding Gibson Fletcher. Fast.

I grabbed my car keys and headed to McGregor's bond shop, determined to have it out with him.

Bobby Four-Fingers was sitting at his usual workstation. He had his earbuds in, his head nodding along to whatever tunes he was listening to. He didn't notice I'd arrived until the shouting started.

McGregor had me in his crosshairs. He strode around his desk to face off with me, his expression grim. I'd had my mind on apologising. Knew I needed to call a truce between McGregor and me, and that an apology was no doubt what he'd be waiting on.

I forced out the words even though it felt like they might choke me. 'Last night didn't work out good for either of us. I'm sorry if my methods don't sit well with you, but we need to find a way to make this work.'

McGregor shook his head. 'What's that meant to be? An apology?' He laughed – it sounded bitter. 'You put my people in danger, Lori. I don't want you on my team, and I've told Monroe that.'

'Yeah, so he said. But he says I'm staying and we need to work together, so here I am.'

McGregor cussed. 'You've got no place being here.'

I felt the anger rising again. 'Why? Because I'm a woman?'

He looked surprised. 'Why would I have a problem with you being a woman?'

'Because you've treated me like a second-rate bounty hunter ever since I arrived. You've never given me a chance; you were territorial right off the bat and got more hostile ever since.'

McGregor shook his head. 'I—'

'And it's not just how you've treated me. The way you were with Rosas last night; the spotter's mistake was down to her *and* Ortiz, but you directed your frustration only at her.'

'That wasn't my intention.' McGregor's voice was loud, but I heard a slight undertone of doubt that hadn't been there before. I wondered what that was about, whether he recognised the truth of my words, or if he was just irritated at me calling out his prejudice.

'Yeah, right.' My tone was sarcastic. 'You're all about the macho bullshit. Guys like you make me sick, you don't think women have a place in this kind of business.'

Bobby had heard our voices over his music and pulled his earbuds. He caught my eye and shook his head, warning me off.

I ignored him. Glanced slowly, deliberately, around the office. 'Tell me the last time you hired a woman?'

A muscle pulsed in McGregor's cheek. 'I don't remember.'

'I guessing never. Am I right?'

He glared at me, curled his lips into a snarl. 'Leave it alone.'

I'd hit dirt. He was prejudiced against women in this line of work, maybe women full stop for all I knew. 'Why should I?'

His expression was grim, his tone hard. 'Because it's not relevant to catching Fletcher, and that's why you're still damn well here, isn't it?'

'It's relevant to me. You can't—'

'Stop!' McGregor shouted. 'I'm ... We're not having this conversation.'

I forced myself to hold my ground. Looked at Bobby. 'You think it's right to treat someone bad because of their sex?'

Bobby put his hands up. Looked real uncomfortable. 'Don't drag me into this.'

I glared at him. Shook my head. 'Coward.'

I stormed out of the bond shop onto the sidewalk, the frustration of the job, the unfairness of McGregor's treatment, the fear for JT's life exploding inside me like fireworks. I wanted to punch something, McGregor and Bobby in particular.

I slammed the heel of my fist against the wall. Felt pain jolt through me. Stared at the blood rising to the surface of my skin. Fuck. I felt like I was losing it. Right then, at that moment, I needed to talk to someone. I needed a friend.

I called the only real friend I could talk to about this stuff. He answered after four rings. He didn't give a greeting, just waited on me to speak first.

'Red?'

'Sure is, Miss Lori. You doing okay?'

I inhaled. Stepped along the sidewalk to the Jeep. I leaned against it and took a moment to get my head together. Then I told him everything – from Dakota's drawings and JT's heart attack, to the unsuccessful pick-up in Mexico, and my fight with McGregor. 'I just don't see how I can work with him, Red. It's impossible. We can't even stay in the same damn room as each other without fighting.'

Red whistled. 'If Monroe's insisting you work with McGregor you need to find a way to make it work.'

'Didn't you hear what I said about him hating women?'

'Sure, I heard, but he works with a female spotter and from what you said he only got tough with her after the pick-up went bad. It's understandable he was pissed they'd got the target wrong.'

It felt like Red was taking McGregor's side. 'So, what, you're saying he *should* have taken it out on her?'

'Don't put words in my mouth, Miss Lori. From what you've said she was the one in charge out of the pair. It's logical he'd focus on her.'

'So what's his problem then?'

'Sounds like your man McGregor has a tight chain of command

set up. He has a particular way of getting things done and you're not fitting into it.'

'Yeah, because I'm female.'

'Maybe.' Red paused a moment. 'But chances are it's not personal.'

'Like him never hiring a woman isn't personal?'

Red sighed. 'So he doesn't like working with women; that's not so unusual in your line of work, you know that. By my way of thinking there's something else at play here, too. If I remember rightly you didn't take to this McGregor guy from the start. Maybe you need to try a little harder to get along.'

I clenched my fist tighter around my cell phone. '*I* have to try harder? I just damn well apologised and he threw it back in my—'

'I'm not trying to get into an argument with you, Miss Lori. You called me for advice, and what I'm saying is that you don't trust this McGregor to help you and that's what's got you fighting like alley cats.'

I said nothing. Red was right, I didn't trust McGregor, but that didn't mean I wanted to talk about it. I changed the subject. 'How are you doing?'

'I'm okay; little bit sore in places but it'll pass. I'm back working the job. No sign of Gibson's ex-wife and her husband. I'm still working on the rest. I'll let you know when I've got something.' He paused a beat, then said, 'Find a way to trust McGregor, professionally at least, otherwise I don't think you'll be able to get past the stand-off you're in.'

I rubbed my forehead. Thought of JT's rules. 'I was taught not to trust.'

'You trust me. I'm pretty sure you always did.'

'You're different.'

'Why?'

Truth was I didn't rightly know. But I did trust Red, always had done. Maybe it was the sense of calm just being in his company brought me. Maybe it was because he reminded me in many ways of an older JT. Maybe it was because he'd never doubted my ability or resolve. Whatever it was, I trusted him now, and I knew he was right – I did need to rescue the situation with McGregor. Problem was, I just couldn't see any way I could bring myself to trust a man like him.

I ended the call and walked down the block to a sandwich shop. I got pastrami on rye and sat down at one of the tables in the back, thinking I'd try and figure out my next move as I ate.

I'd taken two bites when my cell rang.

'This is Lori.'

'My husband's gone out.' Mia sounded breathless. 'I can check those dates, but I need your help. He's locked the door to his study.'

I jumped to my feet, shoved the rest of my sandwich into my purse and headed for the door. 'I'll be with you in ten.'

It was time to find out exactly what Marco Searle had been getting up to.

36

My cell phone started ringing for the fifth time in as many minutes. I parked up outside Mia's place and checked the screen. Five missed calls, all from Bobby Four-Fingers. Then one message: *Momma don't be mad. Call me ASAP!!*

I guessed he was feeling guilty about not backing me up earlier with McGregor, but right then I was all out of compassion. I didn't want another argument, and I sure as hell didn't want to talk to Bobby, McGregor or any of that crew for a little while. Besides, I had a job to do here; the chance to see whether my hunch was right and Marco Searle was the man who'd been masquerading as Fletcher's brother Donald on the monthly prison visits. So I threw my cell back into my purse and hurried up the driveway to the house.

Mia had the door open before I reached the porch. 'He's out, but I don't know for how long. We can check his scheduler, but he's locked the study and I can't find the key.'

'Show me.'

We hurried along the hall. Expensive and understated, the oak floorboards, soft grey walls and smiling family portraits created a calm environment that was at odds with the tension I could feel radiating from Mia.

She turned to me, frowning. 'You can't be here when Marco gets back. He hates me having visitors.'

'No problem. I'll be quick.'

She nodded, but the frown remained.

'I really appreciate this, Mia.'

'I'm doing it for Gibson. So that you believe me when I tell you he didn't kill those people. Then you'll help me clear his name.'

I nodded. Didn't tell her how he'd assaulted me in the parking lot, or say that all the evidence pointed to him being guilty. Instead I let her believe I was her friend, and that I'd help her. And if she was right, although it was unlikely, I would help her clear Gibson's name.

Mia stopped. 'This is Marco's study.'

The door was high-quality oak. Sturdy. Not easy to force, not without making a mess anyways. A more subtle approach was needed. I rummaged in my purse, pulled out the black pouch containing my lock-picks and got to work.

Marco Searle's office was real neat; white shutters shielded the windows, only allowing thin shafts of light through their narrow slats; white floor-to-ceiling cabinets lined the walls and a huge white desk with a computer and two screens dominated the centre of the room. There was no paper visible anywhere. I looked at Mia. 'You said he kept his scheduler online?'

She nodded. 'It's on the computer. I don't know the password, though.'

I went to the desk. The computer was password protected, as Mia had said. Glancing around the room, I tried to figure out what it could be. It was odd; there was nothing personal in the room: no pictures, trophies or diplomas. No clues.

I typed Mia's name into the password field. Incorrect. Then I tried 'password' figuring it was worth a try – a lot of folks used that even though you shouldn't. Again incorrect.

I looked at Mia. 'Does he have a hobby, something important to him he might use as a password?'

She shook her head. 'Nothing I can think of.'

Damn. There had to be something. Most people used the name of something on their mind, consciously or subconsciously, at the time of creating their password; that's why photos around a desk were usually a good clue. The only things on Searle's desk aside from the computer, a pen-tidy and a silver letter opener in the shape of a dagger, were a wooden box of Cuban cigars and a crystal ashtray with the butt of two cigars in it. The brand name on the cigar box was Monte Cristo. It had to be worth a go. I typed Monte Cristo into the password field. The screen unlocked.

'I'm in.'

Mia fiddled with the cuff of her sleeve. 'Be quick. Please. If he comes back and finds us in here...'

I nodded. Got to work. Opening the scheduler, I scrolled back through the months, checking the dates of his trips against those on which Gibson Fletcher had been visited by his 'brother'. The first two matched. My heart rate accelerated. This could be the break I needed; I could be right – Searle could be the man who had impersonated Donald. I checked further back; the next date matched but the one before didn't and nor did the two previous to that. Damn.

I looked over at Mia. 'Your husband wasn't visiting Gibson.'

She frowned. 'Of course he wasn't. Marco despises Gibson.' Her voice faltered. 'He said he was going to kill him.'

Searle hated both brothers. Helping Gibson escape, then killing him and framing Donald could have been on his agenda, but if he'd been involved he hadn't got his own hands dirty, not according to his whereabouts recorded in the scheduler. Yet the coincidence of both Walker and Searle having connections to the Chicago Mob was still on my mind. Searle was mixed up in this somehow, I was real sure of it. I just had to figure out how.

The last date on my list was when the package had been sent to Southside Storage, allegedly by Donald Fletcher. I flicked to it. Inhaled sharply. Marco Searle's schedule was clear that day. I checked the days before and after; there were no entries for eight days straight. In all the months I'd looked through, no other days had been blank, unaccounted for.

I looked at Mia and pointed at the screen. 'What happened in the first week of March, two and a half years ago? Where was Marco?'

Mia pulled the loose thread she'd been fiddling with away from her cuff. Avoided my gaze. 'I don't know.'

I kept my eyes on her. I was pretty sure she did know. I made my tone soft, hoping she'd confide in me. 'You sure about that?'

She was silent a long moment, then she said in a quiet voice, 'That's when he found out about Jacob.'

'Your son? What did he find out about him?'

Mia looked away, her cheeks and throat flushing pink. 'Until then I'd let Marco believe Jacob was his. They both have black hair, brown eyes; it wasn't so hard for him to believe…'

I stared at her as the truth about Jacob's parentage dawned on me. 'He's Gibson's son?'

'Mine and Gibson's.' She looked at me, defiant. 'Marco making us move here had been the last straw. I hardly got to see Gibson, it was too hard … we couldn't carry on like that. We wanted to be together. So Gibson was divorcing his wife, and I was going to leave Marco. But before I told him I had to be sure Jacob wasn't his; I couldn't have him getting custody. So I had a DNA test done. Marco found the letter with the results.' She shuddered. 'He went crazy. Ranted and hit things, hit me … threatened Jacob. He said if we left he'd find and kill all three of us. I couldn't let him hurt my boy. So I stayed, and Marco left for a while, said he needed to be alone – needed time to process.'

From what I'd heard of Marco, he hadn't sounded much like a 'time to process' kind of guy, but I guessed finding out the kid you'd been raising wasn't yours would mess with your head.

I tapped the screen. 'And these eight days were when he was away "processing" things?'

'Yes.'

'And you've no idea where he went?'

'I told you I haven't.'

'It's just that—'

Mia put her hand up. 'Wait.' She looked out to the hall, listening.

I heard it too – the sound of the automatic garage door opening.

Mia's expression turned to terror. 'Marco's back. We have to get out of here.'

I shut down the computer, made sure everything was exactly as we'd found it and hurried out, closing the study door behind me. I couldn't relock it without the key. Hopefully Marco would just assume he'd forgotten to lock the door.

'He'll see you if you try to leave now. In here, quick,' Mia said, pushing me into a large, light family room decorated in lemon and white. Long white drapes hung floor to ceiling from the windows; at one end of the room stood a white baby grand piano, a vase of white roses blooming on top. Just like in the other rooms, there were no photographs of Marco, Mia or Jacob. It was a beautiful space, like something out of a magazine, but utterly soulless.

I sat down on the nearest couch. Mia re-entered with two glasses of iced water and sat on the couch opposite. I grabbed a glass and gulped down half the water.

I heard a door open. Mia laughed loudly and started talking about a shop downtown. I nodded along, said I needed a new outfit. It wasn't far from the truth.

A black-haired man, handsome in a dark suit and tie-less shirt, appeared in the doorway. He had a strong jaw and full lips that turned down just slightly at the edges.

He looked from me to Mia. 'I didn't realise we'd be having company this afternoon.'

Mia stiffened at the sound of his voice. She turned. 'Marco, this is Lori, a friend of mine. She dropped by as she was in the neighbourhood, letting me know there's a sale on at my favourite store this week.'

Searle strode across the room to me. Held out his hand. I saw that between his thumb and forefinger he had a scar in the shape of a starburst. He smiled. 'Pleasure to meet you.'

I stood and shook his hand. It was soft, like he'd never done a day of manual labour in his life. Like he always paid others to do the heavy work for him. He held my hand a moment longer than was necessary and said, 'Mia doesn't have many friends. Don't think she's mentioned you before.'

I forced a smile. 'Well that's because we only met recently; I'm vacationing here. Lucky for me I got chatting to Mia at beach yoga and she told me all the best places to visit.'

Searle let go of my hand. Glanced at Mia. 'Very lucky.'

'Anyways,' I continued. 'It's time I got on my way.'

Mia looked tense and withdrawn. I could only imagine what it was like for her living with Searle – him hating her while she resented him.

They both led me to the front door, and I stepped out onto the porch. 'See you soon, Mia?'

She nodded. Didn't quite meet my gaze.

Marco Searle put his arm around her and pulled her to him. She flinched as his fingers pressed deep into the flesh where her neck met her shoulder. His message was clear: you're mine; I'll never let you go. He smiled at me and wished me a good afternoon. His smile was broad, warm, and at odds with the cold hardness of his eyes. I shivered. He reminded me of my late husband, Thomas Ford – another man well used to using anger and cruelty to get his way. A man who liked pretty things that did as they were told.

Mia was a trapped in a loveless marriage by a violent man. I'd been in that position before. I'd felt that hopelessness. I'd felt that longing to escape. And I knew what had happened when I had managed it: people had died.

I wondered if that was a price Mia was willing to pay too.

I wondered if the people Gibson had killed already were a part of that price.

37

The more I thought on it, the more I felt sure Gibson wouldn't leave town without Mia. Their affair had lasted more than twenty years, and when Searle had uprooted her from Florida to California, the distance between them had been unbearable enough for them to decide to leave their spouses and run away together with their son, Jacob. It stood to reason that, if Gibson was running now, he'd want Mia with him.

So rather than heading back to McGregor's bond shop I ignored the three missed calls I'd had from him and drove out to the beach and Pier 61, the Coastal Surf Cottages. Mia said she rented the place as a retreat from Searle, but she'd also admitted Gibson had met her there before he went to Mexico. Maybe that was the truth, but I still wanted to be sure there was no one staying in cabin twenty.

The sun beat down on me as I walked along the wooden pier to the end cabin. I let myself in through the whitewashed gate and stepped up to the cabin. The pale-blue shutters were open, giving me a clear view inside through the half-glass frontage. The living space looked as neat as before, but things had been moved since I'd last been there; the plate by the sink was gone, as was the half-drunk bottle of red wine that'd been sitting on the counter. The place now looked empty, unused.

I turned to go, then stopped. When I'd followed Mia here a few days previously she'd put a note in the mailbox asking: *Where are you?* My money was on that note being for Gibson.

Turning back, I strode to the mailbox and opened it. Inside was a folded piece of paper. I pulled it out, unfolded it and read the loopy scrawl.

Almost done. Be ready.

38

I was still thinking on the note as I arrived back at McGregor's bond shop. The writing had been Gibson Fletcher's for sure, but Mia had told me that the day after I'd followed her there he'd run off to Mexico without her.

He'd lied to her or she'd lied to me. Either way, someone wasn't telling the truth.

The bond shop was closed. I tried the door but it was locked. Wondering why McGregor had shut the place up early, I banged on the door.

I heard raised voices inside. Then the bolts disengaged and the door was flung open. Jorge stood there, serious-faced and unsmiling. 'You'd better come inside.'

Compared to the heat of the sun, the bond shop felt like an icebox, and not just because of the air-con. McGregor was waiting for me, his expression like thunder. I'd taken five paces into the room when he started yelling. 'Where the fuck have you been? And why haven't you been answering your cell?'

I glared at him. I was still pissed from our argument, and was made more pissed by his shouting. 'I've been following up a lead. And I don't answer to you.'

He cussed. Slammed his hand down onto a filing cabinet. 'Four-Fingers was calling you. You never picked up.'

I glared at McGregor. 'Like I said, I was busy.'

'This morning Rosas and Ortiz had another sighting of Fletcher over the border. They needed assistance.'

Damn. Now I felt bad for not answering; I should have been on that job. 'Was it Fletcher? Did you get him?'

McGregor shook his head. 'I don't know if it was him. Jorge and me were on another job. Four-Fingers was the only one here. He tried to reach you, but you never picked up so he went in alone.'

I glanced around the office; it was empty aside from McGregor and Jorge. I felt fear ripple through me. 'Where's Bobby?'

'He called me from the road, left a voicemail. Fletcher had been spotted close to the border, but Rosas and Ortiz got held up en route so Four-Fingers went in solo.'

Shit. 'What happened?'

McGregor looked at me with disgust. Shook his head. 'You don't deserve to know.'

My mouth went dry. 'Tell me, please.'

McGregor looked away. Cussed under his breath.

'We don't know for sure,' Jorge said. 'But Rosas and Ortiz arrived to find Four-Fingers bleeding. No sign of Fletcher. Looks like it was a set-up, more than one man waiting on us to show.'

'He's in the hospital. Out of action for days – weeks most likely. Busted ribs, internal bleeding, face a mess,' McGregor spat. He stepped towards me, his hands all up in my face. 'It's your fault. You should have been there, should have had his six. *You* put him in the hospital.'

The blood rushed to my cheeks. 'If I'd answered his call I—'

'You didn't think. You didn't answer.'

I stayed silent. I was in the wrong and I knew it. Bobby had been hurt because I'd been too pissed at him to pick up when he called. I hadn't helped him when he needed me. I'd let him down.

McGregor looked at me like I was dirt. 'You're a prima donna – a selfish bitch who's only interested in what's in anything for her. I'm sick of you.'

'I just want to find Gibson. I never meant to—'

McGregor put his face close to mine. His breath was hot against my skin. The fury in his glare burned into me. 'You did this. You got one of my best men half killed. I can't have it. I can't lose another team member. You're a liability, a danger to my team, and I won't tolerate it any longer.'

'But we need to catch—'

'I'll find Fletcher and bring him in, but not with you.' McGregor pointed to the workstation I'd been using. 'Get your shit together and get out of here. I'm telling Monroe you're benched.'

The panic had me in its grip and I couldn't wrestle free. When McGregor called Monroe he'd demand I was taken off the job. Given the situation with Bobby, I figured Monroe would agree. But I couldn't let that happen. I had to find a new lead, catch a break and get us closer to Gibson. I had to prove to Monroe he still needed me.

I returned to the hotel. Needed to go through everything to do with this job. Made a strong coffee, and went back to the beginning.

Two things seemed to have been pulling Gibson Fletcher to San Diego. One was Mia Searle, and the other was the package at Southside Storage. If I could confirm what had been in the package, maybe I could find out who helped Gibson with his escape, and that would help me crack this.

I pulled out the documents that Clint Norsen had photostatted for me and spread them out on the bed. I double-checked the signature on the sender's docket, and compared it to the prison visitors' log signature; as I already knew, they were a definite match. Other than that, at face value, everything looked normal. But there were a few stand-out things for me. First was, why had the person masquerading as Donald sent a package to Gibson in a city he didn't live? Second, why had the sender left the package at Southside Storage after Gibson had been sentenced and put in jail. They could have had the package returned to sender, so why hadn't they? Was the jailbreak planned even then? My third question concerned the contents of the package.

Monroe had led me to believe the package most likely contained the stolen gold chess set that Gibson had taken before the double homicide. The shipping documentation told me different.

The weight of the package was recorded as 69.3 grams. Grabbing my cell, I Googled the chess set. Wikipedia listed its worth when last valued at 1,345,000 dollars. The weight of the set was recorded at just over 2,000 grams.

I looked back at the documentation. The weight was clearly written – 69.3 grams on the sender's docket, and 69.3 grams on the collection slip. Whatever was inside the package, one thing was for sure; it wasn't the gold chess set.

I called Monroe. 'I've been going over the package documentation from Southside Storage again. The package weighed just under seventy grams, it wasn't heavy enough to be the chess set.'

'Your main priority is finding Fletcher.' Monroe's voice was hushed, like he was trying not to be overheard. In the background, I could hear phones ringing and conversations. I wondered if he was in the FBI offices. 'Once we've got him I can question him about the chess pieces.'

I frowned. At the start of this Monroe seemed real keen on getting the chess set back. 'I thought this was one of the reasons you wanted Fletcher found on your terms?'

'Yes, obviously.' He sounded irritated. 'But catching Fletcher is the priority. He's been on the loose too long, Lori. My bosses are questioning if we'll get him back.'

'I'll find him.'

'Just be sure that you do. And fast.'

He didn't mention McGregor having called him, so I didn't bring it up. Instead I said, 'Any word on that CCTV from the jail? I could really use a break about—'

'I've asked, but nothing yet.' He sounded frustrated. 'I'll tell you if I get it.'

He hung up before I could reply.

I put the burner back in my purse. Thought it weird Monroe wasn't pushing harder for the CCTV and that he hadn't been more surprised that the package couldn't have contained the chess set. Was he deliberately hiding things from me, or was this just more of his need-to-know bullshit? Whatever was behind it, I didn't appreciate being kept in the dark. It was only a matter of time before McGregor called Monroe and tried to get me taken off the job. If I didn't have a solid lead by then everything would have been for nothing.

I couldn't let that happen.

39

It was late, and much as I hated to admit it, I just needed to hear his voice.

The infirmary nurse was different from the one that'd spoken to me the night before and was a whole lot more resistant to letting me speak with JT. But after I'd held for what seemed like forever for them to check the authorisation from Monroe, they finally gave JT the phone.

Would he talk to me? Would the trauma of the cardiac arrest have changed him somehow? Nervous energy fizzed through me as I said, 'How are you doing?'

'I've been better.' His voice sounded fragile, his breathing heavier than usual, but he was able to talk and that counted for a lot. 'You still in California?'

'Yeah. We've had a few false sightings of the fugitive but nothing concrete.' I decided not to mention Gibson threatening me, the problems with McGregor, and the problems me and Red had had in Florida. 'I've got a few leads though.'

'Go home. Be with Dakota. Don't put yourself in danger.'

'I want to get you safe.' I needed to tell him about Dakota; about the cancer that could return, and the donor she might need; about how he was her best hope. 'Dakota needs you, she—'

'Not on the phone ... another time...'

I would tell him, surely I would. 'I owe you.'

He exhaled hard. 'You don't owe me a damn thing, kiddo. I'm in here so you can walk away.'

'And if I don't want to?'

He said nothing. All I could hear was his laboured breathing and the rhythmic beeping of a heart monitor. It felt like his silence would snap my heart clean in two.

'Lori?' he said at last.

'Yes.'

'You're strong. You don't need me.'

'I know.' My lip trembled, and I was glad that he couldn't see it. I was a survivor, I could get through anything, but sometimes I wished I didn't always have to be so damn strong. 'But I'd still like you to be with us.'

He sighed. A few beats passed before he said, 'I'd like that, too.'

His words jolted me hard. Him saying he wanted to be with us – I'd not expected that. I'd gotten so used to him never expressing how he felt, it was a shock now he had. I didn't speak. Wondered what he meant … if he really meant it.

'You'd—'

'But, the thing is, if you're with me you'd never be safe. That price on my head means they won't stop until I'm—'

'That's why I have to get you out of there. I need this job, because I need Monroe to deliver his end of the deal.' If there was a chance we could be together, I had to make it happen. I didn't know if me, Dakota and JT could work as a family, but I sure wanted to give it a try. 'I'm not asking for your permission.'

I could hear the smile in his words as he said, 'I wouldn't expect you to.'

'Good.'

He lowered his voice. 'But what got set in motion all those years back, when your husband disappeared, is still in play here. They won't rest until the debt is squared. I have to find a way to do that.'

'You shouldn't have to. *I* killed him, *I* should be the one taking the blame.'

'No.' His voice was stronger, firmer.

'Then we'll find a way to square it together.'

'There are a lot of men loyal to the Old Man in here. They'll come for me again.'

He nodded.

We sat in silence a few moments. Joni Mae dozed in her stroller. Tight in her little fists she clutched a fluffy green rabbit with one eye missing. Clint watched her. From his blotchy complexion and watery eyes I knew he was fighting back memories and emotion. I stayed quiet. Waited for him to get back his composure.

He cleared his throat. 'I never did it, you know. Never went to college.'

'You had a lot on your plate, what with the baby and all...'

'Yeah. I thought about being a cop, but Monroe said to sit tight at Southside Storage. Told me he'd have an assignment for me soon.'

'And did he?'

'Not until the other week.'

'You waited over two years?' I couldn't hide the surprise in my voice.

'Two years, five months and eight days.'

I had an idea of what the assignment was, but I needed to know for sure, to hear it from Clint without prompting. 'And when your assignment came, what was it?'

'Monroe sent me a photo. Told me to watch out for a man who'd escaped jail in Florida and was likely heading this way. His name was Gibson Fletcher.'

Monroe had Clint in position at Southside Storage two and a half years before he was needed. He'd made sure he didn't leave, but had waited until Gibson had escaped before giving Clint any kind of job. 'What day did he give you the assignment?'

Clint thought a moment. 'July nineteenth. In the afternoon.'

I felt a chill creep up my spine and shivered in spite of the sun's warmth. Gibson Fletcher escaped from the hospital on July twentieth. Clint had been put on alert a day earlier. There was an explanation, but it didn't make sense: Special Agent Alex Monroe knew the prison break was going to happen *before* Gibson turned fugitive.

41

Never trust no one. Not even if they're FBI.

I'd made the deal and taken the job to catch Gibson Fletcher, but now it seemed Monroe had known all along when Gibson was breaking free and where he'd be heading. I'd taken a chance, played the dice and hoped the odds would work in my favour, but Monroe had been playing me for a fool. The question was, why?

Back at my hotel, I reached for my cell phone and dialled Red's number. Put it on FaceTime and hoped he knew how to work it. I needed to see a friendly face.

He picked up after six rings. His image was clear on-screen – his face still bruised, but the cuts healing. Behind him the ocean shimmered. He sat down on one of the deck seats. 'Why're you calling on video?'

'I needed to see how you're doing.'

'I'm doing just fine, and you could have just asked me.' He gestured at the screen. 'You know I hate this stuff.'

'Sorry,' I said. Then I told him what I'd discovered about Monroe and Clint's history.

Red was silent for a long moment, then said, 'What's your take on why Monroe wants Gibson so bad?'

I thought back to what Monroe had said about this job, and why he wanted Gibson Fletcher. It all seemed to centre around the gold chess set stolen ten days before Gibson's arrest and bail for thefts on the vacationers' yacht *Sunsearcher*. I'd been put on his tail when he skipped that bail, and ended up catching him. But I'd not got to him in time to save Patrick Walker and his wife from Fletcher's attack on their luxury yacht. I now knew the package sent to Southside Storage had been despatched earlier in the day on which the Walkers were murdered.

According to Monroe there'd been no sign of the chess pieces since they'd been taken, but any further information about them was need-to-know, and as far as Monroe was concerned I didn't need to know.

'I think it's all connected to the missing chess pieces, but none of the facts fit together right.'

Red frowned. 'Run me through them.'

'Donald Fletcher allegedly sent the package to Southside Storage, but the signatures don't match and Donald denies it. It doesn't wash for another reason – the brothers were estranged by then and so there's no sense thinking Gibson had any contact with Donald or knowledge of what he was doing. Yet whoever sent the package told Gibson where to find it, as he was the one who picked it up two and a half years later.'

'So whoever sent it was in contact with Gibson and knew where he'd be heading if he got free.'

'Yup. But Monroe told me he had no reason to believe Gibson Fletcher would go to San Diego. He'd sounded surprised when I told him about Gibson and Mia, and asked me to look into it. Now it seems he's known all along. Why else station Clint Norsen at South-side Storage? He'd been in place over two years in advance of Gibson's jailbreak, and Monroe briefed Clint to look out for Gibson the day before he escaped. Monroe could have had a tip-off about the bust, but surely he'd have had the hospital watched if that'd been the case; far easier to prevent Gibson running in the first place than trying to catch him once he'd gone.'

'True,' Red said, looking thoughtful. 'Unless he wanted Gibson to run?'

I remembered the night I'd been attacked in the parking lot of my hotel, of how certain I'd been it was Gibson who attacked me, and how he'd leaned close and said, 'Tell Monroe to leave me be. He owes me that.'

'Why would he?' I said.

'That's for you to find out, Miss Lori, but it's not sounding good.'

'Yeah.' My head hurt. None of it stacked up. It was like adding two plus two and making thirteen. I crossed the room to the coffee-maker and made myself a cup of strong coffee.

'What's your next move?'

Oftentimes my way of dealing things was to go in straight, and I considered that in this situation, but something held me back. Sure, I could lay down the facts and have Monroe tell me how they added into something good and within the law, but I wasn't convinced that would be the truth. I figured he was either keeping a bunch of things from me due to his 'need-to-know' way of working – in which case he'd be unlikely to share more anyways; or he was dirty and hiding facts to pervert the course of justice – which meant revealing my hand was at best stupid and at worst real life-threatening.

'I need to know more before I tackle Monroe,' I said. 'Have you got anything I can use?'

'Not yet. I stopped by Gibson's ex-wife's place out in Lake County, but there's still no sign of her and her new husband. Looked like they'd not been there for a good while – the mail was stacking up in their mailbox – so I spoke with their neighbours. Nice couple, elderly, with time on their hands to watch and talk, if you know what I mean. They said they'd not seen Gibson's ex-wife or her husband since the day his escape hit the news.'

'That's over a week. Is that typical for them?'

'I asked that, and they said no. They also had a key to the place that they held onto in case of emergencies. So I asked them to open it up and I took a look around. The place looked neat, well cared for. Odd thing was that in the kitchen they'd left their breakfast all laid out on the counter – eggs, hash browns, bacon and pancakes – half eaten and abandoned. One of the coffee mugs had been tipped over, the coffee had pooled on the counter and dripped onto the floor.'

'Signs of a struggle?'

'Other than the coffee, nothing was messed up. It looked more like they'd left in a real hurry. All their clothes seemed to be in the closets, no obvious gaps. The neighbours had a cell number for her. We tried it, but it went straight to voicemail. They told me that's unusual; she's usually one of those types with her cell permanently in her hand.'

It didn't sound good. 'Before I might have told Monroe about it, but with what I've just learned I don't want to give him any more information than I have to.'

Red said nothing for a long while. When he spoke, he sounded real serious. 'You know, I'm thinking you should maybe head back here. Tackling an FBI agent who might've turned rogue, that's real dangerous. Could be time to forget the deal. That's what Tate told you to do anyways.'

Red was right, JT had told me to walk away at first. The irony now was that he'd accepted my deal with Monroe was his best shot at walking free.

'Not an option,' I said.

'Then you need to be real smart. A man like Monroe, he's got the resources and the law on his side even if he's doing something bad. You go up against him and fail, you'll be running your whole life, or worse.'

'I know.'

'And you're still thinking of taking him on?'

'When I have the facts, yes.'

Red whistled through his teeth. 'You know you might never get them. He's going to have covered his tracks real careful.'

'Then we need to look hard.'

Red was silent for a few beats. He looked deep in thought, then said, 'I'll do what I can from here, you know that.'

I nodded. I'd known Red wouldn't fly out to California. 'Can you try and get a copy of the CCTV from the prison Gibson was at? I need to see who was signing themselves in as Donald.'

'I'll do my best, but be careful, you hear? A lot of these federal types, they've got no honour, no kind of code.'

I felt the fear twist inside my belly. Ignored it. I was going to finish the job and get JT free, that was for damn sure. 'I'm fine. I'm a long way from anyone who's got my back is all.'

'You got some folks there in California you trust to help you?'

I thought of McGregor. 'I don't trust easy.'

'Maybe you need to try a little harder.'

Red was right. All I had was questions; a bunch of cards which added up to a busted flush. I needed to find someone with an ace.

42

The burner beeped. A message from Monroe:

Situation critical. McGregor refuses to work with you. I need Gibson caught asap, with or without you. I'm flying to San Diego in the am to take control. Meet midday at McGregor's.

Shit. I'd known it was only a matter of time before McGregor spoke to Monroe, but now it'd happened the clock was ticking double fast. From what Monroe had said before, he reckoned he needed McGregor more than me; meaning if I hadn't found Gibson before midday the next day, or was as close as dammit to doing so, I'd be off the job and the deal I'd struck with Monroe for JT's release would be null and void.

Whatever concerns I had about Monroe and the stuff he was keeping from me, I couldn't let that happen. JT and Dakota had to be my top priority.

I checked the time; it was 17:51. I had eighteen hours to finish this. I couldn't rely on any help from McGregor; he'd made it real clear he didn't want to see me again. But what Red had said about needing to accept help resonated. I needed to do whatever it took to bring Gibson in or, if that wasn't possible, I had to get McGregor to let me back on the team. Either way, it meant I needed to pull in some favours.

The list of folks I could call on was short. Only two people I'd met came to mind: Mia Searle and Bobby Four-Fingers. I felt an affinity with Mia – we both knew violence at a man's hand, we both wanted our messed-up families to be together, and she'd helped me before. But there was a danger there, too; she wanted me to help her get Gibson free, and although I'd said I'd take any evidence she found of him being framed to Monroe, given my objective was to bring Gibson in it was likely we'd ultimately be on opposing sides.

Which left Bobby Four-Fingers. He'd been kind towards me at McGregor's bond shop, always respectful and helpful, and we'd had a laugh. The worst he'd done was not speak up when McGregor had gone for me after the failed raid in Mexico. I'd been angry about it, but now, having cooled off outside of the heat of that situation, I felt real bad that I'd ignored his calls and messaged apology. Because he'd tried to make a pick-up alone he'd been hurt. He hadn't deserved that. I needed to go visit with him, make nice, and see if I could get him to help me.

I called Bobby and asked if I could come over. He'd agreed, although he hadn't sounded super keen. He lived in a condo just off Park Boulevard over in East Village, close to the Gaslamp Quarter. It was a fine location, close to nightlife and amenities, and it was a clean building with a gym, a pool and a roof terrace. I parked the Jeep in the underground parking lot, and took the elevator to the fourteenth floor. From the quality wood floors and the flawless presentation I could tell the place was high end – far higher end than I'd have credited Bobby having the taste for. I felt bad for judging him. I also wondered where he got all his cash from; a place like this wouldn't leave much change from two thousand bucks a month. The bounty-hunting business must be real good in San Diego.

I pressed the buzzer beside number 1417 and waited. I felt a little nervous waiting on him to answer the door. Knew how much I needed his help to persuade McGregor to let me stay on the team.

I heard the sound of bolts being pulled back and the door unlocking then Bobby opened it wide. I gasped at the sight of him, couldn't help myself.

'Shit, Bobby. What the hell did they do to you?'

He smiled. The bruising around his jaw made it look more like a grimace. 'Pretty, aren't I?'

I'd heard he'd been beaten but I hadn't expected this. His face was mottled purple and red, one eye was completely closed from the swelling around it. He was stooped, one arm curled protectively around his ribs, the other bound in a white bandage and resting in a sling. He shuffled back to let me inside, a pronounced limp hindering his gait.

'Why did they—'

'They don't like bounty hunters in Mexico. Occupational hazard.' He hobbled through the open living space towards the kitchenette. 'You want a beer, soda, tea or something?'

'Soda would be great.'

Bobby took a beer and a soda from the refrigerator. Handed the soda to me before twisting the top off his beer one-handed. He took a long draw on it. Looked back to me. 'It's medicinal, you know.'

'I bet.' It was hard not to stare at his injuries. 'I should have been there. I'm sorry, truly I—'

'You should have, but you weren't and I decided to charge in alone.' He chuckled, then winced and pressed his arm against his ribs. 'Guess a bit of your gung-ho style rubbed off on me.'

'Sorry about that.'

'It's okay.' He took a gulp of his beer. Narrowed his eyes. 'So now we've got the apologies out the way, what's it you wanted to talk over?'

'McGregor won't work with me anymore. Monroe's flying out tomorrow to take control of the operation. If that happens I'm screwed.' I told Bobby the bare bones of my deal with Monroe. 'If I don't catch Gibson before Monroe arrives, he'll work with McGregor and I'll get cut out. That means my ex-mentor will get convicted of multiple homicide, maybe even get the—'

'Okay, I get it. So what do you need from me?'

'I need you to persuade McGregor that he should keep me on the team.'

Bobby shook his head. 'I don't got that kind of sway over him. The boss is mad at you, thinks you're a liability. I can't see him changing his view anytime soon.'

I cursed under my breath. 'Because he's a sexist prick – I'm sick of the way this business treats—'

'You know, momma, McGregor isn't a bad guy.'

I frowned. 'Could've fooled me.'

'Look, I know the two of you don't get along so good, but it's not a personal thing or a woman thing, it's—'

I raised my eyebrows. 'You think? Sure seems like it is from this angle.'

Bobby took a swig of his beer. 'You told him he never gave you a fair shot, but from the way I saw it you never gave him much of chance, either.'

'I gave him plenty.'

'No, you didn't. You got mad at him and all, but you didn't talk to him about his concerns. If you had it could've—'

'So you're saying it's my fault?'

Bobby held his good hand up in mock surrender. 'Not saying it's anyone's fault. I'm just saying if you knew him a little more you might have cut him some slack.'

'Is that right?' I glared at Bobby. I wanted his help for sure, but this men-sticking-together bullshit was making me mad. 'Why don't you tell me why I should have done that?'

Bobby sighed. 'It's not my story to tell.'

'Well ... shit. Thanks for the soda. I'll see myself out.' I turned to go.

'Momma, wait.' Bobby gestured to the couch. 'Look, take the weight off. Chill. I guess it'd be okay to tell you; might stop all the fighting.'

I narrowed my eyes. Undecided.

Bobby walked to the refrigerator and took out two beers. 'Ditch the soda. Have this, and listen up.'

I took the beer and sat down on the couch. 'Okay. Shoot.'

Bobby perched on the edge of the bed. 'McGregor used to run the business with his wife, Talisha. They set it up together after coming out of the army. Things went well. They got a good rep and a lot of business, started expanding the team. Took me on after I'd retired as polis.'

'Okay, then what? She ditch him? Is that why he's so bitter?'

Bobby's expression got all serious. He shook his head. 'Back then we hunted alone or in pairs. Talisha was the best of us – had a knack for finding the trickiest skip traces.' He smiled. 'She was one of those people you opened up to. Everyone did – made her real good at getting information.'

I took a gulp of beer. 'And?'

'Meant she worked on her own a lot of the time.' He sighed. 'She was alone the night she got jumped. Bunch of guys took her – gang-bangers whose mate she'd pulled in a few days earlier. They held her captive for ten hours. Took turns with her – rape, beating...' Bobby swallowed hard. 'Filmed it all and sent it to McGregor.'

Shit. 'What happened to her?'

'Her body washed up on Torrey Pines Beach out near La Jolla a few days later.'

I felt sick to my stomach. 'How did he cope?'

'He didn't. Cops found the men eventually, locked them up. But it made no difference to McGregor. He took it all on himself, convinced it was his fault she'd been caught, that they'd violated her. She'd been almost four months pregnant with their first child. He lost them both.'

I shook my head. Didn't know how anyone could come back from that.

'He cut himself off from the team, hit the drink, and hit rock bottom pretty soon after. The rest of us kept the show on the road. After about six months he started talking again; a few months after that he quit the drink. The day after the anniversary of Talisha's death, he showed up for work and focused like a maniac on the business.'

'But he never hired a woman again?'

Bobby nodded. 'Something like that. Rosas is different – she's Jorge's contact. Otherwise McGregor doesn't work with women – it brings back memories he wants to keep buried.'

I understood now. Shit. The man's wife and unborn child had been murdered, and I'd called him a sexist asshole. I felt like a total bitch. 'I didn't—'

'You couldn't have known. It was a while back now.'

But Bobby was wrong. I could have done my homework on McGregor better, I could have checked out his background more thoroughly. Instead I'd only glanced at his credentials, keeping my focus on Gibson Fletcher and the job. That lack of preparation had cost me dear.

'I need to make this right,' I said.

Bobby shook his head. 'No, momma, you don't. You go in talking about McGregor's personal shit and he'll kick you to the kerb faster than you'll be able to apologise.'

'Then what the hell do I do? Monroe will be here tomorrow. I'm as good as fired.'

'Find Gibson Fletcher.'

I laughed. Shook my head. 'Yeah, if only I'd thought of that.'

'I'm serious.'

I looked at Bobby; he did look serious. 'I've got a whole bunch of questions and not so many answers right now. Why did he come to San Diego rather than heading straight over the border? He picked up a package from a storage place near the airport: what was in it? There's so many—'

'Then focus on the question that'll get you closer to Fletcher right now – what's keeping him here?'

I raised an eyebrow. 'Thought you believed he was in Mexico?'

Bobby looked down at his battered body. 'Changed my view on that a little bit.'

'How so?'

'The man I went after – who jumped me? He wasn't Gibson Fletcher. He was similar-looking for sure, a close-enough lookalike from a distance, but like that man in the shack we raided, it wasn't our guy.'

'Rosas and Ortiz made another mistake?'

Bobby frowned. 'Thing is, those spotters haven't made any mistakes before. And now there's been two in a row as we hunt for the same guy? Doesn't stack up right to me.'

I leaned in closer to him. 'You think they set us up?'

He considered it a moment, then shook his head. 'No, Rosas and Ortiz are good people. I think someone's been playing them.'

I caught his meaning. 'Decoys?'

'That's my thinking.'

'But why?'

'Because someone with a hell of a lot of power doesn't want us to find Gibson Fletcher.'

I thought about what Bobby was saying. Monroe had more clout; was he deliberately sabotaging our hunt? 'Monroe?'

'Wouldn't make no sense.'

True. But then I knew a whole lot more about Monroe and the things he'd done that didn't add up. I kept that to myself though, and asked Bobby, 'Who, then?'

'Don't know, momma. Who has the most to gain from Gibson staying free?'

The answer was easy. 'Mia Searle. She's got a child with Gibson; she wants them to be together.'

'You think she's behind the decoys?'

It was possible. Mia wanted her family together and I knew she'd been in contact with Gibson since he'd come to San Diego. I also knew that she'd lied to me before. 'Maybe.'

'Tell McGregor then. I'll call him and tell him my suspicions about the decoys. Then you tell him about Mia.'

I hesitated. Something Mia had said back when we first met in the diner came into mind. I shook my head. 'I don't think it's her. But she did say her husband, Marco Searle, is after Gibson; that he wants him dead and has friends in Mexico that'll help that happen. She's really afraid, and I believe her. I reckon Searle's behind the decoys. He wants Gibson Fletcher for himself.'

'You need to tell McGregor about Searle, then.'

Tell McGregor? I wasn't there yet. I was sorry about what happened to his wife, for his loss, the pain and the heartbreak and all, but I was still a long way from trusting him. 'He'll cut me out. I can't risk that. I need to do this myself.'

'He won't. Take him proof and you'll get him on your side.' Bobby looked at me real serious. 'McGregor's a good man. When shit goes down you'll want him in your corner.'

Get proof? Bobby was right, I needed to be sure Searle was responsible for the decoys before I busted him. I'd only get one chance with Monroe, so I had to be sure I had the right person, and a lead on Gibson, before I took this to him.

I had until midday tomorrow. I needed to move fast.

43

When I called Mia back in my hotel room, she wasn't convinced. Searle was home, in his study, she told me. She couldn't see a way of getting what I needed anytime soon.

I took a deep breath and asked again. 'It's important, Mia. I think Marco is deliberately sabotaging our search for Gibson so that he can find him first. We talked about this before; you told me what will happen when Marco gets to him...'

'I know, but I can't just barge in there. I never go in his study – it's off limits. I have to wait.'

'We don't have long.' I drummed my nails against the nightstand. 'If I can't get proof of who's behind the sabotage I'll get thrown off the job. That means my leverage with the FBI will be gone, and that retrial you want for Gibson? Any hope of that'll be gone, too.'

She inhaled sharply. 'I want to help, okay. It's just he could be in there all night.'

I could tell from her tone she wasn't going to budge on this. She was too afraid to go in the study while Marco was home. 'But you'll do it?'

'As soon as I can.'

'I need emails, messages – anything that links to the decoys in Mexico. Print them or take a photo – I need evidence.'

'Yes, okay.' Mia's voice sounded harder. 'I heard you the first time.'

It was a long shot that he'd have left the details on his devices, but if he didn't expect anyone to go looking, maybe he wasn't too careful. 'And you think you can get into the study on your own?'

'I watched how you picked the lock, and I remember the password for his computer.' She sounded determined. 'If it helps Gibson, I can do this.'

'I appreciate you taking the risk.'

She was quiet a moment. 'I'm doing it for Gibson, and for Jacob.'

'I understand that. Thank you.'

'Just talk to the FBI and get Gibson another chance, then we'll be even.'

I was in no position to promise Mia anything and I hadn't agreed to talk to Monroe. But I didn't tell her that, even though I knew I was giving her false hope. 'I'll do what I can.' I felt bad as I said it.

'So will I.'

I was too wired to sleep. Instead I flicked through the recent pictures Dakota had messaged me; one taken by a counsellor of her grooming her favourite horse – a chestnut mare called Widget – and more pictures of her artwork. The happiness of the first picture seemed eclipsed by the darkness that inhabited the final few. But I couldn't think on that right then. I missed my baby. Knew there were things we'd need to talk about, work through, once this job was done. For the moment though, I was just thankful that she was safe.

My cell buzzed in my hand. The caller wasn't Mia but Red.

I answered. 'It must be real late for you?'

'It is, but I think you're going to want to hear this.' Red's tone was businesslike, not his usual laid-back drawl. He sounded like he was walking. 'I've been trying to put together the missing data from the Walker homicides. I just met with the retired detective who worked the case. Found something real interesting.'

I sat up a little straighter. 'Oh yes?'

'Seems Gibson wasn't the only visitor to the Walkers' yacht that night.'

I'd not anticipated that. 'He didn't act alone – he had an accomplice?'

'I'm not sure if they were in it together. The timings are a little hazy – the kids were confused, apparently. They couldn't agree on how many people had visited with their parents that night. One said two men, the other was adamant there was only one. The cops had a good description of Gibson from both kids and his prints were all over the murder scene. Seems they figured it'd be easier to pin it on him alone.'

'That's why they "lost" the girls' initial statements?'

'That's what the retired detective said. He didn't like it, but the order came from higher up the chain of command.'

'Shit.'

'Yep. Especially if you're Gibson.'

'So what do you think? Was Gibson acting alone?'

'Hard to say without seeing those statements, but from what the detective said, the kid was convinced she'd seen a second man. Way she told it, her sister was back in their bunk sleeping, but she'd wanted a glass of water so she got out of bed and headed to the living area. The door had been ajar, and through the gap she saw a stranger – a different man to the one who'd arrived earlier, before the kids went to bed, and who'd introduced himself as Gibson.'

'Did she describe him?'

'Apparently, yes, but the detective couldn't recall the details. He did remember one thing though: the kid heard the man introduce himself to her mom. He called himself Fletcher.'

I frowned. 'But it wasn't Gibson?'

'That's what the kid said.'

Shit. 'You think it was Donald?'

'Impossible to say, but that was my thinking off the bat.'

My mind flooded with questions. Was that why Donald Fletcher had changed so dramatically in the past couple of years? Had the strain and guilt of murdering the Walkers and leaving their two daughters orphaned eaten away at him until he was a shadow of his former self? Was he waiting to be found out? Was that why he needed so much security around his property?

'We need a description of the man.'

'That's what I said. Luckily the detective liked to keep records. He's digging out his old notebooks for me, said he might have more details written down.'

'I didn't think cops were allowed to take things home relating to—'

'True. He shouldn't have kept them, but he did; and for that we might be thankful.'

'You said the timings were hazy – what did you mean by that?'

'Gibson was at the yacht that night, no doubt about it, but the time he arrived and left was a matter of dispute. The kids initially said he came just after dinner – they'd been doing the dishes – and left a half hour later. But the medical report put the Walkers' time of death at gone eleven o'clock, a good three hours later.'

'Did your detective friend have a theory on that?'

'He did.'

'And?'

'He always thought Gibson Fletcher was innocent of the homicide. He said a man like that, skilled at burglary and getting away with it, wouldn't have made the mistake of leaving his prints at the scene.'

'If he'd not killed before, the stress of the situation could have...'

'It could have, but the detective didn't think that's what happened to Gibson. He said he interviewed him as part of the investigation – several interviews over many hours. They deprived him of sleep, they tag-teamed him – the good cop, bad cop routine; they even offered to cut him a deal. Nothing changed Gibson's stance – he said he was innocent, that the Walkers had been alive when he left, and that he had nothing to add aside from his deepest sympathies to the two girls who'd lost their parents. The detective, real experienced, with over twenty-five years on the job, believed him.'

I thought back to the first time I'd hunted and caught Gibson Fletcher. He'd seemed like a stand-up guy for a career criminal: polite, respectful. He didn't fight when I found him, just put his hands up and said he'd come easy. Yet, if the timeline was to be believed, he'd have killed the Walkers just a couple of days before I picked him up. I shook my head.

'Honestly, I didn't figure Gibson for a killer either,' I said.

'So what's your next move?'

'Same as before: find him and bring him in. He's a wanted man. Us thinking he is or isn't guilty doesn't change that.'

'True. But if the man was framed...'

'Then he needs a retrial. If he runs, he'll always be running. That's no kind of a life.'

'And your job is to bring him back.'

'Yes, it is.'

Red paused a beat. Then said, 'Alright then.'

I didn't like the judgement in his tone. 'You got something you want to say about that?'

Red whistled. 'I'm dog-tired and I'm aching bad, Miss Lori. I don't want a fight. All I'm thinking is that being a PI is a whole lot easier than your job. Sometimes I just choose not to say I found someone.'

I thought about what I had riding on this job – JT's freedom, Dakota's health. 'That's not an option for me.'

'I know. One man's freedom in exchange for another.'

I clenched my cell phone tighter. Didn't like the truth of Red's words. 'Gibson shot those guards when he escaped at the hospital. If he wasn't a killer before, he is now.'

'It's not me you have to convince.' He paused. 'I know you. This thing's going to eat at you till you know the truth, isn't it?'

He was right. I had to take Gibson in, but I wouldn't let him rot in jail if he was an innocent man. 'For sure.'

'Then I'll keep digging. I'll call as soon as I know more.'

I was silent a moment. Thought about how Donald had convinced me it wasn't his signature on the parcel docket and the prison visitor logs, and wondered just how good a liar he was. Had he been involved all along? Was he playing me?

And what about Gibson? Maybe Mia *was* right about him. The evidence stacking up pointed to him being innocent. The Walkers' homicides could have been a wrongful conviction; he could have been framed. If that was right I had to make good on my word to Mia – I needed to do what I could to get Monroe to see the cops had got the wrong guy and to get Gibson a retrial. But first, I had to catch him.

I cleared my throat. Felt the weight of the undertaking heavy in my chest as I said, 'Red. Thank you.'

And then I waited. I hated the waiting. It made me feel powerless. I fetched a sausage biscuit from the hot vending machine along the corridor, made herbal tea to calm me, and tried to think on what I'd say to Monroe the next day. The clock was counting down to his arrival and all I could do was wait for Mia.

My reliance on her made me restless. Sure, she was helping me find the information about Marco, but I couldn't be sure she wasn't hiding Gibson's location from me. I'd followed her, challenged her, and asked her to trust me, but I could sense she was still holding back; holding out on the hope that Gibson would come back for her and they'd ride off into the sunset together, looking for a happy ending.

But this wasn't a fairy tale, and Gibson was no kind of prince; he was a thief and a killer with multiple homicides to his name – maybe the Walkers and definitely the cops at the hospital. The irony that these were the exact same charges JT had been arrested for back in Florida wasn't lost on me. I got that me and Mia weren't all that different – both wanting our messed-up families back together; both doing what we could to try and get the men we loved off the charges against them. The thing was, though, I knew exactly what JT was guilty of. I'd seen what he'd done on the ride from West Virginia to Florida, because we'd faced the criminal gangs side-by-side. I knew that if he hadn't have been there, I'd never have gotten my Dakota back safe, and if he hadn't taken the blame for my husband, Tommy's disappearance, the Miami Mob would have killed me. I owed both our lives to him, and now he needed me to save his.

I sure as hell was going to deliver.

44

He woke knowing he wasn't alone. The lights were out, which was normal for the infirmary during sleeping hours. But the presence he detected wasn't a doctor or a nurse. Medics didn't press their sweaty palm across your mouth and pinch your nostrils shut. They tried to save you, not end you.

He struggled against the man's grip. Knew he'd tire quickly. Slammed the heel of his right hand into the side of his attacker's head.

A grunt. The hand released. JT inhaled hard. Got a proper look at the man.

Black uniform. Taser. Cuffs.

Not a medic. A guard.

He was leaning over the bed, blond and pale, more fat than muscle – no match for JT on a good day. Hell, no kind of match on an average day, but right then, not long after being shot, and stabbed, and having a cardiac arrest, this guard was enough to cause him some trouble.

His doughy face was inches from JT's. He had the bloodshot eyes of a drinker. Bad breath and bad body odour. 'The Old Man doesn't want the patsy,' he hissed. 'He wants vengeance for Tommy's death and he's waited a long time. An eye for an eye and all that Bible shit.'

'I killed Thomas Ford.'

'You sure?'

'Real sure.'

The guard shook his head. Smiled cruelly. 'But you see, that gives us a problem, because we know you didn't. We heard your conversation on the phone with her. Heard her say she killed Thomas Ford – her own husband. Confirmed what we'd suspected.'

JT's chest tightened. His breath came quicker, shallower. 'No.'

''Fraid so. And the Old Man, well, he can't let that go. Justice needs to be served. An eye for an—'

JT punched the guard in the face.

He rubbed his jaw. Smirked. Walked around the bed to the small sink. Spat blood into it and rinsed it away with water. 'You're riled, huh? Guess you really do got a soft spot – or a hard spot – for that bitch.' He wiped his mouth with a tissue. Put it in the yellow trashcan for bio waste. 'But you need to get yourself over that. The Old Man wants her ended; and sure, we could snatch her up, but he thinks it'd be better if you brought her to him.'

'Never going to happen.'

'She betrayed Tommy for you, is that about right? Helped you when you were hunting him, but somehow Tommy got dead?' He gave a little laugh. 'The Old Man thinks it'd be poetic if you're involved. You betray her – an eye for an eye.'

JT didn't speak. Glared at the podgy guard. Clenched his fists. 'I'm not for sale.'

'Everyone has a price.' The guard smiled. 'Cute kid she's got. Wonder who the father—'

JT snarled, 'Tell the Old Man the answer is no.'

45

The ringing of my cell jolted me awake, the beeping dragging me back from the twilight zone between sleep and wakefulness. It wasn't dark outside any longer – the sun was filtering through the voile covering the window. Still groggy from sleep, I groped for the handset on the nightstand and answered, expecting it to be Red.

'He ... I...' The woman's words were too distorted from crying to make out.

'Mia? Slow down, tell me what's wrong.'

I heard her gulp the air. 'I got into the study ... I...' More sobbing.

My heart rate accelerated. 'What's happened? Did he hurt you?'

'I'm ... okay. Marco ... he ... he...'

'I need you to take a breath, Mia.'

I heard her wracking sobs slowly subside.

'First, are you safe?'

'It's okay, he's ... not here ... he doesn't know that I...'

'Good. Now tell me what happened, slowly.'

Mia spoke fast, her words running into each other. 'Marco got up earlier than normal and went out for a run. I knew you needed the information fast so I thought, okay, I'll go in the study now; I should have an hour before he's back. So I managed to get into the study ... and I typed the password into the computer and it worked.' She took a loud breath.

'And?'

'I didn't find anything. There was nothing on his email that mentioned Gibson or Mexico. I searched for as long as I could risk it, checked the sent and deleted folders then shut down the computer. It was when I came back upstairs I saw it.'

'What?'

'His cell. He'd left it in his dressing room. I managed to unlock it – the grease marks from his fingers showed me the passcode. He'd been sending messages to a person...'

'Who, Mia?'

'It said "Dodge". Dodge had been paying men who looked like Gibson to be decoys for your spotters – Rosas and Ortiz, right? – I found their pictures in the message exchange. Marco wanted to find Gibson first ... Dodge would get a bonus if he took Gibson alive so Marco could ... so he could kill him.'

'Have they got Gibson?'

'No ... no, not yet ... but ... the pictures made me think there might be others, maybe of the people he was working with or something. So I went to his camera folders and that's when I found the ... the ... I...' Her voice sounded strangled. She started crying again.

'What did you see, Mia?'

'More pictures, but ... I ... I ... can't believe he ... It's too...'

I kept my tone gentle. 'Can you tell me about them?'

'Snuff pictures, that's what I thought first off ... a man and woman ... covered in blood and...' She took a ragged breath. 'I thought Marco's need for hard-core porn had turned from forced sex to ... to murder and...' She was sobbing too hard to speak.

'Mia, deep breaths. Tell me what else.'

'I recognised them.'

'You knew the victims in the photos?'

'I never met them, but I knew of them.'

Realisation started to dawn on me. Searle was involved in far more than sabotaging my hunt for Gibson. My voice was urgent as I asked, 'How?'

'Their pictures were all over the media. They were the couple Gibson was convicted of murdering. Their name was Walker – a husband and wife.' She blew her nose. 'Why does Marco have images of them dead? I ... It makes no sense ... How could he have those pictures on his cell unless he ... unless he was...'

Involved in the murders? Responsible for the Walkers' deaths?

Her voice was almost a whisper. 'He hates Gibson. He said he'd do anything to keep him away from me.'

Anything.

Even murder?

46

The photos suggested Searle was balls-deep in the murder of the Walkers and I was starting to believe Gibson Fletcher might have been wrongfully convicted. The pieces of the puzzle were moving closer to each other, yet exactly how they fitted together still escaped me. That said, the photos Searle had were new evidence. They put a different slant on the Walkers' murders, adding another player to the game. Although I didn't trust him, I needed to tell Monroe.

I grabbed the burner from my purse and checked Monroe's last message. His flight would arrive just after eleven. Right now, he'd still be in the air and our burner phones were too basic for internet calling. I couldn't wait two hours. I needed to act now. Mia was in a mess and if Searle figured out what she'd discovered there was no accounting for what he might do. I had to help her, even if it meant getting in the line of fire between her and Searle. I couldn't let him hurt her for helping me.

I sent a message to Monroe: *Call me asap.*

Then I slipped my vest on under my shirt, fastened my shoulder holster over the top and put on my leather jacket. Grabbed my Taser and headed for the door.

I'd just climbed into the Jeep when my cell phone buzzed. The message was from Red: *Urgent! Watch now: CCTV visits Donald Fletcher – Gibson Fletcher.*

I clicked the video file. The footage was medium quality but it didn't matter; the identity of the man impersonating Donald Fletcher was an easy spot. I recognised his gait as he approached the counter, but his face was hidden, so for a brief moment I held on to the hope that I was wrong. Biting my lip, I waited for him to turn. Prayed that it was someone else.

It wasn't.

As the camera view changed to one positioned behind the desk officer's shoulder, the impostor's face was framed dead centre. His clothes were more casual than I was used to – blue jeans, a white tee and a sport coat – and he'd altered the shape of his face somehow, most likely with temporary cheek fillers pushed up over his gums; he'd also added a neat moustache and black framed glasses. But his brown hair was the same – just a touch too long and rather wayward. His piercing stare was fixed on the officer.

I cussed loud, slamming my palms against the steering wheel. I didn't need to hear him speak to know he had a Kentucky accent. Gibson's brother had been telling the truth; it wasn't him visiting at the prison. FBI Special Agent Alex Monroe was the man impersonating Donald Fletcher.

I felt paralysed. I knew I needed to drive to Mia. I had to make sure she was okay. She'd taken a risk to help me out, and now – unless she could act like nothing was wrong – what she'd discovered would put her in danger. I had to keep her safe. Couldn't let Searle hurt her. I owed her that.

But I couldn't take my eyes off the CCTV image freeze-framed on the screen of my cell phone. I watched each of the short clips, corresponding to each of the prison visit dates. In every one the visitor was the same man: Alex Monroe – the agent who was supposed to be leading the hunt for Gibson Fletcher; the man who was supposed to be able to get JT's charges dropped just so long as I brought Gibson in. It made no kind of sense.

Or maybe it did.

Monroe was the law, so why was he impersonating Donald Fletcher in order to visit Gibson? He had access to prisoners if he needed it for his job – he didn't have to sneak in under another person's name. But

I had the proof that he'd done just that on the screen in front of me. That told me he was hiding something. By bringing me in to chase down Gibson rather than sending an FBI team after him, Monroe had managed to keep his co-workers at a distance from Gibson. I reckoned now that whatever he was up to with Gibson, it wasn't part of his work. That's why he wanted time with Gibson before he took him back to jail.

The puzzle pieces were starting to fit.

Gibson Fletcher must have colluded with Monroe; he kept meeting with him every time he turned up as 'Donald' on the first Tuesday of every month for the same length of time – one hour. Except the last visit hadn't been on a Tuesday, and it only lasted seventeen minutes rather than sixty. The next day Gibson Fletcher had got a ruptured appendix and been rushed to the emergency room at Florida Medical. The smart money told me Monroe was the one who'd helped Gibson escape.

He must have thought he was bulletproof. Because, while Monroe might not have got the prison CCTV for me, he'd given me access to the prison visitors' logs. He must have let me see them because he was confident his deception would hold. He'd never imagined I'd go back and talk to the real Donald Fletcher. I remembered Monroe's anger at me having flown back to Florida to speak with Donald without telling him first. I knew now he'd have done his damnedest to talk me out of going.

He also hadn't figured that I'd check the signature against the Southside Storage package docket. He must have known there was no CCTV from back then to incriminate him. But the signature on the Southside Storage sender docket was the same as the one in the prison visitors' log: Donald Fletcher's signature, signed wrongly by Monroe.

It hit me like a sucker punch. Monroe sent the package; which meant he already knew what was inside. Given his interest right back at the start of this job had been to find Gibson in order to find the stolen chess set, there had to be some connection. But the package wasn't heavy enough to contain the pieces, and if Monroe had sent it, surely he could have just picked it back up. No, there was something else at play here, something that Monroe and Gibson were in on.

I glared at the screen of my cell phone, at the image of Monroe's face staring back at me, and felt a white-hot fury ignite deep within my core. He'd underestimated me, and that would cost him, because now I knew his secret. This was not a jurisdiction issue. There was no need-to-know bullshit, no wiggle room. Monroe was dirty. I just needed to figure out his end game.

I fired up the engine and stepped on the gas. Felt shaky as hell inside, but on the outside I was all business. Monroe was still in the air; I could do nothing until he landed. Getting Mia safe was my most urgent priority. She couldn't end up a casualty of this messed-up game.

47

I sensed something was out of whack from the moment I pulled up outside the house. The garage was open, the connecting door into the kitchen ajar. I could see Mia's SUV parked up. Beside it was a blue convertible – Searle's I assumed. Someone had arrived or left in a hurry.

Ditching the Jeep at the kerb, I sprinted up the driveway. I heard raised voices from inside, angry, snarling – Mia and Searle. I rushed through the garage into the kitchen. Spotted car keys and shades on the island unit in the centre of the room, a half-drunk smoothie with red lipstick on the glass beside them.

I kept moving. Checked the family room, glanced into the utility and the half-bath: all empty. As I headed along the hallway towards the study, the voices grew louder. I heard a crash, the sound of glass shattering. Mia screamed.

I hurtled into the study. Searle had his hands around Mia's throat. She was thrashing against him. Papers scattered from his desk onto the floor.

'Let her go.'

Searle turned when he heard me. His features contorted in rage. 'Get the hell out of—'

'I know what you did, Searle.' I moved closer to him. 'You framed a man for murder. You're going to jail.'

He snarled at Mia. Flung her away from him. 'Fucking traitor.'

She cannoned into the desk. Fell heavily to the ground.

'Back-up is coming,' I bluffed. 'There's no way out.'

He charged me. His shoulder ramming into me, and thrusting me back into the wall. I ducked out of his reach. Pulled the Taser from my holster. He was too close for me to get a full shot off so I dry-fired into his shoulder.

Searle bellowed in fury, whacked me with his forearm, batting the Taser away. It slipped from my fingers and I heard it clatter onto the floor. Shit. He kept fighting, raining blows down on me, the voltage not enough to stop him. I blocked him. Got a couple of punches in before he pounded me in the chest, knocking the air from me.

I doubled over, wheezing. Saw Mia drag herself upright using Searle's desk as support. There was blood smeared across her face. Her top was ripped. Scarlet marks around her throat showed where Searle had tried to throttle her.

She picked up the letter opener – the silver dagger – and took a shaky step towards us.

'No,' I croaked – to Mia not Searle.

He misunderstood me, thought I was pleading with him. Raised his fist again. 'You shouldn't have poked your fucking nose into our business.'

'Is that why you had me followed? Why you had my investigator beat up?'

Confusion flickered across Searle's face. 'Haven't nothing to do with—'

'Leave her alone.' Mia's voice quivered with emotion. Her hand shook as she raised the dagger.

Searle ignored her. Didn't even turn to look.

I held her gaze. Shook my head. Then, moving fast, I bent down, reaching for my Taser.

Searle hit me again, real hard. The heel of his hand struck my left temple and my knees crumpled. I hit the floor.

As darkness clouded my vision, Mia lunged for Searle.

I woke sometime later. Felt groggy, a dull ache throbbing down the left side of my head. I blinked, clearing my vision, and saw crimson blood was smeared across the oak-wood floor. Bloody handprints smudged against the pale grey of the study wall. The desk drawers had been yanked open, and papers flung out of them littered the room like oversized confetti. The crystal ashtray lay shattered on the floor. The cigar box was overturned; the prize Cubans stomped into a brown mush.

'Mia?' I called. My Taser was lying on the floor beside me, I grabbed it. 'Are you okay?'

I heard a wheezing, gasping sound coming from the other side of the desk. Getting up, I lurched towards it. Spotted a pair of feet sticking out from behind the desk wearing bright-orange Nike training shoes, white socks ... tan legs – man's legs. 'Searle?'

No answer.

I kept moving. Found Searle slumped against the empty drawer unit. His chest was heaving. His neon-green training top was soaked in blood. Beneath his tan, his face looked ashen. The handle of the dagger letter opener was sticking out of his gut.

I put my hand on his shoulder. 'Searle, can you hear me?'

His eyelids flickered open. He glared at me. Muttered something I couldn't make out.

I leaned in closer. 'What's that?'

He muttered again. Still I couldn't understand him.

'I'm getting help,' I told him. I took out my cell. Dialled 911.

He shook his head. Sweat beaded across his forehead. 'No cops.'

I paused, my finger ready to connect the call. 'You need them.'

'No cops,' he repeated. His breath came in gasps. Blood gurgled from his mouth as he fought to form the words. 'Bitch thinks she knows where it is. She's told him. If they find it, they'll run.'

'Where what is?'

Searle's eyes rolled back. I was losing him.

'Marco! Tell me. What are they after? Where are they heading?'

Searle grimaced. The blood had stained his teeth red. 'What they've been ... looking for...' He hyperventilated a few breaths. His body was trembling. 'Chess...'

The gold chess pieces; it had to be. Searle had had them, hidden them, and now Mia knew the location and had told Gibson. 'Where?'

'Home-from-home ... she should've never...' Searle glanced up towards his desk. Tried to speak again. He coughed. Blood poured from his mouth, bubbled over his chin. He gasped. Made strangled sounds but no words.

I pressed dial on my cell. The call connected. I told the operator I needed police and medical.

I looked back at Searle. His lifeless stare told me they'd arrive too late.

48

I didn't have long. The house was a crime scene and I couldn't be there when the cops arrived – I didn't have time to answer their questions. I had to find Mia and Gibson.

I put the Taser back into my holster and stood up. I remembered how Searle had looked at the desk when I'd asked him where Mia had gone. Stepping around him, I moved to the computer. There were multiple windows open: emails, a realtor's website, Google maps.

I looked at the map. Co-ordinates had been put in for a location a few miles from Lyons Valley. I switched the view to satellite and saw what looked like a small ranch with a house and some barns, rocky land surrounding it for miles. The terrain was undulating and rugged. The ranch had no close neighbours. My heartbeat quickened. This could be the place Mia and Gibson were heading for.

I flicked to the email app and scrolled quickly through the trail of messages. The cops could be here any minute, but I needed to be as sure as dammit I was right. If Mia and Gibson were stopping once on their way to Mexico, I only had one chance to get this right.

The first chain of emails was with a realtor, the second with a legal firm; Searle had arranged to view then buy a property near Lyons Valley. It was out in the hills towards Mexico. He'd paid cash and put the documents in his name only. The reference number on the realtor's email linked with the listing number on the realtor's website. I clicked through the photographs; a basic ranch house, horse barns, rough pastureland filled with scrub and rocks, trees surrounding the buildings. I figured the house was the one on the map. Everything pointed towards the property.

Switching back to the map, I took a photo of the co-ordinates with my cell phone then wiped the surfaces I'd touched with my sleeve to erase any prints and turned to go.

I glanced down at Searle's body. I didn't feel sad. He'd beaten Mia for years, and most likely killed the Walkers and framed Gibson Fletcher for the murder. When he'd arrived home he must have discovered Mia going through his files. Or maybe she came right out and accused him, and that's what started their fight. I'd seen her terror as he tried to strangle her, and the wrath in her eyes as she'd moved towards him with the letter opener in her trembling hand. She'd killed her husband, and I knew how that felt – the relief and the guilt. The consequences.

She was free of him now. But I couldn't let her go.

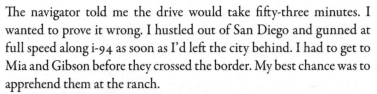

The navigator told me the drive would take fifty-three minutes. I wanted to prove it wrong. I hustled out of San Diego and gunned at full speed along i-94 as soon as I'd left the city behind. I had to get to Mia and Gibson before they crossed the border. My best chance was to apprehend them at the ranch.

Assuming the ranch was where they were heading.

Assuming Mia and Gibson would rendezvous there.

Assuming that was the place Searle had hidden the chess pieces.

JT had always taught me not to make assumptions, but right then, assumptions were all I had. I didn't have time to waste. I had to make a move for checkmate, and this was it.

I felt the buzz of my cell phone in my pocket. I answered the call. 'Red?'

'The detective found his notes on the original statements with the Walker daughters.' Red sounded excited. 'I've messaged you pictures of them, but there's something you need to know. The guy – the one girl saw – he had a scar shaped like a star on his hand.'

'Searle had a scar like that, I noticed it when he shook my hand.' With the photos Mia found, and the eyewitness statement of one of the Walker girls, it looked certain that Gibson was innocent, that

Searle had killed the Walkers and framed him for it; a high-stakes play to get Gibson out of the game and away from Mia for good.

'Had?'

'He's dead, I...'

'You in trouble, Miss Lori?' Red sounded worried.

'Mia is.' I told him about Mia's call, and about Searle being dead. 'I'm heading to a ranch near Lyons Valley. I'm thinking Mia and Gibson could be there.'

'You with back-up?'

I didn't answer. Didn't want Red fussing on me.

He raised his voice a little louder. 'Did you hear me? You got back-up with you?'

'I'm going alone.'

'You're a grown woman. I know you don't need me to tell you what to do but—'

'Then don't.' I kept my foot pressed hard on the gas.

Red whistled. 'You told Monroe?'

I laughed. 'After the CCTV you sent? No way! He's dirty. I don't know why for sure, but I'm guessing it's because of the gold chess set. 1,345,000 dollars is a hell of a lot of money, and it seems it's enough to turn an agent.'

'You need to tell someone where you're heading.'

'I told you, didn't I?'

'Someone closer who can have your back.'

I thought of Bobby all beat up. Shook my head. 'There's no one here I trust who can help me. Anyways I know Mia, she's a good person.'

'She's a good person who just killed a man. And she's helping a known fugitive leave the States. If she's in possession of that chess set I doubt she'll want to give it up. Gibson, too.'

I stayed silent. Knew there was sense in Red's logic, but I didn't want to think on it. I liked Mia. She'd helped me.

'She's not your friend, Lori.'

'I get that.'

'Then call in back-up. You only have a basic knowledge of the terrain and the property, you'll be miles from help, and it's two against one. Monroe doesn't know you're onto him. If you call him, he'll come. You can sort the rest out later.'

'There's no way I'll—'

'Don't be a hero, Miss Lori. Remember Dakota's waiting on you. What happens to your little girl if you don't make it home?'

Twenty minutes later the country was changing, the terrain had become more mountainous, the neatly manicured vistas of San Diego replaced with rocky wildness.

I took a left onto the Skyline Truck Trail. Kept driving. There were few properties and I hadn't seen another vehicle in miles. This place felt real remote and the further I drove the more acutely aware I became of the isolation.

The midday sun was high overhead and the air above the blacktop seemed to warp and shimmer in the heat. In the Jeep the air-con kept things cool. Inside my head I was having a battle.

Red's words about Dakota had hit home, just as he knew they would. If something happened to me she'd be alone. I'd not seen my family in years and her father was in jail. She'd be as good as orphaned, put into the care of the state. I couldn't let that happen. I had to get home to her.

I glanced at the burner phone lying next to my purse on the passenger seat. It'd been ringing every couple of minutes since ten after twelve. No doubt Monroe wanted to know where I was, why I'd not met him at the bond shop as instructed. But I didn't want to speak with him. I needed to figure out his game, and until then, I wasn't ready to confront him.

Switching off the burner, I picked up my own cell and dialled the number of the one man I knew in San Diego who could help. Keeping my foot hard on the gas pedal as the call connected, I told myself that, although we'd never seen eye-to-eye, he was an honest man. Bobby Four-Fingers had convinced me of that. I didn't have to like him.

The call connected. The voice on the recorded message was gruff. 'This is McGregor. You know what to do.'

I waited for the voicemail to beep, then said, 'It's Lori. I know where Fletcher is and I'm on my way there, about twenty minutes away.' I read out the co-ordinates. 'It's a ranch owned by Marco Searle. He's dead – stabbed at home less than an hour ago by his wife, Mia. Everything points to her being with Fletcher now.'

I ended the call. Knew I'd done what I could. Stepped on the gas and kept driving towards the ranch.

49

I halted the Jeep at the side of the highway.

When I'd raided the cabin in Mexico with McGregor and his team we'd not used stealth. Rosas and McGregor had agreed that hard and fast was best, and in that case, I was inclined to agree. But high in the hills above Lyons Valley my situation was real different. I was alone, no team. And there was no way to get a clear line of sight to the ranch house from the highway, only brief glimpses as the trees thinned momentarily before getting denser and screening the property again. I needed a strategy that'd work best in the here and now.

In fact, all the ranch buildings were hidden behind scraggy trees, their planting and canopy a whole lot denser than I'd reckoned on from the satellite image I'd seen on Searle's computer. I spotted the outline of the ranch house through the occasional gaps and saw that alongside it were two vehicles – a blue convertible that looked like Searle's, and a red truck. It seemed Mia and Gibson had arrived.

I had to act fast. Couldn't risk them leaving.

Stealth was therefore the best approach. On foot worked best for that. It'd let me get the lay of the land – to assess my surroundings and what Mia and Gibson were up to – before I made my presence known. It'd give me the advantage of surprise if I needed it, and in a two-on-one scenario, I'd likely need whatever advantage I could create.

I checked my cell. No signal. I'd had no word from McGregor and I didn't know whether he'd gotten my voicemail. But I couldn't check now, and surely I couldn't wait for him.

Looked like I'd be going in alone.

Red's words of caution repeated in my mind. Even though it seemed Gibson hadn't murdered the Walkers, and he could have had help when he escaped from Florida Medical, three prison guards had still been left dead. I remembered his anger as he threatened me in the parking lot of my hotel. He'd been far stronger than me. If he turned hostile I had to be able to defend myself.

I looked at the glove compartment. Flipping the catch, I opened it. The gun Bobby Four-Fingers had given me was inside. I clenched my jaw. My whole being rebelled against picking the weapon up. I told myself to just do it, that I needed to give myself every protection. That Dakota was depending on me. I didn't know what would happen inside the house, but I knew Gibson wouldn't want to go back to jail, not when he was so close to freedom.

I reached in and forced myself to grab the gun. Then threw open the door and started running.

I slowed my pace as I got closer to the house. Stayed alert. Fortunately the trees kept me camouflaged and I moved between them light-footed, navigating the jagged boulders and pitted earth. All the while I maintained my focus on the house, scanning for signs of Mia and Gibson. Saw none.

I stopped, hidden behind a gnarly old tree, and listened hard. My pulse pounded in my ears and I battled to shut it out, trying to concentrate only on the unfamiliar surroundings. The birds were noisy above me in the canopy, making it hard to hear anything other than their song. I clenched my fists. It was no good, I needed to get closer.

I moved further towards the house.

The trees thinned as I approached. Here my cover was less dense, my presence more exposed. Still I saw no one, but that didn't mean they hadn't seen me. I moved quicker. Kept low. The dirt gave way to a makeshift driveway, its tarmac old and broken, weeds growing through the cracks. Without the shade, the heat of the sun reflected back off the surface like a blowtorch. My skin flushed and I felt the sweat cascading down my back. I kept moving.

The house looked more run-down than it had on the realtor website, but it was the same property for sure. It looked uninhabited and untouched, and if it wasn't for the two vehicles parked outside, I'd have figured it was.

I moved across the tarmac to the convertible. Put my hand on the hood. It was still warm. Whoever had driven it had arrived recently. I hoped they were still here, but I didn't want them leaving until I had them restrained.

Reaching into my pocket, I pulled out the Swiss army knife JT had given me when I first started training with him. It was the twin of his. 'They're real useful,' he'd told me. Pretty soon I'd realised he was right.

I knelt down beside the convertible and stabbed the knife into the front tyre. Repeated the action with the other three tyres, then did the same to the truck. That evened the odds; we were all on foot.

Putting the knife away, I skirted back around the truck to the front. The windows were open, and on the passenger seat was a carton, about the size of a shoebox. The cardboard was faded and battered around the edges, but the address on the label was real clear – 'Gibson Fletcher, c/o Southside Storage, San Diego'. This had to be the package Clint had seen Gibson collect.

I reached into the truck. Opened the box. Took what was inside. Didn't think on it, didn't have a plan. All I thought was that, if I had it, and they somehow got away, it would be leverage – a measure of last resort – to bring Gibson back.

I pushed it into my left pocket and looked towards the house. The front door was shut. I saw no one. I wanted to avoid making myself known for as long as I could; so, keeping low, I moved around to the back of the house. To the left of the back door, a broken porch swing creaked back and forth. The door was ajar.

I paused. Heard nothing from inside. Reaching under my jacket, I withdrew my Taser and stepped up onto the porch.

Nudging the door open with my toe, I entered. It was gloomy inside, the air tasted thick and stale. I found myself in a basic kitchen. It was neat, everything tidied away aside from two plastic water bottles, half drunk. I moved through the room to the next: a family room. One couch against the far wall; aside from that no furnishings. Moved into the dining room. Found it empty.

Back in the hallway I looked up the stairs. Were Mia and Gibson up there? Had they seen me arrive? Were they lying in wait, ready to jump me? My heart pounded in my chest, and I gripped the Taser harder. Stepped onto the first stair.

It creaked loudly beneath my weight and I near jumped clean out of my own skin. *Keep it together*, I told myself. *Stay focused; you've got this.*

Pulse racing. Heart pumping. I kept going up the stairs to the second floor. I searched each room in turn – three bedrooms and a master bath. All basic, all empty. Mia and Gibson weren't inside.

Damn. They had to be here.

I hurried down the stairs. Slowed as I reached the back door, thinking I'd heard something. I felt the fizz of anticipation, the potential of finding a clue. Listened hard.

I heard it again. A crash. Like a bunch of glass bottles smashing. It came from outside.

Through the door, I saw no one. The crash had sounded like it was further out back, a little ways off. In the distance, along a dirt track that zigzagged up the hillside between the trees, I spotted one of the barns.

I moved quickly across the porch and over the scorched dirt towards it. Avoiding the path, I headed into the trees. The shade of the canopy blocked much of the sunlight but, where it managed to break through, it cast mottled shadows across the ground. The air was hot and humid. The earth was pitted beneath my feet, the lumps and boulders challenging me to stay upright.

I kept running. Heard another crash, a dulled sound this time; not glass breaking – something else. Then another. I wondered what the hell Mia and Gibson were doing.

I didn't have to wait long to find out.

50

The door of the barn had been forced off its hinges. Taser in hand, I pressed myself up against the sun-bleached wooden cladding of the wall and peered inside. It was gloomy, but I saw that, rather than being one huge space, the barn had been divided into sections. The doorway led into a storage room lined with shelves. In the far corner, a dark-haired man in a plaid shirt had his back to me. He had the bulk of Gibson Fletcher and was using his strength to yank wooden crates from the shelves, then searching through them and tossing them aside. There was no sign of Mia.

I glanced around me. Checked she wasn't close.

Nothing. The trees were still, the land around them, too. The only sound was the ever-present birdsong. The air was chewy on my tongue. Sweat glistened along my arms and between my fingers, making the Taser slippery in my hand.

Swapping my Taser into my left hand, I wiped my palm on my jeans, took the gun from the waistband and stepped into the barn.

'Gibson Fletcher, put your hands high.'

He stopped moving but didn't raise his hands. My heartbeat banged harder. It felt like déjà vu from the shack in Mexico.

I raised the gun and the Taser, kept them trained on his body mass. 'Hands up. Now.'

'I heard you didn't use guns.' It was Gibson's voice for sure.

I took a step closer. I couldn't cuff him easy from this position – the broken crates lay between us – and he was out of Taser range. But I didn't want my only option to be the gun. 'Can't believe all you hear,' I said.

He dropped the crate he was holding back onto the shelf and turned towards me. He gave a little shake of his head when he saw the gun. 'Guess I got that one wrong, then,' he said, raising his hands.

I kept both weapons aimed at him. 'I guess so. Where's Mia?'

'She's not here right now.'

'There are two cars. She's here someplace.'

He shrugged. 'If you say so.'

I stayed alert, scanned my peripheral vision. Knew Mia could appear at any time. I gestured to the broken crates and their spilled contents – old bottles of moonshine, rusty-looking yard equipment and the like. 'What are you looking for?'

'Something that got taken.'

'The chess pieces?'

He nodded. His eyes darted right, and I wondered for a moment if he was about to bolt. I took a half-step forward. Needed to get him cuffed. 'Why'd you take them?'

He laughed, a deep belly laugh that sounded joyful for a moment, then cut off as abruptly as it had started. 'It was my job. I had no choice.'

I cleared my throat. The barn was dusty as hell; I could feel it on my skin, in my mouth. 'There's always a choice.'

He frowned. 'Spoken by someone who's never been in a position where there isn't.'

'I've been in plenty of bad situations. Just because you don't like the choices, it doesn't mean there aren't any.'

He cussed. 'You know what? I never figured they'd send a bounty hunter after me. Cops yeah, and Feds as soon as I crossed state lines, but not you.' He squinted a moment. 'I was right before though, wasn't I? Monroe put you after me?'

I nodded. The longer I could keep him calm, the closer I could get without spooking him.

'Bastard. I should have known...'

'What did he promise you? If you stole the chess pieces you could split the profits?'

Gibson laughed again. It wasn't a happy sound. 'It was never about money.'

I inched a little closer. Another few feet and he'd be in Taser range. '1,345,000 dollars didn't appeal to you then?'

He shook his head.

'I find that real hard to believe. A thief and a dirty FBI agent in business together – you were going to sell the pieces and run. Is that why you beat up on an old investigator and had me followed in Florida?'

A pulse at Gibson's temple throbbed. 'You've got this wrong. I'm one of the good guys. I never beat up your investigator or had you followed. I wouldn't have hurt you in the parking lot of your hotel if you hadn't fought against me so hard. I worked for Monroe. I was his asset.'

I frowned. So now both Gibson and Searle were claiming they'd never had me tailed or beaten Red in Florida. And now Gibson was saying he'd been working for the FBI? I didn't believe it.

'Prove it,' I said.

'My skills are useful to a guy like Monroe. People would often approach me to procure specific items for their collections...'

'And by "procure" you mean steal?'

'Yeah, steal. So I stole the chess pieces as bait for a deal with the Chicago Mob. It was a theft to order. I was supposed to deliver them to the top guy – he was a real fan of the game, total chess addict – and Monroe was primed to storm in and arrest him for handling stolen goods. It was going to be an iceberg situation – the stolen chess pieces would be the tip. Plan was I'd give up all the information on the transaction in return for a reduced sentence. Monroe would make sure I served none of it. Then after, he'd let me walk away from him and the Bureau. My debt would have been settled. I could move away, have a chance at a better life.'

'With Mia?'

'And my son.'

'So why didn't you deliver the chess pieces?'

'I did – at least most of them. But at the last minute the top guy got twitchy. He sent his accountant – Patrick Walker – to collect them instead. Well, that didn't suit Monroe; he needed clear attribution of guilt from me stealing them to the top Chicago guy taking possession.

So he had this idea: give all but one of the pieces to Walker and tell him to call me once his boss had authenticated them, and then I'd hand-deliver the final piece to him. Monroe said it couldn't fail; the guy was known for being totally OCD – he'd need the full set.'

'So why did Walker and his wife have to die?'

'They didn't. That wasn't part of the plan.' Gibson shook his head. 'We talked, and I gave Patrick Walker the product. They were all fine when I left.'

I didn't trust him, but based on the evidence Red and I had collected on Searle, plus the pictures Mia had found, I figured Gibson was telling the truth.

I inched a little further forward. 'But you let them bang you up for it. Why?'

He glanced to the right. Looked back at me. 'It was safer that way. I had my suspicions about who'd killed them and why. I needed Monroe's help to handle it.'

'Searle?'

'Yeah. He found out about Jacob and about Mia and me. He wanted revenge. I guessed he'd found out it was me who took the chess pieces, and found out who I was delivering them to and when. He's friendly with the Cabressa family, so it would have been easy enough for him. Then all he had to do was frame me.'

'But you stayed in jail for two and a half years. Why run now?'

Gibson's cheeks coloured. His arms lowered a few inches. 'Because I realised I wasn't ever getting out. The Bureau would have left me to rot. I couldn't do it ... I told Monroe I needed an out. He owed me that at least.'

He was still out of Taser range. I needed to get closer. I slid one foot forwards. 'Why'd he owe you?'

He clenched his fists. 'Because he got me into this in the first damn place, and I knew he wanted the final chess piece. Unlike the rest of the Bureau *he* wanted me to finish the job. His career took a fast ride down shit creek when the Walkers died during his sting operation.'

'So he visited you every month and you made a plan.'

'Something like that.' He lowered his hands a fraction. Sounded sad as he said, 'You know, I never hurt anyone before those hospital guards. Monroe made me a killer. I just wanted to be free to see my boy grow up.'

'Tell that to the families of those dead guards.'

Gibson looked grief-stricken. 'It was the only way. Monroe said I was on my own until—'

'You weren't going to help him again, were you?'

'I've worked for him more than twenty years. Sure, it started when he caught me in a tight spot, but I thought we'd become friends.' He shook his head. 'When it came down to my skin or his, he threw me to the wolves.'

'He helped you though.'

'Only because he thought it'd salvage his career.' Gibson fixed me with an angry stare. 'Whatever that bastard promised you, he won't deliver. Only thing he cares about is himself.'

I nodded. Tried to ignore the bite of fear his words made. Focused on moving a little closer. 'So you decided to run?'

'That last chess piece, it's worth a lot, but not as much as the whole set.' He looked down at the broken crates. Grimaced. 'You know, I wish you'd let things go, just like I asked.'

I narrowed my eyes. 'From the bruises you left, it didn't feel like you were asking.'

'And yet here we are.'

'Yeah.' I inched forward again. Finally, I had him in range. 'And it's time for the running to stop.'

Gibson moved real quick. He faked right, then jumped the ruined crates between us and ran at me like a bull charging a dislodged bull-rider. I squeezed the trigger and the Taser fired. The probes hit him square in the chest and discharged fifty thousand volts. He stumbled, but kept coming. Fast.

Shit. I yanked the trigger again. Fired the second cartridge. Another fifty thousand volts ripped through his body.

He crumpled at my feet. His body convulsing, his hands tensed into claws. His bladder released, pee spreading across the front of his jeans. His eyes rolled back into his head.

I heard a howl behind me. Turned.

Mia. Gun in hand. Tears streaming down her face. 'You killed him!'

'No, he'll be okay...'

I needed her to know I wasn't going to hurt her. So I threw the Taser down. Lowered my gun. Put my free hand out towards her. *Trusted* her.

She pulled the trigger before I had time to say more.

51

Never trust no one. I'd broken JT's rule, and it was going to be the death of me.

Time seemed to slow from the moment she pulled the trigger. I watched the gun leap in Mia's hands, jerking them upwards. Saw the shock register on her face.

Then I felt the pain. Like I'd taken a roundhouse kick to the chest, but a thousand times more powerful. My legs buckled, and I fell backwards. Gasping.

Can't breathe.

Oh Jeez.

I ... can't ... breathe.

My vision blurred. It felt like the world was spinning, tilting. I couldn't feel my legs. Couldn't feel my arms. It wasn't supposed to go this way. I'd miscalculated, badly. Got distracted by Gibson and failed to make my move fast enough. A fatal error; a losing move in this game of strategy; checkmate played out to the death.

Breathe. Must breathe.

My body was in pain. My chest felt on fire.

Footsteps rushed past me. Mia's voice said, 'Gibson ... Oh god ... Can you hear me? Baby ... please ... are you okay?'

I tried to gulp the air. Needed oxygen.

Must breathe.

I tried.

Failed.

Retched and tasted bile. Tried to swallow, but I couldn't. It hit the back of my throat. Hot. Sour. I gasped. Wheezed. Felt like I was drowning.

The gunshot repeated in my ears. Ricocheting around my brain. I tried to turn my head. Needed to get up but couldn't move.

Breathe. Please. Breathe.

I tried real hard to force oxygen into my lungs. Didn't work. They were too weak, the air too dense and heavy. Fear crashed through me. My baby, Dakota, I couldn't leave her. I'd promised I'd be back to pick her up. Promised. I had to fight.

Breathe. Do it.

Dakota's face hovered in my mind like a mirage, then dissolved into nothing. I roared out loud. Inhaled hard through my mouth, my nose. Forced the breath. Inhaled ... and a trickle of sweet, cordite-scented air entered my lungs.

I heard Gibson's voice, weak but nearby. 'I'm okay ... I'll be okay ... I can't find them though ... The plan's not ... I...'

'It doesn't matter,' Mia said, her voice trembling with emotion. 'Let's just go. I'll get you safe and fetch Jacob just as we planned. The plan *will* work. '

'Need to ... together...' Gibson's voice was fading.

Footsteps. Coming closer. A human shape came into view. I blinked, trying to clear my vision. Failed. It felt like my consciousness was slipping away.

'Why didn't you let us go?' she asked. 'Why?'

I forced open my eyes. Mia stood at my feet. Something in her expression made her look different, tougher.

I was as good as dead.

'You saw what Marco did. You know Gibson didn't kill those people on the yacht. He's innocent,' she said.

I wanted to tell her she was wrong. Gibson wasn't innocent. He'd killed three hospital guards. He'd attacked me in the parking lot, and he would have attacked me right here if I hadn't Tasered him. But I couldn't speak. My breathing was too laboured; every breath was an effort. It felt as if my ribcage was crushing my lungs.

Mia raised her gun. Aimed it at my head. 'I didn't want this to happen.'

Struggling to breathe, I forced out the words. 'Don't ... do—'

'I have to.'

'You're not ... killer.'

'You told me back when we first met that we all have the capability to kill. I've killed once already today...' Mia's voice was determined but she looked sad. 'If I don't do this you'll never let us go. You'll keep chasing us.'

I used every last bit of my strength to shake my head. A tiny movement was all. I kept looking her right in the eye. Didn't blink. Wouldn't flinch. Wasn't going to make this easy.

Mia's hands were shaking, the gun unsteady. 'Don't lie to me. We both know you're lying. I looked you up. Your man's in jail. You're out here separated from your kid. Gibson told me you're working for his handler and I know exactly what a conniving son-of-a-bitch he is. I bet he's offered to get your man out of jail, hasn't he?' She paused, watching my face. Nodded. 'Yeah, I thought as much. And if that's what he's offered, I know you'll never give up. You'll never stop chasing us, because you want your fucked-up family back together just as much as I want mine.'

I'd liked her. I'd *trusted* her. A bond forged in shared pain and the desire to reunite our families; but it was a desire only one of us could achieve, I saw that now. I thought of Dakota waiting for me to pick her up from camp, and JT waiting in jail for me to fulfil my deal with Monroe and get him free. Neither of them knew Monroe was dirty and that if the FBI found out the deal would be off because Monroe would be implicated in Gibson's jailbreak. They were depending on me, trusting me, and I had let them down. I looked up at Mia. 'I...'

Mia's expression hardened. She re-aimed the gun at my head, her hand steady now. Her finger moved on the trigger.

Memories kaleidoscoped through my mind: Dakota warm in my arms the first time I held her as a baby; teaching her to ride her red bike; her first gold star at school; laughing as we made mango and chocolate ice cream. Dakota, JT and me together. Mine and JT's last kiss.

I clenched my fists. Felt anger. Fury. Thought of the life we could have had. Stolen now. Tears poured down my face. Who would look after my baby?

The gun fired.

I heard the crack of the shot. Felt the slam of the impact.

My world turned scarlet.

52

Blood. Everywhere.

It was in my eyes and on my clothes, but it wasn't mine. I still felt paralysed, helpless, spread-eagled on the floor of the barn. Gasping.

I heard wailing somewhere to my right. I tried to move my head to look, but the effort was too great. Heard footsteps, running. A man passed in front of me, a shadow across the red of my vision. I heard the sound of something being kicked across the floor – Mia's gun, I presumed. Then a man's voice, talking to Gibson. 'Stay down. Don't be a hero.'

The wailing turned to sobs. Between them, I heard the sound of metal cuffs being fastened.

I tried to look towards where Mia had been, but I still couldn't raise my head enough. I called out. 'Mia?'

No reply. The only sound was Gibson wailing.

'Mia?' I gasped again. 'Answer me.'

I wanted her to be fine, but I knew that she couldn't be. A millisecond before she'd pulled the trigger, another gun had fired; not mine, not Gibson's. I'd seen her eyes open wide, and a fine mist of blood spray out from her body as the bullet hit. I'd felt it coat my face, my neck, my arms, as I'd lain helpless in the dirt. I'd cried her name as I watched her fall.

'Lori? Are you okay?' McGregor kneeled beside me. He pulled up my shirt, and released the tabs of my concealed body armour. As the vest released, air flooded back into my lungs. I thought I was going to vomit.

'Thanks.' It was too little a word for saving my life, but the only one I had.

He nodded. 'No problem.'

My legs and arms tingled as the feeling returned. I managed to lift my head. Looking down, I saw the two bullets embedded in the vest just below where my heart was. I was real lucky. I'd only had to deal with the agony from the force of the shots, each one slamming like a jackhammer into my chest as the vest took the brunt to slow the impact. I'd be badly bruised for sure, but I wasn't dead. Whether Mia had missed the headshot she'd been going for, or had changed her mind at the last moment and put a second bullet into my chest on purpose, I didn't know, but the implication was clear either way. Mia hadn't known I was wearing concealed body armour, and the vest wasn't visible beneath my shirt. So there was no room for doubt; Mia had meant to kill me. If it hadn't been for the vest and for McGregor she would have succeeded.

I looked at her then. She lay a few feet away from me. There was a ragged exit wound in her chest and the blood had poured from it, across her lilac T-shirt and onto the floor, mingling with the dirt. Her long black hair was fanned out around her face. Her sightless gaze was fixed on me.

I thought back to what she'd said, why she felt she had to kill me, and I knew that she'd been right. We both wanted our families back together; we both had complicated relationships – messed-up versions of a family; and we both wanted to try and make it work out. Thing was, in the situation we were in, one could only get it at the expense of the other. She'd meant to kill me, but I couldn't blame her. Instead of anger I felt sadness that she was gone. Instead of relief to be alive, all I felt was guilt.

Behind me, Gibson's sobs grew louder and for a brief moment I felt glad that it wasn't JT or Dakota crying over me. Then the sadness twisted in my stomach. Mia had wanted me to help her and I'd led her to believe that I would. Now she was dead.

Leaning forwards, I shuffled through the dirt and pressed her eyes shut.

'You. Did. This.' Gibson's words were slow and pain-filled.

I turned and saw the shadow of the man who'd been tough as hell a few minutes earlier. Tears streamed down his face. He held my gaze, his eyes filled with anguish. Then folded in on himself, rocking, while his hands stayed cuffed behind his back.

'I'm sorry.'

He didn't answer. Kept rocking. I could hardly bear to watch him.

McGregor stood up. Put his hand out to help me up.

Tearing my gaze from Gibson, I took McGregor's hand and got to my feet. I felt wobbly, like a colt taking its first steps. Had to tough it out though. Had to get through this.

McGregor kept a hold of me. Looked concerned. 'You need to sit down?'

I shook my head. Felt nausea from a sudden wave of vertigo – the shock I was still feeling from the bullet's impact. I waited a moment, before saying. 'There's something I have to do.'

I looked around, searching for something to cover Mia with. All I could see in the barn was a box of dusty rags and a tattered tarpaulin. Neither seemed good enough, respectful enough, to do the job right.

Wincing, I struggled out of my plaid shirt, then knelt on the ground beside Mia and covered her face and her body. I stayed with her a moment, put my hand on her still-warm arm. Stared at the blood congealing in the dirt. Thought of the life that she'd wanted, and the one she'd been dealt. Whispered, 'I'm so sorry.'

Close by, McGregor bowed his head. Gibson grew quiet.

A long moment later, I stood up. I moved to McGregor and asked, 'What happens next?'

He looked out towards the highway. 'We sit tight and wait for Monroe.'

Two bullets to the chest, both at close range. Despite the vest, I was lucky to be alive, real lucky. But with Mia dead, I didn't feel lucky. The sorrow of the situation eclipsed everything else. I was thankful for McGregor arriving when he did, for intervening as my back-up, but as the two opposing emotions tumbled around in my mind I knew I needed to turn my attention elsewhere, to focus on what happened next. I had to figure out how to play things when Monroe arrived.

McGregor had told Monroe he was coming to the ranch. He'd messaged him the co-ordinates. We sat on two of the crates, waiting. Gibson had shuffled across the floor to sit beside Mia, her face and body still covered by my shirt. He was silent now, ashen-faced from loss. There didn't seem any sense in moving anything.

McGregor had a haunted expression in his eyes, and I wondered if the realisation that he'd shot a woman dead was taking its toll on him. I knew he hated violence against women. I knew the grief he still felt at the murder of his wife and unborn child, and knew that beneath his work-focused exterior he took things hard.

He caught me staring. 'Good work taking out the tyres on their vehicles,' he said, offering me his water bottle.

I took the water and gulped it down. I'd have found his words patronising under previous circumstances, but not anymore. 'Thanks.'

He nodded. 'I should've given you a chance before.' He gestured towards where Gibson was sitting beside Mia's body. 'Everything that's happened here you've handled like a pro.'

I kicked at the dirt with the toe of my boot. Wrestled with my emotions. Didn't ever want someone dying to be just another thing that happens; never wanted to get used to handling it. But I knew McGregor was trying to be kind, looking to make me feel better, so I ignored the emotions and said, 'A pro that got shot.'

McGregor shrugged. 'Happens to all of us at one time or another. That's the job.'

'Yup.' I stared at Mia covered with my plaid shirt. Could hardly believe she was dead. 'But this was my mistake. I should have—'

'If you hadn't got to know her we would never have found Gibson. She called you because she was in trouble, and you found Searle and the location of this place because you went to check she was okay.' He lowered his voice. 'I was wrong before. I should have listened to you. They'd have got away if you'd not been here.'

I shivered, feeling cold despite the heat of the sun and my T-shirt and the undone vest. I didn't speak. Kept staring at Mia's body. If I'd not followed her she'd still be alive. Her son Jacob would still have a mother. Gibson and her would've had a chance at their own kind of happy ending. All I'd brought instead was an ending. Again guilt twisted in my stomach.

McGregor's voice drew my attention back to him. 'What did she mean about you wanting the same things?'

I looked at him. I supposed telling him the truth couldn't hurt. 'She told me before that all she wanted was a chance to live with Gibson and their son Jacob as a family. They'd never had it. Her husband, Marco, beat her, murdered innocent people and manipulated the law to frame Gibson when he learned Jacob wasn't his. Mia had wanted to escape him for years.'

'So what are you looking to escape from?'

I shook my head. 'I'm not trying to escape anything. I made a deal with Monroe that if I found Gibson and brought him in, Monroe would get the father of my child off the false homicide charges he's awaiting trial for.' I didn't say we'd been estranged for ten years. I didn't say my child barely knew her father. I didn't tell him that I feared living together in case it broke us. 'I want my family together, too.'

McGregor nodded. His jaw tightened, and although he didn't speak about it, I figured he was thinking about his wife and unborn child. From what Bobby Four-Fingers had told me, and the emotion-filled expression on McGregor's face, I knew he'd have given everything to bring them back.

I put my hand over his.

We sat that way for a few minutes – until we heard engines approaching.

I glanced at McGregor. 'Was Monroe coming alone?'

'I thought so.'

Something was wrong. There was more than one vehicle. Their engines were loud. Their speed too fast, too urgent.

I leaped up, hurried to the doorway and peeped round the frame.

Two cars skidded to a halt, dust blooming around them. Doors opened. Men approached, their guns trained on the doorway to the barn.

I turned to McGregor. Mouthed the word, 'Cops.'

He looked real surprised.

'You're surrounded,' the officer in the left-hand car said into a loud-speaker. 'Drop your weapons, and come out slow.'

We weren't going to argue. Just needed to move slow enough not to spook them. We didn't want to get caught in friendly fire.

Inside the barn, McGregor strode over to me. Unbuckled his holster and raised it high. I nodded and we stepped into the doorway together, hands high.

The cops put us on the ground before we could tell them who we were.

53

Being face down in the dirt with my hands cuffed behind my back had not been part of the plan. My chest was aching from taking two bullets in the vest; fear clawed at my throat, dust coated my lips, making me cough. What if we got arrested? What if Monroe let the cops take us? What if I didn't get to see Dakota again?

I looked at McGregor. He'd been put face down on my right. 'We need to tell them who we are, why we're here,' I whispered.

'We will.'

He was too unconcerned for my liking. The cops had left us and were inside the barn. They were first responders, not detectives. Most likely they'd put Mia and Gibson together and add it up to something different than it was. I couldn't have that.

'Sir?' I called out. 'We need to speak.'

No answer. But I could hear them moving around in the barn; footsteps, the noise of crates being moved.

'Sir? I need to speak to the officer in charge.'

'Shut it, yeah,' said a male voice from above me. A pair of black boots attached to legs in black pants came into view. I couldn't see higher than their calves.

'We're bounty hunters,' I said. 'The man in there is Gibson Fletcher – Gibson "the Fish" Fletcher. He's a wanted fugitive. We've called it in, so the FBI will be here real soon.'

The cop laughed. 'Yeah, sure, whatever you say, lady. And I'm the queen of England.'

'She's telling the truth.' McGregor's voice was firm, no bullshit. 'My licence is in my right back pocket.'

'Give it a rest, yeah. We'll take a look when we're ready.' From the way he spoke, it was real clear he'd tried and convicted us in his mind already. He never checked our pockets.

'But it's important. If you just take a moment to look…'

There was a shout from inside the barn. The boots turned. I heard footsteps retreating. Glanced around as best I could. The cop had gone. I never thought I'd think it, but right then I sure hoped Monroe would arrive real soon.

'Some polis are real assholes,' McGregor said.

The fear tightened around my throat, threatening to choke me all over again. I couldn't go to jail. Dakota needed me. Needed at least one of her parents. I tried to keep my voice steady as I said, 'For sure.'

McGregor seemed to sense my fear. He held my gaze. 'Monroe will fix this, don't worry.'

I nodded. Tried to act like I knew it would be fine. Gibson had thought Monroe would fix things for him, and I'd seen how that'd turned out. I hoped McGregor's relationship with Monroe held more currency.

'How'd you get to know Monroe anyways?' I asked. 'From what I hear he's the country-club type. Doesn't seem like that'd be your scene.'

McGregor grimaced. 'I wasn't always a bounty hunter.'

I narrowed my eyes. 'Monroe's always been FBI.'

'True. And sometimes even the FBI need help.'

'Like on this job?'

'Yes and no.' McGregor's expression told me that was as much as he wanted to tell.

I wasn't satisfied with that. 'How?'

McGregor clenched his jaw. Fixed me with an intense stare. 'You and me, we're friends right now, but don't push me, okay? I can't tell you, so I won't. That's the end of it.'

I frowned. The secrecy made me wonder all the more on what had brought Monroe and McGregor together. McGregor had been military before becoming a bounty hunter, I wondered if that had been something to do with it.

Before I had the chance to ask, I heard an engine getting closer. I strained my neck to look past the cop cars and saw another vehicle approaching along the track. I glanced at McGregor. 'Monroe?'

'Let's hope so.'

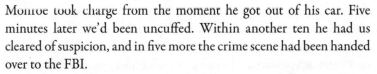

Monroe took charge from the moment he got out of his car. Five minutes later we'd been uncuffed. Within another ten he had us cleared of suspicion, and in five more the crime scene had been handed over to the FBI.

The cops didn't put up much of a fight. It seemed they were happy to sit this one out, so long as they could claim the glory for catching Gibson. Monroe made the deal, and the cops took him away.

I won't ever forget the anguish on Gibson's face as they forced him to his feet and dragged him from Mia's body. The way he twisted his head back, straining for a last look at her. He dragged his feet as they all but carried him from the barn, the Taser wires still hanging from the probes embedded in his chest. Mia's blood was smeared down one side of his face and across the front of his shirt. With his hands still cuffed he wasn't able to wipe it off.

I stepped towards him. Asked the cops to stop a moment.

Taking a tissue from my pocket, I wiped the blood from his skin. He didn't look at me, kept his eyes trained on the earth. The man who'd attacked me in the parking lot a week ago had disappeared. This Gibson Fletcher was broken by loss, and I doubted he'd ever recover. I knew, deep down, that I was responsible.

I stepped aside and watched as the cops manhandled Gibson towards their cars. I thought of Mia never getting the chance to live with her man, of their son Jacob never experiencing a real family life, and I wanted to cry.

Monroe's bark pulled me back into the moment. 'Now get the hell out of here. I'll handle things. Then we'll meet back at the bond shop in a few hours.' From his tone it was real clear the situation had made him pissed.

Well, I was pissed at him, too, for lying to me from the get-go. I wasn't going to let him push me around. 'How did the cops find us?'

'They got a call. A couple of hikers on Pine Pass heard the gunshots and called 911.'

Shit. 'How'd they even get a signal?'

'No idea. But they did, and so the damn circus came to town.' Monroe looked over at Gibson. The cops were loading him into the back of one of their cars. They weren't none too gentle about it. 'Now I've got to clean up the mess.'

I rubbed my wrists. I'd not been cuffed long, but the cops hadn't been gentle with me either, and the metal had chafed against my skin. 'What'll happen to Gibson?'

'They'll process him. Then he'll be transferred back to prison.'

'Did you get to—'

'Get out of here, okay.' Monroe's tone was hard. 'Go, now.'

I knew then I needed to prepare myself for trouble.

54

Monroe was going to burn me. He'd burst into McGregor's bond shop ten minutes earlier with a face like a grizzly that'd eaten a bee, and things had got worse from there. I was perched on the edge of Bobby Four-Fingers' desk. Monroe was standing beside the spare workstation.

McGregor moved past him to the front door, flipped the sign to 'Closed' and turned the lock. He faced Monroe. 'You were saying?'

'You screwed up. It's over,' Monroe said. 'Gibson's on his way back to Florida.'

'And the chess set?' I said.

McGregor raised an eyebrow at Monroe. I figured he'd not been party to that bit of information.

'Gone.'

I said nothing. Felt the heaviness in the left pocket of my jacket a little more acutely, and was glad the cops hadn't searched me too closely before Monroe had called them off.

McGregor shook his head. 'We got Gibson back; that's a win in my book.'

'Back to jail, yes, but that wasn't the only objective.' Monroe ran a hand through his hair. It stayed sticking up at the back. Would've looked comical if he wasn't being such a dick.

'It was our objective – my objective,' I said. 'You got to see him before the cops took him away, you had time for your "chat".'

Monroe glowered at me. 'I needed more than a chat.'

'Yeah. I heard about what you needed.'

He narrowed his eyes. 'What are you implying?'

'Gibson told me all about your deal.'

'Rubbish,' he said, but his expression didn't match the anger in his voice. He looked riled. 'There's nothing to tell.'

'He said you'd say that, too.' I put my hand into my left pocket. Felt the cool metal. Decided not to show Monroe, not yet. Thought of it as insurance. 'So what about *our* deal?'

'You didn't do what I asked.'

'I caught Gibson, didn't I?'

'You turned a pick-up into a bloodbath, and the deal was that I'd get time off the books with Gibson. That didn't happen, ergo, no deal.'

And just like that he turned the tables. Bastard. I remembered Red's words, how he'd warned me not to get involved in some dick-waving federal bullshit, but I'd done it anyway. The lure of getting JT free and clear had been all that was needed to catch me, and Monroe had played that move real smooth.

'But we—' I began.

'There's nothing on paper.' He put his hands up. 'There's nothing I can do.'

Shit. I glanced at McGregor. His expression was hard to read. I looked back at Monroe. 'You lied to me just like you lied to Gibson. You used him, and you've used me. But I won't let you get away with it.'

Monroe shrugged, acting all confused. 'Get away with what? I've been doing the Bureau's work...'

'Bullshit. You knew Gibson was innocent of the Walkers' double homicide but you let him go to jail for it anyways. You had the local PD remove the eyewitness statement that put Searle at the scene because you wanted to get the chess set back yourself. You left Gibson in jail for two and a half years, until he was desperate enough to agree to anything to get free, then plotted to break him out so he could finish the sting on the Chicago Mob.' I stabbed my finger at him. '*You* broke the rules, and a lot of people died. This gets out, your career isn't dying, it's buried six feet below.'

'You don't have any proof.'

'I've more than enough to get you mothballed – probably enough to get you jail time.'

'You're lying. Desperate to—'

'You can act dumb all you want,' I interrupted. 'But I've got the prison CCTV showing you signing in as Donald Fletcher, and the fake signature on the logs matches the one on the package sent to Southside Storage two and a half years ago.' I decided a little white lie wrapped up inside the truth was okay as I continued: 'I can't prove that one of the chess pieces was in that package, but I know you gave Clint Norsen a heads-up to look out for Gibson a full day before he escaped.'

'You wouldn't—'

'I've got this as well.' I pulled out my cell phone and swiped to the voice recorder. Pressed play.

Gibson's voice through the speaker was clear and strong: '...*Because he got me into this in the first damn place, and I knew he wanted the final chess piece. Unlike the rest of the Bureau he wanted me to finish the job. His career took a fast ride down shit creek when the Walkers died during his sting operation.*'

I stopped the recording. 'There's a whole lot more where that came from. I had it recording in my pocket the whole time from the moment I got to that ranch. Mia's on it.' I smiled at him. 'You too.'

'You fucking bitch.'

I nodded. It was a fair comment under the circumstances. I tilted my head to the side. 'Who's feeling desperate now?'

Monroe clenched his fists. 'You think you can blackmail me into—'

'Can't I?'

He glanced at McGregor, who shrugged. Then Monroe turned back to me. 'Be careful, Lori. You're playing a dirty game.'

I held his gaze. 'I learned it all from you.'

'Believe me when I say you don't want to make me your enemy.'

'Ditto.' Straight talking and fair play was my usual mantra, but sometimes you've got to play a little dirty to stay in the game. I wondered if Monroe had been the one having me followed. If he was the person who'd ordered Red's beating. 'Now, as far as I see it, I've got a whole bunch of evidence, and you've got a deal to keep.'

Monroe thought for a moment. Narrowed his eyes. 'There isn't anyone else knows about this. I'm FBI, and you're, what, some small-time bounty hunter? I could bury you.'

McGregor spoke for the first time in a while. 'But you won't. Because you gave her your word, and the Alex Monroe I know, he does the right thing. Keeps his word.'

A vein pulsed in Monroe's forehead. He looked from me to McGregor and then back again. We had him in check-mate. Looked like he knew there was no sense in arguing. 'Okay. A deal's a deal. I don't go back on my word.'

Not when you know you'll lose, I thought. 'Good. Then we're done here?'

Monroe nodded. 'Yeah. We're done.'

'So make the call.'

55

Monroe moved across the room, pulled out his cell phone and dialled. 'That problem I had going on in...' He turned away as he carried on talking.

I looked at McGregor. Sometimes allies are forged from the most antagonistic beginnings. 'Thanks.'

He nodded. 'You deserved as much. Monroe is a good man ... well, he used to be.'

'You hope he still is?'

'Something like that.'

'Hope can't make it true.'

'For sure.' McGregor held my gaze. 'Four-Fingers said he told you about my wife. Well Monroe was there for me when she died. He investigated the case. Made sure the local PD had every resource they needed. The gang-bangers who mowed her down had been on his radar a while. He made sure none of them would see freedom again.'

'So what happened to *that* guy?'

McGregor shook his head. Glanced across at Monroe, who was still speaking on his cell. 'Who knows? The job. The bullshit. Life.' He frowned. 'It gets us all one way or another.'

I nodded. Understood. However Monroe had changed, theirs was an alliance, a friendship forged in loss and revenge. McGregor felt he owed Monroe. It made him backing me up even more impressive. 'Like I said, thank you.'

'Look, I know you're going to be keen to head back to Florida. But if you ever fancy some work out this way, look me up. You're always welcome on my team.'

I smiled. It was funny how things had worked out; the man I'd thought of as my nemesis was now my ally. Bobby Four-Fingers had been right, McGregor was an honourable man. 'I'll bear that in mind. Give my regards to Bobby and Jorge.'

'Will do.'

Monroe ended his call. Walked towards me. 'It's done.'

So he said, but I was far from trusting him. 'Tell me the details.'

'He'll be released without charge. New evidence will have come to light.'

I exhaled. He sounded sincere, though I wouldn't believe him until JT was out of that place, a free man. I forced a smile. Knew better than to burn my bridges with Monroe. An FBI contact, even one with dodgy working practices, could be useful to me, especially now I knew his shortcomings ... and he knew that I knew.

'Good.' I exhaled.

Monroe nodded. 'I'd say it's been a pleasure but...'

'It's been something, for sure.'

'Yeah. That.' Monroe turned to go, then changed his mind. 'One other thing. Tate isn't well enough to leave medical care right now. They'll check his insurance, then move him to Florida Medical.'

I frowned. They were transferring him to the same place Monroe had set up Gibson's escape from; that made me real suspicious. 'You're kidding me?'

Monroe held up his hands. 'Not my decision. I'm just passing along the message.'

I didn't like the sound of it. Wondered if this really was over, or if Monroe had another plan, some other play to make. I put my hand in the left pocket of my jacket and gripped the chess piece – a knight on a rearing charger – tight. If Monroe went back on his word, I'd need a bargaining chip. I figured I'd best hold onto this one for a little while longer.

56

As things went, Monroe's word wasn't as important as I'd reckoned it would be. The officer in charge of the investigation called me while I was at the hotel, packing my things into my backpack before leaving to get my plane.

Turned out that the state trooper shot by the man who'd taken JT, Dakota and me hostage when I was on my last job, and forced me to drive him across state, had regained consciousness in the early hours of the morning, Florida time. By midday, he'd told the local cops his story. He'd seen that the man on the backseat of the Mustang had been holding me and my child at gunpoint; so our story checked out. On another thing he was real clear, too – it wasn't JT sitting on the back-seat, it wasn't JT who shot him, but he did remember a man hollering from inside the trunk.

Whether it was the state trooper's words, Monroe's influence or a combination of the two I wasn't real clear, but the precise why of it didn't matter none. What mattered was that all charges were dropped and JT was released without charge. His insurance company had made the arrangements for him to be transported to Florida Medical.

I thanked the officer and ended the call. Relief rippled through me. JT was a free man and soon he'd be well enough to come home. I stopped in the middle of folding my jeans. Gripped the denim a little tighter.

Home?

I'd been thinking so hard on getting him free I'd not given any mind to where he might go when he was. I'd been heading to my home – mine and Dakota's apartment – but now JT was getting released, we'd have to talk about what happened next for us. Would we live together, as a family? Would he want that, or would he head straight back to Georgia? We'd never discussed what might happen after. All we'd been focused on was getting through the now and the hope that we might be reunited. The question mark over what would happen next made my stomach flip.

Me and JT, we'd always been like fire and gasoline. There was passion for sure. Love, too, on my side, and I reckoned also on his, although he'd never said the words. But could I live with a man – any man – after all these years? Did I want to let someone into my space, into the workings of my life, into my daughter's life?

Now that it came to it, I wasn't real sure. It hadn't ended so well the first time.

I thrust the jeans into my backpack. Told myself I was being ridiculous, getting ahead of myself. I didn't need to think on that right then; what I needed to do was finish my packing and get on the plane.

I stuffed the rest of my clothes into my backpack and tucked my Taser into the inner pocket before zipping the pack shut. Back in Florida, Dakota was waiting for me to collect her from camp. Seeing her could not come soon enough.

57

I'd dropped the Jeep off at the rental company and was walking through the terminal building to the gate when my personal cell buzzed. Pulling it from my purse, I checked the screen – a withheld number. Oftentimes I don't answer them, but given everything that had happened I didn't want to miss the opportunity of speaking with someone connected to Gibson's case, or my own. I pressed answer.

I only heard his breath at first.

My body tensed. My throat went dry. I gripped the cell a little tighter.

Then he spoke. 'Lori? That you?'

My breath caught in my throat. 'JT?'

'I'm getting out. They'll transfer me tomorrow.' His gravelly voice sounded stronger, more like him, than the last time we'd spoken. 'You did it.'

I blinked back tears. Nodded, even though JT couldn't see me. Felt glad that he couldn't see I was crying. 'Yes, I found Gibson.'

'Good job.'

I said nothing. Bit back the emotion that was raging within me. Didn't tell him that it didn't feel like a good job, that it felt like I'd trusted the wrong person, and that I'd been going to betray them anyways. The job had conflicted me on many levels, and people had died. I had yet more blood on my hands.

'Lori? You okay?'

I forced a smile into my voice. 'Sure, I'm just tired. It's been a crazy few weeks.'

'For sure.'

I felt guilty then. JT had been locked in jail, stabbed and had a heart attack. If anyone had been having a rough few weeks, it was him. 'How are you doing?'

A pause. Then he said, 'Better.'

'Good.'

The conversation was stilted. It felt like there was so much to say, so much to talk about that it was impossible to begin. I didn't know how to move forward, and JT never had been one for many words.

So rather than talk about how I was feeling, I focused on logistics. 'I'm flying back tonight. I'll get Dakota from camp, then we'll come visit with you.'

'I'd like that.'

'Me too.' And as I said it, I knew it was true. Whatever else was unspoken and undecided between us, I did want to see him. On that I was real clear.

JT would be out of jail. He was a step closer to safety, and I was a whole lot closer to having my family – my daughter and her father – reunited. That's why I'd taken the job, to get him free and clear, and give Dakota the chance of a proper future, whatever her cancer threw at us. I'd gotten what I wanted. Now I'd have to learn to live with it.

My flight was called for boarding. Ending the call with JT, I switched off my cell and strode towards the line. At the plane, I handed my boarding pass to the attendant. She smiled, and directed me down the aisle to the back. As I walked between the seats, I wondered why I felt so weird. I'd succeeded. I'd done all that I'd come out to California to do. I shook my head. Why, if I'd done all that I'd come here to achieve, did I feel so bad?

Four rows from the back, I found my seat and buckled myself in. Unzipping my backpack, I took out the gold knight and held it in front of me. A lot of people had died for this chess piece – Mr and Mrs Walker, three hospital security guards, Marco Searle. Mia. I turned it over in my hand, looking at it properly for the first time. It was heavier than I'd expected. The craftsmanship was impressive – fury seemed to burn through the eye slits in the knight's helmet; the rearing charger looked ready to burst into gallop. Running towards trouble or away from it? I wondered. Was I a fool to have kept the piece?

Later, when we were in the air, the thought struck me: where was the rest of the chess set? Gibson thought Searle had taken it from the Walkers' yacht after killing them, and Mia must have thought Searle had bought the ranch as a place to hide it. But Mia and Gibson had turned the ranch inside out looking for the pieces and had no joy. Had Searle taken it, or was there something else going on here?

I zipped the knight into my backpack, asked the flight attendant for a strong coffee, and started thinking through the facts I knew. As I reached up to take the coffee from her, I spotted what looked like a familiar face.

I froze. What the hell was he doing on the plane?

I faced forwards again. Gripped the coffee cup tight. Behind me, in the back row on the opposite side of the plane, sitting in the window seat, was the dark-haired man who'd tailed me in Florida.

My heart was leaping in my chest like a rodeo horse. I turned, glancing back over my shoulder for another look at him. Inhaled sharply. It was definitely the same guy. Shit. I was stuck on the plane, a sitting target. I wondered what his move was and when he'd make it.

I waited. Nothing happened. The cabin lights were dimmed. The man didn't move.

As the time ticked by I felt the tension building higher. I needed to know who he was working for and what they wanted.

Tired of waiting, I got up, moved to the back and slid into the empty aisle seat beside him. He sat up straight. Looked surprised.

I leaned in close to him. 'Why are you following me?'

He shook his head. 'I don't know what you—'

'Don't bullshit me,' I hissed. 'You were tailing me the last few times I was in Florida. Did you beat on my investigator, too?'

He said nothing.

'If you don't start speaking I'm going to scream like hell and shout that you grabbed me on the way to the restroom and indecently assaulted me. I'll cry and these people will believe me. You'll get detained, and I'm betting you don't want that.'

He scowled. 'I didn't beat anyone. And I only arrived in San Diego two hours before this flight. My orders are to watch you is all.'

'Did you leave the note on my truck?'

He nodded.

The plane started to judder with turbulence. I ignored it, pressed him for answers. 'Why?'

'The Old Man wants you to admit what you did.'

My stomach flipped. 'I didn't do anything.'

'We know you killed your husband. The Old Man wants you to tell him how.'

'And you're to take me to him?'

'He wants you to go to him voluntarily.'

'Bullshit.'

The plane rocked more. People in line for the restrooms hurried back to their seats. The fasten seatbelts sign pinged on.

'He thought of you like a daughter, he wants to give you the chance to—'

The plane lurched left, the engines roaring. Using the turbulence as a distraction, I jabbed my elbow into the guy's temple. Knocked him unconscious. I couldn't have him following me once we got to the other end. Old Man Bonchese didn't talk things through or give people chances – he was an old-school Mob boss. An audience with him wouldn't end well.

Taking the man's shades from his shirt pocket, I put them over his eyes and positioned him against the seat as if he was sleeping.

'Ladies and gentlemen, we've started our descent into Orlando. It's a little bumpy, so please return to your seats and fasten your seatbelts. We should be on the ground in twenty minutes.'

The plane touched down at a quarter after eleven. As I hurried to the exit I saw the dark-haired guy was still slumped in his seat. I knew Old Man Bonchese would get another tail on me soon enough, but I couldn't dwell on that. I still had things to do, and puzzles to work out. Until the chess pieces were all accounted for, for me the job with Monroe would never be finished. 1,345,000 dollars was a hell of a lot of money to go missing. And in my experience loose ends always unravel in the end.

The Deep Blue Marina looked real ghostly in the moonlight. I walked along the wooden walkway, my boot heels sounding real loud against the silence. The boats on either side of me bobbed against their moorings. Most were in darkness, but as I neared the end of the jetty, I heard music – blues – playing softly, and saw a light was on inside Red's houseboat.

I stepped onto the deck and knocked on the door to the cabin. Thought I heard voices inside. Waited.

The door was opened. Not by Red, but by a woman. She was younger than Red, but not by much. Her long blonde hair was pulled up in a messy bun. She wore a man's shirt, Red's no doubt, over a bikini. 'Hi. Can I help you?'

I felt bad. It was late, and I'd turned up without calling first. I should have realised Red would have company. 'Sorry to disturb you. Is Red here?'

The woman smiled. 'Don't worry, you're disturbing no more than me losing badly at cards.' She turned back into the boat. 'Red, honey, there's someone to see you.'

A moment later, Red appeared. The bruises on his face had faded and the swelling had disappeared. He smiled when he saw me. 'Miss Lori, you doing okay?'

'I am. I just had something I wanted to talk through. Didn't realise you had company, I can come back...'

The woman waved her hand. 'Oh don't leave on my account. It's late, I should get going anyway.' She went back inside and disappeared into the sleeping cabin.

Red stepped out on deck. Gestured for me to take a seat. 'Beer?'

I nodded. 'Thanks.'

He reached into the cooler and took out a couple of beers. Twisted off the tops and handed one to me. 'I saw you found Gibson. Want to tell me what happened?'

I took a deep breath, and told him the full story: Gibson getting arrested. Me getting shot. Searle and Mia getting dead. Bobby Four-Fingers and McGregor saving me. Monroe and his side deals and promises. The man following me, and Red himself taking a beating all because Old Man Bonchese wanted to talk with me. JT being released. Jacob Searle, Mia and Gibson's son, all alone in the world.

Red let me talk. Didn't say anything until I'd finished. We sat in silence for a moment before he said. 'Don't feel guilty.'

'I—'

'I can hear it in your voice, the way you talk about Mia Searle's kid.' He shook his head. 'Sad, for sure. A bad deal for the kid, absolutely. But not your fault.'

I bit my lip. Right then it sure felt like my fault. 'I could have let them go though. Like you said before, there's always a choice, I could have chosen not to finish the job, I could have—'

'Could you?'

I looked down at my feet, at the condensation on my beer bottle dripping onto the varnished wooden deck.

'If you'd walked away you'd have chosen Mia's family over your own.'

I stared at the damp patch on the wooden deck. 'I know.'

'So you did what you had to.'

I nodded. Red was right. Didn't make it any easier to live with though.

Red cleared his throat. 'Gibson's ex-wife called me the day his capture hit the media. Turns out her and her new husband fled their home as a precaution. There'd been no love lost between them during the divorce, and she figured he might be going after her.'

I nodded. Took a swig of my beer. Didn't speak. The memories of Mia dying and of Gibson's sorrow were still replaying in my mind.

'And I found out about Donald Fletcher, like you asked,' Red continued. 'He told you the truth. Was clean of anything dodgy. The money he lives on came from a medical insurance payout; critical illness cover – bowel cancer, untreatable.'

I remembered how gaunt Donald had looked, how different from a couple of years previously. 'Figures. What about the security at his place, any idea what that's about?'

'A little. Seems Gibson's parents weren't the only ones who got grief over Gibson's conviction for killing the Walkers. Donald took a severe beating one night after the verdict. He was found on the street a couple of blocks from the bar he'd been drinking in. Apparently there'd been some harsh words exchanged at the bar – Donald threw a punch or two. CCTV showed a group attacking him as he walked home.'

'Were they convicted?'

Red shook his head. 'Donald refused to press charges. It was soon after that he added the security to his property.'

Shit. So many lives had been changed or lost, and everything had been for nothing. In the end, the sting on the Chicago Mob top man had failed and Monroe had tried to cover up the fallout. That wasn't a satisfactory conclusion. Something more needed to happen. 'What do you—'

I stopped, interrupted by the woman reappearing in the doorway and stepping out onto the deck. She'd changed into Capri pants and a chiffon top, a wicker basket swung from her shoulder. She looked real elegant, yet relaxed – a look I had no idea how to pull off.

Red stood as she walked towards him. Kissed her on the mouth. 'See you soon.'

She kissed him back. 'Till next time.' Then she gave me a little wave. 'Lovely to meet you, Lori. Nice to put a face to a name.'

I watched her step off the boat and walk away along the jetty. I turned to Red. 'Sorry to mess up your evening.'

He shook his head. 'You didn't mess it up.'

'Who was she anyway?'

Red smiled. 'That's Patsy. My wife.'

He had a wife? I'd never have figured Red for the marrying kind. 'She doesn't live here?'

'God no! We work better from a distance. If we live together we damn near tear each other's throats out within a week.'

I thought about me and JT, wondered if it'd be the same for us.

'So Gibson's back in jail and JT is free?' asked Red.

I nodded.

'So the job's done...'

'I guess.'

Red narrowed his eyes. 'You want to tell me what else is eating you?'

I frowned. 'How'd you mean?'

He tapped the side of his head. 'I can see you've got a whole bunch of stuff going on in here. Just asking if you want to talk about it.'

I gave a half-smile. Red always was super perceptive. I guess that's one of the things that made him a great PI. Reaching into my pocket, I pulled out the knight and placed it on the seat between us. The figure's gold shield glinted in the moonlight.

Red picked it up. Turned it over in his hand. 'This what I think it is?'

I nodded. 'One piece from the chess set. The rest are missing.'

He frowned. 'And you have it because...?'

'The package Monroe – pretending to be Donald – sent to South-side Storage two and a half years ago was on the front seat of Gibson's trunk at the ranch. I recognised the label on the carton. Looked inside and found this. I took it then because I figured it could be a bargaining chip if things got tricky.' I shook my head. 'I don't really know why I kept it. I guess because I didn't trust Monroe to keep his word and thought I might need to wait a little longer to reveal my hand.'

'And now JT's free?'

I looked up. Met Red's gaze. 'I want to find the rest of the chess set. A lot of people died for these pieces and the sting they represented. I can't move on without knowing where they are. It feels unfinished.'

Red whistled. 'You know sometimes you have to just let go.'

Letting go? Oftentimes I could do that. Walk away, no problem. This time though, things had gotten personal. I needed to see it through to the end. 'Not this.'

He chuckled. 'Okay, got any ideas where they might be at?'

'It seems pretty clear Searle took the set from the Walkers' yacht when he killed them.' I nodded at the knight in Red's hand. 'That one Gibson had already given to Monroe.'

'So Searle had the set?'

'I think so.' I ran my hand through my hair. The night was muggy, my T-shirt was sticking to my back and I felt like I needed a shower. 'And Monroe does, too, but I don't think he found it. He had his people turn that ranch inside out. Gibson and Mia had done the same before we arrived. There wasn't any sign of it. They've been through the Searles' house in San Diego, too. Again, nothing.'

'Maybe he sold it on.'

'I don't think he did.'

'Why are you so sure?'

I thought about Marco Searle bleeding out on his study floor. I'd asked him where Mia and Gibson where going. He'd said the word 'chess' and looked up at the computer. I'd found the map of the ranch on the screen and assumed the two were connected. What if they weren't?

'It was something Searle said – the way he said it.'

Red nodded. Encouraging me to go on.

'Searle knew Mia and Gibson wanted the chess set. He didn't want them to find it.' I remembered Searle grimacing as he talked about the chess pieces, like a smile without joy; thinking he would get the last laugh.

Shit. He knew they were heading to the ranch, and he knew they wouldn't find what they were looking for there. It was a red herring; a trap to lure them into checkmate. I gripped my beer tighter. Looked back at Red. 'He hid it someplace Mia would never think to look.'

'Where?'

Good question. Where would Mia never look? I stared out into the blackness of the ocean. Thought back to my conversations with Mia, to her life, her routine. Mia had talked about the Coastal Surf Cottage on Pier 61 as her bolt hole. She'd said it was somewhere to retreat when life with Marco got too much, a kind of home-from-home.

Home-from-home.

I'd heard that from Searle, too. When I'd asked him where the chess pieces were – 'Home-from-home', he'd said, 'she should've never ...' He'd used the exact same expression as Mia. Was it coincidence?

I felt the familiar buzz of adrenaline as the last few puzzle pieces clicked into place. Looked at Red. 'I think I know where the chess pieces are.'

59

At dawn they told him the transfer to Florida Medical was arranged. By 08:30, he'd been loaded into an ambulance. No cuffs, no shackles. Back in civilian clothes, the grey tracksuit gone. His personal effects were handed to him in a manila envelope. He didn't say thank you, they didn't say sorry.

They wouldn't let him walk to the ambulance. He had to take a wheelchair. An orderly pushed him – a young lad, not so strong. Made a big deal of it. JT guessed pushing two hundred pounds of human around was a heavier load than he was used to. Didn't say anything. Just breathed in the hot morning air and wished he had a pack of Marlboros.

The guard came to say goodbye when he was sitting inside the ambulance. Same man as attacked him in the infirmary, blond and podgy. Bad breath, bad body odour. He sat down on the bench seat opposite. Smiled. 'You thought anymore on what we talked about?'

JT didn't speak. Didn't look at the guard. Stared straight ahead.

'The Old Man wants an answer.'

'I gave you my answer,' JT growled. 'It's a no.'

The guard shook his head. 'Shame. Because you and your bitch are a problem.'

JT shrugged. 'Get over it.'

'You know that isn't going to happen. Word is she's responsible for the death of another of our associates – Marco Searle – a friend of the Old Man's grandson. He's real cut up about it. Wants action taken fast.'

JT remained silent. Stared straight ahead. Showed nothing on his face.

The guard got up. Before he reached the doors, he turned and leaned down, whispering to JT real quiet. 'What happened in the showers, that was a warning. Next time we'll get you proper. You and the bitch.' He smiled. 'Your little kid, too.'

JT roared with anger but the guard jumped down from the ambulance. He watched the doughy man stride away. Saw him raise his hand in a wave. Heard him laugh as he mouthed, 'An eye for an eye.'

Bastard. JT knew it wasn't an idle threat. The Old Man always followed through. They'd come after him, after Lori, and after their daughter. None of them were safe. Dakota wasn't safe.

The ambulance driver slammed the doors shut. Moments later the engine fired up and they lurched forward, through the air-lock gate system, exiting the prison.

JT considered what to do. He thought about calling Lori when he got to Florida Medical, telling her about the threat, about what the Old Man was planning. Decided no. He'd figure out what to do first. He was the one who'd got her into this. He'd approached her ten years earlier; he'd involved her, put her on the path to killing her husband. He'd changed her. Was responsible. He would figure out how to neutralise the threat.

One day soon he'd tell her about it. Not today, though. Not yet.

He gripped the seat hard. Thought about Lori and Dakota, about the time they'd missed out on, about the time they could have together. He squeezed the seat cushion until he felt the muscles in his arms burning and the beeps of the heart-rate monitor attached to him accelerated into double time. He exhaled as he punched the ambulance wall with his fist.

He couldn't let them be hurt.

60

Tanned, smiling, relaxed – the way Dakota looked was a million miles away from the bruised, brave, but sad kid I'd dropped off at camp a couple of weeks before. I'd spoken to the girl in the office and walked out to the horse barns to surprise Dakota. Didn't want to wait a moment longer to see my baby. Couldn't bear us to be apart another minute more.

She was round behind the barns, inside one of the square pens outside, grooming a tall chestnut horse with a wide white blaze down the front of its face. I could hear her singing to the animal as she worked. I stopped in the shade of the closest barn and leaned against the end stall, watching. As I stood, I breathed in the smell of hay and horse. Looked at the recently raked dirt yard and the polished tack sitting on the timber fence, and was content to rest a while, here in nature, with my baby.

I tried not to let my mind wander. Didn't want to think on the realisation I'd had the previous night – that Searle could have hidden the chess set in the one place Mia would never think to look for it. I wanted the set found, but had spent a restless night trying to figure out who to tell. Whatever way I came at it, the best person had to be Monroe; he knew the history, and he'd wanted to finish the job. Problem was, I just couldn't bring myself to make contact.

So I watched Dakota grooming her horse. When she'd finished, she crouched down and reached under the fence to pull a few strands of grass from the pasture beyond, before holding them out for the horse to eat. It seemed to appreciate the gesture. It wasn't until she ducked under the rail to leave the pen that she saw me.

'Momma!' she squealed.

Dropping the brush, she sprinted across the yard and pulled me into a bear hug. I tried not to wince as she pushed her head against my chest; didn't want to let on about getting shot. Didn't want her to worry. I kissed the top of her head. Held her tight.

She looked up at me. 'Are you visiting or…'

'It's time to go home,' I said. 'If you'd like that?'

Dakota grinned. 'Yes, but come meet Widget first. She's the best horse in the world, seriously. Come on.'

She took my hand and led me to the pen. The chestnut horse turned to face us, put its nose over the fence. 'Okay, so hold your hand out like this.' Dakota demonstrated. 'Let her sniff you.'

I smiled at her confidence and how at ease she was with the horse. Did as she instructed. 'Hello, Widget,' I said.

Widget put her muzzle on my hand. It was softer than I'd expected. Then she opened her mouth and licked me. I pulled my hand away fast.

Dakota laughed. 'She likes you. She only licks the hands of people she likes.' She put her own hand out again and Widget licked her. 'She never bites.'

'She's great,' I said, smiling.

Dakota threw her arms around the horse's face and hugged her. Widget didn't seem to mind.

I knew from the photos that Dakota had sent me of her paintings that there was darkness lurking somewhere inside her. That the experience she'd had of being kidnapped by Randall Emerson and his men had changed her in some way. But right then all I saw was a happy kid, and for that I was thankful. It gave me hope that she would be okay; we would be okay. 'You ready to go home?'

Dakota grinned. 'Yes, Momma.'

As we walked back to my truck, Dakota chattering away to me about all the things she'd done at camp, I felt waves of emotion flooding through me: love, joy, guilt. I'd gotten back to my baby girl. But every step we took together reminded me that Jacob Searle would never see his momma again, and that his father would be jailed for life. Gibson's final job had been a failure, and he'd spend the rest of his days paying the price. As for me, I'd done my job. But the outcome…? It didn't feel like the right kind of justice.

Something needed to happen.

Pulling out my cell phone, I selected Monroe's name from my contacts and tapped a quick message: *Remembered something Searle said. Think chess set in Coastal Surf Cottages – number 20, Pier 61.*

Now it was down to Monroe.

61

He was waiting out front when we arrived. Leaning against the pale stucco wall outside the main entrance to Florida Medical, real casual. One knee bent, the sole of his boot resting flat against the wall. He looked like JT; his dirty-blond hair flopping over his forehead, the faded denims, the plaid shirt, the scuffed work boots. Like him, but not exactly himself; something was different.

I parked in the lot. He hadn't seen us yet, which was good. Gave me time to get used to how he looked, work out what was different. Gave me a moment to compose myself so I didn't let my shock show on my face.

While Dakota, unaware of JT, continued playing a game on her cell phone, I studied him. What was different? He was still a big guy by anybody's standards, but to me he looked gaunt, like he'd lost a lot of weight and had too many hollows where there shouldn't be any. It was as if jail had sucked some of the life force out of him. And in a way I guess it had – the incarceration, the stabbing and the heart attack each taking their toll in a different way. He was free, though, and that was what mattered.

I checked the mirror. In the past couple of days I'd been real vigilant, watching out for anyone following me, but I'd seen nothing. Maybe the guy I'd knocked out on the plane had told the Old Man to back off and he'd decided to leave me be a while. I doubted it, though. The Old Man was used to having things go his way. I figured he was just waiting on the best moment to make his move. But that didn't matter right then. In that moment, it was all about me, Dakota and JT.

Unclicking my seatbelt, I turned to Dakota. 'You ready to go get him?'

She grinned, and handed me the cell I'd given her for camp. 'Yes, Momma.'

We got out of the truck and strode towards the building. It was early, barely nine in the morning, but already the heat and humidity of Florida's summer was cranked to the max. I pointed towards the entrance. 'Do you see who's waiting?'

Dakota squealed with excitement. 'JT!'

She let go of my hand and sprinted across the tarmac towards him. She stopped a couple of paces from him, then launched herself at him and hugged him tight. As I got closer I heard him chuckling, hugging her back, but saw that there was pain in his eyes. I guessed he was as frail as he was gaunt right now.

'Hey,' I said. Real sudden, I felt nervous.

He looked at me with those big blues of his, the light making them look azure, and gave a half-smile. 'Hello, yourself.'

Dakota released him from the hug and he stepped towards me. I saw him wince with the movement. Saw the lines around his eyes were a little deeper than a few weeks ago, and that he was paler despite his tan. 'You got a smoke?'

'Of course.' I took the pack of Marlboro Reds I'd bought him on the way over from my purse. Opened the pack and tapped one out.

He took it. 'Wouldn't let me have them in there.'

'It's a health centre.'

He nodded. 'For sure.'

'And I thought I was supposed to collect you from the cardiac wing?'

'They wanted me to wait in a wheelchair.' He shook his head. 'Wasn't ever going to happen. I'm not sick.'

I said nothing. Knew he needed to tell himself that.

'You got a light?'

I reached into my purse, took out his Zippo and handed it to him. 'Said I'd hold onto it until you were out.'

'Yes, you did.' He smiled. Flipped the top of the Zippo and lit up. Inhaled long and slow, then exhaled with a sigh. He reached out and took my hand. 'It's good to see you.'

'Good to see you, too.' I held his gaze. My heart was banging hard against my ribs. Smiled. 'You want to get out of here?'

'Thought you'd never ask.'

62

One week later

I'd never expected to hear from Monroe again. Was real surprised to see it was his number calling me. Let the call ring out and go to voice-mail twice. Me, JT and Dakota were at the grocery store at the time, trying to act like a real family, trying to find a routine, a normality that we'd never known before.

We were staying at my apartment while JT carried on with his recovery. He and I hadn't had a conversation about what we'd do longer term. He never had been one for forward planning, and I knew better than to push him on it before he was ready. I knew we'd need to face the threat of Old Man Bonchese, too, but wanted JT at full strength before we did so.

Enjoy the now, I kept on telling myself. *Whatever happens later – this right now is good.*

We were in the fresh-fruit section. Dakota was picking out a water-melon. She was addicted to the thing after camp; wanted watermelon with every meal. I supposed there were worse things for an addiction. She was healthy, and that was all that mattered. I still hadn't had the conversation with JT though – still hadn't told him about her illness, about how, if the cancer came back and she needed a bone-marrow transplant, that he'd be her best chance, because I wasn't a viable donor. I knew I needed to tell him. He was her father, so he deserved to know. And I'd kept him out of her life for so many years already. There was also the risk Dakota would tell him about the disease herself. They were getting close enough for that.

I sighed quietly. No more secrets. That had to be the way forward.

I smiled at the two of them: father and daughter together, something unimaginable a little more than a month ago. JT was helping Dakota, lifting down the watermelons from the top of the display and holding them out for her to look out. She shook her head at his latest offering just as my cell started ringing a third time. JT looked at me, raised an eyebrow. 'They seem real keen to talk.'

'Yeah.'

'Answer, it's fine.' He put the watermelon back and selected the next candidate Dakota pointed at. 'We've got this.'

I nodded, stepped away from them and answered. 'What do you want?'

Monroe told me they'd turned the cabin inside out before they'd found the chess pieces. Searle had hidden them in a hole in the wall, covered by the wooden cladding behind the bed. I didn't know what his intention had been, other than to keep them from sight and keep the blame for the Walkers' murder on Gibson Fletcher. I wondered if using the place his wife retreated to from him had brought him some kind of twisted pleasure. Mia had never known how close she was to them. If she had, her and Gibson would never have gone to Searle's ranch, and I'd never have caught up with them. Mia would still be alive.

I was thinking on that, on the irony and the tragedy, when Monroe's voice down the line pulled me back into the moment. 'Lori? Did you hear what I said?'

'Sorry, no.'

He sighed, impatient. 'I've got an idea about how to finish the sting Gibson started.'

'Good for you.'

'Maybe.' He paused. 'I'll need your help.'

Shit. 'Like I'm going to work for you again. You lied to me. Hell, you broke the damn law yourself, and you are the law!'

'Just hear me out.'

I glanced at JT. He smiled, oblivious. 'Why?'

'I know you took the missing knight. You're not done with this case, and you know it. You feel bad that Mia died, that Gibson is back in jail.

You want a resolution to what Gibson and I started two and a half years ago just as much as I do. If the operation works out, there's a chance I can get Gibson out early.'

I looked at Dakota laughing with JT. Knew that Jacob – Mia and Gibson's son – would never get to see his momma again, and probably not his father, either. Mia's death, I felt responsible for. Gibson had only killed the guards because he was backed into a corner, desperate. It wasn't fair for Jacob to suffer because of that. I couldn't change what had happened, but maybe I could make some kind of amends.

I turned away from the fresh-fruit section and said to Monroe, 'So what are you suggesting?'

'I need you to take the chess pieces to the Chicago Mob.'

Acknowledgements

Writing a book can be a rather solitary process, so I feel really lucky to have an amazing bunch of people around me who coax me away from my laptop and out into the world on a regular basis. It keeps me sane, gives me ideas, and prevents me from developing an even bigger 'writer's ass'.

I'm forever grateful to my crime-writing sisters, Susi, Alexandra, Helen and Karin, for the laughs, the advice, and all the 'you can do it' chats. Oh, and the cocktails (with a shout-out to Jamie H for all the post-cocktails toast!). To Caroline and Kirsten for the horsebox wisdom and the many, many cups of coffee (especially during the editing process). And to Red for keeping my feet warm while I write.

Special shout-outs go to Andy for encouraging me along the journey and reading the draft – your insights and support are appreciated always. To Rex, a real-life bounty hunter and proper gent, who taught me the bounty-hunting ropes; he's a professional, any errors in this book are entirely mine. To Bobby for inspiring the character of Bobby Four-Fingers – I hope you like your namesake! And to Nigel and his family for acting as great location scouts in San Diego.

I'm super lucky to be part of a brilliant writing group who kindly look at my early scenes. Big thanks to the City Writing crew – Rod, Laura, David, Rob, James and Seun. I hope you like the final version, and here's to many more wine-fuelled critique sessions!

The crime-writing community is a wonderfully generous place, so a massive 'Yay!' to all those fabulous crime writers who hang out in the scene of the crime – your wit, humour, advice and smut is the stuff of legend!

To all the fabulous bloggers and reviewers who championed *Deep*

Down Dead, the online book groups like the legendary TBC on Facebook, and the readers who read the book and got in touch to say they liked it – thank you so, so much. I hope you enjoy this next installment in Lori's story.

Huge thanks to my family, who have always been so positive and encouraging about my writing: Mum and Richard, Dad and Donna, Will and Rachael, and Darcey – you really are a wonderful bunch of dears.

A super massive thank-you to my awesome agent Oli Munson and the brilliant team at AM Heath. And, last but absolutely not least, a massive cheer, whoop and high five to the fabulous Team Orenda – Karen Sullivan, West Camel, Mark Swan and Sophie Goodfellow. You guys are pure amazing.